Praise for
THE GLASS HOUSE

'A masterfully told, character-driven novel that will have you laughing and crying in equal measures' *THE AUSTRALIAN*

'Stunning, engaging . . . Expect sadness, despair and even a few laughs from this unique novel that's so timely, given ever-emerging issues in our mental health system' *DAILY TELEGRAPH*

'A compelling story about mental health that is told with plenty of heart, humour and insight' *WHO WEEKLY*

'Highly engaging. Brings alive the frontline of mental health care'
PROFESSOR PATRICK McGORRY AO

'Embraces the complexity of what it means to be human'
MEREDITH JAFFÉ

'A great read that combines laugh-out-loud moments with those that bring tears to your eyes. An honest, sensitive look into mental health care in Australia' PROFESSOR JAYASHRI KULKARNI AM

'Gripping, rich and insightful, and brimming with compassion'
ARIANE BEESTON

'A remarkable exposé about mental illness and its treatment . . . told with an engaging, light touch reminiscent of *Eleanor Oliphant is Completely Fine* and Simsion's *The Rosie Project*. A timely, innovative book' BOOKS+PUBLISHING

ANNE BUIST &
GRAEME SIMSION

THE GLASS HOUSE

hachette
AUSTRALIA

'We all move uneasily within our restraints.'

— Kay Redfield Jamison, *An Unquiet Mind: A Memoir of Moods and Madness*

hachette
AUSTRALIA

First published in Australia and New Zealand in 2024
by Hachette Australia
(an imprint of Hachette Australia Pty Limited)
Gadigal Country, Level 17, 207 Kent Street, Sydney, NSW 2000
www.hachette.com.au

This edition published in 2025

Hachette Australia acknowledges and pays our respects to the past, present and future Traditional Owners and Custodians of Country throughout Australia and recognises the continuation of cultural, spiritual and educational practices of Aboriginal and Torres Strait Islander peoples. Our head office is located on the lands of the Gadigal people of the Eora Nation.

NATIONAL LIBRARY OF AUSTRALIA

A catalogue record for this book is available from the National Library of Australia

ISBN: 978 0 7336 5323 0 (paperback)

Cover design and illustrations by Alex Ross
Cover image courtesy of Shutterstock
Author photographs courtesy of Max Deliopoulos
Typeset in Sabon by Bookhouse, Sydney
Printed and bound in Australia by McPherson's Printing Group

FSC www.fsc.org MIX Paper | Supporting responsible forestry FSC® C001695

The paper this book is printed on is certified against the Forest Stewardship Council® Standards. McPherson's Printing Group holds FSC® chain of custody certification SA-COC-005379. FSC® promotes environmentally responsible, socially beneficial and economically viable management of the world's forests.

ONE

DISPLACEMENT

It's an unremarkable Victorian terrace in an inner suburb of Melbourne. Only the closed curtains on a summer morning suggest that anything is amiss.

Behind them, the open living space is in disarray. Household items are scattered on the floor: cooking pots, cleaning products, a baby's rattle. But there has been method in their placement. Below the sink, three rows of tinned food mark the start of a trail that runs to the front door: literal stumbling blocks for an intruder who wanted to take the shortest route to the kitchen bench.

A woman – small, dark-haired and visibly agitated – enters from the back garden in her dressing-gown, carrying a pot plant. She deposits it in the hallway outside the nursery, then fetches a stool from the kitchen. She climbs up with the plant and balances it on top of the door.

A laugh – unnatural, fractured – escapes her. It's partly the image of the booby trap going off, partly a perverse satisfaction that they've chosen the wrong woman to mess with, and, perhaps, the only way her mind can deal with what she has to do next.

Back in the kitchen, the baby carrier is sitting on the bench. Matilda was crying all night and now she's crying again. Sian pulls a kitchen knife from the block.

If I'd wanted an image to sum up everything that's disturbed me in my first three weeks of acute psychiatry at Menzies Hospital – and, in a strange way, what I've loved about it – I have it now.

A slight woman in a Tweety Bird nightie and untied blue satin dressing-gown is walking down the white hallway of the Mental Health Service's Acute Unit, flanked by two uniformed police officers. Powerless, vulnerable, and probably with no idea why she's here.

Acute psychiatry is the emergency medicine of mental health: for the stuff nobody saw coming. Until someone close to them becomes paranoid or overdoses or begins cutting themselves. Or waving a knife around, as Sian Tierney, the woman being brought into the ward, did a few hours ago.

Today may be the lowest point of her life. In the next hours and days, we'll have a chance to do something about it: to work out what disease or situation is behind the crisis, to treat it and to find a path forward.

The cops, a tall male and a wide female, swaggering to accommodate the equipment on their belts, look relaxed – smiling, chatting – but they're not touching her. Seems wise. I'm reading in her body language the irritability that sometimes accompanies psychosis. *Don't poke the bear, guys.*

The Crisis Assessment and Treatment Team briefed me over the phone. No previous psychiatric episodes – meaning only that she's not in our system, not that she's never had one. Not coherent; her name was provided by the neighbour who'd seen her behaving oddly in the street and called the police. The police called the CATT guys. When she pulled a knife on them, they called the police again. The police took her to the Emergency Department, who sent them on to us. And it's still only 11 am.

The female officer leans in and says something to Sian that I sense is meant to be reassuring.

Sian shakes her head, face set. She looks to be in her early thirties, perhaps five years older than me, but reminds me of some of the foster kids my family took in, delivered to our house overwhelmed and out of their depth. Attitude was all they had left.

Police, a knife, a person with mental illness. The consequences could have been way worse.

Omar, one of the nurses, steps out to meet them. He's a big teddy bear with a tuft of corkscrew curls and a gap-toothed grin. His smart remarks and innocent expression have been circuit breakers on more than one occasion. I like him a lot.

He takes the paperwork from the cops and leads Sian into an interview room. I'm watching from the staff base, where we hang out to write notes, check test results and debrief. *We* being consultant psychiatrists, trainees, interns, nurses, our lone psychologist, social workers, occupational therapists and the occasional student. Plus me, a registrar, one step past house medical officer and two steps past intern on my medical career journey, working in psychiatry, but not yet in the official training program.

The staff base is crowded with computers, chairs and filing cabinets, with a reception desk at the entrance. Windows on all sides, like a fish tank. In fact, it used to be called the fishbowl, but patients assumed we were referring to their spaces rather than ours, and, understandably, weren't happy with the implication of constant exposure and surveillance – and objectification. So it's now the glass house.

There's a noise behind me: Sonny, the martial arts instructor with schizo-affective disorder and a habit of exposing himself, has kicked the glass. Now he's pacing, singing loud enough for us to hear: 'We Gotta Get out of This Place'. In his current state, it'd likely be the last thing he ever did.

He's in the High Dependency area: four bare-walled bedrooms and a common space with chairs bolted to the floor and a TV fastened high up near the ceiling. It's for the patients who need a higher level of care and monitoring; in practice, that means those at risk of harming themselves or others. There's a spare bed and, thanks to the knife, it's about to be Sian's. That knife has also disqualified her from a bed in a private facility, no matter what health insurance plan she's on.

Omar joins us in the glass house and gives Sian's file to my boss, Nash Sharma. He's leaning back in his chair, legs stretched out, looking like a businessman at the end of a long day – stubble, open-necked white shirt, tailored pants slightly creased.

'They did a drug screen in ED,' says Omar. Most of our patients come via the Emergency Department. 'No results yet. She says she hasn't used. Ever, in her whole life.'

'All yours, Hannah,' says Nash, passing me the file. 'I hope you realise I'm skipping an online course on bullying so we can do this together.'

The joke's a bit close to home. The admin director's position has been vacant since he was fired for bullying. If Nash is skipping a non-clinical training module, it won't be the first time. And it won't have anything to do with supervising me.

Nash catches my disbelief and smiles. 'You know what turns people into bullies? Same as what we see with patients: there's an underlying propensity, then along comes a trigger. Like trying to do a difficult job with inadequate resources, and then you're asked to do just one more thing. Like a bullying course.'

We head to the interview room through the L-shaped Low Dependency area, which has views into two sides of the glass house. It serves the twenty-four inpatients who can be trusted, more or less, not to attack the furniture or each other. I suppose the glass walls to the garden are intended to create a feeling of space, but they only serve to highlight the high brick wall on the far side. Not much grows in its shadow. It's still nicer than the concrete courtyard that the High Dependency guys get.

Sian is sitting forward in a stained vinyl chair, her blue eyes darting around the room. I sit opposite her, with Nash beside me and Omar off to one side, and give her a few moments to take us in, though I can sense Nash's impatience. The interview room's decor doesn't inspire sharing of confidences: grey-tiled floor, nothing on the white walls except the emergency evacuation instructions. I remember how disorientating I found the Acute Unit when I first came here, less than a month ago. Without a mental illness.

I try to envision Sian in her normal life, out with a couple of girlfriends. She's the bolshie one, dealing with the guy hitting on her friend. What is she making of us? Does she realise she's in a hospital?

In the psych wards, we don't wear white coats or scrubs. I'm in my usual short skirt and Doc Martens. My black fringe and glasses probably say law clerk more than psych registrar. Or government agent, if that's what the voices are telling Sian.

I make a start. 'My name's Hannah Wright. I'm a doctor here, and this is Dr Sharma, our consultant psychiatrist. Omar's one of our nurses. Do you know why you're here?'

Sian takes a breath. There's the tiniest quiver at the edge of her mouth but her voice is forceful. 'It's a screw-up. The cops said I just had to talk to you guys and then I can go home.'

'How about you tell us what's been happening first, and then we'll talk about what we're going to do.'

She sits up straight, hands in her lap, and tries out a series of expressions, from aggressive to accommodating, before settling on slightly too bright.

'I had a bad night's sleep, that's all. My partner's away and I'm not used to . . . being alone in the house. Noises. You know what I'm talking about.'

'What sort of noises?'

'Nothing. Just the house moving. I need to get home and . . . I've got washing to put in the dryer. It'll start to smell if I leave it too long.'

Amazing what you learn in this job.

'Where's your partner?' I ask.

'Interstate. Western Australia. Working.'

'Would you like us to call him?'

'It's got nothing to do with . . . I mean, he's at a mining site. He has his phone off during the day. Please. Just let me go.' She's radiating so much anxiety that I'm feeling it myself, but I'm no closer to understanding its source. Time for the checklist: mood, anxiety, psychotic symptoms, medical history, developmental history . . .

She answers all my questions, but too quickly. No, nothing out of the ordinary has happened. Family in Melbourne; no problems with them. She isn't feeling sad; she's just been sleeping badly for the last week. Because her partner's away and there are things to be done. Which is why she has to get home. To get that washing in the dryer. *Let's get this out of the way and we can both get back to what we were doing.*

When I ask her if she works, she rubs her hands up and down her bare legs, sinews taut. 'I'm a union organiser. On a break at the moment.'

For mental health issues? She's being cagey. Like she needs to do something or be somewhere. And not the laundry. Nash leans forward.

'You seem pretty stressed,' he says to her. His accent is mainly Californian, but there's a trace of Indian; it's a reassuring mix.

'Of course I'm stressed – wouldn't you be? My neighbour's a . . . she calls the cops and I get hauled in here. I haven't done anything wrong, and I want to go home. I *have* to get home.' She's wringing her hands, speaking faster.

'Why the urgency?'

Sian seems to soften; there are tears forming in her eyes. I'm not sure how much control she has over these quick-fire switches. She whispers something and I pick up the word *safe*.

'What we still don't understand,' says Nash, 'is why you were out on the street in your nightclothes, and why you were carrying a knife.'

Incongruously, she laughs. 'Must have put it in my pocket by mistake when I emptied the dishwasher. That's what happens when you don't sleep. I need to go home and get some. Sleep.'

Her eyes dart past Nash, over his head and to the door. It's not easy keeping up a conversation while there are voices in your head: *They're out to get you; you're not safe here.* Not that she has admitted to hearing them, but it seems likely.

'We need to talk to your partner,' says Nash. 'If not him, a family member.'

'There's no-one I can call.'

'You told Dr Wright you had a good relationship with your parents and siblings.'

'My parents are overseas, visiting my sister.'

'And your other siblings?'

'There's only one other. I don't speak to him. He's a right-wing nutjob.' Her body tenses; she's so brittle she could snap.

'I'm sorry,' says Nash, 'but we're going to have to keep you here until we get the blood test results and are sure you're safe to go home.'

In an instant, Sian's expression hardens. 'You can't do that. You have no right . . .'

'I'm afraid we do. Do you understand this is a psychiatric facility?'

The CATT team have put her on an assessment order. It's the first stage in what they used to call being *sectioned*. Before that, it was *certified*. As in *certified insane*.

There's nothing insane about Sian's response to Nash's question, unless you count the sheer intensity of it. Her desire to get out seems to have enabled her to summon the mental resources and eloquence she likely uses in advocating for her union members.

She turns to Omar. 'I want this recorded.'

'I'm sorry,' says Nash, 'but we can't do that. Dr Wright will make a note of anything you want to say.'

She looks at me, hard. 'I want you to record that I'm being held against my will and am not liable for any consequences of that decision. I am not insane, and I have a right to refuse treatment. I refuse any drugs. I refuse anything that affects my thinking. No hypnotism, no . . . electric shocks.'

The mention of electric shocks seems to have stirred something up. She stops, looking terrified.

'No shock therapy. Under any circumstances.' She looks at me, then Omar. 'You're my witnesses. I demand to go home. Now.' She stops, apparently exhausted.

I ask for her partner's number, and she hedges. It's on speed dial in her phone, she says. Which is . . . guess where?

The police secured the house. No-one else home but 'stuff all over the floor, like a madwoman's shit', they'd told Omar. Nice.

—

'No drugs, no ECT, no hypnotism,' Omar says when we're back in the glass house. 'Definitely no hypnotism. I guess that only leaves lobotomy.'

I wonder if he jokes with everybody like this or is just messing with the newbie.

'What do you think?' Nash asks.

Sian is now in the High Dependency common area, watching the door. Looking for a chance to escape?

'What she said about treatment: paranoia?' I say. *You're my witnesses* is weighing on me.

'Hard to tell,' says Nash. 'Could be the psychosis, but if I had to speculate, I'd say she's like that when she's well.'

'She seemed totally freaked out about electroconvulsive therapy.'

'May have had it in the past. May have watched some bad movies.'

'But should we take some notice of her objections?'

'The problem,' says Nash, 'is that she doesn't believe she's unwell, so she isn't taking into account the single most important fact she needs to make a rational decision.'

'I guess.'

'In case you're wondering about the recording, the reason we don't allow it is that if it ends up in court, you'll have some other psych picking apart our interview technique and our conclusions. Second opinion is one thing, that's another.'

Carey, one of the admin staff, has wandered over, apparently having nothing better to do. In a place where you have to try hard to stand out, Carey succeeds. The androgynous look, overwhelming aftershave and all-red outfits – including a striped suit, hat and red-framed glasses – are just the beginning. Autism spectrum disorder has to be in the mix. They perch on a chair, too close, listening in.

I turn back to Nash. 'She's not telling us everything.'

He nods. 'Signs on mental state?'

I summarise the results of my examination. 'Perplexed, anxious affect. Guarded. Possibly responding to internal stimuli.' Meaning voices in her head.

'Which suggests?'

'Drug-induced psychosis, bipolar one or schizophrenia.' This is Carey. Diagnosis at ten paces, by a ward clerk.

Nash says what I'm thinking. 'And you decided this how?'

'I read the CATT notes.'

And now – like we need another opinion – someone else chimes in. 'We're talking about Sian Tierney?'

The new participant in our impromptu case conference has swiped in at the corridor entrance, so she's on staff, but I don't know her. Mid-to-late thirties and slightly taller than me – I'd say 170 centimetres – but only because she's in four-inch heels. Which means she's not nursing or medical. Glossy blonde hair, designer clothes: she looks like a Fox News presenter.

'Who are you?' says Nash.

'Nicole Ogilvy. I'm the director.'

'Of?'

'Of Mental Health.'

It seems Nicole is our new administrative boss. If so, I didn't get the memo. Or it's one of the constant stream that arrive every day in my inbox that I didn't have time to read.

'I think you missed the turn,' says Nash. 'Offices are back down the corridor.' *This is my domain: you don't come in here asking questions until you've introduced yourself and asked my permission.*

'You must be Dr Sharma.' Now she checks my identification badge. 'Good to meet you, Dr Wright. You're going to see me around quite a bit, getting a sense of how the service runs.'

'And Hannah will be trying to do her job,' says Nash.

I'm enjoying this exchange more than I should be.

Nicole ignores Nash's barb and gestures toward Sian, sitting alone in the High Dependency common room. Sonny is pacing in the concrete courtyard. 'Does she have a history?'

Nash looks like he might explode, but doesn't say anything – lets the silence speak for itself. Carey decides to help out.

'No record on CMI under the name and date of birth she provided to the CATT. In case you were unaware, CMI is the client management interface that records mental health admissions. And CATT stands for Crisis Assessment and Treatment Team. Although the word "team" is frequently added – redundantly.'

'I was aware. Thank you . . .' She trails off, waits, but Carey doesn't offer their name, and the badge poking out of their red shirt pocket is the wrong way around.

She gives in. 'Who are you?'

'I'm Carey Grant. Non-binary, so *they* is the appropriate pronoun.'

'What do you do here?'

'I'm Professor Gordon's research assistant.' Ah. I did not know that. I'm still getting my head around who's who in the glass house.

'And you're researching what?'

'Professor Gordon and I are investigating patient perceptions of the admission process. I also manage his data. And perform various other tasks.'

'Who pays you: us or the university? Don't bother – I can guess.'

'Good. Because it's confidential.'

'Of course it is. So, unless you can show that you don't report to me, I have a job for you. I'm guessing you're pretty good with computers?'

'I'm guessing that your guess is based on a stereotype which we should be avoiding here, but yes.'

Amazingly, Nicole nods and smiles, but her tone is condescending. 'You're quite right. Thank you for calling it out. But CMI only covers public psychiatric admissions in this state. Is that correct?'

'That's correct.'

'Use your data management skills to find if she's been admitted privately or interstate.'

Nash's hand bangs down on the bench, hard enough that Carey jumps. Omar and a couple of the other nurses are barely suppressing grins, and Sonny, back in the common room, starts thumping the glass. Nicole just looks at Nash and waits.

'This is *my* patient we are talking about.' Nash's voice is calm but emphatic.

Nicole is very still. 'And this is *my* mental health service, which I have been brought in to drag – apparently kicking and table-thumping – into the twenty-first century, as per the Mental Health Commission recommendations. One of those is integrated patient treatment, which we can't deliver if we don't know the history.'

'You're proposing to use a busy person to do what a phone conversation with the patient's partner will resolve in thirty seconds.'

Omar looks at me: 'You got a plan for getting that number out of her, Hannah? I think we're going to need the truth drugs.'

I shake my head and Nash turns back to Nicole. 'If Carey finds something relevant, they report it to me. Here, in this ward.'

'I may join you for the case meeting,' says Nicole. 'Does four o'clock work?'

Nash holds it in, for now, and nods.

As Nicole walks away, there's some shouting in High Dependency, and I follow her gaze to see that Sonny has undone his pants and has his penis in his hand. I've seen him do this in front of a female patient before; she barely reacted. But Sian is right in his face. Giving it to him. Sonny has a history of violence: he's not a guy to mess with.

I'm right behind Omar as he runs in. But by the time we get there, Sian has won. Sonny is zipping up, apologising.

'Lucky we took the knife off her,' Omar says, miming to Sonny what she might have done with it. He escorts Sonny to his room and I'm left with Sian – who turns her anger on me.

'You saw what just happened. This place is the *definition* of unsafe.' She lays it out: Why should an unwell person have to deal with shit that would never be acceptable anywhere else? She's going to sue. She'd be safer at home. In fact, if we let her go . . .

I'm sympathetic to what she's saying and impressed with her taking it up to Sonny and now to me. But she's not going home.

Omar, back from settling Sonny, interrupts. 'That was pretty gutsy of you,' he says to Sian. 'But be careful. You're not in Kansas anymore.'

Perhaps it's this realisation, along with her unaccustomed powerlessness, or maybe it's her inner psychotic thoughts, but when I get back to the glass house, I see that Sian has retreated to her bedroom and is banging on the wall with her fist. The nurse hurries over, but by the time she gets there, Sian has sunk to the floor, like a child needing a mother's comfort.

—

I've started typing up Sian's notes when Nash's mobile rings.

'Yes? For god's sake, can't you . . .'

I'm only hearing one side of the conversation, but it's enough to work out that the psychiatric nurse over in ED can't do whatever it is Nash wants. He sighs. 'I'll be there in a few minutes.' As he ends the call, he laughs. 'Come with me.'

'What's happening?'

'There's a member of parliament insisting on being discharged. The nurse doesn't want to get it wrong.'

'Why's he here?'

'Jumped in front of a truck. On purpose, obviously, or they wouldn't be calling us.'

'And he's refusing treatment?'

'Physically, he's fine, but apparently the truck's not: don't ask me why. So the driver was unhappy – road-rage unhappy. Someone called the CATT team, who brought the politician here, and the police brought the truck driver.' Nash grins. 'Our man isn't out of danger yet.'

'You want me to observe?'

'I want you to make sure the truck driver doesn't run into the politician—again. Can't rely on the ED team; they'll be flat out.'

'On a Monday morning?'

'The psych team are on a training day.'

'What about Sian?'

'Write her up for five milligrams of olanzapine stat.'

I guess that's Nash's way of telling me he's diagnosed her as psychotic, and that her passionate speech about declining drugs and other treatment has meant zip. Intuitively, I agree with his assessment, but we've hardly got a full history.

'Not too much?' I say. It's a big dose for a small woman who may not have had it before.

Nash shakes his head. 'She'll sleep like a baby.'

—

The Emergency Department is at the other end of the campus, in one of three new glass-and-steel towers. We cross the tree-lined road, then negotiate corridors and stairs because Nash doesn't want to wait for the lift.

The state-of-the-art facility has two large workspaces of nurses and white-coated doctors surrounded by cubicles full of patients, relatives, trolleys and machines. A year ago, as a house medical officer getting a taste of different specialties, I worked in a place like this. For a while, I thought emergency medicine might be my career.

There's a room, rather than a regular cubicle, for psych patients, with a window in the door. Nash looks in.

'That'll be the politician,' he says. 'The triage nurses will know where your truck driver is. If he's settled down, you should be able to send him on his way.'

He knocks on the door of the psych room then enters, and I turn to see Carey striding down the hallway toward me. What are they doing here?

Carey at least seems to know what I'm doing here. 'You're seeing the truck driver, aren't you?'

'That's the plan. But –'

'Prof wants you to find out if he's aware that the person he almost hit is a VIP. He's hoping the answer is no, so probably not a good idea to ask directly.'

'Thanks for that advice.' And thanks for the heads-up that Prof's involved. He and I have some history. I'm trying to stay out of his way for the next six months, at least until I get into the training program.

'Actually,' says Carey, 'he's not really a VIP. Xavier Farrell, backbencher. More an IP.'

'You are looking for me?' The voice – with a strong accent that sounds Middle Eastern to me – is coming from a cubicle adjacent to the psych room; its entrance is around the corner.

Carey smiles. 'If that's the truck driver,' they say, 'we know the answer to Prof's question.'

I pull back the curtain to see a man of about forty seated inside: solidly built, eyes so dark I can't see his pupils. A brief smile reveals crooked teeth.

He stands up and introduces himself as Ahmed. He's been waiting for the nurse, who has presumably been distracted by the IP.

'I can go now? I've settled down.' He smiles broadly; he's heard what Nash said. Out in the waiting room, there will be people literally screaming to be admitted but, like Sian and Mr Farrell, this guy only wants to go home. Everybody wins.

Nevertheless, now that I'm here, I feel I should do a risk assessment to determine whether he is a danger to himself or others. And for practice. With any luck, it won't take long; I still have my inpatients to see, results to check and a family discharge meeting to attend. I need to complete Sian's admission, reassure her and talk to her partner. Plus there's the 'case meeting' with Carey and Nicole at four. I haven't left work before 7 pm since I started in Acute, despite Nash pushing me to manage my workload. Like he's a good example.

I've just begun Ahmed's assessment when the psych nurse shows up holding a clipboard with his notes. I step out of the cubicle to speak with her.

I'm in her territory, and she makes sure I know it.

'Happy to have you do my job, but I called Nash because of Mr Farrell, not this guy. Apparently the braking damaged his tyres, and he cracked the shits. Been fine since they dropped him here, but if you think you need to see him . . . you're going to learn a lot about tyres.'

I scan the single page of notes. Brought in by police, calm since arrival. Focused on the damage to his tyres.

I return to Ahmed.

'I was hoping to talk with you about what happened.'

'What is there to say? An idiot walks onto the road. I only see him because I am always on the lookout. I hit the brakes, hard, and the tyres . . . poof! Now they're fu – . . . finished.'

'We can write a letter for your employer, if that would help.'

'The employer is me. Can you write a letter to the idiot? Tell him to pay for the tyres that were sacrificed to save his life. I have a small business, three trucks only, second-hand, so no advanced braking system . . . Do you know the cost of truck tyres?'

'How are you feeling now?' I ask. 'I understand you were agitated earlier.'

'I am okay. The idiot is okay. Only the tyres are not okay.'

'Does the thought of driving make you anxious?'

'On unsafe tyres . . .'

'At worst you'll have a flat spot,' I say. 'And it might not be on all the tyres. How many kilometres did they have on them?' I'm a country girl; I know about utes, roos and not throwing away anything that's still usable.

'I bought them only three months ago.'

'I can see you're worried. Do you often worry about things?'

'Nobody has destroyed my tyres before.'

Okay. This isn't going to work.

'You want to go home?'

Emphatic nod.

'Then you're going to have to answer some questions that aren't about tyres and don't have tyres in the answer.'

Another nod. He just wants to get out of here.

'Do you take pills to keep you awake?'

Of course not. Nor does he have any mood problems, and he sleeps eight hours every night. His business is doing well, so long as he doesn't have to . . . deal with unexpected expenses. Came to the country as a refugee and runs a support group for other Afghans. He's never seen a psychiatrist, does not have suicidal thoughts, has no forensic history – 'Not even a speeding ticket.' Anyone would get angry if some idiot . . . caused reckless damage. There's an edginess beneath his desire to please, to tell me what I want to hear so I'll let him go. That's the second time today – and the second time today that something doesn't feel right.

My mind drifts back to Sian. Why is she taking time off work? What was she doing with a knife? Why the fixation on going home? I'm probably making a mistake by trying to figure it out logically, while she's thinking she needs to get back to the mothership.

'What would you do if you saw the man who stepped out in front of you?' I ask Ahmed.

'Mr Farrell? Can I answer honestly?'

'Of course.'

'Then I will need to mention tyres. I would ask him to pay for them. Four hundred dollars for each one. If he's an important person, he can afford it.' *I'm rational and safe – let me go*. But also: *I know who's responsible for my distress.*

The curtain of the cubicle isn't drawn all the way, so I see Professor Gordon sweeping down the corridor – sweeping is what he does – with Carey in his wake. I excuse myself from Ahmed and step out into the corridor, doing my best to look anonymous.

Prof Gordon is maybe sixty-five, could be older, clipped Freudian beard, steel-grey hair, shiny pointed shoes: a small man radiating authority and narcissism. I'm hoping he's forgotten me.

'Ah, Hannah, it's you,' he says. 'Carey tells me you've seen the truck driver. Has he been discharged yet?'

I point to the cubicle, and we move out of Ahmed's earshot. I give the prof a precis that demonstrates I've taken a history and made what I hope is a sensible formulation: simple road rage, which isn't in *DSM-5. The Diagnostic and Statistical Manual of Mental Disorders* – the psychiatrists' bible – is a catalogue of syndromes, not symptoms. You don't need to be mentally ill to lose it at a guy in a suit who's cost you money and probably given you a massive scare.

Prof nods his approval. I've done my job, and I may have clawed back a few points. Except . . . even as I've been summarising the case, I've felt an uneasiness brewing. I have to say it.

'He's holding something back.'

Prof smiles. I used those exact words nine months ago in reference to a different patient, starting a chain of events that ended with Prof blocking my admission to the psychiatry training program, and putting my dream of becoming a qualified psychiatrist on hold. I've got a little less than six months to redeem myself with him – or for him to get over it – before I can reapply.

'Suicide risk?' he says. He might not actually raise his eyebrows, but it's there in his tone.

At least I can give a different answer this time. 'No reason to think so. But he's deflecting. I think he's made a safe space for himself to avoid . . . being open with me.'

Ahmed has poked his head through the curtain.

'That's our driver?' says Prof and, when I nod, he walks toward him. 'Where's he from?' Because people of colour are always from somewhere.

Ahmed answers for himself. 'I'm from Afghanistan.'

Prof enters the cubicle and sits down; he's hijacking my patient mid-interview.

'You saw a lot of terrible things, I imagine, in Afghanistan.'

'It was normal.'

Prof nods. 'Dead bodies?'

'On the way to school we would see limbs. One time, a head.' Ahmed is calm, but he no longer sounds dismissive. And there's no mention of tyres.

Now, Prof waits. Eventually, Ahmed fills the space.

'I was visiting my cousin at a hospital in Kabul. They came through . . . shooting the women in their beds . . . my cousin too.' He's shaking and his eyes are filling with tears. 'What reason to kill women in a hospital?'

It takes Prof less than ten minutes to get a history. Ahmed had already been accepted to come to Australia as a refugee. Since arriving three years ago, he has been having nightmares, reliving what happened in the hospital. So much for the eight hours sleep. And he was hit by a car in the aftermath of the hospital attack. Though he was uninjured, it added to his trauma and, I'd guess, anxiety about hitting pedestrians.

'And when you saw the man step in front of you today?' asks Prof.

'I saw blood. Like in my dreams.' He hesitates. 'I wished it had been me.'

Prof explores Ahmed's post-traumatic stress and survivor guilt. With all the extra information, he reaches the same conclusion as the nurse – and me: Ahmed can go home.

But Prof's not going to let me off without a lecture – in front of his research assistant.

'His suicide risk is currently low – the wish that he had been the one stepping in front of the truck today belongs to his flashback. But you shouldn't have been so quick to make that judgement, especially when your intuition told you there was something you'd missed.'

Maybe I wouldn't have missed it if he'd let me finish the interview.

'Next time, you won't need to rely on intuition. War-torn country, police, firefighters, paramedics, train drivers, always ask. Give the PTSD program a call and get him in the next group intake.'

He adds: 'You need to reflect on why you miss a symptom or diagnosis or risk – or overvalue one. There's a tradition in psychiatry of undergoing therapy yourself, and that can help with understanding your blind spots. It can also prepare you for dealing with cases that may awaken past trauma.'

I bite back my retort: *Maybe* you *need to talk to* your *therapist about why you're still so butt-hurt about a junior doctor seeing something that you didn't, to the extent that you want to take her down in public.*

As he walks off, I remind myself, not for the first time, that there's a guy who's still alive today because my sixth sense told me something that the Prof, with all his years of experience, had missed. If that's prevented me from getting into the training program, I guess my patient – Jùnjié – and his family would think it was a good trade.

As for getting therapy myself, it's not at the top of my to-do list right now. For some trainees, their own psychological problems are a big issue, maybe even the reason for their choice of profession, but I figure my upbringing has made me resilient. A lot of what happened with the foster kids was traumatic, but I dealt with it.

Since then, I've told patients they're going to die, seen them die, counselled their families. And in my own life, I've dealt with the end of a relationship that I thought would provide love, stability, a family. I've had to give a lot of emotional support to my own family. Intuition and resilience are my superpowers. My challenge is going to be learning the theory I need to qualify: five years of study and assessment *after* I get into the training program.

All the same, Prof's comment about blind spots is bugging me. What am I missing with Sian?

—

At the ED hub, I ask Carey when they'll be seeing Sian to do her admission survey.

'As soon as she's capable. Earlier is better, before their impressions are influenced by later interactions.'

'Can you do me a favour?' I say. 'Ask her why she's on leave from work.'

'Why can't you ask her?'

'I think she's hiding something; maybe you can catch her unawares.'

'You want to know if there's some reason she's not working which may be relevant to diagnosis or treatment?'

I smile. 'That's what I want to know.'

'That's clearer. Better to specify the problem than tell me how to solve it. I'll do my best.'

Nash appears with a man I assume is Xavier Farrell, member of parliament and destroyer of tyres. Suit and tie, maybe fifties, thinning hair, solid and jowly, ears that stick out. Someone who's probably used to owning the room, or at least the church hall. Not today. He looks wretched, wrecked.

Then he spots Ahmed, who's wandered out of his cubicle. I'm trying to signal to Nash – *keep them apart*. But it's too late. Farrell breaks from Nash and walks toward Ahmed. I can sense him trying to pull himself together, to set his world back to normal.

'Mate, I want to apologise . . .'

Ahmed freezes. Then he starts shaking, his chest heaving from hyperventilation. Farrell gets the message; he backs off, toward the consultation room he just left.

Prof shepherds Ahmed back to the cubicle with Carey and me a few steps behind. He sits Ahmed down, pulls a pen – a *fountain* pen – from his jacket pocket and holds it up.

'Concentrate on this pen,' Prof says to Ahmed with the sort of authority you don't question. 'Now, keep your focus there as you take deep breaths.'

It takes Prof only a couple of minutes to lead Ahmed to a state of calm.

We return to the ED hub, where Nash is waiting.

'You've seen Mr Farrell?' Prof asks him.

Nash nods. 'I've convinced him that he needs to be admitted. He didn't want to; it was just an impulse and it wouldn't happen again. But he's not ready to tell us why he did it. I told him I'd make him involuntary if I needed to.'

Prof leads us to the psych room, where Farrell is pacing; Carey and I wait awkwardly in the doorway, unintroduced. I guess I'm learning something from all this standing and watching.

'We'll pop you over to Riverbend,' Prof tells him. 'Discreetly. It's a private facility just next door.'

'How much out of pocket?' says Farrell.

Prof starts an explanation, but Farrell has worked out that the answer is something more than zero. 'I'll stick with public.'

As Prof leaves, he takes me aside. 'Carey tells me that your patient knows who Mr Farrell is. Is he likely to make trouble?'

I doubt Ahmed wants trouble of any kind, but . . . 'He's very upset about his tyres. Hundreds of dollars each, apparently.'

Prof gives me the smile of privilege. 'I'm sure Mr Farrell's colleagues can put that right. I'll have a word.'

—

I've left reviewing Sian till after the 4 pm meeting, in case Carey's found something. I have to hope that the antipsychotics haven't put her to sleep – if she's taken them. The nurses won't force her to. Not yet.

Carey and Nicole are right on time, Nash a few minutes late. Carey looks at their watch meaningfully.

'So,' Nash says, 'I'm guessing no previous admissions.'

'It's been an interesting exercise in using public data resources,' says Carey.

'Just tell me what you found.'

'No unified system in private and they won't tell you anything, so you need to get the information via someone you know who works there. Subtle support for hierarchy, privilege, personal connections.'

Carey opens a laptop. 'Riverbend allows access to eleven private hospitals across Australia owned by the same company – no admissions of a Sian Tierney. I checked her partner's name also: Della Rosa. Three states have not got back to me –'

Nash has heard enough. 'So, nothing.'

'Nothing from the health systems. So I looked her up on Facebook.'

'You did *what*?' Nash and Nicole, in unison.

'Hannah had a question about her personal life.' Thanks for that. 'And I almost certainly have the answer. Maternity leave.'

Nash looks like he's been slapped.

Carey fills in the detail. 'She had a baby three weeks ago.' Then: 'Oh shit.' Even they get it now.

Sian has postpartum psychosis. She *was* trying to hide her reason for being off work.

Nicole's face is a mix of triumph and horror. 'So, where's the baby?'

TWO

COMPULSION

The barrister addresses the half-empty courtroom as if he's on stage at the National Theatre.

'I could argue that my client was not in full charge of his faculties. I say "could", because it's obviously not true, in a mental health sense; he's as sane as you and me and the late Charlie Manson. But as he's the first vice-chancellor I've had the pleasure to represent, it seems a shame not to make the joke. You'll note that I've avoided the low-hanging fruit around vice. And fruit.'

The posturing has exceeded the limit of the Honourable Michael Haggerty's tolerance. 'Thank you, Mr Kennedy. I think you've made your point.'

'Not in the least. To quote, or indeed misquote, a man less educated than thee and me, but with an intuitive turn of phrase that leaves us crying, forever dying in his wake – Sir Roderick Stewart – my respect for you is immeasurable, but –'

'Mr Kennedy, thank you. Please sit down.'

'Oh, don't be a stick in the mud, Michael. We're just having a bit of fun.' And suddenly he's doing a full-throttle impression. 'Wake up, Mikey, there's something I want to say to you . . .'

'Jealous husband?' says Alex.

Omar has steri-strips on his forehead and a black eye. I guess he deserves the occasional smart remark thrown back at him, and Alex Ashwood is the guy to do it. He's a registrar like me, but, unlike me, is in the psychiatry training program, accepted into the intake that I'd hoped to be a part of. Slim, untidy blond-brown hair, hazel eyes and ambitions of being a Freudian therapist in the mould of Prof. He and I do basically the same job and have eight of the Acute patients each.

It's the morning handover in the glass house, and Alex has just arrived. He missed last night's drama. Nash has set – or reflected – the mood, sitting quietly, listening. I can see Sian through the glass sitting alone, her face blank with grief.

Omar considers Alex's question for a few moments then seems to decide that the truth is more bizarre than anything he can make up. 'Tripped over a tin of cannellini beans and a pot plant fell on my head.'

Nice to know I'm not the only one who trips over things.

Last night, after I'd finally gone home, my wine glass ended up in pieces on the landing after I had an encounter with the edge of the carpet. My apartment is one of four in a converted Edwardian mansion, a kilometre from the hospital at the shabby end of the suburb, and has its share of frayed edges. I've lived there three months – ever since the break-up with the guy who was meant to be The One.

Jess, my brother's ex-girlfriend, has had the second bedroom for the last four weeks. I left her watching *Emergency*, took my replacement glass into the garden, with its old-fashioned beds of azaleas, roses and rhododendrons, and sat under the big elm. Thought for a while about the fragility of life.

Omar and a nurse from the Mother Baby Unit had gone to Sian's house. None of us left the ward until they called in. They found Matilda in a cupboard under the kitchen sink. She was okay, and soon drinking from the bottle they'd brought with them. High fives all around. She was placed with Sian's parents – who were not overseas, as Sian had claimed – until her partner could get home from Western Australia. Meanwhile, Sian had withdrawn into her psychotic thoughts and showed no reaction to the news. I'm hoping when she sees Matilda alive and well, she'll reconnect. Despite the jubilation, we're all shaken by what we almost missed.

We move on to Alex's new patient: Xavier, the politician I'd never heard of until his suicide attempt. Omar tells us that Xavier's keeping to himself and keen to leave: 'No babies to kiss in Acute.'

'Well-educated man with good reflective functioning,' says Alex. 'Married, three children. Says he has no current suicidal thoughts. His near miss has shocked him and his family, made him realise how much pressure he was under. He's agreed to take desvenlafaxine.' He looks at Nash. 'I'm thinking he'd be a good candidate for psychotherapy.'

'In addition to his antidepressant?'

'Absolutely. But I was thinking about my psychotherapy case.'

Psych trainees have to see someone, under supervision, for forty sessions. But hardly anyone starts until the second year of training.

'Not now,' says Nash. I'm not sure whether he means 'not at this meeting' or 'not till you've done a year and are working for someone who has at least some interest in psychotherapy'.

After the meeting, I'm wondering whether to share something with Alex. He's been a bit stand-offish, though it could just be that he's busy. There are only three first-year psychiatry trainees in the Menzies Mental Health Service: Alex, plus Jon Homann and Ndidi Edozie who work in other units. They're the nearest thing I have to a peer group, and I should be making an effort to connect.

I catch Alex as he's heading into Low Dependency.

'Something about your politician I thought might interest you.'

'Not in the notes?'

'Probably not. Prof offered to move him to Riverbend, but . . . let's just say he's the sort of guy who gets his hair cut at the hairdressing academy.'

Alex laughs. 'He's going to find the public health system a bit more challenging than a haircut. But' – he pauses, smiles – 'thanks, Hannah. I owe you.'

Trainees' psychotherapy cases are undertaken at no cost to the patient.

—

There's a new admission at lunchtime. Max is a barrister – obviously, as he's still wearing his robe. And, equally obviously, he's manic.

'Good heavens, young woman,' he booms, shoulders pulled back as if he's about to address the court. 'You can't possibly be a doctor.'

He's middle-aged heading toward old; portly and pompous; switching between sitting, standing and pacing, as I suppose he'd do in court, though probably not so rapidly. A caricature of a British barrister of generations past, with a touch of Basil Fawlty. On steroids. Or, more accurately, off his meds. Manic patients can be violent occasionally, but I'm not too worried about Max, especially since Omar is sitting in.

'I'm Dr Wright, one of the registrars, Mr Kennedy,' I say.

'Very good, excellent; don't suppose there are many women in your profession,' Max says, incorrectly. 'Did you know that the first woman – actually, she may not have been the first, but that's not essential to the story – to play in a so-called men's cricket match – which actually means open, so women can technically play – I imagine you didn't know that; I certainly didn't; well, I hadn't actually thought about it explicitly – so, in an *open* cricket match – dismissed the great Brian Lara, holder of the record for the highest test – and first-class – score . . .'

I am typing as he segues to a model named Lara and his speech gets faster. *Flight of ideas*, I type, and my computer slides off my lap. When I pick it up from the floor, the screen is blank.

Max hasn't missed a beat, so I talk over the top of him – no easy job. 'Have you been taking your medication, Mr Kennedy?'

'Call me Max, dear girl. Do you realise that lithium can cause confusion and poor memory? Is this going to enhance or diminish the lucidity of a legal argument?'

I figure that's a 'no' to the meds. Ostensibly, reducing his lithium helps energise him: 'lifts my spirits when the weight of the quotidian world is upon me'. What it's done in reality is put his job in jeopardy. Not for the first time, according to the notes. And there's been at least one suicide attempt. The other face of bipolar disorder. On the surface, he's entertaining. Underneath, he's battling a life-threatening illness.

'Once we've got him back on the lithium, we'll have a few more days of free stand-up and then he'll settle.' Omar confirms what I know in theory and what he's seen countless times in practice. 'Then we'll transfer him to Riverbend.' Private care.

—

I've barely finished documenting Max's medication on a clunky replacement laptop when Sian's partner, Leo, arrives. T-shirt and jeans, unshaven, guarded.

Rather than asking to see Sian, he wants to talk to us, and we move to one of the interview rooms.

Nash keeps it brief. 'You've probably heard of postnatal depression: this isn't that, so forget whatever you've been told. Your wife has postpartum psychosis – happens in one in six hundred births. It's usually short-term; most women make a complete recovery. But right now, she's not thinking clearly and may have some strange ideas. Again, this will respond to treatment.'

'When can she come home?'

'Mr Della Rosa, your wife is very unwell. Women this unwell have killed themselves – and their babies. She's currently an involuntary patient and I'll be placing her on a treatment order.'

'What does that mean?' There's a hint of combativeness in Leo's tone.

'Legally, it means she stays here until I'm persuaded that she's ready to leave – unless you can convince the Mental Health Tribunal otherwise. But the medication should start working in a few days.'

'You're . . . *committing* . . . her. That's what you're saying?'

'We're making sure she gets the help she needs.'

With the shortage of resources in mental health services, being an involuntary patient at least guarantees you a bed.

A nurse appears at the door with Sian and guides her to the sofa beside Leo. Her eyes flicker when she sees him, then she looks away. It's hard to believe she's the same person who took down Sonny yesterday.

'Sian?' says Leo. 'You okay?'

Nothing. No expression. Rather than reach out to her, Leo turns to Nash.

'You've given her some sort of sedative?'

'Antipsychotics,' says Nash. 'They're extremely effective in treating this illness. But, yes, they have a sedative effect.'

'Wait. How did you get her to take them? She won't even take a Panadol.'

I think of Sian dictating her instructions, insisting that we didn't medicate her. You don't need a psychosis to have beliefs – beliefs we may not agree with, but that we're supposed to respect. I'm sure she needs the meds, or at least I'd have them if I were her, and I'd want my sister or mother to take them . . . but how to have that argument when she isn't rational?

'She wasn't in a position to make that decision,' says Nash.

'So you made it for her.'

Forced to choose between an injection or pills, she'd opted for the latter.

'We weren't able to contact you,' says Nash, 'but it was what she needed.'

We're interrupted by another nurse at the door. Nash waves in a couple who must be Sian's parents. If I were looking for a stereotype of latte-sipping inner-city progressives, they'd do, not least because

Hugh Tierney is carrying takeaway coffees with 'L' scrawled on the lid. His wife, Jenny, is holding a baby. She looks to Nash before showing the baby to Sian.

Sian face stays blank.

'Do you want to hold Matilda?' asks the nurse.

'That's not Matilda,' says Sian.

I feel the shock go through the room.

'Sian . . .' says Leo. Softer now, bewildered.

'Matilda is gone, Leo. They took her.'

Her voice is flat, eyes empty – a mother who, in her reality, has lost her baby.

—

At the end of the week, Nash calls in Professor Sandra Byrd, who runs the Mother Baby Unit across the hall. We've seen no improvement in Sian, even after increasing her medication and switching it from tablets to wafers, which she can't spit out. She's stopped eating and is barely drinking.

I'd guess Sandra is in her late fifties. She's dressed like a rosella: red glasses (large and round, in contrast to Carey's rectangular frames), red streaks in frizzy grey hair, and a red-and-green dress that reminds me of an artist's smock. You'd have to be a professor.

Sandra brings one of the first-year trainees, Ndidi, with her. Cream-and-brown pants suit, long braids. Ndidi is Nigerian Igbo, probably a couple of years older than me, and grew up in Canada, where her father was a diplomat. She divides her time between the Eating Disorders Unit and the Mother Baby Unit.

We've seen each other in the registrars' room, but haven't spoken much. A casual remark about having to work back earned me a lecture on unpaid overtime. Nothing to disagree with, but she was talking about the issue in general rather than how she or I were managing the work–life thing. I guess that was my answer: no time for personal stuff.

Sandra and Ndidi interview Sian then debrief us in the glass house. We're all standing up; another case conference on the run.

'The delusion is entrenched,' says Sandra. 'She thought she was protecting the baby from conspiracy theorists – and that she failed. Thanks to us.'

The family – Leo, Matilda and Sian's parents – have been waiting in the Low Dependency common area. Nash leads them into the interview room, along with Sandra, Ndidi and me. Ndidi and I grab extra chairs. It's cosy.

Nash gives them a summary. 'Our best option at this stage is ECT. Electroconvulsive therapy – what we used to call shock treatment – is very effective in postpartum psychosis. Frankly, it would have been my first choice.'

'And mine,' says Sandra.

Hugh and Jenny exchange glances, but Leo doesn't hesitate. 'No way.'

Nash waits a beat. 'What do you do for a living?'

'I'm a mechanic. Heavy equipment.'

'So,' says Nash, 'you understand how things work. People trust you, and I imagine you trust other people to know their business. You want your wife home; you want her well. I'm telling you that in order for that to happen, we're going to need to use medication and possibly ECT. I need you to trust us to do what we have to do.'

Sandra adds, 'The sooner we can get mother and baby back together, the better for Matilda.'

Leo looks at the ceiling, then at Sian's parents, who are nodding, then he nods himself. 'Okay.'

Afterward, her parents want to pin down how long Sian will be in hospital.

I repeat what Nash has told me. 'Maybe a month, but there should be a lot of improvement before that.'

'Sorry if I sound pushy,' says Hugh, 'but there are practicalities to consider. I'm supposed to be on a sabbatical in Italy. We've changed our flights but we can't delay much longer. And we have another daughter in Europe.'

I don't say anything.

'Regarding the ECT,' says Hugh, 'you should know there's a bit of a family history.'

Jenny nods. 'My aunt, Sian's great-aunt, had a series of nervous breakdowns, and was in and out of hospital. She told some pretty hair-raising stories about shock therapy.'

'Which Sian heard?'

'Couldn't not have,' says Hugh. 'With respect, she was the archetypal crazy aunt. And frankly, the treatment probably helped. As far as Sian's concerned, Dr Sharma said that ECT would be his first choice. If so, we're sorry he didn't start it earlier. I mean, we want Sian back to normal as quickly as possible.'

—

Nash asks me to enlist Leo in persuading Sian that ECT is her best option. The tribunal hearing to approve it will go ahead regardless, but it will be better if Sian has already agreed to it. It takes some persuasion to get Leo to come in, and he brings his mother, who has flown in from Port Hedland in Western Australia, to help with Matilda.

'Deirdre Walker,' she says to me, proffering a cool, bony hand. 'I remarried.'

Our meeting is held in the Low Dependency area, where Sian is now staying, and Max the barrister gets to them ahead of me. All of us in Acute – staff and patients – have become accustomed to being bailed up by Max offering his rapid-fire, loosely connected thoughts on everything from politics to popular music – or music that was once popular – and his plan to expose Judge Michael Haggerty for some 'abomination' committed at law school which will ruin Haggerty's career, and eclipse the notorious incident involving a British prime minister and a pig. (I had to look it up.)

'Ms Tierney's partner, may I presume?' Max says to Leo. 'Word has it your wife's fronting the tribunal. No secrets here. Walls are thin. Lips are loose. And you would be her sister, madam?'

Deirdre rolls her eyes.

'I have some small experience in legal matters . . .'

'Come again?' says Leo.

Max showers Leo and his mother with legal advice only tenuously related to the case, until the expression 'thick as a brick' sends him off into a critique of the works of Jethro Tull – the seventies rock band, not the eighteenth-century agricultural reformist ('make no confusion with him, my boy'). I step in and break up the conversation, but not before Max has slipped Leo a note.

Omar has confiscated Max's phone despite his strident protests, but even prisoners find ways of communicating with the outside world, and the hospital is not a prison.

Leo gives me Max's note. 'He's mad.'

I want to say, *No shit. You're in a psychiatric hospital.* But I take the opportunity to reinforce the message I need him to pass on to Sian. 'It's a word we avoid, but yes, he's unwell, which is why he's here. He's being treated and, in a week or two, he'll be back with his family and you can guess what sort of work.'

It's a good lead-in to asking for Leo's help in persuading Sian to have the treatment she needs. He agrees to try, but I don't see a lot of enthusiasm.

'You know, Sian's the one who wanted a baby,' he says.

'And now she isn't coping,' says Deirdre. 'I have to say, it's no great surprise to me.'

—

Back in the glass house, I read Max's hand-written note. It's a letter, accompanied by instructions that it be sent to newspapers, the Legal Services Commissioner and the University of Melbourne. Like Max himself, it would be funny if it didn't have such potential to cause harm. I can believe that he and Judge Haggerty engaged in offensive activities as students, but the thought-disordered way in which he describes them would be more damaging to himself than the judge.

Alex spots me reading the note. I fill him in on the story and ask if he has any ideas for dissuading Max from sabotaging his career.

'Shoot him full of olanzapine and shut him down till the lithium kicks in. Isn't that what we're supposed to do? Medicate patients to stop them doing harm to themselves and others?'

'And the alternative?'

'Recognise his autonomy, his essential underlying personality. Work with that.'

'And I'm going to do that when?'

'Five years' time. You'll be in private practice. And he'll be able to afford you.'

'If he's still got a job.'

Back in the Low Dependency area, I hear Max's booming voice again, and the equally unmistakable voice of Carey, matching him for volume. They're in one of the interview rooms. I don't like Carey's chances of keeping Max focused long enough to do the patient experience survey. Their exchange reminds me of my dad in front of the TV, competing with the panellists on *RocKwiz*.

Max booms: 'As in Cary Grant or Carey with the cane? Or like "Carrie Anne"?'

'Two out of three. My family name's Grant. I had to choose a new given name, so I chose something memorable. But the spelling's like the Joni Mitchell song. Gender neutral.'

'You're a Joni Mitchell fan?'

'No. Not a Hollies fan either.'

'"Sorry, Suzanne".'

'Suzanne taking you *down*. Leonard Cohen. Slow *down*.'

'No way to. "Locomotive Breath".'

'"Breathe",' says Carey, like a meditation coach.

'Pink Floyd.'

'And Taylor Swift. "Just Breathe".'

I pass the door ten minutes later and they're still at it, Carey consistently managing to send a message of slowing down. They'd be *very* good on *RocKwiz*. Max *may* be slowing down.

'When are you coming down?' Carey asks, and Max hesitates.

'I don't know,' he says. 'It's a depressing thought, isn't it? But for the record – or the CD or cassette or cartridge or MP3

– you're misquoting one Reginald Dwight, better known as Elton Hercules John.'

'Wrong. Bernie Taupin. Lyrics go with the lyricist.'

'You're a smart guy. We'd be a riot in court.'

'My turn: give me some answers, so I can fill in a form.'

Max laughs. 'Too easy.'

'And here's the form. On a scale of one to seven, where one . . .'

I think this is going to take a long, long time, but suddenly Max is cooperating.

'No need to explain. "Ready Teddy".'

Later, I run into Carey in the tearoom. 'I overheard you doing your survey with Max.'

'Third attempt. He's going to be transferred to Riverbend and I wanted to get in before that. But: success.'

'You were pretty amazing.'

'It's called empathy. I had an idea of how he was feeling and I did my best to join him. Too many psychiatrists never really try to understand the patient. They're always on the outside looking in. Not in – *at*. You've heard about lived experience? Be good if they put some weight on that when they picked people for the training program.'

Well, we agree on something. And Carey has established a connection with Max.

I explain the Judge Haggerty issue. 'Max is at risk of doing himself some damage and I thought you might have a solution.'

'Possibly. Anything else you'd like me to do?' It'd be sarcasm if it wasn't Carey.

'Persuade him to stay on his meds.'

If Carey can do that, they can have my job.

—

I've organised a meeting of the new psych registrars to be held at my place. By taking the lead, I've made sure the guys who've made it into the training program can't exclude me. Given I'm working alongside Alex, doing the same job, I'm basically one of them. And I would actually be one, if not for that screw-up with the Prof. When I do get in – *which I will do* – I'll still have five years ahead of me before I qualify as a consultant. So-called 'study groups' are as much about support as study and I figure it's a good idea to get mine going now.

Naturally, I get held up at the hospital. By the time I've walked a kilometre to my apartment in the evening heat, collecting sushi on the way, my clothes are sticking to me and I've only got fifteen minutes to get ready. I open the door to the smell of garlic cooking. Jess is not good at keeping a low profile.

Jess dated my brother Lennon for a couple of years. I knew her from school before that, even though she's two years younger. We caught the same bus, and for a while she came to our place once a week so I could tutor her in maths. She's a freckled ball of energy and insecurity, with a shock of bouncy red curls, and is, as Dad might say, smarter than she looks.

She goes for cost and comfort over fashion, and animal prints over everything. Back home she was a hairdresser: 'Everyone says it's like being a therapist, but it's actually totally different from what you do.' She's come to the city with plans to become a paramedic and is applying to study for a diploma in emergency health care.

I park the sushi in the kitchen, wondering if I've bought enough, and head for the shower.

Of course, somebody turns up early. I hear Jess laughing. Alex is in the kitchen with her, opening the wasabi and soy sachets. I told them I'd cater, but he's brought a bottle of wine, which is a good thing, as I'd forgotten about drinks. It's interesting to see him in a more social setting; he hasn't gone home to change, but the loose trousers and polo shirt work on him. He turns around and his look tells me that he thinks the shorter-than-work-length blue skirt works on me. I had *not* expected that. Ndidi and Jon arrive before I have time to think about it.

Ndidi is in white shorts and a singlet top, carrying a bottle of mineral water. I've met Jon briefly. He's a Bilinarra man who's just moved to Melbourne after doing his medical training in the Northern Territory and is immediately likeable: shirt untucked, full of enthusiasm, modest about his experience. He smiles broadly at Jess and gives her a hug. Like they've recognised each other.

Jess seems to have taken over the kitchen, so we move the table into the living room. It's so small our knees are knocking. Since Jess has been in the spare room, the living space has become my study: desk and bookshelves at one end, TV and sofa at the other.

'Anyone prepared anything?' says Alex.

'Sushi,' I say. 'I was thinking tonight would be basically, *My name's Hannah, I come from the Grampians and I work in Acute. And my secret to surviving five years of this is . . .*'

'Running,' says Ndidi.

'Ditto,' I say. I've been doing it since school: the sport option that required the least physical coordination. I'd pick Ndidi as a marathoner. She's on the skinny side of thin.

Alex waves his glass as an answer, and Jon laughs. 'If I had a drink every time I got stressed . . .'

'C'mon,' says Alex. 'There's no stress in Extended Care.'

'Wander over and take a look sometime. Back in the day, before antipsychotics, you'd have all been there with me.'

'Not necessarily,' says Alex. 'We had psychotherapy.'

'Which is your thing, right?' says Ndidi.

Alex nods. 'Don't get me wrong: I don't want to miss a psychosis when it walks in the door, and of course there's a role for medication, but . . .'

'In my father's house there are many rooms. Looks like you're choosing the den with the comfortable couch.' Ndidi drums her fingers on the table. 'Since this is orientation day . . . why didn't you do psychology? Or social work? Anyone can be a therapist, but seven years of medical study is a hard slog.'

'A lot of work just to be able to prescribe drugs, which I'm going to try to avoid doing. Not to mention I was taking the place of someone who needed a medical degree to become a surgeon or a biologically minded psychiatrist. You're not the first to point that out –'

'But you thought you were among friends,' says Ndidi.

'Still do. In my family, my school, it was all doctors and lawyers. Therapists and artists and carpenters, not so much.' He laughs. 'Definitely no carpenters.'

I can see Ndidi's tempted to keep pushing, but she changes her mind. 'So – all that study, internship . . .'

'Two years as a house medical officer.'

'And now you finally get to do what you want to do.'

'For fifty minutes a week. But today's the day.' Alex raises his glass. 'I've got my psychotherapy case. Hopefully the first of many.'

'The politician?' I say.

'Famous or not famous?' calls Jess from the kitchen.

'Mr X,' says Alex. Not the ideal choice of pseudonym for a guy named Xavier. 'Nash agreed I could do it if I was closely supervised, and now that I've got you guys –'

'Shit,' says Jon. Alex laughs, and it takes the rest of us longer than it should to realise he was kidding.

'I asked Prof if he'd supervise me, and he said he would.'

'Nice work,' I say. 'I didn't think Nash would approve it.'

'He wasn't going to. But Nicole dropped in to check up on Mr X.'

'She's seriously testing some boundaries.'

'He's an MP, so she's all *keep me in the loop.* Nash says, *I've given him to my first-year trainee to practise on.*' Alex is laughing. 'Not quite those words, but that was the message. Then he had to follow through.'

'Your turn, Hannah,' says Jon.

'I told you. Grew up about four hours from here, escaped being a third-generation hippie, had a bit of a struggle to get into medicine, got through . . . lived with a guy for a few years, here I am.'

'Tell us why you chose psychiatry.' Alex is looking at me like he's actually interested.

'As soon as I started the psych term last year, I realised it was what I wanted to do.'

'Because . . .' says Alex.

I buy a little time picking up the last piece of sushi, but at the moment of its greatest height above the soy sauce it slips from between my chopsticks and splashes black liquid over the table. Fortunately, Ndidi's white shorts seem to be okay.

'What you just saw is one of the reasons I did psychiatry. Nothing to break.'

'You're kidding,' says Ndidi.

'In biochem, did you guys have to stand at your cupboard at the end of term to check off the contents?'

Jon nods.

'At the beginning, I had maybe five beakers, three flasks, a dozen glass pipettes. At the end, I had one beaker.'

Alex smiles. 'Now I get why you use stemless glasses.'

'They started out with stems.'

He laughs at my joke, but I've broken two already.

'I was thinking about emergency medicine for a while,' I say. 'But you know what it's like – *hold this, pass me that*. Some resuscitation equipment ended up on the floor. Nobody died, but . . .'

That *get another resus kit and get her out of here* moment was the nail in the coffin of emergency medicine.

I might as well tell the whole story.

'The glassware was how I met my partner. Ex-partner. Marcus. He was the tutor – final-year med student – and made it all into a joke.'

'Not another psychiatrist?' says Alex.

'Obstetrics.'

Nobody actually rolls their eyes, but I have a feeling of being understood, of not having to explain how he looked down on my change in specialisation, or how our final argument was over his dismissal of a patient's clinical anxiety.

And then Jess appears with – *ta-da!* – a huge platter of roast chicken and potatoes.

'Hannah's so busy she doesn't have time to cook, and you can't live on sushi. Save room for ice cream.'

I look around for the reaction, half-expecting a smirk from Alex at the country girls and their roast dinner. But his smile looks genuine. I definitely didn't buy enough for four.

Jon insists that Jess join us, and we end up talking about her paramedic ambitions and growing up in the country. And, having overshared my professional dreams, screw-ups and love life, I realise at the end of the evening that Jon and Ndidi haven't told us anything much about themselves. Jon's just quiet; Ndidi, I'm still not sure of.

But as she's leaving, she turns back to me: 'You said you run? Are you up for a park run Saturday morning?'

'Sure,' I say casually, but I feel like punching the air.

Then Alex sticks around.

'First here, last to leave,' I say as we stack the dishwasher.

'You're going to interpret that?'

'I'm not the analyst,' I say. If I were, I'd say there was something happening between us.

'No, but since you mention it, you're my pick as the one most likely to do psychotherapy.'

'If you mean setting up in a wealthy suburb, talking to people who've got marital problems . . .'

He smiles. 'Sounding defensive.'

'Sounding like I need to sleep.'

'I haven't forgotten I owe you,' he says.

'Awesome group,' says Jess later, digging into rocky road ice cream on the couch. 'Your guy's pretty hot.'

—

At the reception desk the next morning, there's a visitor who looks like she's on her way to a cocktail party – or a seniors' singles night, though there's nothing senior about the short skirt, stilettos and big earrings.

'I'm after Max Kennedy's doctor,' she says in a loud voice. 'Suzi Quatro with glasses, I'm told.'

The receptionist has spotted me, and beckons me over, trying not to laugh.

The woman extends her hand. 'Lillian. Three l's, two in the middle.'

'Hannah Wright. Two h's, one at each end.'

She laughs. 'I like you. We could have fun. Do you drink?'

'You wanted to speak to me. I'm guessing it's not about that.'

'Funnily enough, it is. I understand you're looking after Max Kennedy. He's my partner – partner, not husband. We live in sin.' She laughs. 'Eight years now, and they said it wouldn't last. People actually said it. To our faces. And look at us now.'

From her substantial handbag, she produces a bottle of wine. 'I know this isn't strictly allowed, but at Riverbend . . .'

I put on my responsible-doctor face. 'Riverbend's a private hospital. Different rules. Alcohol interferes with medication and some of our patients –'

She interrupts. 'I thought that might be the case. Which is why I asked, rather than sneaking it in.'

She makes no move to leave.

'Is there anything else that's worrying you?' I ask.

It turns out there's a lot worrying her – which is hardly surprising, given her partner's in a psychiatric hospital after skipping his meds. We move to an interview room.

'I couldn't believe how lucky I was,' Lillian says. 'After all these years, I found my soulmate. He's smart and fun and . . . well, you're not seeing him at his best. A lot of people find me tiring, but I can match it with him when he's up and try to lift him when he's down. But . . . he goes over the top: we've lost all our friends. All of them. He bought a Ferrari for one of them – an actual Ferrari – to apologise, and she just took the car. Then, when he's down, he regrets it and it adds to the depression.'

'You know, if he took his meds . . .'

'Oh, I know. It was an Australian who discovered lithium – discovered what it could do. Before that . . . Max's father had manic depression, which is what they used to call bipolar disorder. Sorry, you'd know that. He was a brilliant writer, but the only medication he had was alcohol.' She shrugs. 'What we need is something that keeps people like Max in the sweet spot. That's what he's trying to do when he changes the dosage. If he found the magic formula, we'd all take it. Even me.' And just like that, the wind goes out of her sails. 'Because I'm not sure I can keep this up anymore.'

—

Leo can't persuade Sian to agree to ECT. A Mental Health Tribunal hearing is convened for the afternoon anyway. Nash assures me it's a rubber stamp and that I can get some practice in case presentation.

'We didn't need a tribunal to compel her to take medication; it's all about public fear of ECT, which is only reinforced by treating it differently.'

Usually the tribunal would meet online, but there's some IT problem so we're doing it in person. Nash and I head to a seminar room in the ivory tower, one of the hospital's original buildings, dwarfed by the new towers across the road. It's home to a random collection of hospital services as well as university outposts, including Prof's team.

The room, with its noisy air conditioner, mangled venetian blinds and coffee station, has none of the trappings of a court of law. The modular furniture has been assembled into a single big table.

The tribunal members are seated in the middle of one long side. They look senior and serious: a male lawyer of about seventy, who will chair the session; a dour-looking community representative, perhaps a little younger. The third member – a psychiatrist – hasn't arrived yet.

Sian is on the other side of the table, huddled at one end with her parents and Leo, who has again brought his mother, Deirdre – and a lawyer. Sian allows her parents to pull her into a family hug, while Deirdre radiates disapproval – possibly of the process, but my sense is that it's of the public display of affection and vulnerability. She's in a pale pink dress: sheep's clothing.

Nash and I take seats at the other end from Sian's team. Nash is here for moral support. And possibly to make sure I hold the party line. He turns toward the door and indicates a tall, imposing woman of about sixty.

'The psychiatrist is Margaret McDonald,' Nash says. 'I haven't seen her before.'

I'm looking at her companion. It's Prof, as usual taking up more space than his physical self. It looks like he's at the tail end of giving Dr McDonald the grand tour of his fiefdom.

Now go back to your office.

Prof sees me. He pulls a chair away from the table and sits down to watch.

Behind her smile, Margaret reads as sharp, in every sense. 'Doesn't look like a rubber stamp,' I say.

Nash shrugs and I know what he's thinking. She's a psychiatrist. One of us.

The tribunal lawyer asks me to summarise the case.

'Sian Tierney is a thirty-two-year-old mother of a three-and-a-half-week-old girl, Matilda, living with her partner of five years . . .'

I avoid looking at Sian and her family, or Prof, as I outline the patient's family history, admission, treatment and response, finishing with our immediate concern: 'She isn't eating and only drank two hundred mils of liquid yesterday – and that took a lot of persuasion.'

When I'm done, the psychiatrist, Margaret McDonald, is the first to speak. She doesn't get much out of Sian, whose head keeps dropping onto her mother's shoulder. She turns to Leo. 'This must be difficult for you.'

'It's a nightmare,' says Leo. 'Look at her. They're bombing her out. Can you tell me how that's helping?'

'I'm sorry to be blunt,' Margaret says, 'but you understand that her refusal to drink could be fatal?'

'Of course I do. But how do you know it's the . . . postpartum . . . and not the drugs that's stopping her drinking?'

'You've indicated you're supportive of an alternative treatment – electroconvulsive therapy.'

'Only if it's going to work. Which the drugs haven't, after Dr Sharma said, "Trust me, she'll be right in a couple of days".' He glances at Sian and her parents. 'We're asking you to tell us what's best for her.'

Margaret turns to me. 'Have you thought of a less-sedating neuroleptic?'

'We believe that ECT is the most effective treatment.'

'That wasn't my question.'

I know what Nash would want me to say: *We've looked at all the alternatives and ECT is our best option.* But the reality is that Nash has no interest in trying alternative medication. It doesn't sit well with his – and the healthcare system's – need to get her better as quickly as possible and free up a bed. He's been open about that.

'No, we haven't considered other antipsychotics.'

Sian's lawyer, silent until now, is on it.

'But if you did try something else, you could delay the decision on ECT. And if it worked –'

Nash speaks before I can. 'We'd be going back to square one. While we waited for a therapeutic effect, we might need a special nurse, and possibly an IV and nasogastric feeding. We're not in a position to be able to accommodate that on the ward.'

'You can't set up a drip in a hospital ward?' This is the community rep, sounding incredulous. And demonstrating that she doesn't know much about psych wards. Psych patients are mobile, often non-compliant and might use someone else's pole and tubes to harm themselves or others.

While Margaret is having a word in the community rep's ear, Professor Gordon weighs in from the back of the room.

'It's always fascinating to hear patients' and community representatives' suggestions for treatment, but as the clinical director, I'd want Dr Sharma to be using ECT, regardless of the availability of nursing support for other options. It's the most effective treatment for postpartum psychosis. There's minimal risk, and usually only minor side effects.'

'Can you describe those side effects?' asks the community rep. 'So the family is fully informed?' She looks to Prof then Nash and, finally, me.

I start. 'Headaches, confusion, temporary loss of memory –'

Nash interrupts. 'Would you like Dr Wright to describe the side effects of the alternatives, or do we only have a problem with ECT?'

The community rep drops the line of questioning and hands over to her lawyer colleague, who asks Sian's parents' for their view.

They're prepared to 'do whatever's best'. Of course.

The tribunal chair turns to Leo. 'Mr Della Rosa, will you give assent on your wife's behalf for her to have ECT?'

'If I say no, will it make any difference?'

'We'll certainly take it into account,' says the chair. 'But you've heard what Dr Wright and Dr Sharma have said.'

Leo confers with his mother. 'I'm not going to go against their advice,' he says.

Sian mutters something, and the chair hushes the room.

'Sian, did you want to say something?'

It's a struggle, but she gets it out. 'I don't want it. I'll take the drugs, but I don't want the shock treatment. I'll try to drink.'

'I hear you.' The words are out of my mouth before I've had time to think them through. I had hoped Leo would speak for her. But she's my patient. She asked me to witness her objection to treatment. It was probably misinformed, based on her aunt's stories and, just as likely, *One Flew Over the Cuckoo's Nest*. But she has a right to be heard.

Margaret McDonald looks taken aback, but it's the chair who addresses me.

'Did you want to say something to the tribunal, Dr Wright?'

'I'm sorry. But on admission Sian was insistent that we record her refusal of medication and, quite specifically, ECT.'

'While psychotic,' Margaret points out.

'With respect, having spent some time with the patient, I think that what she's saying now is what she would say in the absence of the illness.'

The Mental Health Commission was big on allowing patients to make their own choices, so perhaps they consider this when they retire to consider their decision.

Perhaps not, given how quickly they return. The ECT is approved.

Sian is expressionless: powerless, rendered silent by a combination of grief, fear and delusions that I can't begin to imagine. But she gives me a small nod when I catch her eye. I'm glad that someone appreciates me sticking my neck out; she's likely to be the only one.

Sure enough, Prof draws me aside as we file from the room.

'Are you satisfied with what you said?' he asks. 'On reflection.' His tone is mild.

'I've worked closely with the patient and felt it was important to ensure her wishes were heard.' I take a breath, tell him what he wants to hear. And what, *on reflection*, I might as well have done, given the outcome. 'I probably should have just supported Dr Sharma.'

'Not *probably*. When we're assessing people for the training program, we have a responsibility as gatekeepers. Most people who are accepted have the ability to pass the exams, so what do you think we're looking for?'

I know the answer he wants. 'Judgement.'

'Quite. When you hear of a psychiatrist messing up, it's seldom because they don't know their neurology or pharmacology. It's because of an error of judgement. Why do you think people make errors of judgement?'

'Pressure . . .'

'That may be the trigger for some. We're all different. Which means we need to reflect on our own circumstances, our sense of self, our vulnerabilities . . .'

Same message as before: *I'm still pissed off at you; 'judgement' is the hammer I'll keep hitting you with; therapy is my solution to everything.*

—

'So, do you think we should go ahead?' Nash asks me as we walk back to the unit.

'I guess we just have to hope that, when she's well, she'll be happy with the decision.'

'For what it's worth, I've never had a situation where we went ahead over the objections of the family. But you're focusing on the ethics rather than clinical effectiveness. Are you comfortable going ahead?'

'I wouldn't say comfortable, but yes, I am. I accept that ECT is the appropriate treatment.'

'Good,' says Nash. 'You can come in Friday and administer it.'

—

I get back to the ward to find delivery guys piling boxes in the corridor. Max the barrister is directing traffic.

'I thought you were at Riverbend,' I say.

'Dear girl, I've been discharged. Can't keep me in your madhouse.'

'So why are you here?'

He indicates the boxes. 'Wine. A case for each of the fine professionals who set me on my feet again. Two for Carey Grant, not to be confused with the late actor, who has allowed me to join their pub-trivia team in exchange for allowing the inconsequential reputation of an inconsequential judge to remain unsullied – which, in the clear light of day, was likely a wise course.' He pauses, then adds in a lower voice, 'And maintaining the optimum medication to ensure no embarrassment for our team.'

'Carey spoke to you about medication?'

'For three hours. Medication, money and – another "m" – moderation. They gave me a very comprehensive – and, I would add, unforgivably overdue – explanation of how lithium works. I've been chasing a chimera.'

M for mixed feelings. If I'd had three hours free to spend with Max, maybe I could have done that. As a doctor, rather than a research assistant with Google.

Except that Max adds, 'Yesterday evening. On their own time. But back to the wine.' And back to expansive mode: 'One for you, Dr Quatro. From the Vallée de la Loire. Chinon. *Why Chinon?* you ask, or I ask on your behalf. *Shine on*. Like the movie. Like the harvest moon and the stars and the sun and the crazy diamond. Crazy is not politically correct, but I'm reclaiming it for the purposes of conveying my appreciation. Thanks for helping the crazy people shine on.'

He spots Omar, who's come to see what's going down.

'And for you, my friend, something infinitely more valuable than alcohol. When you are inevitably sued for infringing a patient's autonomy under the Mental Health Act, I shall defend you pro bono. I salute your courage in putting right ahead of rights.'

'He's still manic,' I tell Omar as Max departs.

Omar shakes his head. 'Not enough to be held involuntarily. He's making sense, relatively speaking. Back to normal. For him.'

THREE

POWER

It's an ordinary suburban living room. Ordinary suburban parents, disciplining their fifteen-year-old daughter. Brianna is crying and her parents are being painfully reasonable.

'All we're asking,' says her mother, a pinched woman in her early fifties, 'is that you don't call them. If you promise us that, you can have it back. Okay?'

Brianna nods, defeated.

Brianna's father is holding her phone. 'We're a family,' he says. 'We stick together. We make decisions together.'

Another nod.

'I need to hear you say it.'

'I promise.'

'Because if you break your promise again . . . this time, I'm warning you . . . you're not our daughter anymore.'

'David!'

Brianna is crying hard. She gets up, snatches her phone and heads to her room.

Her father's voice follows her. 'I meant what I said.'

Brianna slams the door. Dials. 'It's Brianna Young. Chloe Young's sister. She's dying.'

Masked and gloved, I'm standing with Nash and an anaesthetist in a tiny room off the main operating suite on the shiny new surgical floor of Menzies Hospital. I'll bet that nobody mentioned electroconvulsive therapy at the grand opening. This so doesn't feel like psychiatry.

Sian has been wheeled in. The anaesthetist tells her: 'You'll just feel a pinprick. Now, close your eyes and count backward from ten . . .'

Sian opens her mouth, but no words come out. She was fearful but resigned when I saw her a few minutes ago.

As she sinks into unconsciousness, the anaesthetist eases her head back and fits a mouthguard. 'If she was still pregnant, I'd be taking extra precautions,' he says. He's supporting her chin and is monitoring pulse and blood pressure. He adds, for my benefit I assume, 'But she still needs close observation, as her musculature will be more flaccid than usual, easier for her to have reflux and aspirate.'

Minimal risk, Nash told the tribunal. And her mother and father and partner. I pull myself up: every treatment has risks and the anaesthetist is only telling me that he's on top of them.

I called Leo last night to tell him we were going ahead. He didn't say much and wasn't around this morning. Summer is stretching well into March, but the sun was only just up when my alarm went off for a 7.30 am start. We have to finish before the surgeons come in.

As I arrived on foot, Nash was being dropped off by his wife, with three pre-teen kids in tow. The youngest looked like he had pretty severe cerebral palsy. When Nash kissed them goodbye – the kids; not his wife, who was sitting stone-faced in her sari – he was all goofy dad, and the kid with a disability went off into peals of laughter.

The ECT machine looks innocuous. I've read the guidelines and watched the video Leo was given. Troy McClure: *You may remember me from 'Why Electric Shocks are Good for You'*. Big on the evidence of its effectiveness, not so much on the mechanism. I realise I'm allowing the latter to affect my emotions. How much harder is it for people without a medical background?

Sian has several electrodes attached with sticking plaster across her temples. A nurse secures her arms and legs in case her response is unusually violent. As per the guidelines. Non-invasive; no marks will be left.

Nash shows me the controls on the machine. 'Because it's her first ECT, we'll apply the lowest stimulus.' He adjusts the dial. Frankenstein. *Crush that thought.*

Nash places the paddles in my hands and shows me the button to push with my thumb. The anaesthetist is talking to the nurse and not paying any attention to me; if he was, he'd see my hands are sweaty and shaky. *Don't drop the paddles.*

Nash pushes my hands down so the paddles are firm against Sian's skin. I take a breath and squeeze the button. I half-expect her to jump, and there *is* a jump – but it's me, backing into Nash. And dropping the paddles.

The machine purrs and spits out a paper graph like an ECG. It's showing Sian's brainwaves: an upward spike, then steady at the new level.

Nash points to Sian's feet and I see there is a slight fluttering, which stops as the brain spike settles to a lower level.

'Thirty-five seconds,' says Nash, pointing to the chart. 'A bit short. We'd like forty-five to sixty to produce a clinical result, so we'll increase the stimulus next time.'

And just like that, it's over. The anaesthetist removes the mouthguard and Sian's breathing on her own. After all my trepidation, it's been pretty simple – mundane, almost. I saw way more drama in emergency medicine.

We'll do it again in two days' time: 7.30 am every Monday, Wednesday and Friday for eight sessions – unless we see a marked improvement in her condition before that.

Sian is returned to the ward where she wakes and complains of a headache. The nurse suggests analgesia and rest. After the state-of-the art dials and displays, a cliché from the last century: a Bex and a good lie-down.

I meet with Leo and Sian in her room later that day and tell them the ECT went well. Which is to say there have been no severe side effects.

Leo looks at his partner then back at me. His expression isn't giving much away, but I sense he's feeling out of his depth and isn't used to it. 'When will it work?'

I repeat what I've read and been told. 'After three sessions there are likely to be signs of improvement.'

Back in the glass house, Omar senses my concern. 'Chill. By the time we've finished with her, she'll be asking for a socket at home.'

—

Nicole enters the glass house after handover, looking for Nash or the unit manager. Both are in a meeting. Alex and I are her third choice.

'I need to brief one of you on an admission.'

'That'll be me,' I say; Alex has been slow in discharging his patients. But Nicole is crossing the line between administration and clinical – not for the first time. Nash won't be happy.

'The medical ward she's in needs a bed. The chief medical officer has asked me to find one here. She's a long-term Eating Disorders patient. Tell Nash to call me when he's back.'

As soon as Nicole has left, Alex asks the obvious question. 'How did we get lucky?'

Easy enough to find out: Ndidi spends half her time in the Eating Disorders Unit. I call her and find she's all over it.

'We've got four beds, and since I've been here we've had the same four women. It's a nice little racket. Daniela Popa – she's the consultant – pokes her head in three times a week to check the meds: *How are you feeling – showing Ndidi the ropes, are you?* And gets paid for three sessions. Your patient's Chloe Young. Anorexia nervosa. Nicole was here half an hour ago looking for a bed for her. She says, *Maybe time to discharge someone?* But Popa says *nopa*.'

Alex turns the computer screen toward me: he has Chloe's history up. 'Guess how many admissions,' he says. '*Long-term* is your clue.'

'Eight,' I say, aiming high.

'Eleven. Mostly to Eating Disorders.'

I flick through the tabs. 'Plus five to Child and Youth. First diagnosed at twelve, first hospitalised at fifteen, longest admission forty-two weeks.

'My god,' says Alex, and for a moment I'm with him. But . . .

'Would we say the same if it was sixteen admissions for asthma?' A friend from school spent eighteen months in hospital after a motorcycle accident. We do think differently about mental illness.

—

Chloe comes in the ward's front doors, pushed in a wheelchair by a nurse and accompanied by her parents. She's in a hospital gown, which looks out of place. Our patients usually wear their day clothes.

Elena Karras is in the glass house with me. She's the only psychologist who works in Acute and we share her with the Eating Disorders and Mother Baby units. She's maybe early forties, noticeably short, dresses in a kind of chic bohemian style – long sleeveless jackets, huge earrings and beads – and is always smiling.

Okay, not always. 'Holy Mother of God, is that Chloe again?'

Chloe is twenty-nine, two years older than me. On admission, she weighed twenty-eight kilograms. I haven't weighed that since I was six. Her body is that of a child but her skin could belong to an eighty-year-old. She's a wizened crone at an age when she could be out partying or building a career or having children.

In the past two years she hasn't been admitted or, as far as I can tell from the notes, seen a psychiatrist. Her choice, supported by her parents. This admission to the general hospital was officially for bedsores, but it could have been for a dozen reasons. Her ulcers weren't healing because her immune system is shutting down.

I'm used to illness being unattractive. I'm not hung up on the idea that anorexia nervosa is self-inflicted. It's a disease and it *looks* like a disease. But I struggle to picture Chloe in a normal-life scenario – without the disease – because it's so all-encompassing: mind and body. Her eyes are the exception. In her thin face, they're large and clear, attentive, as though all her remaining energy has concentrated itself in them.

Her parents hover around her like she's a terminally ill cancer patient. I wonder how that feels for her. They're both in beige; his trousers, her skirt. Neat, tired, ordinary people you'd walk past without noticing.

My experience with patients facing death is that they are often upbeat for others, while pissed off at being ill, often through no fault of their own. And the smokers, drinkers and reckless drivers who *have* contributed to their situation are in no position to undo what they've done. But Chloe will have had to deal with others telling her, 'If you'd just eat . . .' As if she doesn't know that.

I figure I'll make a start before Nash returns, but even before we're seated in the interview room, Chloe's parents, Sue and David, are on my case. He's an accountant and she works part-time as a receptionist in a GP clinic. They come across as intelligent people, but seem to have colluded in denying the obvious severity of their daughter's illness.

'She's been eating,' says David. 'We thought they'd be discharging her.'

'She really doesn't need to be here,' says Sue.

In my five weeks, I've heard that more than once from patients and relatives. Chloe's parents have probably accepted the advice of the physical-medicine doctors without question, including their recommendation that Chloe be transferred to a psychiatric unit, but now she's here, they figure their opinion is as good as ours.

If Chloe wants to go home, we can't stop her unless we make her an involuntary patient.

'She's always had a very sensitive stomach; she can't absorb things the way most people can,' says Sue. I don't know what point she's making but it gives me an opening.

'So, Chloe,' I ask, 'are you vomiting?'

'No. Not for years.'

Is she lying because her parents are in the room? It takes a few minutes, but I persuade them to wait outside.

Once we are alone, I change tack. 'When you were twelve, Chloe, what did you see yourself doing when you were thirty?'

Chloe looks surprised by the question; those eyes brighten.

'I loved school. I was really into sport; I played netball for years. Maybe I should have trained harder – aimed to join the Diamonds. But I had to study.'

She's fitting the mainstream psychiatric view of anorexia nervosa. It wasn't enough just to play netball: she had to qualify for the national team. And dieting . . . I knew a girl at school with bulimia who thought people with anorexia nervosa were just more successful than her at what she was trying to achieve.

Out of the corner of my eye, I see Nash is back. I figure he'll join me when he's ready, so I push on.

'What was your favourite subject?'

'Art.' She seems to lose concentration and only half-follows the thread. 'I'm doing an online course in social work.'

'When you look in the mirror, what do you see?'

Now I'm going through the diagnostic criteria, as I'm supposed to, but even as I ask the question it seems clunky and insensitive.

After sixteen admissions, we don't need to check whether she has anorexia nervosa.

Chloe grimaces. '*You* look in a mirror and wish your hair was longer or shorter or blonde . . . *I* see ugly.'

Not quite the same thing, which is why she's the one in the wheelchair, but it's an attempt to relate.

In the glass house, Nash is on the phone, but glaring at me. Alex motions for me to join them, so I open the door and ask the nurse to wheel Chloe to David and Sue.

Nicole arrives before I can speak to Nash. The nurses scuttle out into the ward; the unit manager, back from the meeting, stays. Alex busies himself with his computer – hanging around to watch the show. Clinician versus manager. Tribally, I'm in Nash's camp – we care about patients; they care about numbers – but it doesn't always play that way with these two.

'The Mental Health Service has been asked to take her,' says Nicole.

'The service needs a doctor to look after her, and that's not going to be any of my team,' says Nash. 'We've done all we can for her.'

Nicole is leaning against the doorway. Nash sits down heavily and his chair shoots backward, bumping into me.

'You've seen her, Hannah. Does Chloe think she should be here?'

I clear my throat. 'None of the family thinks she should be here.'

Nash nods.

Nicole nods back. 'You can make her involuntary if you have to.'

'I won't be doing that. It's not considered appropriate when treating eating disorders. And this service has previously followed that advice in Chloe's case. It's what we call best practice.'

Nash lays it out: 'Chloe's cognitive functioning is severely compromised by virtue of her BMI being under fifteen for years. She can't learn.' He looks hard at Nicole and speaks slowly. 'Her immune system is shutting down. We can't help her. She's *going to die*.'

'That may well happen, Dr Sharma, but not before we've explored the full range of treatments. Including the *best-practice* option.'

Here we go. Nash straightens in his seat. 'And suppose you tell me what a social worker thinks is best practice for treating anorexia nervosa?'

I didn't know she was a social worker.

'Nash,' she says, and after *Dr Sharma,* it sounds like she's speaking to a child. She's still standing, literally talking down to him. 'I once trained as a social worker. That's an important part of my background, and I draw on it frequently. But, unlike just about every doctor I know, I don't define myself professionally by the first thing I did. I have a doctorate in managed care. I don't expect you to call me Dr Ogilvy, and I don't expect you to take any notice of my opinions on clinical matters, but I do expect you and every clinician in this hospital to respect evidence and best-practice guidelines ahead of your personal biases, habits and pet treatments. Do you understand what I'm saying?'

Before he can respond, Nicole drops her voice. 'The Butterfly Foundation specifies that family therapy is a mainstream treatment of choice. They're not the only ones saying this. Yet nowhere in the notes can I see that it has ever even been suggested for Chloe.'

'Are you serious?' says Nash, and there's an intensity in his voice that I haven't seen before. 'Do you know the difference between some . . . *consumer* . . . pamphlet and *medicine*? One of the reasons I left America was to escape having to spend hours negotiating for the most appropriate treatment for my patients, and I can tell you that the Mental Health Commission did not intend for administrators here to start behaving like insurance companies there. I will not be using family therapy on a terminally ill patient. If you want her to have family therapy, she can get it as an outpatient.'

I don't know if it's Nicole, the situation with Chloe or his history in the US, but something has pushed Nash's buttons.

Nicole just addresses his argument.

'You know perfectly well that these things don't work in isolation. She'll need medical support, supervision, meal plans . . . The Eating Disorders Unit has agreed to organise those.'

Seems some deals have been done.

Alex leans into me and whispers. At first I'm only aware of the intimacy, and it takes me a few moments to register what he's said. 'Odds-on Nash wins.'

'I've said my piece,' says Nicole. 'I'll ask Professor Gordon to decide.'

'Even money,' Alex whispers.

Credit to Nicole for finding a way to walk away without conceding. Prof is Nash's boss, and Nash will be obliged to accept his decision. But Prof will surely support the psychiatrist who works for him, right or wrong, as he did at the tribunal.

When Nicole has gone and Nash has stormed off – presumably to see Prof – I put my theory to Alex.

'I'm leaning to Nicole,' he says. 'Three reasons: first, Prof reports to the chief medical officer, who wants us to take Chloe. Second, Nash will respect that, and Prof will owe him one.'

'So, I only got it wrong because I thought Prof would stick up for the guy under him. He's so arrogant that I forget he has a boss to suck up to.'

'Maybe, but I think he's actually looking sideways. Nicole and Prof haven't sorted out who runs Mental Health. Prof was supposed to retire and give her a clear run, but he cut some sort of deal to stay on and now they're equals. Prof will want to build bridges. And then Nicole will owe *him* one. That's my third reason.'

'You realise nothing you've said has anything to do with Chloe?'

'I do. But I don't have any insights to offer there.'

'I thought you'd have been on Nicole's side – psychotherapy.'

He shakes his head. 'The behaviour's been entrenched since she was twelve. I doubt any sort of therapy is going to make a difference. And she wouldn't want it. Maybe, after all the treatments that have failed, we should respect that. And let her die.'

—

I tell Chloe's parents we're sorting out some administrative issues and David looks at me impatiently.

'I was told this would be streamlined. Dr Ogilvy said' – *Dr* Ogilvy? That'd be Nicole, who doesn't use her title – 'that you'd be trying some alternative treatment. But if Chloe wants to come home . . .'

In the absence of word from above, she'll be here overnight. I'll need to sort out meds and a skeleton management plan – bad choice of words – likely without any input from Nash.

I spot Omar talking to Elena, the psychologist, and hit him up for advice. He has plenty.

'The Eating Disorders staff will see her and set up a meal plan – she'll be watched for an hour after each meal. It's worthwhile giving her a small dose of diazepam half an hour before. We'll have to keep an eye out for any signs of refeeding syndrome.' In case I've forgotten my physical medicine in the past five weeks, he adds, 'The body not coping with the transition to metabolising food again. Could kill her.'

I shake my head, just a reaction.

'First anorexia nervosa patient?' says Omar.

'Yep.'

'We struggle with them.'

'I've noticed. Nash was pretty . . . emotional . . . about not wanting her in the unit.'

'Nash is different. But for nursing staff, they're manipulative, superficial, dishonest . . .'

'. . . and almost all female,' says Elena, pointedly. 'And you can't help thinking, *Why can't they just eat?*' She raises a hand to forestall our objections. 'It's what we all think at some level, and you'll get different answers from different people.'

'You know the family,' I say. 'Is there some issue?'

'There's always something – but that doesn't mean it's the cause. We don't really know what the cause is.' She takes a breath. 'You're seeing the hard end of eating disorders. The majority of patients get better or learn to live with their condition. That's with treatment. Untreated, they have a worse outcome than for just about any other psych illness.'

'Which is what we're seeing here?' Though sixteen admissions isn't exactly untreated.

'I think the severe cases are the result of a perfect storm: genetics, personality, family dynamics, peer pressure – and no treatment, or maybe the wrong treatment, or the wrong time or the wrong therapist. It's not simple. Not much of what we do is.'

'If she stays, Nicole wants her to have family therapy.'

Elena takes another breath. Sighs. 'To help them let her die?'

—

Alex's prediction turns out to be right, more or less. Carey fills us in. 'Dr Sharma was advised that if, and only if, the patient and her family want treatment, we should offer it.'

Neat solution – politically, at least. Nash accepts her, so it's a technical win for Nicole, but then Chloe discharges herself: a win for Nash.

Nash comes back to the ward, obviously in a hurry. He doesn't look like a guy who's had a win.

I give him a quick summary: parents ambivalent about family therapy; Chloe wants to go home.

'Good. I'll see her first thing tomorrow and tell her she's free to leave.'

He glances at my management plan and approves it. Carefully considered, precisely documented treatment until the morning, when Chloe will go home to die.

I'm struggling with this. Suicide is not always predictable, even in hindsight. Afterward, you wish you'd done something to prevent it – if only you hadn't missed the moment. Now, that moment is playing out in front of us, and we have so many resources to hand.

Nash guesses what I'm thinking.

'None of them want help – not the sort we're able to give.' He gives me a wry smile. 'I thought you were all about patients' rights.'

He's referring to Sian and the ECT. Unfairly. Sian's issue was choice of treatment, not of life or death.

'They aren't saying they want her to die,' I say. 'If it were cancer, we'd try surgery, chemo, radiotherapy.'

'Until we had nothing left to try. Eventually, we help the family and patient come to terms with the body's failure.'

'Can't we help the Youngs come to terms with the mind's failure?'

'If they want to seek the help of a counsellor, they can – but that's not us.' Nash turns to go, then turns back. 'Talk to Chloe before she leaves. Decide if she'd be happier here or at home.'

—

I'm on my way to the registrars' room to write up discharge summaries when Alex suggests we grab a drink. Omar is right behind him and will have heard, which is a good reason to say no. But I need a debrief. And a drink. Someone to open up with other than Jess.

Plus, there was that moment between us at the study group meeting, and the confidential whisper today; I'd like to see if there's anything there. Not that I want to pursue it, necessarily; at this stage I'm just curious. And the alternative is discharge summaries.

As we leave, I turn to see Omar grinning knowingly; he clearly thinks there's more to Alex's invitation than an opportunity for colleagues to debrief.

The hospital is on the eastern fringe of the city; there are plenty of bars close by. We walk along the main street, then Alex turns into an unmarked entrance and we head up a couple of flights of stairs to a rooftop garden with a bar and a few restaurant tables. The bar section is crowded with corporate types drinking and watching the sun set over the city, behind the Menzies' towers.

'Do you have a favourite cocktail?' Alex asks.

'Whatever you're having.'

He takes that to mean 'choose something for me' and orders me a bathtub gin. I guess there are cocktails with more suggestive names, but I'm thinking that Omar picked it right. And Jess, too – though 'hot' isn't the first word I'd use to describe Alex. Cute maybe. Smart; I guess there's no argument there. And intense – behind the easygoing facade.

My one rule of dating post Marcus was supposed to be *no doctors* – especially not doctors I was working with. Burnt once; small world; has to be a sign of lack of imagination.

Jess disagreed. 'Doctors date doctors. Or nurses. But female doctors – always doctors. And they meet them at work.'

'And you know this how?'

'Television.'

She's not entirely wrong. The rule about not dating colleagues doesn't seem to apply to medical people; plenty of my fellow students paired off at uni for such compelling reasons as being allocated positions next to each other for lab work.

The cocktail tastes good, but it would be just as good if it came in a glass rather than the miniature bathtub with the tiny yellow duck.

Alex clinks his boulevardier – yep – against my bathtub and smiles. 'So, tell me about yourself, Dr Wright. Why did you really end up in psychiatry? Besides wanting to stick it to your ex.'

'Is this a work question or a date question?' Might as well get that sorted now. I have to work with him. And the vibes he's been sending make me feel I'm not way off the mark. But I've dropped the straw. I try to take a sip without swallowing the duck.

'Your call,' says Alex.

'Pass.' We laugh, a mutual acknowledgement that he was playing analyst by throwing my question back at me. 'I didn't do psychiatry to stick it to my ex. More the other way round – he couldn't deal with me doing something he wasn't on top of.'

'So he needed to be in control,' says Alex.

'Possibly. But you asked about why I want to get into psychiatry. I'm not in yet. And right now, the question is more –'

'Whether Prof will let you in.' He laughs at my expression. 'Gotcha. He hasn't said anything to me, but there's some issue, isn't there? Spit it out.'

'We had a disagreement over a patient.'

'And you were right?' He smiles. 'Wouldn't have been a problem if you were wrong.'

'You want to tell this story?'

'Just being an active listener. I'll shut up now.'

He does and I tell him the story.

'The patient was a gymnast, training for the Olympics. Knee replacement at seventeen – dream over. A big deal psychologically, but the surgeons didn't want to hear about that.'

Which was why I was asked to see him. I was only a house medical officer, second year out, getting a taste of psychiatry as part of the smorgasbord on offer. I'd made up my mind it was the direction I wanted to pursue, and had applied for the training program, but at that point, I knew little more than I'd learned as a medical student.

But I had time. Time to do more than a fifteen-minute history, time to listen to what Jùnjié said, all of what he said, and how he said it, and to what he didn't say; time to begin to understand him as a person rather than the host of some disease or a broken object.

I'd got halfway home that night before I jumped off the tram and headed back to the hospital. Jùnjié had triggered a memory of one of the foster kids who'd lived with us. I spoke to Jùnjié again, then I phoned the psychiatrist on call – who happened to be Prof.

'I think he's holding back something,' I said.

'Seventeen-year-old Chinese men will often not reveal things to you.' I could hear people in the background; the professor was out to dinner or maybe at a party.

'I think he's having suicidal thoughts. He needs a special.' Meaning a psych nurse dedicated to a single patient.

'Dr Wright, I saw him today.'

'I saw him a minute ago.'

I was prepared to push it, right up to 'blood on our hands', and if that didn't work, I was prepared to stay all night myself. But Prof gave in; he must have wanted to get me off the phone so he could get back to his party.

'I'll authorise a special for tonight and review him again in the morning.'

Which he did. I was already in the corridor outside Jùnjié's room when he arrived. So was the crash team, quietly packing up their cart. The nurse gave him the news.

'The special took a break. Jùnjié went to the toilet alone. I'm afraid there was a communication problem.'

Jùnjié had asked a friend to bring in a stretch band to 'exercise his arms'. They found him hanging from the door handle. It wouldn't have happened in a psych ward, where the fixtures are specifically designed not to take that much weight, but this was a surgical ward.

I look back at Alex, realise I've been staring into space while I've been talking. I finish the story.

'He was found quickly; he wasn't hanging there long enough to suffer brain damage.'

Alex exhales. 'Jesus. But . . . Prof had a problem with that?'

'He took something I said the wrong way. Just a statement of relief. But it was in front of the nurses.'

'Go on.'

'I said it was lucky that one of us had seen the signs.'

'Ouch. Not a good way to manage a narcissist.'

Like I don't know. Prof had pulled me aside, told me that I'd just been overcautious, and had happened to strike a case where there was a real danger. 'On the facts in front of them, your senior clinicians made a reasonable assessment. Caution is a good thing, but there's more to it for you, isn't there, with suicide? It's a risk we have to manage every day, and our judgement needs to be unaffected by unresolved issues of our own.'

I'd nodded. It wasn't like he was totally wrong.

But then, the kicker. 'As you probably know, I'm in charge of selection for the psychiatry training program. If people have issues that may affect their clinical judgement . . .'

And just like that, my certain place in the program became an offer of a non-trainee position with no guarantee I'd ever get in.

'You think Prof had a point?' says Alex.

'Maybe. But I don't think everyone's a suicide risk – just this guy.' *And I was right.* 'You know Prof; any advice?'

'Show that you've listened to him. Don't make waves. Maybe think about therapy?'

'You know how long the waiting lists are for people who really need it?' I'm possibly sounding defensive. 'I've thought about it. Not right now.'

The sun has gone, and the after-work crowd is being replaced by people who've come for dinner. It's still warm, and we can see the city lights.

Alex has kept his promise to shut up and listen. Maybe he's just practising his psychotherapy skills, but I'll take it. Where I grew up, nobody had time to listen.

'Your turn,' I say.

He smiles. 'Can I ask you about one of my patients?'

It's Xavier, the politician – Alex's psychotherapy case. I'm not sure I want to go there. The guy stepped in front of a truck; I don't feel ready to share responsibility for what he might do in the future.

'I thought Prof was supervising you. Too tough for him?'

'This isn't about the process. It's about understanding something that happened – its impact. Frankly, I'd trust you more than Prof on this.'

Well, that's a pretty effective line.

Alex leans in to be sure no-one can hear us. 'He disclosed *why* he made the suicide attempt.'

Xavier, an older man of the world, a VIP, is sharing his deepest personal stuff with a guy way younger, totally new to the job, because he's a *therapist.* I wonder how this feels for Alex. But I have a pretty good idea about Xavier's secret.

'He had an affair, right?'

Alex shakes his head and I guess again.

'Sexual harassment.'

Alex nods; I've picked it.

'How long ago, what level, and who?'

'A few months ago, after a work party. Just a proposition, he says, though I'm guessing maybe a kiss, too – stuff his generation didn't take too seriously.'

'I'm guessing she wasn't his generation.'

'Works in his electoral office. She flirted with him at some function and suggested they go somewhere, and then backed out – or freaked out. Later, he followed up . . .'

'You mean he tried again.'

'The way he tells it, he was trying to make sure everything was okay. But she'd already made some sort of unofficial complaint, and now he's scared it might come out.'

I play psychotherapist and let Alex fill the silence.

'So, I'm wondering, first, was he really trying to kill himself or was it just to send her a message?'

'I hope you're just wondering and not expecting me to answer.' It's not something I want to get wrong, though the guy I saw in ED didn't look like someone who'd pulled off a well-judged strategy.

'Okay,' says Alex. 'Second question, to a woman of about the same age: should he talk to her?'

This one I can answer. 'No,' I say, finishing my drink. 'But ask Prof whether it's your job to tell him that.'

'Fair enough. Another cocktail?'

'I'm good. Usually a glass of pinot gris is enough for me. The duck drink has a kick.'

'Feeling better, then?'

'Meaning?'

'You came here stressed out about Chloe and now you're looking relaxed. The question – the big question for us as we go forward – is whether it was the talking or the drugs.'

'Both.' I am feeling better. I need to learn to let go, but not at the expense of becoming an alcoholic. 'Do you still want to know why I did psych?'

'Trying to make sense of a dysfunctional family, right?'

I shake my head. 'An undergrad degree, four years of medicine, two years' residency, and then ninety per cent of the time treating serious mental illness with medication. Not the obvious way to get help with your issues.'

'But . . .'

'Not the reason I did psych, but my family *is* pretty crazy. Three kids. And fifty foster kids, give or take. Plus anyone who could play music or sing or chop wood on the weekends. Or needed somewhere to crash.'

Alex's eyes widen.

'Soup queues, mismatched shoes, top-to-toe in the beds. Mostly they only stayed a few days or weeks. But there were a few who lived with us for years. So, I'm used to chaos. The glass house is nothing.'

'Can't have been easy.'

It hadn't been easy. The kids we took in were disturbed. Quite a few were seriously disturbed. Like the one who defecated in my clothes drawer. My parents responded with unconditional love. I guess I could have become accommodating, but instead I learned to hold my territory. At school, there was the usual group of mean girls. I was the top student academically, dressed in hippie hand-me-downs, wore glasses. They never touched me. And the kid who shat in my drawer only did it once.

Looking back, I did some pretty shitty things to some kids who really needed psychological help. I've got a lot of making up to do.

I'm at the point of suggesting we stay for dinner – or go somewhere less fancy – when my phone buzzes.

It's Omar: there's some issue with Chloe.

Alex understands. As other doctors do.

—

Omar is laughing when I come into the glass house. 'That bad?' he says.

I look at him blankly, and now he's really laughing.

'Oh shit. I was just giving you an out. Now I've ruined your hot date.'

'You saved me from telling him why I did psychiatry. Is Chloe awake?'

She's sitting alone in the common area in her wheelchair.

Talk to Chloe before she leaves, Nash had said. *Decide if she'd be happier here or at home.*

'How are you?' I ask her.

It takes Chloe a minute to place me. She shrugs.

'The consultant is going to let you go home tomorrow if you want to.'

She doesn't react.

'Is there any reason you wouldn't want to go home?'

'No reason.' After a long pause she says, 'Just Brianna. My sister.'

'There's a problem with her?'

'She's the one who called the CATT team.'

'Why do you think she did that?'

'She's always fighting with my parents.'

'And it's hard going home to that conflict?'

'It's hard when I'm thinking my sister is going to call you guys to bring me in here to force-feed me.'

Maybe she's given me an opening.

'I know being here is tough . . . but what we're suggesting this time isn't so much about eating,' I say. 'It's about working with your family. *Family* therapy. To sort out how they cope and support you. How they can work together.' In the absence of a response, I add, 'That includes Brianna.'

'They'll talk to Brianna?'

'With you and your parents.'

I watch her think about it.

'You said that being here isn't all about eating,' she says. 'Maybe you could tell the nurses that, so I can have my meals without them standing in my face.'

Her eyes tell me we're close to a deal. 'I can ask them to give you a bit more space. Do you think you could you stick it out for a few sessions with Elena?'

There's the smallest hint of a smile. 'You're the doctor.'

FOUR

DENIAL

Sister Carmella is not wearing a habit, but the substantial cross hanging over her blouse makes her religious affiliation clear. The class is called Body, Mind and Spirit. At this top-tier Catholic school, she feels comfortable confining herself to the third.

She doesn't know many of the final-year boys and girls by name, but she has a favourite, James, a shining example of what the Jesuits used to call 'muscular Christianity'. He could well be destined for the priesthood, though he tells her that his father has other ideas. And lately, he seems to have been struggling, not his usual self.

Today, he's not here. The boy sitting beside James's customary place in the front row shrugs in response to the unasked question. She's about to begin the lesson when, as one, the class looks to the doorway.

James is standing with his hands raised and elbows at his sides in the priestly orans posture, his expression either beatific or stoned. He is completely naked.

The class is, for a moment, stunned into silence.

'James,' says Sister Carmella, in something between a whisper and a squawk.

He lowers his hands, opens them, and when he speaks, it is with a serene authority beyond his years. 'You shall know me no more as James. I am the Christ returned.' He pronounces *returned* as three syllables: *re-turn-ed*. Nobody laughs.

One of the boys pulls off his jumper and walks toward James, offering it to him. 'Hey, buddy . . .'

Up go the hands again and the voice is now thunderous: 'I am come to judge the living and the dead.'

Sister Carmella has had time to collect her thoughts, after a fashion. 'Gentle Jesus.' It's a two-word prayer, but an unfortunate choice. 'Would you like to speak to one of the wellbeing team?'

'All heads shall bow, or ye shall surely burn in the fires of hell.'

A girl bows her head, slips out of her seat and kneels on the floor. Her neighbour reaches for her, then changes her mind and drops to the floor beside her. Others begin to follow her lead.

Sister Carmella watches, dumbstruck. Her eyes return to the tall boy surveying the class, promising to divide the saved from the sinners. Slowly, she sinks to her knees.

Saturday morning I find myself at a park halfway between Ndidi's place and mine and halfway into suburbia, thinking we're going to have a relaxed jog, talk shop and enjoy the open space.

It seems a couple of hundred other people have had the same idea, including kids and dogs and the seniors you see in the paper swimming in the ocean at dawn in winter. There's a coffee van, marshals, and a guy with a megaphone.

Ndidi finds me. She's wearing pink Nikes, a matching crop top and tight shorts.

'You haven't heard of parkrun?' she says. 'Every Saturday morning, around the world.'

I shake my head.

'Five kilometres,' she says. 'Is that too far?'

I'm a pretty good runner. I manage a forty-five-minute jog most mornings, when weather and work don't get in the way. Five kilometres will be a piece of cake. I just nod. 'Should be okay.'

We line up at the boathouse by the river. Ndidi positions us a couple of rows from the front, behind a woman with a three-wheeled pram. 'She's here every week. Outperforms most of us while she's wrangling a baby.' She laughs. 'Like I need that in my face.'

There's a surge of humanity, and pram woman is away quickly. Ndidi starts at a faster pace than I'd have expected, and we run for a few minutes without talking until the field begins to string out.

'Anything happening?' I say, trying to sound like I'm breathing easily.

'On call Thursday night. Seventeen-year-old with a first-episode psychosis. Hearing voices, paranoid. And the father just wants me to tell the kid about the evils of weed.'

'Could be the trigger.'

'Sure. Still got to deal with the psychosis. But Dad wants a consultant's opinion. Consultant comes in the next morning and basically lets him bully her into saying what he wanted.'

We finish a loop, and head over a bridge. Breathing *hard*.

'How's Alex?' she asks, looking straight ahead.

What sort of question is that?

'Doing his share. He's okay – not trying his Freudian stuff on patients like your seventeen-year-old. How's the Mother Baby Unit?'

'I'm coping.'

Then suddenly she's ahead. I pick up my pace but can't catch her. The faster runners are passing me in the opposite direction, on their return leg. Thirty seconds later, Ndidi passes with a thumbs up, then I do my own U-turn and head back.

Now it's my turn to pass the slower runners. And coming toward me, with three kids and a big curly-haired dog tied to the smallest, is someone I know: Xavier, Alex's psychotherapy patient, the MP I saw in ED right after his suicide attempt.

He sees me, smiles and nods as we cross, but I don't think he places me. I guess he meets a lot of people. My expression as I gasp for air won't be helping.

Ndidi is waiting at the finish line with coffees. She puts an arm around me.

'Nice work. I signed you up – did you get a finishing token?'

I nod. 'You do this quite a bit.'

'Most weeks. If you want to come along, I'd love the company. I won't ask about you and Alex. But if you want someone to talk to any time . . . it's what I do for a living.'

I'm about to tell her there's nothing going on – yet – but change my mind. 'Thanks.'

As we're walking over to register our tokens, she gives me the answer to the question she ran away from.

'You asked about the Mother Baby Unit. To tell the truth, I'm finding it pretty challenging. And I don't mean technically.'

Ndidi's married with at least five years of study in front of her before she qualifies. Dealing with babies all day . . .

Before I can say anything, she laughs. 'We do psychiatry, we're going to have to deal with our own stuff.' *I've shared all I'm going to share.*

As I sip the last of my coffee, I spot Xavier and his family crossing the finish line. Almost immediately, they're accosted by a couple, in a friendly sort of way. I often try to picture my patients in their normal lives, but it's not often I have an opportunity to see the reality. I'm guessing the couple are constituents wanting to get in his ear. He's nodding seriously. And his kids are watching their dad, big man in the community.

He's looking okay, or at least he looks the way he did when he tried to apologise to Ahmed for jumping in front of his truck. The dog looks pooped.

When I get home, I find an email telling me I'm a registered parkrunner with a personal best of twenty-three minutes and six seconds. Sixty-four seconds slower than Ndidi's. She'd moved fast to get those coffees.

—

Jess interrupts me as I'm doing some research at my living-room desk.

'I thought you were going home this weekend,' she says.

'I'm exhausted. I don't think I can drive four hours. We'll do it on Zoom.'

Jess is all sympathy: *You work such crazy hours, so much responsibility and you have to study.* I don't tell her my fatigue is the result of a pissing contest in the park this morning with a fellow medical professional.

I haven't been back home since I started at the Menzies. I've just had too much on. Mum phones regularly to check on my social life, which should make for a short conversation but doesn't. My sister, Melanie, is usually in the background, just dropping in, again.

My younger brother, Lennon, doesn't phone, but we text a lot. He's the reason I was planning to visit.

He's about to go jackarooing in Far West Queensland. He doesn't have to tell me that Mum and Dad want him to finish his electrical apprenticeship; that's been a constant theme since he started. But there's more to it than that. They don't deal well with anything that threatens to divide the family.

We were all about family growing up – us and the foster kids – and we don't seem to have the tools for separating. Lennon seems to think that I'll be able to blow in and deal with dynamics that took a lifetime to brew. But I do need to see my family. If it wasn't such a long drive . . .

'I'll drive you,' says Jess.

'I thought your car . . .' Forget it. We'll be taking mine.

Jess's own family has the tyre dealership in Halls Gap, half an hour from us, but I suspect that's not the reason for her offer.

'You want to say goodbye to Lennon, right?'

Jess nods and looks at my screen. 'What are you buying?'

'Training materials,' I say as I hit *print*.

She looks at the screen. 'For running?'

—

In the end, I drive. Now that I've recovered from the run, I'm feeling invigorated. We head out through the football traffic and across the West Gate Bridge. My car is an eighteen-year-old white Corolla; a hand-me-down from Mel, which Dad cleaned up for me when she had her third kid. That's our family in a nutshell.

Jess kicks off the conversation in her usual way. 'Suppose there's a guy on the road, legs and arms crushed, chest crushed, head injuries: what do you do first?'

'Pray. Then get some warning triangles out. Actually, do that first. Seriously, they'll teach you all this when you do your paramedic course.'

'Only if I get in. I need to know as much as I can for the interview.'

We talk for a couple of hours about first aid. She knows a lot for someone without any training, and I sense she's trying to compensate for a lack of self-confidence.

We stop for fuel and Jess returns from the shop with burgers and drinks.

'Protein, carbs and water. I've probably left it too late. When you exercise, you should have them right after.'

'Thanks, coach.'

She beams. 'I've been doing some reading about general health. When you're a paramedic, people expect you to know all the answers.'

'Nobody knows all the answers. And you can get in a heap of trouble pretending you do.'

'You knew the answer to everything I asked you, and emergency medicine isn't even your thing. You're so going to ace the psychiatry exams.'

So, partly because I want to prepare her for the fall if she doesn't get into paramedics, I tell her the whole story about Prof blocking me from the training program. It takes a while. By the time I finish, we've left the freeway and the mountains in the distance are shimmering in the afternoon sunlight.

I can sense that she's shocked, and I'm expecting her to offer words of encouragement, and I guess she does, but in a way that makes me feel more pressured, and her sound over-invested. 'Hannah, you have to. You can't not make it.'

Glad she's going to be an ambo and not a psychotherapist.

After the turn-off into the national park, the native bush is dense around us, branches hanging over the roads that twist around narrow corners. A steep drop on one side, cliff face on the other.

We pass through town, where I wave at one of our neighbours, then head up the dirt road to Casa Wright. I park fifty metres from the house and check the range we've crossed, looking for smoke, as we all do at this time of year. It'll be a week or two before the risk of bushfires eases.

A badly damaged Corolla of about the same vintage as mine has been added to the collection of useful and could-be-useful hardware spread over the property: car bodies, trailers, several caravans, oil drums. I check to see if any of the tyres have more tread than mine. Nup.

My father, Merv, is on the verandah. He's a grey-bearded bear of a man who used to be able to scull a yard glass of ale, thinks anything can be fixed and whose ideal weekend is jamming with a bunch of folkies. He believes that everyone is basically good, which is a nice philosophy, but wasn't the most practical approach to a house full of dysfunctional kids.

I breathe in the eucalyptus and prepare myself.

'Engine's in reasonable nick,' says Dad, apparently referring to the Corolla. He gives me a hug and offers his usual comment: 'You've lost weight.' Jess gets a hug too: 'And you're looking healthy.'

The rest of the family is in the kitchen. My mum, Genevieve, her long, grey-streaked fair hair tied loosely halfway down her back, is searching for her glasses. Maybe because I've been away a while, or perhaps because psychiatry has made me more aware of family dynamics, I see her with fresh eyes. Anxiety on a stick: a mess of love and good intentions. I give her a hug and think 'brittle' as she fusses a cake onto a serving plate.

'Gluten-free,' says Mum and rolls her eyes at me.

That's new. 'Is someone intolerant?' I ask.

'Wasn't part of the ancestral diet,' says Mel, running her finger along an edge of the frosting and tasting it. Like cavemen ate icing. She's three years older than me, a short version of Dad with a mane of black hair, baby number three on one hip and phone in hand.

Lennon is talking to Jess. He's a little guy, not much taller than me, with Mum's hair and freckled complexion.

'You seeing anyone, Lennon?' I hear Jess ask.

'Nah,' he says, and Jess looks disappointed. Their relationship has morphed into friendship, which is probably what it was for the most part anyway.

One of the ex-foster kids, Kayla, has dropped in or is staying. Who knows? She's wrangling a toddler and a baby. The place is a zoo. As expected.

Kayla hands the baby to Mum.

'I'm helping with the sleep routine,' Mum says, and disappears.

'How fast does eczema get better?' asks Mel.

'Bugger off, she can help you later,' says Lennon, but I take a look at Mel's baby and suggest some ointment. Which will need a prescription from the GP, who'll make their own assessment.

Mum returns, minus foster granddaughter, and she and Dad pepper me with questions.

'Have you sorted out that problem with your professor?' asks Dad. I've only mentioned it to Mum once or twice on the phone, but now I've got them worried.

'All good,' I say. 'It's just the system.'

'She's amazing,' says Jess. 'She saved a baby.'

I have to explain about Matilda – how it was a team effort and all that – but I'm glad to have an opportunity to show them that my job isn't about keeping people locked up forever, or lying on the couch talking about their mothers. To my relief, no-one asks about Marcus or whether I'm seeing anyone now. Maybe they listened last time.

The afternoon disappears in overlapping conversations, and I need to escape for a walk before dinner.

I get back to find Jess has taken my car to go to her folks' place for the night, and a bunch of neighbours have arrived with beer and dips and a catering-sized pot of vegetarian chilli. I'm looking at a scene from my past: the same players, in the same places, but everybody older.

Dad picks up his acoustic guitar. The guy I waved to going through town starts plucking an upright bass. Another has a harmonica, Mum's got her harp, an older woman's on bongos. Then everybody's singing, with Lennon, Mel and me doing the harmonies. Lennon's deeper-than-you'd-expect voice will be missing next time.

Mum gives us an intro to 'Teach Your Children', and we pick it up, counter-melody and all. The song is probably from even before her time, but this is all country countercultural comfortable. And that awkward lyric about feeding your dreams to your children and knowing them by the ones they pick? How does psychiatry sit with my parents' dreams? Until today, it hadn't occurred to me that they were invested in it any more than any other career I might have picked.

We finish the song, laughing at how good we were.

After dinner, I finally retire to the caravan where I'll be sleeping; there are spare rooms in the house, but they've been filled with junk and one is Mum's painting studio. There's still a copy of the house rules taped to the caravan wall. *Apologise for your mistakes and forgive others for theirs. Look for the good. Seek to understand before criticising.* I'd have gone for: *Lights out by ten. No drinking. Keep your hands off Hannah's stuff.*

It's almost midnight and I'm trying to get the heater to work when the door opens. Lennon comes in holding a bottle of bourbon, offers it to me – no, thanks – and flops on the bed.

'You're really going?' I say. 'How are Mum and Dad dealing with it?'

Lennon puts his hands behind his head and stares at the ceiling. The white plastic is stained and buckled – it gets hot here in summer and freezing in winter. 'They're still thinking you'll move back,' he says. 'You know. Soon.'

'And get married and have kids and help out, while working as a full-time psychiatrist.' And hosting another generation singing Crosby, Stills and Nash.

He laughs. 'Yeah, probably.' He's avoided the question about Mum and Dad's response. I guess I'll find out tomorrow. 'Don't know if the jackarooing is what I want to do, but I'm never going to find out till I get out of here. I mean, they're awesome, but . . .' Another long silence, which my mother would have filled if she'd been in the room. Then, 'I don't know if I'll ever have kids. After what happened.'

He doesn't want to commit, Jess has said, more than once.

'Shit, Lennon. That's still eating you up?' He'd been thirteen. He'd had counselling but, like me, stopped after a couple of sessions. I guess, being that bit older, I was more able to put it in perspective. 'If you want Mum and Dad to feel better about you leaving, this may not be the best explanation.'

He gets up and heads back to the house. I'm left with what our parents would call 'something to think about' and then not think about it.

—

I start the next day with an eighty-five-minute run up and down hills: tailored training program day one. Then it's an uphill battle to organise my informal family therapy session. It takes me two hours to get everybody around the kitchen table.

'So,' says my father. 'What's this all about?'

'I just wanted to be part of us all saying goodbye to Lennon together, wishing him well as a family . . .'

'Lennon?' says my father. 'Where's he going?' My mother looks stunned. The jollity of last night is gone.

Lennon looks at me sheepishly. *Thanks, Hannah.*

—

Jess picks me up in my car. With new tyres.

'My parents wanted to thank you for everything you're doing for me. They wanted to be sure I was looking after you. I told them about the roast chicken.'

I want to hug her and say, *I love you, but please stop over-functioning about . . . everything.* I settle for the hug.

For the first couple of hours, she has her earbuds in, listening to a podcast about resuscitation.

It gives me a chance to think about the scars my family are still carrying from what happened twelve years ago. Mum and Lennon obviously; Dad more subtly, but it's there; Mel: hard to tell.

What did Alex say about my reasons for choosing psychiatry? *Trying to make sense of a dysfunctional family.*

Jess pulls out her earbuds and I ask how she's feeling about Lennon.

'It's so fucked. He's giving up his apprenticeship; he's got no idea. Do you think he's not over me and it's some sort of projection?'

'Reaction.'

'That's the right word?'

'Yep. Maybe not to the break-up but to what happened in his childhood.'

Jess knows what I'm talking about. Her expression tells me she doesn't want to discuss it.

'Yesterday, you seemed pretty concerned at the thought that I might not get into the psych program. I mean, I want to, and I'll find a way, but it doesn't really affect you – does it?'

She takes a long time before answering. 'This is going to sound weird . . .'

'I doubt it'll be any weirder than a paleo diet.'

'It is sort of new age. Lennon and I talked about it. It's like, after what happened, one of us had to become a therapist to . . . like karma, put the universe back in balance.'

'Something good coming out of it,' I say.

'That's a better way of putting it,' says Jess. 'Not so weird.'

Not as weird as the first word that came to my mind. *Redemption.*

But . . .' starts Jess, and this time the pause goes on for about five kilometres. 'Please don't laugh, but I've promised myself that if you don't make it, or you die or something, I'm going to try. To do what you're doing.' Then she laughs herself. 'So, you better make it.'

—

Monday morning, I have a new patient to admit.

'He was in last week,' says the psych nurse from ED, doing the handover on the phone. 'We sent him home to see a private psychiatrist, but he can't get an appointment for three months.'

James is seventeen, which means technically he can go into the adolescent unit, but they don't have a bed. No bed for Chloe in the Eating Disorders Unit, Xavier the politician wouldn't pay for private psychotherapy, and Sian, with postpartum psychosis, can't go into the Mother Baby Unit until it's safe for her to be with her baby. That just leaves us. Acute: when nobody else wants you.

James is tall, well-built, looks like he'd play sport. But his body language says library rather than football field. Baggy trousers loose on his hips, head in his hands.

His mother, a Filipina woman of maybe forty in a pink tracksuit, has one arm around him and her other hand on his knee. If not for the disparity in size, I think she would encompass him, as if he were still the baby she remembers.

His father is a stocky Caucasian man in a suit, with a notebook. He's standing apart, impatient and making sure I know it.

Omar leads us all into the interview room.

'Michael Huber,' says the man, herding his wife and son in front of him. 'You're the registrar?'

'I am. And this is James and his mother?'

He takes the hint. 'Joy. I'd like to see the consultant.'

'I'll take the history, then Dr Sharma will see you.'

'I take it Dr Sharma's not the consultant I saw in ED last week?' He doesn't put air quotes around 'consultant' but they're implied. Ah. He's the bully Ndidi talked about: the one who pushed the consultant into saying what he wanted to hear and now doesn't respect them. Good to know.

'No,' I say. 'Dr Sharma is the director of the Acute Unit.'

I start to take a history from James, but Michael interrupts several times.

'Mr Huber, Mrs Huber, you are naturally worried about your son, but right now we need to understand what's going on. So I'm going to ask you to step outside for a bit while I talk to James.'

'*You* need to understand that he's been using marijuana.' Michael is waving a finger at me.

'Thank you. My colleague made a note.'

'Can you give him something to help him sleep?' asks Joy. 'He stays up all night, and then he can't concentrate at school.' She speaks quietly, but I have no sense of her being in thrall to the bully.

There's a small gold cross around her neck. 'Religious delusions,' the ED nurse had said.

'Omar, can you escort Mr and Mrs Huber to the waiting area, please?'

Omar gives me a 'go, girl' look as he leaves with them, and James sits up a little straighter.

'Things stressful at home?'

James nods, mumbles something to himself, drops his head back into his hands.

'Are the voices pretty bad?'

He nods again.

'What are they saying?'

'God and the Holy Mother . . . God has laid His commands in my mind: I am called to judge the quick and the dead, divide the sheep from the goats, die that man may be redeemed . . .'

No point trying to look for logic in delusions. Despite him being their biological and spiritual son – not to mention *Jesus* – he tells me God and Mary think he's not worth anything. As well as God's instructions, he's hearing his own voice in his head and trying to answer it, but nothing's working. 'The Holy Mother wants me to kill myself. I guess it would shut them up.'

'We can help the voices go away with medication, James. Are you still using drugs?'

James shakes his head. 'It was only marijuana. I stopped, like, weeks ago, but my dad won't listen. It wasn't working anymore, anyway.'

In James's account, his mother is an anxious helicopter parent, his father critical and often angry: 'Nothing I do is good enough.' Alex would have a field day with the boy's choice of voices.

Family history: a paternal grandmother who was 'locked up' for a while before she died; Michael apparently hadn't seen her for years because she was 'off with the fairies'. James plays football and has recently been thinking about studying theology. That's another thing his father has a problem with.

I look at James, lost and alone in his chair, and think of Lennon, trying to see a path ahead.

—

I want to check in with Nash before discussing James with his parents, but he's tied up with Zac, one of Alex's patients who is starting clozapine for his schizophrenia. There's a lot to explain to Zac's family about the benefits and risks. Top potential benefit: a normal life; number one risk: death by heart attack. James may be just a couple of steps behind him on the psychosis journey.

I take James back to the Low Dependency common area, bring his parents into the interview room and give them my assessment: first-episode psychosis. 'First episode' implies to those who use the term that the underlying cause is schizophrenia. There are other reasons for psychotic symptoms, one of which is drug use. Sian's postpartum psychosis is another. But James hasn't had a baby. And from what I've seen, none of the other alternatives are likely.

'It's the drugs,' says Michael. 'That's the only good reason for keeping him here. So he can't get the stuff.'

I'm not about to undermine Michael's confidence in us, but last week we had to ban Sonny's visitors when the sniffer dog found his stash. No wonder he wasn't getting better.

I don't think returning to drug use is going to be an issue with James in the short term. I believe that he's stopped using marijuana, but he's likely done so because the psychosis was taking over his mind and he was no longer getting a feeling of wellbeing from the drug.

'Certainly, remaining free of illicit drugs is critical,' I say. 'But he's going to need medication.'

'What about therapy? Talking to him? Isn't that what psychiatrists are supposed to do?'

'Not in James's situation. Medication is our best option.'

Michael narrows his eyes. 'For how long?'

'Usually, we'll see an improvement in one to two weeks. But he'll need to stay on medication beyond that.'

'I won't argue with you now. But one or two weeks and then he can get back to school?'

'He might need to take more time off.'

'Or he might not. Where's the director?'

'That would be me.' Nash enters, white shirt and blue jacket, looking the part.

Michael stands and shakes his hand. 'My son's been using marijuana and started having hallucinations. I want to know how long before he's back at school.'

Nash asks to confer with me; we step out and I summarise my findings, including the fact that Michael's mother was institutionalised. I'm guessing that's contributing to his denial.

We return to the interview room.

'James,' says Nash, 'what do you think is wrong with you?'

James seems to be listening to voices; he's mumbling to them, ignoring Nash.

Nash turns to the parents. 'We will obviously ensure other diagnoses are excluded, but given the tests that have already been done, it seems unlikely that there is an organic cause, like a brain tumour. Your son has a first-episode psychosis.'

'This is bullshit. He'll be fine if you keep him off drugs.'

'He may be. But right now, he needs medication.' Nash pauses. 'His illness can be treated. And if we do that early and assertively, it doesn't have to become chronic.'

'I want a second opinion.'

Michael looks angry, but he's also clearly scared. Joy is just scared.

'Of course, though you've had four: two last week in ED and two today. However, you're welcome to bring in any doctor of your choice, or I can refer you to Professor Gordon.'

'Ron Gordon?'

'I think there's only one.'

'He'll do.'

'I suggest you don't tell him anything I've said. So you're confident he's arrived at his diagnosis independently.'

'I wasn't going to,' says Michael. 'I don't want his loyalties getting in the way.'

Not exactly the problem I was imagining.

—

From the glass house, where Nash and I are having coffee, we can see Carey filling out their patient admission questionnaire with James.

'Productive conversation?' asks Nash when they join us, uninvited.

'Adequate to complete the form,' says Carey.

Nash raises his eyebrows. 'Really? I spoke to him an hour ago and was making no connection whatsoever.'

'That's probably because you're not as competent as I am.' Before Nash can react, they add, 'If you focus on one thing, you become very good at it. Obviously, you have a range of other responsibilities.'

'Glad you noticed. So, is he happy?'

'Within the limits of his illness,' says Carey. 'Probably helped by the fact that you didn't tell him the truth.'

That lands as I expect it to land. I jump in before Nash has a chance to respond. 'We also spoke to his parents, without him in the room.'

'Did you tell *them* the truth?' says Carey.

'What would you like me to have said?' Nash says. His tone is mild.

'Just the truth. The differential diagnosis and prognosis.'

'Really?' says Nash. He's lost his jacket and is rolling up his shirtsleeves. 'I expect you haven't had a lot of experience giving people bad news. I've told James and his parents that there's a chance of relapse. This is likely just the beginning for them. If James's psychosis doesn't resolve quickly, they'll be talking to a lot of doctors and they'll hear when they're ready to hear.'

I see a flash of something in Carey's expression that seems wildly inappropriate, even for Carey. Foster Kid Forty-Five – the one whose parents treated him like a dog – gave me the same look.

But Carey holds it in and lets Nash continue rather than punching him in the face and risking having laxatives put in his dinner, as may have happened to Foster Kid Forty-Five.

'You want me to tell them that if he relapses, he almost certainly has schizophrenia. That he may need to be made an involuntary patient, so we can put up a fight against cognitive decline, withdrawal, not getting a job, poverty. Forget about a relationship.'

It's a lecture now, in that measured Californian accent.

'Particularly if he continues to use street drugs, there will be a significant risk of violence, involvement in a homicide, more likely as the victim . . .'

Carey nods. 'Excellent summary. You asked me if I wanted you to tell his parents that. My answer is yes. You're concerned about their suffering, but it's far less than James's, if we include the future scenarios you've described. James is in their care and they need to know everything in order to make the best decisions for him.'

I can see Nash wondering how to respond: whether to take Carey's input seriously or pull rank.

'Maybe we should swap jobs,' he says. 'I could learn how to give questionnaires to psychotic patients and you could head up the Acute Unit. Seven years of study, five years of specialisation, ten years or so of experience, and you'll be all set.'

Carey walks with me – follows me – to the cafe. Not happy. I guess they didn't miss the sarcasm.

'Nash was wrong about something, but I thought it was prudent not to correct him.'

'Good call. How was he wrong?'

'About me not having experience giving people bad news.'

They walk off before I can pursue it.

—

I figure I'm finished with the Hubers for the day, but at 4 pm Omar comes looking for me. 'James's parents want to see you. They asked for Nash, but I've told them he's busy.'

'Is he?'

'When isn't he?'

'Your professor's a wanker,' Michael announces, in the middle of the glass house, to kick off the conversation.

I manage to suppress my smile.

Then he adds, 'As you'd expect, given he's an academic. But he seems to know what he's talking about. And he knows how to communicate with people on the same level.'

Wanker to wanker. I just nod.

'If – and he emphasised *if* – it's psychosis, then it has a physical . . . biological . . . basis. Your boss threw me when he said it didn't have an "organic cause". That made it sound like it was caused by something at home. Anyway, it's an illness like any other, and we throw the drugs at it and get it sorted. What I want you to tell me is what his . . . prognosis is.'

I've no idea what Prof said to him. My attempt to keep my response vague (*they'll hear what they want to hear when they're ready*) doesn't satisfy Michael. He makes it obvious that he thinks I don't know the answer. Joy all but rolls her eyes – at him or me?

Screw it: they're asking for the truth; they can have it. Carey may not have persuaded Nash, but if James was my child, I'd want to know. If I was *James*, I'd want my parents to know.

'About one-third of people who experience a psychotic episode recover completely and return to their lives.'

'And the other two-thirds?'

'Another third have a few episodes over their lives but do okay. And a third have a more chronic course with ongoing problems.'

'We'll make damn sure he never smokes another joint, if those are the consequences.'

'That's part of the answer. But he may relapse anyway, and if he does, he almost certainly has schizophrenia.'

Michael and Joy both flinch, then look at each other. I'm guessing Prof didn't use that word.

'Go on,' Michael says.

'It's a tough disease – maybe what your mother had.' According to James, Michael never visited his mother; what does that mean for his son? 'We have better treatment options now, though. As a family, what you can do to reduce the chances of the less-happy outcomes is to get on board with the treatment, find a good psychiatrist, work with them. Ask questions and listen to the answers. And if things don't go as we hope, then family support is going to make a huge difference to James's quality of life.'

'Thank you for telling us,' says Joy. 'It's better to know.'

Nash walks in then, takes a step back, seeing we're in conversation, but Michael's attention switches immediately to him.

'I've seen Professor Gordon, and as I've told Dr Wright he was straightforward and helpful. At this stage, I just want to ask you two questions.'

His first question is about the diagnosis, the second the prognosis. Nash tells him exactly what I did.

Michael nods. A father's just been told that there's a one-in-three chance his seventeen-year-old son has chronic schizophrenia, and I feel like punching the air. I begin to mentally chastise myself, and Michael finishes the job.

'Alright. I've spoken to five qualified people now, and four of them have told me the same thing – and I suspect the only reason the consultant in ED didn't was to avoid a confrontation. I'm used to that. I'm also used to taking advice from people who know what they're doing, but we're talking about my son here.'

'Our son,' says Joy.

'You get many patients thinking they're Jesus Christ?' says Michael. 'It's the sort of thing you make jokes about without thinking about the reality.'

'Not so much these days,' says Nash. 'More likely to be big pharma or microchips. Whatever's in the patient's head.'

Michael looks at his wife. 'Joy here has made James go to her church since he was born. I've got no time for it and –'

'No,' says Nash. 'If you need to build a house, and you've got straw, you make it out of straw. If you've got sticks or bricks . . .'

Weirdly, Michael laughs. 'Everyone in his class has to have counselling – over seeing a naked kid. Even the boys. Plenty of work for you guys. But the teacher – actually, she's a nun – went down on her knees. Afterward, she said she was just playing along to appease James, but I think she thought the rapture had come.'

Joy manages to cross herself so subtly that Michael doesn't seem to notice, but she holds the tiny cross at her neck for just a moment.

'What do we do to keep James in the first third – the single-episode group?' Michael asks Nash. He glances at me. 'We want to hear from everyone who's seen James.'

'I would just repeat what Dr Wright and I have both told you already,' says Nash. 'We work out what meds suit him. Maybe there'll be a quick turnaround and he can go back to school, but . . . final year? I'd be planning a break and coming back next year, so the pressure is off.'

Michael nods. 'Good advice.'

—

I catch Jon in the registrars' room as I'm getting ready to leave. I haven't seen him since our study group meeting; I don't have any reason to go over to Extended Care and he doesn't visit the glass house in Acute. The registrars' room is hardly welcoming – just benches and bookcases, but it's the only quiet place to escape to.

'Discharge summary,' he says, sipping from a can of Coke. 'My first. Not exactly a river of patients coming out of Extended Care.'

We're heading to Alex's for a study group, and Jon orders an Uber. On the way, I tell him about the Hubers. Jon deals with the third of schizophrenia sufferers who become chronic and are unsafe or don't have family to care for them at home.

'The relatives – well, the ones who still keep in touch – usually just want the best care for their son or daughter or brother or sister,' he says.

'And I guess you and the team do too.'

'But we can't provide it unless we can see what it might look like from their perspective. Not easy when they're thinking so differently.'

I'm on the verge of saying it's something I try to do myself, but I'm glad I don't, because Jon brings it right home.

'Good intentions,' he says. 'My mob has a little experience with those.'

—

Alex's place is not as I'd imagined. It's a fifth-storey apartment on the south side of the city, close to the water, and I'd expected it to be stylish but soulless. I guess I had the apartment I shared with Marcus in mind.

But it's a renovation-in-progress: the kitchen has all the appliances, but no doors on the cupboards and wires poking out of the wall where the splashback needs to go. Floorboards look like they've been recently done but only half of the skirting boards are in place. I sneak a look around as Alex chats with Jon. In the spare bedroom, there's a portable workbench and circular saw. And in the living room, beside a bookcase full of books on psychotherapy, is a piano with a protective sheet beside it.

The highlight of the apartment is a deck with amazing views: city towers with illuminated logos, a water channel with smaller boats moored below and a working dock beyond.

It's obvious that Alex owns this place, and I'm reminded that the failed relationship with Marcus and the lack of rich parents, not to mention the years of study, have made me a late starter in the home-ownership stakes.

Ndidi arrives. 'Ooh-la-la. I know where I want to spend New Year's Eve. Where's the chicken?'

'Starters first. I think Hannah's set the standard at three courses.'

He brings out an olive breadstick with anchovies poked into it, wrapped in foil and toasted in the oven. It's ridiculously good. Carbs and salt.

With the sun setting and a glass of wine in my hand, I'm reminded of the last time I had a drink with sunset views and the same man as host, and ask myself lightly, just testing the feeling, could I get used to this?

I could certainly get used to the cooking. Alex has kept the chicken tradition and tries to pass off the casserole with olives and chorizo as something he picked up and reheated, but the empty olive jar on the kitchen bench is a giveaway.

I talk about Chloe, Sian and James. Jon has touched a nerve with his comment about putting ourselves in the patients' shoes. And that was after Carey's argument with Nash, and my attempt to put James's interests first.

I do my best to describe the cases from the patients' perspectives. Sian's easiest, though not *easy*: I can at least imagine myself in her situation and I've seen flashes of what she's like when she's well. James is more difficult: I don't have such a strong sense of his underlying personality. Surprisingly, Chloe's the toughest, and I'm reminded of Nash's reluctance to take her on and Omar's warning about anorexia patients in general. With all of them, I'm embarrassingly aware of the gap between what I claim to do and what I really do.

I'm being pretty clumsy about it and Jon calls it out, in a good way, explaining what I'm trying to achieve.

'Not sure how it'd play with the examiners,' says Ndidi.

'In the end,' says Alex, 'it's going to come down to how well we know our cases. The more ways we have of looking at them, the better. The way we present them . . . that's window-dressing.'

Ndidi outlines one of her mother–baby cases: a woman with schizophrenia who's had her baby removed from her care permanently, in consultation with Child Protection. Third time for her.

My family were dealing with Child Protection constantly because of the foster kids. The authorities don't always get it right. And the consequences of getting it wrong can be pretty devastating.

Jon, the Bilinarra man, is with me. 'I've grown up seeing the impact of babies being taken from their mothers. It's not only the mother who's going to suffer.'

'There are going to be attachment issues between the mother and baby whatever you do,' says Alex. 'And we know that attachment is a big factor in the baby's long-term mental health.'

We doesn't include me, but I immediately think of Sian and Matilda.

Alex gives us a quick take on attachment theory, which I suspect is all he's able to do. I make a note to do some reading. There might even be some research on foster kids – and the kids who have to share their parents with them.

Alex picks up the bottle of red wine that he and Ndidi have been finishing with some cheese. 'This, by the way, was a donation from Carey.'

'Carey?' Jon hasn't met them.

'Prof's research assistant,' says Alex. 'Think red.'

'Or aftershave,' says Ndidi.

'It's actually a bit awkward,' says Alex. 'They left the wine in the registrars' room and I assumed it was an apology for calling me out on a prescribing . . . technicality in front of Nash.'

'What does Carey know about prescribing?' says Ndidi.

'They know about everything. I'm guessing they pick up a lot from hanging around patients.'

'They're probably autistic,' I say. 'Maybe they realised afterward that they were out of line about the prescribing.'

'So,' says Ndidi, indicating her glass, 'everybody wins. Where's the awkward bit?'

'They want to join this group,' says Alex. 'Apparently to, quote, increase their knowledge, unquote. The gift was intended to open the door to that.'

'They're probably a bit lonely,' says Jon. 'Nobody else is doing the same job as them, and they're obviously interested in the clinical work.'

'You're right,' says Alex. 'And I didn't handle it well.'

'Well enough,' says Ndidi, 'since they let you keep the wine.'

'Well, no,' says Alex. 'I was trying to be subtle about saying no and I don't think they got the message.'

'Ouch,' says Jon.

'I was thinking we should buy them a drink,' says Alex.

I'm wondering if he's going to ask me to stay back to talk about attachment. But he's played it very cool, as he does at work. Good for discretion, not so great for knowing where his feelings are at.

'When's our next meeting, Hannah?' asks Jon.

Seems I'm the convenor.

And Alex decides that makes me spokesperson.

'Do you want to give Carey the bad news?' he says.

—

The next day, I watch Michael and James from the glass house, and for the first time I see the physical resemblance. Michael is wearing a football jersey. James is noticeably slowed down. They're awkward with each other.

James has been spending much of his time sitting with Zac, who has the drug-resistant psychosis and isn't making a lot of sense. And Michael's now had a chance to see the other patients: Chloe in her wheelchair, Sonny singing and flashing, Sian still flat . . . It's a taste of what he, Joy and James may be facing.

James is seeing it too, even if he's not processing it. Yet.

Later, Michael asks to see me.

'I've spoken with the school,' he says. 'They're okay with James having a month off, to start with, but I'll need you to write a letter.' He pauses. 'Make it from the hospital, but no mention of which ward . . . or the specific illness.' He adds, by way of apology for exactly what he's reinforcing: 'Stigma. By the way, I called your professor again. Mentioned you'd handled a tough job well and told me exactly the same things he did.' He grins. 'Twenty-five years in business. You know what's going on.'

I feel a rush of sadness for James, and for Michael too. I hope James gets to study the course of his choice or find a job he's happy with and that Michael learns to be proud of him – whichever third he falls into.

'Happy to write a letter,' I say.

Michael nods. Then he starts crying.

FIVE

SABOTAGE

'Just give it to me straight,' says Sabriya. 'I'm not a child.'

Her lunch companion tops up her glass, then his own. He's late twenties, ten years younger than her, slim, bearded. It's a warm day, and they have an outside table.

'Sabriya,' he says, 'you know as well as I do that publishers make judgement calls; I'm sure it'll find a home.'

'I have to say I'm surprised. I mean, you've published social commentary before.'

'We have. And I enjoyed yours: it's sharply observed.'

'So, what's the problem?'

'As I said, your focus is on the . . . observable. For the space you work in, that's probably entirely appropriate.'

'Sorry – you're saying my piece is shallow? No, that's not really it, is it? You wanted something political.'

'That's not what I'm saying.'

'It's what you mean. I'm not *allowed* to write about everyday life and ordinary human dilemmas because of who I am and where I come from. You're as bad as my mother.'

'Listen, I didn't want to . . .'

She suppresses the anger, manages to turn it into an awkward laugh. 'It's fine. I have great respect for my mother.'

When she gets home, she can't write.

—

Omar is messing with me. I'm trying to leave for the day, and he's managed to turn a quick medication check for Chloe, our anorexia-nervosa patient, into an extended discussion. I look over my shoulder toward the door and see Alex hovering.

Omar laughs. 'Your date. Thought we should make him wait a bit.'

'Date. You really think?'

'If he had a question about something clinical, he'd have interrupted. You never told me how the first date went, by the way.'

'Somebody sabotaged it. Some nurse making work for me.'

'Kept him keen, didn't I? If you're interested in him, tell him you're busy tonight. Make him wait a bit longer.'

'And if I'm not?'

'Go out tonight and enjoy the drink. Advice from a guy who never dates.'

'Seriously?'

'I'm married to my mum. Carer at work, carer at home.'

My own social life right now consists of answering Jess's questions about emergency medicine. *Could two bits of plaque break off and give someone a heart attack and stroke at the same time?*

I tell Alex I'm busy. We'll have drinks on Friday.

—

Elena seeks me out at the glass house. Today's she's in baggy floral pants cinched in at the ankle and a long pale-yellow jacket. Beads as always; she manages never to get them caught.

'Thought you might like to sit in on a CBT session,' says Elena.

'With Chloe's family?'

'You're welcome to watch that too, but you should see some individual therapy first.'

Trainees need to check psychological therapies off on the long list of tasks required to qualify. Cognitive behavioural therapy is one of the options, and I need to see it done before I can practise it myself. It makes sense to observe a psychologist – someone who's using it all the time. I doubt Nash has used it since he passed his exams.

'CBT is a bit old-fashioned,' says Elena. 'But the client is a little old-fashioned too, in her own way. She's one of my private patients, a journalist. Or she was. At the moment, she can barely open her laptop.'

'Because?'

'You'll see for yourself.'

I mention it to Alex, thinking he might be interested, but he's dismissive.

'CBT? Twelve steps to happiness. Too much process, not enough hard thinking. Fine if all you want is behavioural change.'

'Maybe that's what's your Mr X needs. *Stop harassing women* would be a good start.'

'I think he's been shocked into that. If he could turn back the clock, he would.'

'Especially since she said no.' I realise that in my mind I've separated Mr X, Alex's patient, from the guy I saw with his family and dog at the parkrun.

'Fair point,' says Alex. 'You can tell me about the CBT over our drink on Friday.'

—

Elena is doing her third session with the journalist in the private rooms adjacent to the hospital. I walk over, enjoying the mild temperature and the clear blue sky, trying to get myself into a different headspace: from mental illness to the problems of day-to-day life.

I know who Sabriya Tehrani is from her pieces in the press. She generally writes about social issues, often from an Islamic perspective, though her take is more cultural than religious.

I wait outside the therapy room until Elena calls me in. Sabriya is seated in one of three armchairs: mine is to one side of her, out of the line of sight between therapist and patient – *client*. She's dressed in an elegant silk blouse, pants and headscarf. She looks defensive.

Pointing at me, she says, 'You can sit in, as long as you respect that this is absolutely confidential.'

I nod, say nothing; I'm the observer. I've had patients, and more commonly relatives, push back. But there's a different power dynamic here. I feel free not to like her, and I may be on my way to taking up that option.

Sabriya isn't finished. 'I should let you know, as I have Elena, that I don't feel any reciprocal obligation. If I want to write about some aspect of what happens here, I'll do so.'

I'll share my observations with Elena and maybe Alex, and Sabriya can share hers with the readership of her nationally syndicated column.

I look for signs that Elena's conscious of representing the entire psychology profession. I'd have expected her to be unflappable. But no: she's on edge, fiddling with her beads.

Sabriya begins, unprompted. 'You'll be pleased to know I did my homework.' She turns to me. 'I can't see you. Could you sit over there' – she gestures to the opposite corner – 'so I don't have to keep spinning my head to talk to you?'

Being invisible is the idea, but it looks like Sabriya is going to address both of us regardless. Elena nods and I haul my chair over to where Sabriya can see me.

'Writer's block,' she tells me. 'Happens to all of us, but this has been going on for a while, and I need to put food on the table. I thought I'd try something different.'

Elena interrupts. 'We've been working on identifying negative thought patterns. How did you go this week?'

'You could ask if I got any writing done. I suppose it's the same question. To which the answer is no. I sat at the keyboard, and . . . nothing.'

'And the feeling?'

'What do you think? Frustration.'

'But before that; before you realised it wasn't going to come?'

Sabriya rummages around in her handbag and takes out a roll of mints. She offers them to us before taking a couple herself. Behind the aggression – and possibly narcissism – there's anxiety, and I mentally scold myself. Not being able to work could trigger a serious mental health issue. I'm seeing the kind of early intervention that we keep saying we want.

The mint or the break seems to encourage some reflection. 'There was this immediate . . . panic's too strong a word; let's say uneasiness.'

'And the thought that preceded it?'

Sabriya produces an A4 notebook and turns to me. 'I suppose you know how this works?'

She flashes the notebook at me and indicates the four columns: '*Thoughts*, *Feelings*, *Behaviour* and *Evidence*. Therapy as imagined by an accountant.' She seems pleased with her turn of phrase.

'Thoughts precede and drive feelings, but often we're unaware of them, and of the underlying beliefs that fuel them,' Elena explains to me, or to reinforce the message for Sabriya. 'The first step in CBT is to identify the thoughts that occur before the emotion takes over.'

'I don't have a lot of time to spend analysing where my feelings come from,' Sabriya says. 'Do you have kids? Elderly parents who need looking after?'

She's asking me. I shake my head.

Elena takes back control again. 'But you're learning to identify the unproductive thoughts.'

'It's not that hard. I imagine most of us draw from the same well. *Thought: I can't do this. I will fail. I've got nothing important to say*. What I've been told since I was a child. Because I'm female. Because I'm Muslim. Or the opposite. Because I have a voice, I have a responsibility to speak on every damn political issue.' She laughs. 'That's my mother. I've never let it get in my way, then bang, out of nowhere . . .'

I wonder what Prof – or Alex – would say she's guarding against. I'm certain they'd be interrogating that dismissive 'out of nowhere'.

'And that thought created the feeling that stopped you.' Elena leans forward and points to the notebook. 'Any evidence that it might not reflect reality? Maybe you've published an article or two?'

'A few more than two. Never missed a deadline. Until now. My mother would tell me to get over myself: others have it worse. But telling myself that isn't fixing the problem.'

Elena goes over the thought patterns that get Sabriya into trouble, but Sabriya deflects any attempt to dig into their causes.

'Given your profession and the nature of the problem,' says Elena, 'I'm going to ask you to take a different approach to this week's homework. Rather than filling in the columns, write me a short piece about the chain of thoughts, feelings and behaviour, and where you think you could make a change. It's not standard, but you're not a standard client.'

Special homework for a special client. Playing right into the narcissism. But it's a neat idea. Get her to write *something* and go from there.

Sabriya thanks Elena then turns to me. 'I'm serious about the confidentiality.'

I'm not sure who she thinks I'll tell, but it reinforces my assessment of her personality.

'Oh hell, yes,' says Elena when Sabriya has left. 'But she's not ready to dig into that. Frankly, I'm not even sure she's up for the level of self-examination that CBT requires.'

What happened to *the unexamined life is not worth living*? I pull myself up. If I could do for Chloe, or even Sian, what Elena's aiming to do for Sabriya in twelve sessions – get them back on their feet, functioning – or if I could get my own family sorted in twelve sessions, I'd be a very happy psych registrar. And daughter.

—

The receptionist calls to me as I arrive at the glass house.

'I was just looking for you. A woman from Child Protection is here to see Sian Tierney. Omar's organising someone to take her in.'

I'm in time to watch the drama unfold through the glass. Aurora, one of our student nurses, is escorting a professional-looking young woman through the Low Dependency common area toward where Sian and her partner, Leo, are sitting.

They're accosted by an older woman we've just admitted with schizophrenia and cognitive impairment – possibly with a physical cause. She's no threat to anyone, but suddenly she's all over Aurora and the visitor; I can't hear the exchange, but I'm guessing she's asking for cigarettes. Over and over – perseverating. The visitor is freaking out.

She pulls away and heads toward Sian and Leo, but is intercepted again, this time by Sonny, who's been moved from High Dependency. It's been a while since he exposed himself, but whatever he's saying seems to be having as dramatic an impact. I rush through the door, take the visitor's arm, collect Sian and Leo, and we head to an interview room.

—

Sian has now had three ECT sessions, the latest producing a fifty-five-second seizure, leaving her with a headache as previously. She's taking fluids, so is out of immediate danger. But she's still depressed and in the grip of the delusion that her baby has been taken by right-wing conspiracy theorists – she's now quite open about that.

Her parents visited this morning before leaving for Europe: 'We've left it to the absolute last possible moment; we know she's in the best place for her right now; Leo's mother has been wonderful.' And, slightly undermining that confidence in our care: 'When can she be transferred out of here?'

'When she's better,' I told them, 'she'll go to the Mother Baby Unit. It's going to be a little while yet.'

Leo has visited, but he's plainly struggling to see past the psychosis to the woman he knows. I wonder how close they really are.

And now, a woman from Child Protection. Why is she here? I'm not going to find out until she gets her shit together.

'Glass of water?' I ask.

'I'm okay.' She takes a couple of breaths. 'I'm Amber. Amber Reed. We've had a notification.' She looks at her notes. 'We understand that Matilda was left alone for quite some period of time.'

Who would know that, outside family and the staff here? I know better than to ask; she's not allowed to tell me who notified them.

'She was left for a few hours,' I say. 'Her mother was unwell, but she put her somewhere safe.'

'But the infant was left alone,' says Amber. 'Which we wouldn't consider safe.' She looks at Leo. 'And you were . . . ?'

'I work in WA.'

'And the baby is now . . . ?'

'Don't tell her,' says Sian.

'With me and my mother,' says Leo.

'I'll need to talk to her.'

'No,' says Sian. 'You're just trying to find out where she is, aren't you?'

'We need to ensure she's safe,' says Amber.

Amber's just going through a standard list of questions, but Sian doesn't know that. She turns to me and her voice rises. 'They'll take her. Don't tell her anything.' She seems to have realised – if only at some gut level – that the baby in question is Matilda. The real Matilda. And the combativeness is part of her normal personality. Progress.

'It's just routine,' says Leo, then looks to Amber for confirmation.

She switches her attention to him. 'We understand that you're going back to work and your mother –'

'It's none of your fucking business,' says Sian, right in Amber's face. 'You're all fucking Nazis. *This* time, I'm not going to let you –'

I interrupt. 'I think you can see that Sian is quite unwell at the moment.'

I sense Amber's out of her depth, a junior sent to check off a notification that wasn't considered particularly concerning. Hard not to feel for her. It's a tough job without much appreciation. But now she sees a way to assert her authority and channel her own discomfort.

'We'll follow up. But in the meantime, I'm going to insist that the baby not be brought here. The environment is unsafe and Ms Tierney is clearly not able to look after her.'

Leo nods. 'You won't get any argument from my mother on that.'

—

'Where's Nash?' Nicole speaks over the familiar sound of the heels; brilliant blue today. We don't have time to answer – he comes in behind her.

'What the *fuck* are you doing?'

I've been staring at the computer screen but can't resist a sideways glance. It's not the first time I've seen Nash angry with Nicole but she usually gives it right back to him. Today she's looking seriously uncomfortable.

'There needs to be better communication with Child Protection,' says Nicole. 'The relationship has been poor, and I want to do something about it. I was just giving them a heads-up that we had a patient who might come onto their radar, but that we'd done everything right.'

'You were right about the poor relationship. Because your heads-up has some wet-behind-the-ears *social worker* coming in here and seeing my patients, and then calling to tell me who can and can't come into my unit.'

'You're talking about the baby? Is that such a big issue?'

Nash's expression says, *Who the hell are you to ask that question?* But it's a huge issue. Sian's perception of Matilda is at the centre of her psychosis; stopping contact is going to make things worse. Delaying Sian's recovery will get in the way of Matilda's attachment and, therefore, her long-term mental health. I've been doing my reading.

Nash is on the phone to Sandra Byrd as soon as Nicole has gone. They decide to move Sian to the Mother Baby Unit immediately – with Matilda. This will put Matilda in the care of her mother under professional supervision.

Nash is pleased with himself. 'Sandra thought it was a nice solution, and not just for the patient. She doesn't like being pushed around either.'

'I guess nobody does.' I'm thinking of Amber.

Omar calls Child Protection to give them the news. Grinning.

I get to tell Leo we're doing what I told the family a few hours ago wasn't possible. And ask him to bring Matilda in.

—

Chloe weighs in at thirty-one kilograms – up two. After only a week, this seems great to me, but Nash thinks it's too much, too quickly, and he looks at her magnesium levels.

Omar doesn't believe it. 'She has her family therapy session tomorrow. She thinks if she's gained weight, she'll go home.'

'Nobody's making her stay,' I say. 'But if she's eating . . .'

'I doubt it's eating that's putting on the weight,' says Nash.

'Wait and see,' says Omar.

Chloe isn't allowed to leave the Low Dependency common room for an hour after eating or being weighed. If she needs the toilet, they'll go with her – so they can measure how much fluid she loses. It seems draconian, but at the end of the hour I find out why. Her clothes and the chair she's sitting on are soaked. She's held on as long as she could, but appears unconcerned, oblivious even, and refuses to acknowledge she's water-loaded. Been there before, I guess. Bladder empty, she weighs 30.2 kilograms.

While the staff are cleaning her up, I speak to her parents, David and Sue, who've come to visit, and explain what's happened.

'Barbaric,' says her father, and, despite understanding the clinical justification, I'm inclined to agree. *Dehumanising* is the word I'd have used.

'She needs to come home,' says Sue. 'At least she gets love there.'

I remember Nash asking me to consider where I thought Chloe would be most comfortable. Have I behaved like an oncologist who pushes for treatments without thinking about quality of life?

What's just happened is surely outside the spirit of the deal I cut with Chloe, when I agreed to get the nurses to back off a bit. I hadn't taken into account the Eating Disorders staff overseeing her management, and slipping straight into some standard protocol. *It's what we're set up to do.*

'I guess that's something you'll talk about with Elena tomorrow,' I say to Sue.

'Thanks for reminding me,' says David. 'We're cancelling that session. Can you let her know?'

'Because of what's happened here?'

'We'd already decided. She'll know why.'

'I'll tell her. Hopefully we can reschedule quickly.' I take a punt and add, 'I think Chloe may be waiting on the therapy before she's ready to leave.'

I don't think David's the sort of guy who says 'fuck', but his expression does it for him.

—

I walk with Sian to the Mother Baby Unit. Ndidi gives us a tour.

I point out to her that the unit has only six patients, compared with Acute's twenty-eight.

Ndidi corrects me. 'Twelve patients. Six mothers – *parents* – and six babies.'

The corridor walls are covered with posters and artwork, much of it created by the women themselves. There are prints of their own hands and feet next to the tiny ones of their infants, and large coloured-in circles – mandalas. And a picture of a long black tunnel with two figures at the end, one much larger than the other.

Sian pauses, looking at the tunnel picture.

Ndidi leans into her. 'There's light, even if you can't see it.'

Sian can't quite bring herself to smile, but there's something positive in the look she gives Ndidi. I'm more curious about Ndidi's response. For a second I think I see an unfamiliar softness in her expression, before she shuts it down.

Sian and Matilda's new space is like a motel room – minus fixtures that a patient could hang themselves from.

'What's the deal with Child Protection?' asks Ndidi as I'm about to head back to the glass house.

I fill her in. 'Why do you ask?'

'They've got a meeting with Sandra in an hour. I think some serious shit's about to go down.'

—

I have to wait till late afternoon to find out what kind of shit. Ndidi texts me and we meet in the registrars' room.

She pulls out her phone and puts it on the table. 'Listen.'

'You recorded it?' I don't need to ask if she got permission. 'Is that even legal?'

'Employees are allowed to record their boss without asking. I was recording Sandra, in case she bullied me.' She's laughing.

'Shit, Ndidi.'

'Background. Sandra got me to join them, to even up the numbers. She and Cynthia are a fair match, but me and the sweet little junior . . .'

'Amber?'

'That's her. The voice you won't know is Cynthia's. She and Sandra have some history, so this isn't all pretty.'

Ndidi hits play, and I hear a voice that must be Cynthia's. She sounds peeved. '*Can we all put away our phones, please.*'

Then Sandra: '*Dr Edozie is on call. The world doesn't stop for your meetings, I'm afraid, so let's be quick. You've spoken to Sian and Leo. Sian has postpartum psychosis, which has an excellent long-term prognosis. The baby will be here shortly, in the care of her own mother, supported by professionals. In the event that Sian is not sufficiently recovered by the time she's discharged, the paternal grandmother will move in until Sian is able to cope without her. Are we all good with that?'*

'Not exactly collaborative,' I say.

Ndidi nods. 'I warned you. Worse to come.'

'No,' Cynthia is saying, '*we're not good with that. Sian put her baby in harm's way. Not just abandoned her where she might have been found; she calculatedly –*'

'*She was delusional. What she did in the grip of psychosis has no relevance to what she'll do when she's well. It's like you going out and getting drunk and ending up sleeping with someone you don't –*'

'*I know what psychosis is, Dr Byrd. As I understand it, Sian has not recovered and does not even believe Matilda is her baby. If you want to pursue your unfortunate analogy, she's still drunk and at risk of repeating her behaviour. If she recovers, well and good, but right now, out of what my department head would call an abundance of caution, we don't want the baby to be* with *the mother.*' A pause. '*As my colleague made clear and as you've attempted to subvert.*'

So that's what it's about. Nash may not like being pushed around, but nor does Amber. Or at least Cynthia doesn't like it on her behalf. Sandra's voice again. '*You're being ridiculous, Cynthia. Sian isn't at home with no support. Nor is she in the Acute Unit. She's in a specialised unit for mothers and babies.*'

'We've removed babies from mother–baby units before for their own safety. Including from this unit.'

'On my advice, every time. And this time, I'm saying that Sian is no threat to her baby. I take that responsibility.'

'And what if we've reached a different conclusion?'

'Then get a second medical *opinion. Or a third. Including the impact on attachment of having multiple carers. For god's sake, is this the hill you want to die on?'*

'And you? Taking in someone who, according to your own earlier assessment, wasn't ready? To cater to . . .' Cynthia apparently decides that trying to drive a wedge between Nash and Sandra isn't going to play, and sees another way. *'You've obviously decided to make some sort of point. But Amber and I note your assurance that there won't be a problem. Let's hope you're right. And obviously we'll need to review at discharge.'*

Ndidi stops the audio. 'Sting's in the tail. Review at discharge. But we'll be able to give our input.'

'Who's going to be Matilda's voice?'

'Right now, Sandra. Don't forget that when you criticise her for going in hard.'

—

Two days later, I'm about to sit down for a 2 pm lunch, in the slot I'd reserved for Chloe's family therapy before they cancelled, when Elena grabs me.

'Are you still interested in observing?'

'They changed their minds?'

'They've rescheduled. But Sabriya Tehrani has requested an emergency appointment.'

A writer's-block emergency.

Sabriya is waiting when we arrive. She's dressed elegantly again, but I sense a heightened anxiety. She nods at me – her audience – as I take up my corner position in her line of sight.

Elena gets straight to the point. 'You wanted your appointment brought forward.'

'Because what you asked me to do wasn't working. Nothing's changed. Same answers. *Thinking: I can't do this. Feeling: I'm stressed.* And it doesn't matter how many times I remind myself I've done it before . . . Frankly, that's what my mother would tell me to do – for free.'

'This is only the beginning of the fourth session,' says Elena. 'Last session you made a start on asking where those negative thoughts were coming from and –'

Sabriya interrupts, looking at me. 'Maybe you've had some ideas?'

Elena answers. 'That's an interesting question to ask Hannah, because as a psychiatrist she'd have the option of medication. She *might* decide that your anxiety – let's call it that, because doctors need a diagnosis before they prescribe – could be addressed with, for example, benzodiazepines.'

'That's your cure for writer's block?' Sabriya asks me. 'Benzos?' Then, when I don't respond, 'Oh, for goodness' sake, you can have an opinion.'

I manage an apologetic smile. I'm expecting Elena to pull Sabriya up, but she lets her continue.

'If there was a pill, we'd all be taking it.' She turns back to Elena. 'But you're not a writer. If you were, you'd understand what it meant last week when you asked me to use my . . . gift . . . as some sort of therapeutic tool. My mother says that I should use it to change the world, that it's a moral responsibility, and I disagree with that, but it's another step down to use it in the service of myself. And to bring my work to you for you to unpick, speculate on, judge . . .'

Judge. It fits: the fragile narcissist. Involuntarily, and just slightly, *really* slightly, I raise my eyebrows.

She sees.

Shit, shit, shit. Don't call me on it.

She doesn't: she's smarter than that. She uses her advantage to get me to do what *she* wants: 'Say something. You've been sitting there, listening. I guess it's possible you've noticed something. I'm interested.'

'I'm sorry, but it's not my role.'

'You only do enigmatic facial expressions?'

'Sabriya,' says Elena.

'Let her tell me what she's observed. One thing.'

And Elena indulges the special patient. Nods.

I point out the most obvious thing, without any question or interpretation. 'You mention your mother quite often.' And there was a reference to caring for aged parents in the previous session. I look to Elena, and she gives me a half smile.

Sabriya looks surprised. 'Really? I wouldn't have said . . .' She pauses – wondering, I think, how much to disclose. 'I'll tell you something. I show everything I write to my mother. She never approves, but I show it to her anyway.' She laughs. 'But the last piece I wrote, for a literary magazine, I didn't show her. She'd have *hated* it.'

Elena smiles. 'I wonder if that's a negative thought that's been holding you back . . .'

'I suppose you could look at it that way.' Sabriya laughs again. 'I imagine you look at everything that way. My mother would say I just needed to get on with what I was put on this earth to do.'

—

It seems I was put on earth to be Sian's special buddy. The following day, Nash lets me know that my job isn't done yet.

'Your patient Sian –'

'Not mine anymore. She's gone to the Mother Baby Unit.'

'Turns out that in order to stay there, you have to have a baby.'

Leo's mother has convinced him that Matilda would be better off in her care, which would mean Sian returning to us – and we'd be back where we were. And since I'm the person who knows Leo best . . .

I phone Leo and ask him to come in.

'You can bring Matilda with you,' I say. 'So Sian can see her.'

'She's not here.' He must realise that's a bad answer. 'My mum's taken her out in the pram.'

I persuade him to come in, but he shows up without Matilda. I wait till he's seen Sian before starting my pitch. Ndidi lets us have her office, though the intern is in the corner using the computer.

'Bit nicer than the Acute Unit, isn't it?' I say.

A wry smile from Leo. 'Not a high bar.'

'How do you feel about Matilda staying here?'

'Maybe you tell me why you think she should.'

'There's a lot of reasons, but I guess the main one is that we all want things to get back to normal. And normal is Matilda being cared for by her mother.'

'If she was capable of it. And normal isn't a psych hospital, even if it's got pictures on the wall.' He pauses for a few moments, looks across the room, and I suspect he's playing to the intern. 'Look, this isn't easy for me, but I have to put Matilda first. I have to ask myself: who's doing the better job of caring for her – and it's my mother. And me.'

'You're probably right: Sian's probably going to struggle for a bit. That's a hump we have to get over, and Sian will improve much more quickly if Matilda's there to remind her of what's real. And she'll have a lot of help and support.'

He still looks doubtful. I try another angle.

'Your mum sounds like a really involved grandma. I guess if it were up to her, she'd care for Matilda until Sian got better. As long as you needed. Longer, even.'

I catch the fleeting smile. I was right; Deirdre is the one calling the shots.

'Your mother may not thank you for doing this, but the longer you leave it, the harder it's going to be to separate her and Matilda. And the person who will thank you for doing it, when she's well, is Sian. Your call.'

'For a doctor, you're pretty pushy.'

'You've heard of doctors' orders. Tell your mum that's what it is.'

—

Leo brings Matilda in a few hours later, and I take them over to the Mother Baby Unit, where Ndidi and Sian are waiting for us.

We peer into the pram and Matilda looks up at us, eyes blinking and curious.

Sian puts a shaking hand on the pram handle.

'Leo stole her,' she whispers to me.

Shit. In the interview with Amber, something in Sian's mind told her that Matilda was her baby – why else would she have been so fierce in trying to protect her? But that understanding doesn't appear to have made its way into Sian's conscious thinking. I'm glad Deirdre isn't here.

'Maybe you could pick Matilda up and play with her,' I say to Sian.

She doesn't move.

Ndidi asks if she may, then gently picks up Matilda and holds her so she's facing Sian. The baby catches sight of Leo and smiles.

'Knows her daddy,' says Ndidi.

Leo looks surprised.

I turn to Sian. 'Is there anything you remember doing with your mother when you were young?' Dumb question; she won't have any memories from when she was Matilda's age. And she won't want to play with a baby that Leo stole.

But to my surprise, Sian responds immediately. 'Making daisy chains,' she says and half-laughs; it's dismissive, but I sense that she's recalling the scene.

'You'll make them with Matilda one day,' I say.

But she's not connecting. She can't picture it and doesn't believe it will ever happen.

—

Alex hasn't forgotten about our drinks date; I wasn't planning to let him.

'Place we went last time?' he suggests.

'Bit expensive. I was thinking the pub.'

'On a Friday night? I thought you wanted to tell me about the

CBT. Anyway, I booked a table and, after what you just said, it has to be my shout. You can take me to the pub next time.'

The weather is still warm enough for drinks on the rooftop, and the breeze is refreshing. Alex orders margaritas, then looks at me intently.

'What?' I say.

'I saw your reaction to me ordering the bathtub gin – thought I'd pick something you couldn't analyse.'

'And there was me, expecting Sex on the Beach.'

We both laugh. Work is over for the week and I'm spending the evening with an interesting guy who listens and understands what I do. I'm beginning to see where Jess was coming from when she said he was hot – and where this could be going.

'So,' he says, 'no partner since beaker guy? The one who laughed at you breaking the glassware.'

'Marcus. It's only been three months. And I've been slightly busy. What about you?'

'I was seeing someone . . . a lawyer, but she got a job interstate, and I guess we'd both decided we weren't' – he does air quotes – 'the ones.'

We sip our margaritas in silence; I suspect we're both wondering how to change the subject.

Alex takes us back to the choice that's brought us together. 'You want to know why I chose psychiatry?'

'I'm wondering why you feel the need to tell me.'

He frowns. He jokes a lot, but as soon as I touch on therapy, he is *so* serious.

I laugh. 'Go on.'

'You already know I decided early on to be a therapist, which was a surprise to my family.'

'They wanted a surgeon?'

'My father's a neurosurgeon. They'd have settled for physician . . . if I'd lost my hands in an accident.'

Back at uni, it was accepted that cardiothoracic surgeons were top of the arrogance list, but neurosurgeons were in clear second place.

'It was my parents having therapy that decided me.'

This I hadn't picked. 'Either the therapist did a shit-hot job, or they stuffed up and you thought you could do better.'

'The first. We were in family therapy because no-one was coping with my younger brother refusing to go to school. If he'd been pulling wings off flies, that would've have been alright, but *skipping school . . .*'

'And family therapy fixed it?'

'I was ten. I think I knew they were on the verge of splitting up. I was terrified that talking about it would make it happen. Looking at it now, my brother's staying home from school was a subconscious attempt to distract them, to make them work together.'

'And they didn't split up?'

'They sorted it out, which was quite an achievement. They're not easy people.'

I try to imagine my own family in therapy. If something arose that my parents couldn't deal with, they'd be happy enough to talk but not prepared to look beyond the obvious. Or even to stay on topic. But they'd probably stay together.

We fill the evening with a mix of personal and work stuff.

Alex is passionate about keeping the talking therapies alongside the biological approaches: 'The battle for the soul of psychiatry.'

I'm sympathetic – not to the full-on three-times-a-week Freudian model, but at least to the sort of extended conversations that I want to have with patients like Sian.

It's only once the bill is on the table that he finishes his story. 'My parents did split up in the end. When I finally told them what had inspired me to do psychiatry, my father told me the therapist hadn't saved their marriage. It was *them* deciding to stay together for *us*. Nice work on the part of the therapist, letting them think it was their idea.'

'But you decided to become a therapist anyway.'

'So I can decide what the truth was.' He's smiling.

'And your brother?'

'No way was he going to be a neurosurgeon. He's applying for the cardiology program.'

I'm feeling good. The traditional method of getting to know someone slowly has a lot going for it. The traditional dating your colleagues – not so much. But Alex doesn't ask me to analyse him or equate 'obstetrician' with 'loves babies and relates well to women'.

And then work gets in the way. Last time it was me; this time it's him.

'Day's not over. I've got some prep to do.'

'For?'

'Prof Round. I'm doing a psychoanalytic case.'

Prof Round is a weekly discussion of a patient, with Prof Gordon presiding. I can't think of anyone in Acute who'd benefit from Alex's Freudian interpretations.

'Not the MP – Mr X?'

Alex laughs. 'I don't think so. But if you're looking for something, you'll find it.'

He's not going to elaborate and I'm not going to beg him to.

As we're getting up to go, he says, 'I almost forgot. You saw a journo with anxiety, didn't you?'

'I saw a journalist.'

'Any chance this is her?' He pulls a newspaper out of his bag. It's folded open to a big headline in the arts section: 'The Four-Column Cure'.

He laughs. 'It's not too brutal. She never mentions anxiety or anger – and obviously not narcissism – but they're plain as day. And I'm guessing you're the silent apprentice.'

'Does she say it helped? The CBT?'

'She has a bit of a dig at it: *Therapy as imagined by an accountant.* But she admits she needed some kind of help to deal with her mother's death.'

SIX

CO-DEPENDENCY

Among the tide of pedestrians heading to work on a sunny morning, a thirty-something woman in modest corporate attire, running shoes rather than heels, is standing still, looking about – lost.

A man of about the same age emerges from a coffee shop and spots her. 'Morning, Veronica. Looking for something?'

'Just the office,' she says.

He shakes his head, incredulous, and points to the building in front of them. 'Right there, where it's always been. Nothing's changed. Except you are definitely getting weirder.'

Chloe weighs in at thirty-one kilograms again and we're all suspicious. She didn't water-load this time, but her hair looks odd.

'Omar,' I ask, 'is Chloe wearing a wig?'

'Like she does every day?'

I hadn't noticed before. 'It just looks different today.'

It turns out there's a reason. There are four weights under it – the kind they used to use on scales – taped to her head. She must have brought them in with her, along with the tape. Was the wig part of the plan or did it just provide an opportunity? That's a lot of forethought for someone who's supposed to be cognitively impaired.

As another nurse undoes the tape and removes the weights, Chloe seems barely there. Not embarrassed, rueful or angry: just disengaged. When she's re-weighed, we discover she's barely gained 500 grams since arriving in hospital, even with the nasogastric feeding in the medical ward.

No wonder there's been no sign of a refeeding syndrome. Despite all the monitoring, she must be managing to dispose of food or vomit secretly.

Omar, meanwhile, is disposing of the weights – in his pocket. 'My mum'll remember these. Old school.' He catches my look. 'I know what you're thinking: we had one job. Wrong. Chloe has one job. And it's the opposite of ours. With every other patient here, we're pulling in the same direction, give or take. But not Chloe. That's the real problem we have with her.'

—

The Prof Round is held in the ivory tower seminar room, where the ECT tribunal met. I'm not surprised to see Nicole, who's already a regular, though only clinical staff are invited. These rounds are famous for Prof's ripping-apart of registrars unfortunate enough to get a diagnosis or treatment wrong. So far, I haven't seen anything like that; I guess times have changed.

Alex's patient, Veronica, turns out to be someone he saw in ED when he was on call. She's agreed to return for his show-and-tell, where, I guess, all will be revealed.

There are a bunch of reasons why patients do this. They might want some good to come from their illness, or maybe they just want the extra opinions.

Veronica is led to a chair outside the meeting room by Sally, a nurse I know from my term in general hospital psychiatry. I presume she has helped Veronica find her way here.

I'd put Veronica in her late thirties. She's in a long-sleeved floral dress – no jewellery or make-up. She just nods when Sally introduces me and I get a sense of her being a bit disconnected.

Sally gives me an update on Jùnjié, the young gymnast whose suicide I prevented.

'He's retrained as a diver. Got his eyes on the national championships.'

I see Prof approaching and hurry away to grab a front-row seat in the meeting room. He stays to talk to Sally before entering, leaving her and Veronica outside.

Alex is wearing a jacket, even though it's quite warm, and is introduced by a senior registrar, Oliver. The title of his talk is 'From Little Things Big Things Grow', and Alex sends a smile my way.

Oliver kills that moment by explaining that it's a case study of a toxic relationship bringing out and amplifying underlying vulnerabilities.

Alex starts a little nervously. I haven't really seen this side of him. But it's obvious that he knows heaps more about psychotherapy than would be expected of a first-year trainee and he's enjoying his chance to show it. As the nervousness goes, so does the boyishness. He's sounding like a professional who knows what he's talking about. And I'm playing with the feeling of it being my boyfriend up there.

'Veronica is a thirty-two-year-old separated IT professional, who presented at the weekend to the Emergency Department in the setting of a dispute with her estranged husband.'

Domestic violence? Alex will definitely have asked about that, right?

'She complained that her husband was bullying her to return to him – and to get help. She has lowered mood and appetite, is sleeping poorly, with constant anxiety, poor concentration and poor memory. The medical registrar asked me to speak with her.'

Prof nods but doesn't smile.

Alex continues with an analysis of Veronica's childhood and its effect on her choice of career and husband, and on the deterioration of the marriage as she failed to meet her 'very picky' husband's expectations.

'The husband responded by becoming more demanding, a trigger for her depressive and anxiety symptoms which, in turn, impacted on her capacity to meet his exacting standards. A vicious circle. Their most recent therapist told them – those are Veronica's words – *told* them to separate.'

Prof raises his eyebrows.

'While I'd hope the therapist didn't direct them in quite the way Veronica reports, she – the therapist – may have seen it as their only way out of a deteriorating situation.'

Alex diagnoses a generalised anxiety disorder. He suggests that Veronica, and possibly her husband, enter into individual therapy so they can gain insight and avoid repeating patterns in their next relationships.

Veronica is brought in, Sally in tow. Why is the nurse still here? She's now carrying a large envelope I didn't see earlier.

Veronica blinks and looks a bit overwhelmed.

'It's bit intimidating, I know,' says Prof as he motions for her to sit beside him. He's angled her chair so she won't see most of us.

Prof gently creates an intimate space between himself and Veronica. He has a reputation for being charismatic with patients, but it's another thing to see it in action. Veronica softens.

'I'm just going to ask a few questions: is that all right?'

Veronica nods.

'You've recently separated from your husband?'

'A month ago. I'm living in my parents' apartment. Not with them; they just own it.'

'How are you feeling about that?'

'I'm okay now. It was awful when it happened. After the therapist told us, after we left her office, we both cried and cried.'

'Because?'

'Because we loved each other and thought we'd be together forever, but it turns out we're not compatible.' She laughs, perhaps out of nervousness, but it seems odd. 'I don't have to worry about putting all the dishes in the right place anymore.'

'And these symptoms you came to the hospital for help with? How long have you been having them?'

'A month or two, I guess.'

'Was there anything that happened a month ago, other than being told to separate from your husband?'

Veronica takes a while to think. 'I lost my job.'

'I imagine that was upsetting.'

'I guess. They were expecting ridiculous outputs. I got another job.'

'Flaky' isn't in the *DSM-5* manual of diagnoses, and I've worked with enough flaky doctors to know that it doesn't have to mean unintelligent, but she sounds surprisingly blasé about losing her job. I'm missing something.

'And your new job?' Prof asks.

'It's okay. It's a bit below what I used to do . . . no technology or anything. Just admin. And they're very picky.'

There's a collective intake of breath, everyone letting everyone else know that they've picked up on the word she used to describe her husband. I look at Alex; he wasn't expecting it either.

'So when you came into the Emergency Department, it was because . . .'

Veronica frowns and tugs at her sleeve. And I see something I hadn't noticed before. She's wearing a plastic inpatient bracelet. Shit.

'I guess I was stressed,' she says. 'Upset. I rang the therapist, but it was a Saturday night and the answering service said to ring Lifeline if I was suicidal or to go to a hospital. I wasn't suicidal so I went to the hospital.'

I imagine Carey is nodding in agreement with that logic.

'What other symptoms have you been getting?'

'Headaches. I thought they were stress.'

My skin is tingling. I look at Sally, then at Alex. He wasn't expecting this either.

'What's your memory been like?'

'Oh, complete rubbish,' Veronica says with a laugh. A little more soberly: 'I've been told that's because of the tumour.'

Alex looks like he wishes the floor would open up and swallow him. I look out the window, watch a guy hanging off the opposite building washing the windows.

'Would you like to share with us how you found out about the tumour?'

'My GP was worried about the headaches and organised a scan.'

'Rightly so. And thanks to your GP doing what we expect doctors to do, Sally here tells me that the outcome is looking very positive.'

'I'm having the operation tomorrow morning. They think they'll able to remove it completely.'

Veronica is thanked, with best wishes for her surgery the following day, and Sally escorts her out, leaving the envelope behind. The slide with the unfortunate title is still on the screen.

Prof pulls out the scan and gathers us around the X-ray illumination board. He turns to Alex. 'So, Dr Ashwood, what do you see?'

We all know there's a tumour, but Prof is going to rub it in.

'Ah, there appears to be . . . um . . . a well-defined mass involving both frontal regions.'

'And if you were a betting man, Dr Ashwood, what would you back it to be?'

Alex clears his throat. 'Meningioma.'

'And the prognosis?'

'From what I can see, very good.'

'As she told us,' says Prof. 'But only because it was diagnosed.'

He segues into a short lecture on tumours affecting the frontal lobes, and the importance of timely diagnosis. He's made his point; now he's just being an arsehole.

Back to Alex. 'And if you had a bifrontal meningioma, Dr Ashwood, what would you think of a psychologist telling their *client*, your partner, to leave you?'

'Um, I clearly should have undertaken a fuller assessment before I concluded –'

Prof cuts him off and addresses the audience. 'So, what went wrong here?'

No response.

Then he looks at me. 'Hannah?' He's made it sound as if I have my hand up. 'What do you think went wrong?'

He wants me to say 'judgement'. To show I'm prepared to take Alex down, in public, to score a point with him. Screw that.

'Well, as you've pointed out, the neurological symptoms were missed in ED and apparently –'

'The ED intern is not presenting today. I'm asking what Dr Ashwood did wrong.'

He's made his agenda obvious now. I give him the word he wants.

'I guess when he saw her, he had to make a judgement –'

'Yes, Hannah, judgement. Which begins with remembering that we are doctors, and using all our skills to see the bigger picture, rather than one that suits your own prejudices or agenda, shaped as they might be by experience or, indeed, trauma. And seeing that bigger picture requires us, as doctors rather than psychologists or other purveyors of services, to sit *above*.'

He's been addressing me, rather than Alex, but now he turns to Nicole. 'Which is why we use the word *patient* rather than *client*.'

She doesn't bite, but Prof pushes it. 'Am I out of line, Nicole?'

She smiles. 'Personally, I say consumers, because I don't want to pick a fight with people I need to work with constructively. But since you've invited me to say something . . . excuse me.'

Nicole has been sitting at one end of a row, but now she stands and steps back and we all swivel our chairs, away from Prof.

'Thank you, Professor Gordon, for running these sessions, and you, Dr Ashwood, for putting yourself on the line. This is my third

Prof Round, and I'd been told to expect a bloodbath. Looking at the expressions around me, I guess this is what was meant.'

I glance at Prof. He's irritated. Good.

Nicole continues. 'It's tough to have your mistakes pointed out in public, and, god knows, we all make them. Prof noted that another professional, who also had a responsibility to look beyond their specialist expertise and who had considerably more time with Veronica, missed the diagnosis. I daresay she was also examined by the ED doctors.

'Review and criticism is part of every job. It can't happen if there's a culture of fear and humiliation – or schadenfreude. As long as I'm in charge of this unit, I'll do my best to ensure there isn't.

'And a word to the registrars. Many of you have never failed at anything in your lives. That is not the general adult experience. Some of you may still be more worried about pleasing your teachers than doing your jobs well. Medical training can be infantilising. And, to be clear, this is specific to medicine; we don't have that problem in the psychology or social work training programs. So a little criticism can be traumatic. I'd encourage you to get over it.'

And with that, we're dismissed. The room clears, but Jon, Ndidi and I wait behind as Alex gathers his things.

He sees us and forces a smile. 'We'll be selling tickets next time.'

Ndidi explodes. 'Totally fucking outrageous. Bullying. He's been doing it for so long he knows exactly where the line is, but you almost managed to make him cross it.' She's looking at me. 'I don't have a lot of time for Nicole, but she saw it, and she called it out.'

'Let's do this by the river,' says Jon.

Alex and I walk across the campus behind the other two.

'You okay?' I ask.

'Am now. At the time it felt like having my teeth out without anaesthetic. But the whole "you're a doctor, check everything" crap. How do think Chloe feels being asked over and over about the same shit just in case the specialists who saw her before haven't done their jobs? And I was in the fucking ED; it's not like I had hours and hours with Veronica.'

'Like the psychologist did.'

'The psychologist should have at least sent her for a physical check. You know, in all this, I put myself in the place of her poor partner, being told by the therapist that he couldn't see you . . . sorry, *her* any more. Shit. I'm mixing up my pronouns.'

'Freudian slip there?'

'Sorry. I'm probably more stressed than I feel.'

'That getting-in-touch-with-feelings thing.'

It's kind of sweet, but I'm more impressed that, at a time when I'd expect he'd be focusing on the blow to his ego, he's thinking about the patient and her partner. And, apparently, us.

We sit on the grass just down from the Riverbend private facility.

Ndidi hasn't cooled down. 'You never put your hand up, did you, Hannah? He just wanted you to throw Alex under the bus. And you didn't. Big statement of solidarity.'

Alex is nodding. 'Appreciated. But I'd have been okay.'

'It's not the issue,' I say. 'It's something between me and Prof.'

Alex is the only one I've told about Prof blocking me from the training program. It seems like the time is right, so I tell the others.

Ndidi's angry, looking for a way to make an official complaint, Jon's resigned in a shit-happens-but-we-get-through-it sort of way, and Alex repeats the advice he's given me before: suck it up – and suck up – for the moment. Like I didn't do today. That's two strikes now.

—

As I'm walking over to the Child and Youth unit for Chloe's family therapy, I get a call from Mum to tell me that Lennon got away safely. It takes her a few minutes to reveal what she's really calling about: she doesn't want to feed Mel's kids the paleo diet, but is worried Mel won't let her have them if she doesn't. I tell her I'll call Mel. Better to deal with it now before it grows into something big.

—

Elena sets me up to watch Chloe's first family therapy session. The viewing room is basically a storeroom, not much bigger than a cupboard, with a couple of chairs and a small broken table at one end. A one-way window looks into a larger room with armchairs arranged in a circle.

'Switch over there is for the sound,' says Elena as she turns the light off.

'This is your first session with them, right?'

'First time in family therapy. I've seen Chloe many times. And I've met them all before.'

'Do you know why they cancelled and re-booked?'

'The parents didn't want Chloe's sister, Brianna, to come, but that wasn't negotiable. They're here because Chloe wants it. She's the one who calls the shots in this family.'

Elena sits in the therapy room with her back to me, and I open my laptop to take notes. A few minutes later, Chloe is wheeled in. Elena stands and offers her a choice of the chairs. She shuffles over to the one across from Elena.

David and Sue enter next. Sue goes straight to Chloe and fusses over her, pushing her hair out of her eyes. (The wig's been gone since we found the weights under it). But that tiny action makes my skin crawl. Chloe is not a child; she's *twenty-nine.*

'We'd really rather Brianna wasn't involved,' says David.

I look to Chloe; I'd convinced her to do therapy in the hope of changing the dynamic with Brianna. I'm too far away to read her expression, and her body language isn't giving anything away.

Elena smiles. 'I didn't make myself clear?' She doesn't move, but her tone is firm, in control. I suddenly understand the magic of the room I am in: how much you can observe when you're not part of the conversation. This is a different version of the Elena who might have been chatting with a friend in her interaction with Sabriya the journalist. Chloe's a *patient.*

David hesitates, then leaves the room. He returns in the company of a fifteen-year-old with spiky purple hair and lip and nose piercings. They sit in a semicircle, the parents on either side of Chloe.

'Thank you for all coming,' says Elena. 'You all know me – though, Brianna, I think we only ever met once, years ago?'

Brianna shrugs.

'I need to inform you of the rest of the team sitting on the other side of the glass.'

I start as they look toward me, even though I know I'm not visible.

'At times I may take breaks and ask for their input, and it is possible they will knock and ask me to see them,' Elena continues.

Really? I should have done some pre-reading.

'First, some ground rules. Everyone gets a turn to talk, and we show each other respect in this room.' She waits until they've all nodded before continuing. 'I'd like to start with each of you telling me why you are here.'

David and Sue exchange looks. Brianna is checking out the floor. Everyone whose face I can see looks awkward.

'We'll go around the circle, beginning with me.' Elena pauses. 'Family therapy is a recommended treatment we have never tried with Chloe. I know, David and Sue, you will want to try any approach that might help her. So, my answer to the question *Why am I here?* is that I am a qualified family therapist and happy to provide that treatment for your family.'

She's telling David and Sue that if they refuse to engage, they're essentially saying they don't want to help Chloe, and that the treatment is for the whole family, not just their older daughter.

'Me?' Everyone is looking at Sue, next up. 'Um, well, of course you're right. We've always wanted what's best for Chloe.'

'Give me a fucking break.' Brianna is speaking under her breath, but if I can hear it, I figure everyone else can.

David tenses. 'Brianna . . .'

'Brianna, you'll get your turn,' says Elena. 'Sue, keep going.'

'It's been hard on everyone,' Sue says. 'You too, Brianna – I understand that. Chloe has been ill, with lots of tests and admissions in the past, but she's doing her best and we're supporting her. So, yes, that's all I want to say.'

I watch Brianna and wonder why I can feel the tension in the room so acutely. I'm tuned into tiny movements – Sue clasping Chloe's hand, David edging forward on his seat.

Elena's arms are resting on the side of the chair, her posture open and non-judgemental.

'We aren't medical people,' says David, before the inevitable 'but'. 'But over the years we've learned a lot. And we know our daughter.' It takes a moment before I realise he's jumped the queue: it was Chloe's turn.

'Of course,' says Elena. 'So, specifically, why are you here today?'

'If there's anything realistic you can suggest to help Chloe, of course we'll do it,' says David. *But there isn't anything you can say or do, because I know best.*

Another pause, then Elena asks: 'If we did have an answer, and Chloe did get better, what would change?'

I can't tell if she's looking at David, but he's the one who answers. 'Obviously, everything. I mean . . .' He turns to Chloe. 'I'm not blaming you, sweetheart, but it's been tough on us all.'

Elena waits.

He turns back to her. 'Life would be different. Chloe would be living independently; I'd probably take a step up at work. Sue and I would go on the holiday we've had to keep postponing.'

'Wow,' says Elena. 'That would be a change. Hold on to that thought, will you?' She turns to Brianna. 'Brianna, before you answer the question, I want to acknowledge that I understand you and your parents disagreed recently about what to do for Chloe: is that right?'

Quick look up from under her fringe. At her mother. Then at Chloe, and I think there is a softening there. I wish this was being videoed so I could replay it.

'Yeah.'

'Which is pretty tough to voice when you're fifteen, I imagine.'

Brianna looks at Elena, seems to clock the possibility that she's not automatically on her parents' side.

'So why *are* you here? Because I told your father that you had to come? Because you are an important part of the family?' Elena is leaning toward Brianna as she speaks.

'*He* said it's my fault she's in hospital this time, so I need to be part of the solution.'

'Do you agree with that?'

Brianna takes a breath. She's only a child and it's evident in every expression, though she's trying to project an image of being cool and grown-up.

'I don't think we can help. No matter how much we read or try or cry or yell or buy her special cakes or stop her exercising.'

'Because?'

'Look at her.' There are tears running down Brianna's face. 'We aren't doctors. We can't make her eat.'

'Your father and mother think they can.'

'Because it's easier to believe her lies.'

'Stop it!' This is Sue, not David. Her mask has slipped, and I see the anger there. It's directed at Brianna, of course, rather than Chloe. How can you be angry at someone who is sick and needs help and support? But, fuck . . . My own anger hits me from nowhere.

I take a breath and focus on the Youngs: I've been so engrossed that I've taken on their feelings as my own.

Sue has stood up and so has Elena, putting herself between Sue and Brianna. I miss what she says to Sue, who sits down again.

'One-word answer, Sue,' says Elena. 'What did you just feel?'

'Well, I –'

'One word.'

'Anger, I guess, but –'

'Great,' says Elena. 'Brianna, one word – how do you feel about the lies?'

'Angry,' says Brianna. No hesitation.

'And David? Ever angry about not getting the holiday or the promotion, being tied to a sick child?'

'It isn't like that. We love Chloe. She's our responsibility. Of course I'm not angry at her.'

'Wow,' says Elena. 'That must make you the only member of your family who isn't angry.' She pauses and looks at Chloe. 'Because I saw your face when your dad spoke when it was your turn, Chloe, and you looked furious.'

I'd missed it.

Dead silence.

Finally, Chloe laughs. 'I'm used to it.'

'Do you think Brianna should get used to it too?'

Elena looks so calm and concerned that for a moment I miss the power of the statement. The others in the room are still digesting it. I wish I was close enough to Chloe to read her expression properly, but I think she looks shocked – maybe because this isn't all about her and her weight. Elena has triggered a seismic shift – in my thinking as well. *Screw the meds and CBT. This is what I want to learn how to do.*

'Why are you here, Brianna?' Elena asks gently, in a way that gives her permission to say anything.

Brianna's voice is part sob, part wail: 'Because she's going to die, and I don't want one of us to find her. I don't want to think it's my fault. I just want this to end. I'm sick of feeling sad and guilty and ignored and . . .' She is crying now, and her parents are frozen.

I want to yell at them: *She needs you – just hug her!*

Elena does something better. She shows no sign of reacting to the chaos, a calm adult surrounded by four children.

'We are going to do an exercise. Please all stand up.'

Elena's voice is authoritative but also kind. Nobody pushes back.

'Chloe, I need you here, sitting next to me.' Elena points to the empty chair. Chloe shuffles over. Cognitive impairment: like Veronica, her emotions are blunted.

'David and Sue?'

They nod robotically, though I can see the anger in the twitches at the corner of David's eyes.

'Think back to when you first had Brianna and brought her home from hospital.' Elena's tone says: *Don't let me down.* 'Brianna, do you trust me?'

Brianna nods but looks dubious, even before Elena tells her to take the seat Chloe has vacated, between her parents, and gets them all to sit.

'Now we are all going to close our eyes and take some deep breaths and think of your family dog – Ruben, isn't he? Do you still have him?'

Four nods.

'When he shot out the door as a puppy and fell in the swimming pool, and Brianna was screaming and she jumped in to rescue him, except she couldn't swim very well and David and Sue ended up in the pool too?'

For a few moments there is quiet.

'Now open your eyes. The team will want to give feedback, so just stay where you are and I'll be back in five minutes.'

I'm not sure what sort of feedback Elena is expecting when she opens the door and slips in beside me. She perches on the broken table.

'Amazing,' I say. 'You don't really want my thoughts, do you?'

'Classically, there is a team in here who put together a statement. I mentioned it because I thought I'd need a breather.' She laughs. 'They're hard work, in case you didn't notice.'

We watch them. Everyone stays in their 'new' seats – Chloe is beside her mother. Sue turns to her and says, 'How are you? You're looking peaky, darling. I'm sure they'll let us take you home soon.'

Brianna, on the other side of her mother, slumps in her chair.

'Time to go back,' says Elena.

She breezes in and sits. Pauses. 'The team wish to say this: they are very impressed by the amount of care for each other you show as a family.'

Not according to my notes. The word *care* doesn't feature at all. *Control* is underlined.

'But,' Elena continues, 'they also wonder if sometimes you all struggle with emotions that get in the way of caring for each other and especially for yourselves.'

The family appears to be listening.

'We can't help but notice,' Elena says, 'that Chloe elicits a lot of care from you, Sue and David, even though she is what, nearly thirty? She was happy to have you sit either side, but she seems to be managing over here with me – and even managed alone for a little while. But that was tough for you, Sue, wasn't it?'

Sue shakes her head. 'I was only –'

'And what you didn't notice was that Brianna sat up when you both were on her side to give her the support she needs to be independent. And then, Brianna, you slumped. I wonder why?'

Brianna looks at Chloe. 'Because Mum was back to talking about Chloe.'

'I notice you're sitting up again now, though. Why don't you keep going and tell your mum how it feels when she's preoccupied with a sister who's an adult?'

Brianna crosses her arms, bows her head for a few moments. Then she looks at Sue. 'Mum, I know you love us both. But it doesn't feel like that when you spend so much time running after Chloe. Worrying about her *all* the time.'

'I don't mean to . . . If you had a child, you would understand.' Sue turns to Elena. 'How can I not worry about her? She's unwell.'

Elena nods, and her voice is gentle. 'No-one is asking you not to worry. But as they say, if you keep doing the same thing over and over, you can't expect a different result. You can't change the fact that you worry about Chloe, but maybe you can change what you do in response to that worry. I'm going to leave that as your homework.'

Elena turns to David. 'I asked what would change for you if Chloe were better. For your homework, I am asking you to think about what you might lose if things were to change.'

David starts to protest, and Elena puts up her hand. 'People compromise – make choices about what's most important. I'm not saying you are happy with how things are; I am saying you are not unhappy *enough* to risk something new.'

'Your homework, Chloe, should you choose to do it –'

Why give Chloe a choice and not the others?

'– is to write a letter to your younger self and give it to Brianna. Describe the things you could have done differently.'

Chloe is noncommittal.

'I get enough homework from school,' says Brianna, next in line.

'But if Chloe does give you that letter, can you read it and think about why she didn't do things differently – what stopped her?'

'If she writes it, I'll read it.'

'It's over now?' Chloe asks.

Elena nods.

'So can I go home?'

Elena opens her arms to the family. 'I'd prefer to have two more sessions with you all first. But it depends on whether you are prepared to risk change.'

There is a silence in which Elena looks so much calmer than she can possibly feel.

'We *have* to.'

This is Brianna. To my surprise, she moves her chair to sit between Chloe and her mother. Chloe raises her head and I imagine there's a lifetime of sister history that passes between them. My sister, Melanie, conveying in one hug that she was pregnant and taking on the role of providing grandchildren. 'Chloe, I have never ever asked you for help. I am now.' Brianna hesitates. 'I want a life, a real life. Please let me have one.'

For a moment I am in Brianna's shoes – the child whose only sibling dies or is dying and whose parents devote their lives to one at the expense of the other. A montage of foster kids – needy foster kids – appears in my mind, along with a mix of emotions that could be mine or theirs.

For a strange few moments, as the family shuffles out, I'm envious of them: wanting it to be me with my parents, sitting with Elena, explaining what we did and how we feel. Having a therapist do the work that I've done in a random way since the day I told them I was going to be a doctor. Maybe since way before that.

I am wiping away tears when Elena comes back into the room. 'You okay?' she asks.

I am . . . I think. Something for me to reflect on, I'm sure Prof Gordon would say. And I'll do it – in my own time.

'Is it going to work?' I ask.

Elena sighs. 'Depends what you mean by work. If I can save Brianna, I will feel I have succeeded.'

My instinct is to push back. *Chloe* is my patient. And Elena's patient, too. Growing up with the foster kids, I saw way too much focus put on the hardships of the families who had to cope with difficult children rather than on the children's needs. Chloe is the patient and the problem that is going to kill her seems to have got lost.

Elena must sense what I'm thinking. 'I'm talking about realistic outcomes. You know what the expectations for Chloe are, physically. But, regardless of that, I'm trying to address the family as a whole, because the family dynamics are part of Chloe's problem.'

'Not something we're really set up to deal with.'

'Don't get me started. We should have given them family therapy way back. I wasn't in the Child Unit so I've no idea why they didn't. The parents probably sabotaged it – and were allowed to. Now? The need for control is pretty entrenched; David and Sue don't know any other way of being together.'

'How does it work for Chloe?'

'Her father has controlled her work and study life – why is a whole other question. But she had to be the best and brightest, and it was too exhausting, whereas the sick role is something she can excel in. Sue needs to be needed, and that's just as powerful a motivator. David will probably just control Sue and be happy with that. None of them knows how to have a relationship with healthy respect for boundaries, though I have hope for Brianna. And, I'm sorry, but it's hard to see any future for Chloe.'

—

I've been thinking of texting Alex to invite him for a drink, but the day's got away from me, and I figure I could be a while working through the paleo diet issue with Mum and Mel. Their argument is bound to be a surrogate for deeper issues they're both afraid to discuss. I start with Mel while I'm walking home.

'You're calling about the paleo thing?' says Mel.

'Just wondering how you were feeling about it.'

'Bigger things to worry about.'

That's called *deflection.*

'I meant, how are you feeling about Mum?'

'Fine. All good.'

Right. If I had forty sessions and knew what I was doing, I might take it slower. But I'm going to have to get to the point.

'You don't resent her getting too involved in how you're bringing up the kids?'

'That's just Mum.'

'I guess. But not respecting your choices about what they eat . . .'

'Oh, the paleo thing? We sorted that hours ago. I'm going to give them packed lunches.'

—

The next afternoon, I'm in the glass house when someone approaches the reception desk and asks for Alex. The visitor is a thin, bespectacled guy in his thirties with his shirt tucked in at the front and hanging out at the back.

'In a meeting,' I tell him. A supervision meeting with Prof – that'll be fun. 'But I work with him.'

'He saw my wife, Veronica Quirk.'

'I've met Veronica. She's had the operation?'

'Two days ago. It went well. Thanks for asking.'

'And you and she . . .'

'I think we'll get back together. But I'm looking for the people we saw who didn't diagnose the tumour. I've read up and . . . well, it should have been on their list.'

He's here to shoot the place up. Not so funny. It happens.

'Have you spoken to any of them yet?' I ask.

'Yes, and they've been defensive. "*Thank you for the information; I presume you won't need to see me again.*" Except the therapist who wanted us to come back because there might still be problems to resolve. I told her what she could do with that.'

'Perhaps she –'

'This woman blamed me. I was *oppressing* Veronica. She managed to persuade my wife that I was some sort of monster and that she should leave me. She actually told us we should separate. Based on a wrong diagnosis, which as a psychiatrist, she should have –'

'Psychologist.'

'*Psychiatrist.* I know the difference. She was a doctor, which makes her failure to spot the tumour so much worse.'

Prof had said she was a psychologist; he hadn't let the facts get in the way of the story he wanted to tell.

I just nod.

'After Veronica left, I just kept the dishes in the dishwasher because every time I went to put them away . . .' He's getting emotional and stops himself. 'That's got nothing to do with Dr Ashwood. Veronica said he was the only person in the Emergency Department who was nice to her and listened. And he told her to see the GP about the headaches. That was the most important advice anyone gave her.'

'I'll pass that on.' Would Alex want me to say any more? Probably not: boundaries. I say it anyway. 'Dr Ashwood shared with me how concerned he was that the misdiagnosis had led to you separating.'

Veronica's husband pushes his glasses back up his nose. 'I appreciate that. But he did miss the tumour. Anyway, I thought he might appreciate some feedback. He probably doesn't get a lot of that.'

—

Carey is in the glass house when Chloe is wheeled past for afternoon tea. A couple of times, their observations from doing the patient admission surveys have been insightful. I ask about Chloe's.

'Flat, unengaged, consistent with the history. But Nash did a clumsy job with the parents. As he did with the parents of the young man with first-episode psychosis. He once accused me of being unused to delivering bad news . . .'

'Not an easy job.'

'There's a training module. It's not perfect, but it's not bad. He should do it instead of bumbling along.'

'Probably not a good idea to tell him that.'

'Someone should.'

'I will if there's a good moment. And Carey . . .' My experience with Carey and what little I know of autism spectrum disorder tell me that I need to be direct. 'Please don't give Alex any more bottles of wine. Our group – we discuss first-year stuff. Cases and exams. It's not social.'

'Perfect. When's the next meeting?'

'Sorry, but it's just for registrars. The four of us.'

'I thought Alex agreed . . .' Carey looks devastated. And I realise it's not because we're not letting them join our group, but because they failed to read the room.

SEVEN

ACTING OUT

'What're you looking at?'

The nightclub strip is bustling, the crowd spilling onto the street rowdy and anonymous. A big guy has taken exception to a group of four men of about his own age.

'You, dickhead,' says one of the four.

The big guy explodes, and it's on. As bystanders try to break it up, a tram glides past.

—

A dishevelled man climbs aboard the tram. He ambles over to a couple in their thirties, addresses the male.

'Cigarette?'

'Oh sure, buddy, of course. Any particular brand? Maybe a cigar?'

'Callum.' It's the girl, screwing up her nose: the guy stinks. 'Leave it alone.'

But Callum's having fun. 'Actually, I don't have one. But my lovely lady . . .'

The man turns toward her. The tram lurches and he falls forward.

She screams. 'Get him off me!'

—

The tram trundles past the unfenced front yard, with its neglected lawn and derelict car: a low-rent house in a low-rent neighbourhood. The outfits that Kelly Keane and her two daughters have chosen for a night out in the world's third-most-liveable city do nothing to soften the impression. Taylah and Aleesha are preloading with cheap sparkling; Taylah's boyfriend, Trent, is drinking a can of beer.

Kelly pulls two takeaway meals from the microwave. Taylah turns away, disgusted.

'They've got meat in them.'

'I'm not making you eat it,' says Kelly. 'When you start paying rent . . .'

'I will when you buy proper food. This is dog food. Meatloaf!'

A big Alsatian runs into the room. Taylah throws one of the packages to him.

'Fuck,' says Trent, suddenly animated. 'That's my dinner.'

'You can share with me, darling,' says Kelly.

Taylah grabs the remaining meal from her mother and throws it on the floor. Trent goes after it, trips, and catches his head on the corner of the table. Meatloaf sees his second helping under threat and jumps on him.

'Get the dog off me.'

Aleesha runs over. 'Your head's bleeding.'

Taylah shoves her sister aside. 'Heads don't stop bleeding,' she says. 'He's gonna bleed out.'

Trent puts his hand to his forehead, checks the blood, does it again. 'Fuck.'

Taylah screams at her mother and sister. 'I just wanted to go out with my boyfriend. You ruin everything.' She runs out of the room.

Aleesha looks like she's tossed a coin in her mind. She gets out her phone. 'Ambulance. Major head injury.' Then, knowing her sister, she adds, 'And an overdose.'

It's not like I haven't been on call before.

When I was doing emergency medicine, the long shifts worked by our predecessors were legendary. Our consultants rolled their eyes at our cushy lives, talked about starting on Friday morning and not finishing until Monday night, hot-bedding, sleeping on X-ray tables, falling asleep in the toilets. Our current industrial award – thank god and our union – doesn't allow that. And I had specialist registrars to back me up.

Now I'm one of those specialist registrars. The interns and house medical officers are roaming the wards or flat out in ED. Some of the interns are only six or seven weeks out of medical school. The HMOs have a year or two more, but all of them will handball any patient who looks even remotely like having a psychiatric problem straight to me.

Most of the psychiatric crises come from ED. But there is also the Mental Health Service itself, with all its specialist units, from Mother Baby to Psycho-Geriatrics, Short Stay to Extended Care, plus the general hospital – 600 beds in all. Tonight, as far as mental health goes, they're all mine.

I have a second psych registrar I can call in, but there has to be a nuclear accident before I consider them. There's a psychiatrist – a fully-fledged consultant – on call as well, and technically they could come in too, but that would require a nuclear war. Phone only.

The official advice is: *Don't hesitate to call*; the unofficial advice, passed down from the senior registrars, is: *Don't call the consultant unless there's a safety issue or the rules require it.* Avoid getting your head bitten off and earn a badge of honour for getting through the night without help.

But if I have to make a call on whether to send home someone who presents as a suicide risk, I'll be picking up the phone. In Jùnjié's case, I identified a risk; I was on the side of safety. The worst outcome would have been money wasted on a suicide watch. But once I'm qualified, I'll have to make the harder decision – to let a patient out on leave or go home. Prof thinks it's going to be an issue for me. I think it'd be an issue for anyone.

I was expecting Nash to be on call tonight, but he grabs me as he's leaving.

'Nicole changed the roster. Apparently I've exceeded some quota. You've got Daniela Popa. And Nicole wants to be called if anything's not working.' He grins. 'Probably wise not to include Dr Popa in that category.'

Nicole has managed to pair the most junior registrar with the laziest consultant. At least it's not Prof.

—

Jon rings me as he clocks off from Extended Care. 'Thought you might want to know about one of our guys who hasn't come back from day leave. Has a delusion about a group of people he thinks are destined to end up in hell. He proselytises to them.'

'Go on. What group?'

'Hell's Angels.'

I set myself up in the registrars' room with *Introduction to Family Therapy*. The calls are steady and manageable. A nurse in Acute wants to give Panadol, but it hasn't been written up. A patient from the Post-Traumatic Stress Unit has gone on leave without formal authorisation; I give a verbal okay. Extended Care needs an authorisation for seclusion – solitary confinement – which legally Dr Popa must be told about. I leave a message on her voicemail.

Then at 8 pm the psych nurse from ED calls. 'Hotting up here,' she says cheerfully. 'Full moon. Police brought in a guy you'll need to see; he's been bombed out after he decked the security guard. The usual.' In case I don't know what the usual reason for unprovoked assault is, she clarifies: 'Ice.'

—

Luka is about 190 centimetres tall and weighs, as far as I can guess from the safe distance of the hub in ED, at least 120 kilos. The security team – minus the one he hit, who is being checked out by an intern – are milling about. Luka is lying down but not still.

A doctor in scrubs joins us. Her name tag says *Dr Kate Rigby, Senior Emergency Medicine Registrar*, but I already know that.

'Who are you?' she asks.

'Psych reg.' Deep breath. 'Hannah Wright.'

'About time. Can you give him something?' She heads off, too busy to remember that in the emergency department of another hospital, twelve months ago, amid the contents of a resus kit scattered on the floor, she was the one who yelled: 'Get her out of here!' Life-changing for me; for her, just another HMO screwing up.

Today's HMO says, 'We're going to put on physical restraints. We don't know what he's taken.' If she thinks I'm going to object, she's going to be disappointed. If we weren't allowed to restrain him, with meds and ties, we wouldn't have an opportunity to help him at all. He'd be in lock-up. Another ethical dilemma; another notification to be left on Dr Popa's voicemail.

Grace, the CATT nurse who's bringing in another patient to hand over to the psych nurse in ED, points to Luka and says, 'Picked him up last month, same thing.' Grace is small and wiry – and wired.

Out of curiosity, I ask Grace, 'How did he end up here – rather than with the police?'

'Police called us. He's a clinic patient – supposed to be on depot.' Depot: long-lasting antipsychotic medication in injectable form.

'When did he last have it?'

'A month ago – in here. He's a couple of weeks overdue.'

Meaning he could be psychotic as well as high on ice.

We hear yelling and a code grey – aggressive incident – is called over the loudspeakers. The security guys move fast, out through the door to the waiting room.

'That'll be Kelly Keane, Taylah's mum,' says Grace, grinning.

'Sounds like you know this family.'

Grace laughs. 'Everyone does. After tonight, you will too. Try not to admit any of them, okay? No-one will thank you in the end. Including them.'

'So the patient is Taylah?'

'Tonight it is. Overdose. Aleesha, the younger sister, called us. Usually Taylah does it herself.'

'Must be tough at home,' I say, 'if being admitted to a psych ward is the only way to get any care.'

Grace shrugs. But I've got the kind of patient I was most worried about dealing with. One who apparently overdoses regularly and literally calls for help. 'Is the psych family room occupied?'

'Yep,' says Grace. 'Taylah's in there. I'm way ahead of you.'

She looks down at her phone. 'Sorry. Gotta go. They've found the patient that absconded.'

The noise isn't abating. I wander over and stand at the back of the office where the triage nurses sit, behind secure windows that protect them from physical assault. I can see a full waiting room with several children, a man holding a bloodied towel to his head, and a woman of maybe forty abusing Security and pointing to the nurses. The microphone at the window picks it all up.

I head off to see the patient whose seclusion I've authorised. He's one of Jon's who's taken drugs while out on leave and come back sexually aggressive. I find Extended Care depressing. I guess the faded prints of landscapes don't incite riots, but they hardly offer hope either.

The patient that the seclusion guy has been propositioning is a woman in her thirties with dyed green hair. She's apparently been encouraging him, but there are factors besides consent to consider, among them contraception and sexually transmitted infections in a captive population. On the other hand, there's an ethical issue about denying people something they'd be allowed in the outside world.

Meanwhile, I've had three new messages on my phone: from Brain Disorders, Neurology and the Short Stay Psychiatric Assessment and Planning Unit attached to ED.

I head for Short Stay (six beds and a seventy-two hour maximum stay to stabilise and discharge), dealing with the messages from Neuro and Brain Disorders by phone en route.

The nurse in charge of Short Stay wants me write up some sleeping medication. No problem.

'I hear the Keane family are in ED,' she says. 'Last time they came in, Taylah talked the registrar into admitting her.' *Are you going to be that naive?* 'I'm not going to tell you what to do, but I'd rather Taylah than Aleesha. Preferably neither.'

I've got the message. But it'll be easier to admit Taylah than to discharge her. If I want to discharge someone who's even notionally a suicide risk, I'll need an okay from Dr Popa. And I'll have to wrestle with my own fears of getting it wrong.

I head back to ED, passing the array of Friday night casualties. It's half GP waiting room, half war zone. The bleeding-head man is still there. He's with a bored-looking woman of about twenty, short jet-black hair and a crop top too brief for the weather.

No sign of Taylah's mother, Kelly. Turns out she's been given her own cubicle and is standing outside it, speaking on her mobile and at the same time conducting an argument with a doctor.

On the phone: 'Hang on, some Nazi is trying to make me turn my phone off.' To the doctor: '*You're* the one being disrespectful. Do *you* get told to turn *yours* off? No, because it doesn't do any harm. If they could really crash planes, terrorists would just turn their phones on. Ever think about that?' Back to the phone. 'Nah, she's not going to do anything.'

Kelly's right: the doctor walks off.

Luka is awake and not happy to be in shackles, but at this stage he's just jerking against them occasionally. I look around for Security. For the emergency psych nurse. For anyone I recognise. Acute may be just across the road but I might as well be in a different country.

I head to the psych room and find the psych nurse there. She's with Taylah: early twenties, platinum hair with dark roots, too much make-up (by my standards, anyway), short dress, bare feet, scars up both arms and some fresh cuts that don't appear to be too deep. She looks reasonably settled.

'I need Security if I'm going to see the man in cubicle ten,' I tell the nurse.

Her phone rings and she answers it, then indicates that she's going to be a while.

I think back to my time as an intern and go outside. Yep, that's where they are: smoking. They're not overjoyed to be called back in to deal with Luka.

'Fucken lemme outta here,' Luka slurs when he sees me. I guess he's in his late twenties – I could've been at school with him. Some normal kid, maybe dreaming of doing what I'm doing now. Except, before he was even born, the genetic dice had been thrown. Maybe the reason he started taking methamphetamines was to shut down the voices.

I have a guard either side of me and we're all a half-metre away from him.

'Is there anyone you'd like me to call?'

'Fucken LEMME OUTTA HERE.' He jerks his arms and we all jump back.

I lean on a trolley that unfortunately has wheels.

Back on my feet, I realise there's no way I'll be able to assess Luka. He has to sleep it off. Tomorrow morning, if he's still in the same state, we can put him in Acute. I write him up for some intramuscular olanzapine and hope it will be enough, but not too much – no-one will thank me if I bomb him out so much he can't breathe and psych takes another ICU bed.

Now for Taylah's mother, Kelly. The psych nurse informs me, with an eye roll, that she's 'acutely distressed'. In fact, Kelly's still on the phone, outside her cubicle, showing no signs of distress, acute or otherwise.

I skim the online discharge summary of two years ago; she was in for two days for an 'adjustment disorder' – basically feeling bad after a trigger. I have to read the notes more carefully to discover that the trigger was her boyfriend cheating on her, which resulted in her threatening him and the other woman, assaulting a police officer, becoming hysterical and claiming to be considering suicide. The police decided that we could sort her out. Less work – for them.

Kelly is wearing tight jeans, a very low-cut top and high-heeled shoes. Dyed red hair. Make-up light and carefully applied. Attractive but hard.

'Haven't seen you before,' she says, as I motion to her to put her phone away and follow me into the cubicle.

'Guess it's our lucky day.'

She's not sure how to take this.

'What happened?'

'Bitch fed our dinner to the dog.'

It takes some effort to keep my face straight. I want to ask, *By accident?* but only out of curiosity. Instead, I say, 'Do you guys fight a lot?'

The long answer involves a daughter who won't pay rent; a boyfriend (likely the guy with the bloodied head); and another daughter, Aleesha (the one who's apparently even less desirable as a patient than Taylah as far as Short Stay is concerned), who seems to have her own interest in the boyfriend. Who in turn would take Kelly over either of them, if she gave him the opportunity. Apparently.

The short answer appears to be that, since Taylah has returned to live at home, they do indeed fight a lot.

'So . . . you wanted to see the doctor too?'

'It's put me on edge. I mean, after Aleesha calls the ambulance, she calls the cops. I say to her, *Why are you calling the cops?* And she says, *They might want to lay charges*. I mean, this is, like, my daughter. And the cops come. Before the ambulance. What do you think of that? And they want to arrest *me*. Why? I'm asking you.'

I suspect the answer may lie in the bits that Kelly hasn't told me. 'How are you feeling now?'

'Shocking. Traumatised. My daughter's tried to kill herself, Trent's had a brush with death, didn't get dinner. Heart racing, stressed, won't be able to sleep.'

'I'm sure if you go home and take things quietly, get something to eat, go to bed, you'll feel better in the morning.'

'Taylah's taken all the pills. I need more Valium.'

That's why she's still here. With all the necessary symptoms.

'I'll give you two Valium now, but if you need more you'll have to go to your treating doctor.'

Kelly protests, but when she sees I'm not going to budge she yells after me: 'Ten-milligram ones!'

I organise two five-milligram pills. It'll take a while.

'Keeping Taylah, are you?' she asks, when I come back and tell her the deal.

'I haven't seen Taylah yet.'

'Tell the bitch to go live with her boyfriend. I don't want her back.'

One down, one to go.

Then the loudspeakers announce a code blue: medical emergency.

—

It's Acute. *My* unit. And because it's a psych unit and not yet 10 pm, I'm part of the response team. I'm already running. I'll count it as parkrun training: 500 metres at four-minute-per-kilometre pace, with stairs and a road crossing. I'm the first doctor on the scene, breathing hard, but the crash cart has got there before me.

It's one of Alex's patients, Zac, a guy in his twenties who's been started on clozapine: the current drug of choice for treatment-resistant schizophrenia. It has to be monitored closely because of cardiac side effects. Which is what I'm seeing now.

He's flat out on the floor and a nurse I don't know – I guess she only works nights – is applying chest compressions while another is attaching him to an ECG machine. A familiar place rendered unfamiliar.

I glance at the swirl of paper which comes out of the machine just before my foot catches on the cord and shuts it down. There's no missing the QT prolongation: myocarditis. Now, I need the intubation tube, and some idiot's taken it out of the drawer. I kick something else on the floor as I flail around trying to find it.

'Ambulance on its way?' From ED. Looks like I've outrun it.

'Yes.' The nurse is outwardly calm, as she has to be, but I sense she's shaken.

I'm okay: I may be a little awkward with equipment, but I don't panic. *Realistic trepidation isn't panic.*

'I need to intubate him,' I say.

Another nurse passes me the tube. Ah, that's where it was.

I've seen this done dozens of times in my surgical and anaesthetic terms. I've done an intubation myself – once. Supervised by an anaesthetist in a non-emergency situation. And, as I've been reminded by running into Kate Rigby tonight, I spectacularly failed to do it on a second occasion.

I tip Zac's head back, drop the first pair of sterile gloves, slip on a second pair, grab the tongue depressor, slip the tube down what I hope is his trachea, attach the bag and squeeze gently. Zac's chest expands. I let out my own breath. *Steady when it mattered.* I hand the bag to one of the nurses and go to Zac's arm to put in an IV line. I've had more practice at this, but I'm not sorry when the ambulance crew arrive and take over.

'Good work,' says one of the paramedics as she checks the intubation. 'But Jesus, it looks like a tornado hit this place.'

How did the tongue depressor get all the way over there? And the box of equipment I stumbled over has spread out a little. Still, tornado seems a little harsh.

Zac is put on a stretcher, bound for Intensive Care.

The chest-compression nurse is shaking. She's a psych nurse and quite possibly has no background in general nursing. I don't even know her name; maybe Zac does. But every time he wakes up in the morning, for the rest of his life, he'll have the day in front of him because of what she – and I – just did.

—

Back in ED, the intern has seen Taylah and done bloods; she's been given the all clear. She'd taken paracetamol, but it's below the toxic level. Taylah looks like a softer version of her mother, and softer too than the wannabe biker chick in the waiting room – her sister, Aleesha, I'm guessing.

The psych nurse answers her phone and leaves us.

Taylah looks me up and down. 'You're new. Can I see Dr Ashwood?'

Alex must have been the registrar who admitted her last time.

'I'm afraid he's not on tonight. I understand you've been here before.'

'Comes from being with my mother in her shitty house.'

'You have a dad on the scene?'

'Nah. Mum's boyfriends are all losers.'

I hear her story of the night's events. In this version, her mother started it by ordering dinner for everyone but her.

'My bitch sister calls the cops and Trent takes her side, because . . . I told Dr Ashwood about what my sister wants to do with him.' She catches my expression. 'I mean with Trent, not with Dr Ashwood. She actually said it. Where he could hear.'

Alex took pity on her. I get it.

Taylah starts crying. 'My life's a total mess. I started cutting because it helps sometimes, but then I thought I just wanted to die and I grabbed some pills.'

According to the notes, Taylah and Aleesha both had admissions to the adolescent unit and since then several to Acute and Short Stay, all in similar circumstances. As has Kelly.

'I'm still feeling suicidal,' Taylah says. She must sense my scepticism, because she adds, 'I don't want to be like this, you know.'

The case notes tell me Taylah has a borderline personality disorder; even with my limited experience, I'd have guessed that. She has trouble regulating her emotions, going from calm to hysteria to uncontrollable anger in ten seconds. She's never been able to trust anyone, let alone herself. She's seen rejection at every turn, and this service is set up to do it all over again. Nowhere can take her long enough to make a real difference.

Short Stay is the suggested management in her file – but only if absolutely necessary. Three days' care and containment. Patch up, send off again.

'What do you think would help, Taylah?'

'I just . . . I want to be, like, normal. Have a boyfriend, go out and enjoy ourselves. I just . . .' Her voice catches. She looks much younger than she is. 'Things always go wrong.'

'Have you had counselling? Like regularly, for weeks, to help you make sense of why? And learn how to change things?'

'I started,' says Taylah. 'But she left. And the guy that replaced her charged a fuck-load. Couldn't afford it.'

'Your boyfriend is still waiting to be sutured. Could you go home with him?'

'His parents threw him out.'

'What about your mum? If she calms down.'

'It'll take her a few days.'

I'm guessing she means three – the maximum time in Short Stay. Taylah knows it's easier for me to admit her, though I can't do it just to provide accommodation. I figure she and her boyfriend will work something out there.

'I'm scared I'll take another overdose,' she says, when I fail to respond. And she *is* scared. At least part of her is. The part that's trying to stay in control.

'There's nothing I can see that suggests you really want to die.'

'You've just met me and you think you know all about me.'

Shit. Have I pushed too early? The Short Stay option is not just easier but safer.

'You're smart, Taylah,' I say. 'You know a few tabs aren't going to kill you. That doesn't mean you don't need help, but I'm figuring what you got from Short Stay didn't last more than a week.'

'They're useless. What I need is an admission to Acute. Long enough to do some good. Like you said.'

I think of all the patients we put on assessment and treatment orders who don't want to come into Acute.

'What I reckon is you'd really like that to work, but deep down you know that isn't enough either. It hasn't been in the past.'

'Stopped me killing myself.'

'Until you were discharged, and then it starts up again.'

Taylah starts to list all the reasons she needs to come to Acute.

I interrupt. 'Taylah, you know that isn't going to happen.'

'Then Short Stay.'

'How about I get your mum in and we talk about sorting this out?' Like I can do some Elena magic. In ED, on a Friday night.

'Fuck that. I'm discharging myself. Where's Trent?'

There's quite a bit of yelling as she bursts out of the psych room looking for her boyfriend.

Kate Rigby's waiting there. 'So, you're done with her?'

I don't think Taylah's at serious risk of suiciding, but what if I'm wrong? She may well make another self-harm attempt; sometimes people miscalculate and die accidentally.

'Not yet. I'd like to talk to her mother again.'

Kelly appears, Valium in hand, and comes at Taylah. 'Don't think you can come back home without saying sorry.'

'Can you escort Ms Keane out?' I say to the hovering security guard and point to Kelly. To Kate I say, 'Can we get Trent in a cubicle and let Taylah stay with him?'

I see something in Kate Rigby's eyes. She's recognised me at last.

'You know,' she says, 'I'm slightly busy with a guy who fell out a tree with a chainsaw. If he makes it, he'll likely lose an arm. But let's see what we can do about finding somewhere for these troubled young people of yours.'

Kelly gives me the finger, but leaves. Five minutes later I have Trent and Taylah together.

I speak to the two of them for nearly an hour while we're waiting for Trent to be sutured, and five more minutes while the job is done. He assures Taylah that he thinks her mother is 'psycho', Aleesha's definitely a bitch and he really needs to get some food. He isn't being especially supportive; I wish he'd hug her; as I wished Brianna's family would hug her in their family therapy session. And which Kelly maybe didn't do years ago, when Taylah needed it most.

But Taylah is smiling and she doesn't bring up admission again. I figure that dissing her sister and mother is close enough to support. For now. She listens to me as I outline a safety plan – what to do if she has suicidal thoughts again – and follow-up. I'm sure she's heard it all before.

When the intern has finished patching Trent, I tell them I'm discharging them both. I phone Dr Popa and leave a message. In the absence of a call-back, the decision is mine.

As Taylah's walking away she stops, turns around. 'If I kill myself, it's your fault.'

—

When I get back to the main section of ED, Grace the CATT nurse is talking with Kate Rigby.

'He'll need to go to ICU,' Kate says.

Grace turns to me and explains. 'The man from Extended Care. Hell's Angels made a mess of him. Last time he did his Jesus-saves routine they brought him in, did the right thing. But this was a different chapter, and for some reason he decided to wreck their bikes.'

I don't know him, but I feel gutted. A guy with a mental illness, possibly fighting for his life, not because of the illness, but because of the way people responded to it.

'That's two psych patients in ICU now,' says Kate. 'Going for the record?'

'The night is young,' says Grace. She sees my expression. 'Let's get a coffee while I tell you about Tim.'

'Created a bit of scene on the tram,' she says, as she loads a capsule into the espresso machine. 'He's homeless, has schiz, no danger but . . . can we just pop him into a bed to get him off the streets?' He's already waited several hours on the non-urgent list.

The hospital system hates admitting people whose primary problem is homelessness. It's a very expensive accommodation option and there aren't enough beds to go around anyway.

Tim is in one of the cubicles, where he's been checked out physically. He's dishevelled and smells. People encountering him would probably think he was an alcoholic, but the way he's talking to himself – or to the voices in his head – is more indicative of schizophrenia.

'Any other ideas?' I ask Grace. 'How about a guardian?'

'He's already got one,' says Grace.

Before I can think about it, I pick up a phone, ask to be put through to Nicole. Nash said she wanted to know if the system wasn't working. At 11.45 pm on a Friday, it's not.

I'm pretty sure I wake her. But she isn't aggressive, the way consultants sometimes are. 'I don't want to admit him,' I say to her after a quick summary, 'because that isn't the issue. His guardian isn't looking after him and I think they should be doing the hard work, not us.'

Silence for a few moments. Then, 'Give me the guardian's details.'

Grace has them.

I end the call with Nicole and turn to Grace. 'Let's keep him here until morning and I'll decide then.' We have key performance indicators to consider. KPI number one is: *Patients can't stay longer than twenty-four hours in ED.* I'll be within that.

—

A little after midnight, there's a lull. I check the man in seclusion then head home. I'm close enough to the hospital to get back if I need to. I don't expect to sleep, because *The phone will go* and *I took a risk with Taylah* are in my head. But I'm out cold when the beeper goes off at 4 am.

They need me to confirm that the guy I put in seclusion can stay there. Anyone in seclusion has to be seen and signed off by a doctor every four hours. Should have remembered that.

I roll out of bed, dress and hurry back to the hospital. When I get to Extended Care, the patient is asleep. No point heading home until I check ED. As I get closer, I hear the helicopter coming. Kate Rigby is waiting for it to land.

'How's your chainsaw guy?' I ask.

'Let's say he won't be playing the piano again. But unlike some, he didn't choose to harm himself.'

Occasionally people equate being from the country with being a little unworldly. But you do learn some things. I look at Kate and say, slowly: 'He was up a tree with a chainsaw? I'll take mentally ill; you can do stupid.'

—

Luka is stirring. I look at his heart monitor – he's indestructible – and order some more medication if he gets aggressive. Tim, the homeless man, is sleeping. I go past Short Stay and they give me the thumbs up, presumably because I didn't admit Taylah or Aleesha. That isn't how it's meant to be, but solidarity helps get you through, and however understanding I try to be about Taylah and her family, they exact an emotional toll on everyone in their orbit. Over in ICU, Zac, my myocarditis patient, is doing well and the Hell's Angels' victim is stable.

I return home and get a couple more hours' sleep before I head back to clear out ED.

I'm feeling better than I deserve, given the amount of sleep I've had. I'd forgotten how this kind of work can make you feel alive: when there's no time to doubt yourself and all the training comes together, as it did when I had to put in the endotracheal tube. The downside is the lack of time to talk and reflect, to help people make more fundamental changes where they can. Not that I'm getting a lot of opportunities to practise that in my day job. But *I survived.* Stumbled and fell, but survived, no help needed – unless you count the call to Nicole.

Taylah hasn't returned to ED. I've asked Grace to check on her, twice. She didn't go to her mother's, which I take as a good sign. It wasn't a hard call to discharge her: history and the conversation we had suggested she wasn't going to kill herself in the immediate future. But there's a nagging feeling that, in sending her home without checking with the consultant, I was trying to prove something to myself, lurching from overcautious to cavalier. *I can make the decision to discharge a patient who's threatened suicide.*

Luka is now coherent. He's still a little cagey, so I have the guards hovering. He agrees to have his depot if I let him go. I agree to let him go if he has his depot – and if someone can take him home, and he promises not to use ice. The promise isn't worth much. I've emailed his case manager. Hopefully they'll organise drug counselling, and hopefully he'll keep the appointment and benefit from it. His mother arrives half an hour later. She's clearly scared of him. Luka hugs me. Someone is grateful, I guess. I suggest he shake the doctor's hand next time. Meanwhile, Tim, bathed and wearing a fresh set of clothes, is digging into sausages and eggs.

'Man, a good day today and let's have another, shall we?'

'Yes, let's,' I say, smiling.

'This is the Menzies, isn't it? I've been here before, haven't I? Must have, could have, don't know, maybe?' He sniffs and smiles – his dental hygiene needs work. Maybe I'll include that in an email to the guardian.

There's no social worker on duty on a Saturday to find him accommodation, so he'll be given a list of places to try.

My phone rings. Nicole. 'Your patient still there?'

'Having breakfast.'

'Handel House, Sturt Street, Hampton. Give him a taxi voucher.'

'Um, thanks. Did the guardian . . . ?'

'The guardian had a boot put up him by the chair of the Guardianship List. Who happens to be a friend of mine. Good work, by the way – the sort of example I need to get support for change.'

—

The sun is up. I run home. Add 800 metres to the weekly total.

Jess is in her pyjamas. She toasts us some pre-Easter hot cross buns ('Drink some water; egg coming for the protein') to go with the interrogation.

'Out all night, huh? How was Hot Guy? It's Alex, right?'

'I was working,' I say, then add, 'And nothing's happening with Alex.'

'But you want something to. Come on, I'm your best . . . flatmate. You can tell me.'

'I thought you'd be more interested in what actually happened last night. I was in ED. Saved someone's life.'

'You're kidding. Seriously?'

'Endotracheal tube and an IV. Just wish Marcus had seen it.'

'That is the worst thing to say. About Marcus, I mean. But how is that psychiatry?'

'I'm a doctor. I see the big picture. From high above.'

I tell her the full story of the resuscitation. 'And there was plenty of regular psychiatry, too. Tricky patient with suicidal thoughts; self-harm but not a genuine risk.'

'How do you tell?'

As a paramedic, she'll see plenty of it. I give her an outline, with a heavy dose of 'abundance of caution'.

Jess looks at me with an expression I can't decipher. 'You know you're going to be great at this, don't you?'

I laugh. 'That's the plan. A way to go yet.'

But her vote of confidence helps. I've dealt with the opposite situation to that with Jùnjié. I'm in the best place I'm likely to be to take it up to Prof Gordon, show him I'm ready. I promise myself I'll do it.

EIGHT

ANGER

It's 3 am and the booze has worn off, as it always does.

There are two good moments in the day: falling asleep as the alcohol numbs the pain, and this space before waking, before the unbearable emptiness of being. And then there's the time between the two, when, if he's lucky, he finds perfect, dreamless sleep. Like death. He's been thinking about death, of it being like the time before 1976 – the year he was born.

Andrew's heart is thumping. He's not going to have another drink; he's finished the bottle anyway. It's sitting by the sink in this grim, undecorated box of a flat.

Before the pain fills him again, he decides. Gets out of bed, pulls on jeans and t-shirt. Takes the stuff he needs from the cupboard and walks out the door to the car.

Time to go back to where he came from. To 1975.

Tonight, our study group is meeting at Jon's. I walk – fifteen minutes along gum-lined back streets, dodging puddles in my Docs.

Jon's rented a rambling weatherboard with peeling paint, but a tidy lawn. There's a younger guy, Kieran, living with him, studying physiotherapy. Alex is talking to him in the kitchen.

'I went for a bigger place, because I thought I'd have family visiting all the time,' says Jon. 'But Darwin's a long way. And Kieran's from home.' I can relate.

There are a few big photos, hung haphazardly, I guess on existing hooks. More are on the floor, leaning against the wall. Outdoor settings, lots of kids – family, I'm guessing. A boy of maybe three with a toothy grin is holding up a fish.

'Which one of you's the photographer?'

Jon smiles. 'Luckily it's only me. Not enough wall space for both of us.'

'And this is what you actually do for stress?'

'I brought these to remind me of the stress I got away from.' He laughs. 'Seriously, the biggest issue in Extended Care is the boss. Dinosaur. I'm managing okay. Maybe I'll get Acute next rotation and I'll be as edgy as you guys.'

It's bring-a-plate night. Jess has made a frosted hummingbird cake and a tin of caramel slice for me to bring. Whatever Jon's got cooking for the main course smells amazing and Ndidi arrives with a huge deli platter.

We all sit around the dining table, and Alex emerges from Jon's kitchen with a bottle of pinot gris. We share a smile; we're the only ones who know the wine's been chosen for me.

Ndidi gives us a quick update on Sian – no psychosis, but still mechanical with baby Matilda.

'Sian remembered her mother making daisy chains with her,' I remind her. 'I realise she can't do that with Matilda, but maybe your art therapist could come up with something.' I'm hoping she can literally paint a picture of the future, which Sian seems to be struggling to visualise.

We move to Alex's psychotherapy patient.

'Mr X is just giving me facts – or his side of the story, at least. I didn't notice at first, but that's *all* he's sharing.'

'There's a surprise,' Ndidi deadpans. 'A politician who wants to control the narrative.'

'I've started thinking I'm just there in case he gets into trouble about the alleged sexual harassment – so he can say, *Look: serious suicide attempt, hospital treatment and I'm seeing someone*. Then he tells me he's been put on some mental health advisory board because of his lived experience. Which I'd say he's pleased about in the sense of an achievement rather than as power to make change.'

'What's Prof say?' Jon asks.

'He thinks I should slip in a few suggestions. More funding for psychotherapy.'

'Seriously?' says Ndidi.

'He said it. I'm sure if I did and it came back to bite him, he'd say he was kidding and that I lacked . . . what's that word, Hannah?'

'A focus on helping the guy? Has Prof talked about ongoing risk?' I'm feeling as though patient and therapist – and possibly supervisor – are colluding to deny the shattered version of Xavier I saw in ED that day.

And without warning, I'm suddenly nauseated, disorientated, in a different place.

It's the middle of summer, my skin's sticky and hot. I smell eucalypt and hear a distant kookaburra. Two disembodied feet are dangling in front of me.

I close my eyes and clench my fists so tight I can feel fingernails cutting my palms. As the flashback retreats, I sense Ndidi watching me. The others don't seem to have noticed anything amiss.

Jon has picked up my concern about Xavier. 'Whoever he is and whatever he did, let's not lose sight of the fact that he presented as an attempted suicide.'

Alex nods. 'That's what he *presented* as. But I'm wondering if what he was really trying to do was send a message.'

I don't think Alex has heard what Jon and I were saying. But that flashback has thrown me. And, short of signing up for psychotherapy, I'm in the best place I can be to do something about it.

'Um,' I say, feeling awkward, 'do you guys ever find that some of your patients stir stuff up for you?'

'Working in a mother–baby unit would put anyone off having kids,' Ndidi says. I suspect her problem is the opposite: having motherhood in her face all day.

'Incarceration, loss of autonomy,' says Jon. 'A bit close to home when you've watched your mob being locked up over nothing.'

'Not a lot in Acute, to be honest,' says Alex. 'Not for me, but I'm guessing Hannah's . . .'

Three quick answers and it's back to me. Jon must sense that I need time to collect my thoughts and drags Alex to the kitchen to help him dish up the meal.

'What happened?' says Ndidi when we're alone. 'A minute ago. You seemed to zone out.'

'Flashback.'

'Had them before?'

'I used to have dreams, but not for a long while. This is new.'

'Are you sure you want to share it with us? If you'd rather talk one on one . . .'

The dangling feet are at the edge of my thoughts. If I close my eyes, I'm certain they will be there again. I nod, committed, as Jon brings out the main course: chicken, of course, but this time with lemon myrtle, saltbush and pepperberry.

'Native ingredients,' he says. 'Thought it might be a conversation starter about how our backgrounds affect the way we approach psychiatry. Which I guess they wouldn't do so much if we were doing surgery or pathology. But eat.'

We serve ourselves. It's really good, though the native spices are pretty low key.

'Do you want to go first?' says Alex to Jon. 'About what our upbringing . . . and culture . . . does to us?'

'I'll give you a very short answer: it affects everything I do. But Hannah's brought up the opposite question. Which is maybe more urgent.' He fixes his gaze on me. 'You want to be the first to take a deep dive into what this job does to us?'

Alex is looking at me intently. But I find myself telling my story to Jon more than the others.

'I get edgy when Alex talks about whether Mr X is playing games. And there's a patient I admitted last week – Andrew, near-miss suicide attempt – who's stirring up the same stuff. And,' – deep breath – 'I just had a flashback.'

I pause, hating the uncomfortable feeling in my chest. 'When I was young my family used to take in foster kids. Fifty-three of them, to be exact, starting when I was eight.'

'Wow,' says Ndidi.

'The last two: Fifty-Two was fifteen – my age – and acted older. Fifty-Three was this scrawny thirteen-year-old with pimples and a smart mouth. Anyway, they were drinking in one of the caravans. I was asked to get them for breakfast next morning. Fifty-Two was hungover and said he had no idea where the other kid was.'

I can see Fifty-Two propped up on one elbow in bed, looking at me with sleepy eyes and a smirk.

'Give me a few seconds.' I take a slug of my wine and push myself to relive the rest: my mother's cry; my father's haunted expression; the click of the Child Protection workers' polished shoes on the floorboards; the ambulance; the police and their cars; slamming doors; the frightened and angry looks of the foster kids as they were taken away.

'I found him.' Another deep breath. 'He'd hanged himself.'

I can see him as if it had just happened. He was unrecognisable: huge protruding tongue; mottled blue skin; eyes almost out of his skull, staring at me. Though he was obviously dead, I got him down on the ground and tried chest compressions until someone heard my screams.

'Oh shit,' says Alex.

'I had no idea what to do,' I say. 'Ultimately, that's why I did medicine. I didn't want to *ever* feel that helpless again. And, later, psych: because that was the only sort of medicine that might have saved him.' Might as well put it all on the table. 'And my parents – they're still carrying it.'

'You couldn't have been expected –' Ndidi.

'Have you considered that your parents –' Alex.

Jon just waits for me to continue.

'It was tough on us all, but Mum and Dad – this was their life's calling. They stopped taking in kids after that.'

After months of the cold shoulder and barely concealed accusations, when Child Protection came calling for help, my mother summoned the strength to say no. It wasn't as much of a relief as I had expected. More a void.

'He'd given me this look, the boy that died, not long before, that I now recognise was a cover-up for despair.' The same look Jùnjié the diver had given me when he had been hiding the stretch band and his intentions. 'But with Mr X and now Andrew – my patient – I'm realising that I haven't really dealt with it.'

It irks me that there's some truth to what Prof has said. But it doesn't mean I need therapy. I just need to face it head on. Some part of me, even as a teenager, recognised the call for help, and as far as my future's concerned, that's a huge positive. The problem is that I ignored it. I didn't want to talk about that with the counsellor, who seemed as happy as I was to move on. But the feeling I'm trying to deal with is guilt. I think.

Alex talks about repression and how it protects us until we are ready to examine our lives. Ndidi suggests patience and being kind to myself and helps herself to a big chunk of Jess's cake. Jon looks at me like he can see what I'm not saying.

Alex hangs about after dinner like he's expecting to walk me home, but I want to talk to Jon. It's as much his photo of the boy with the fish as anything. And maybe not wanting this to be thrown into my relationship with Alex yet. Jon must intuit something, as he hustles Alex out the door. I may have some repair work to do later.

'You want to know why I did psych?' says Jon, when we're alone in the living room. 'I can tell when someone is eating themselves up inside and needs to talk about it. You don't have to, but . . .'

He sits down in an armchair. I take the one opposite and we share the silence for a while.

'It was a pretty awful time,' I say eventually. 'After Fifty-Three.'

Jon leans forward, arms resting on his knees. 'Did he have a name?'

It takes me ages to reply. I haven't said his name – or Fifty-Two's – for twelve years. 'Aaron.'

'You want to tell me about him?'

No. But I do. 'He had his thirteenth birthday with us. First time ever someone made him a cake and sang "Happy Birthday".' Reluctantly, in my case. But I can still see his lip trembling: *This is for me?*

'I imagine he was a little shit.'

I nod. 'But my parents were devastated.'

'And you? How were you?'

How *was* I? Right now, I'm only just holding it together. 'I was meant to be feeling sad. It was tragic. A kid was *dead*.'

'But you didn't feel sad.'

'I was sorry for myself.' I take a breath. 'And I was *glad*. Not that he was dead – I was shocked that someone could die like that, and I really did want to be able to do something about the powerlessness – but glad that he was *gone*. Him and all the other kids competing with me for my parents' attention.'

'You didn't kill him, Hannah.'

'No. But I knew they were drinking, and I didn't tell my parents. And Aaron was always saying life was shit and he wished he was dead.' Except when he was saying the opposite: *Dad's going to take me to the Big Day Out*, and, *We're going to Movie World in Queensland for my birthday.* His parents didn't even show up for access visits. 'Plus that look.'

'Oh, Hannah,' says Jon. Not critical, but not forgiving either.

'Now I feel . . . guilty. I should have checked on him. I should have told my parents. He was only thirteen. And he *died.*'

'You were just a kid.'

'It's really why I wanted to do emergency medicine, and I flunked out there, and now I'm wondering just how . . . whether . . . psychiatrists can stop anyone killing –'

'Stop,' says Jon, getting up and looking around. He dashes out and returns with a toilet roll. 'Sorry – no tissues.'

We both laugh.

'He was your parents' responsibility,' says Jon, and I see him reflecting for a few moments. 'Aaron's parents may or may not have done their best,' he says finally, 'but circumstances left him in a bad place. You didn't put him there and you couldn't have been expected to get him out.'

It's near midnight when I leave. I thank Jon for the listening and for the dinner.

'Can't take credit for the chicken. Except for giving Alex permission for the cultural appropriation.'

'He cooked it?'

'Yep, my mum's recipe, but he volunteered to make it. That's his thing. He didn't want to say anything because it'd look like he was doing something I was expected to do. Guess we're square now.'

—

I don't think I'm going to sleep at all. When I get home, I dig out the rocky road ice cream. Jess gets out of bed and joins me.

'Did Lennon ever talk about what happened when we were kids?' I ask.

'The suicide? Nup. He's not big on opening up. Except bottles. It's why I had to dump him.'

'*You* dumped *him*?' That's not the story Lennon told me.

'Yeah,' says Jess, brushing her red curls off her face. Wearing pyjamas, with her feet tucked underneath her on the couch, she looks younger than twenty-five. 'I mean, I wanted to settle down and he didn't, but I'd have waited. He just needed to sort himself out first, though, and he wasn't showing any interest in doing the hard stuff, you know?'

I didn't. But I'm starting to see.

'The jackarooing might help,' I say.

'Nah,' says Jess. 'He's still running away.'

—

When the alarm goes off, instead of grabbing my phone, I pull on shorts and go for a training run – the long easy one programmed for today. I run without looking at my watch, relying on my body to judge the pace.

We're well into autumn and the mornings are cool. The ground is covered with golden leaves that crunch underfoot as I run in the opposite direction to the hospital, toward the park. There's nobody much about, apart from a magpie that serenades me before flying off with its mate. I take the path by the river and, as I watch the current carry driftwood away and the swirling pools of foam caught in muddy cul-de-sacs, I let myself just *feel*.

I think about Aaron without wanting to cry. I think of the times I did nice things, kind things – including for Aaron. Material for my Evidence column. But I need to do more to deal with my issues. I can start by spending more time with Andrew, my patient with depression who attempted suicide. There's a straightforward, if slightly terrifying, way to justify doing that and prove to Professor Gordon that I'm ready for the training program.

The next day, I ask Nash if I can present Andrew at the Prof Round.

—

Elena is seeing Sian and Leo in a couples session in the Mother Baby Unit, and asks if I want to sit in. Nash is fine with it; he thinks it's instructive for me to follow a patient right through.

I've seen Sian a few times since the postpartum psychosis began to lift. She's gaining insight, which raises questions: *How could I have thought that? How can I trust myself ever again?* But while the delusions are gone and, on an intellectual level, she knows Matilda is her baby, the emotions and connection haven't returned.

She's dressed neatly when she enters the brightly decorated activity room with Matilda in her arms. She goes to hand the baby to a nurse, but Elena says, 'No, she can stay with you.'

We sit in armchairs. Leo is stony-faced and unengaged. Sian puts Matilda on a blanket in front of her with a few toys scattered around.

'I'm a lot better,' she says, but her smile looks forced.

'That's good to hear,' says Elena. 'How about you, Leo?'

'I'm not the one with a mental illness.'

Elena thinks on this – at least, that's what it looks like she's doing. 'It's a bit of a spectrum, though, isn't it? I'm not saying unhappiness is an illness . . .'

'Good,' says Leo. 'Are you surprised that I'm unhappy?'

'At least you can come and go when you like,' says Sian.

'That's exactly what I can't do. You realise I've had to take time off work? I'm having to do all the stuff that we agreed would be your responsibility.'

Elena breaks in. 'Tell me, Leo, what is it you've lost that's hardest to bear?'

'Trust.'

'Fuck,' says Sian. 'I was *sick*. If I'd been hit by a tram, you'd have had to come home to look after Matilda. Maybe forever. But there would have been something to *see* if that had happened.'

Leo stares straight ahead, cold and unreachable. And, I realise, suffering. He hasn't had his partner home with him for more than a month, other than on day leave. He must be wondering if the partner he knew before will ever come home.

'Sian, I imagine this is hard to hear,' says Elena. 'Because you didn't ask to be unwell.'

'I did not. And I did *everything* I could so our baby would have the best chance. And he'd sit right in front of me drinking a beer and . . .' She stops. Whatever way this couple worked before, it isn't working now, and she knows it.

Before I can think it through, I say, 'Leo.' I pause and look at Elena, but she nods at me to go ahead. 'Leo, it's hard being angry at someone you love. It's hard being angry at yourself, too. Which is it at the moment for you?'

Elena isn't giving any indication whether my intervention is helpful or stupid.

'What I can't understand is how she could . . . how she ever thought . . .' He's shaking his head.

'Can you understand what happened, Sian?' Elena asks.

'I've told the doctors, and I've told Leo: I can't remember. I wasn't myself.'

'Does anyone who knows you think you would leave your baby alone?'

Sian shakes her head and – reluctantly – Leo does too.

'So, the first problem is that you are trying to use your usual way of thinking to explain what happened, and that isn't working.'

Leo shakes his head. 'Everyone keeps telling me it's the illness, but whatever the reason, she went . . . she put Matilda in danger and nobody's guaranteeing she won't do it again. And our lives are never going to be the same.'

'Leo is bent out of shape because his perfect world has been disrupted,' says Sian. 'Well, so has mine. And he either gets used to it . . . or he doesn't.'

'Matilda is looking at you right now, Sian,' says Elena. 'I wonder what she'd say if she could talk?'

Sian glances down at Matilda, who chooses the moment to smile at her mother. Leo sees it.

'I need both of you,' Elena says in a soft voice. 'I don't understand your anxiety and anger, but it upsets me.'

With Elena playing the role of child, I feel it's appropriate for me to deliver the therapist message. 'Anger can get in the way of forgiveness.' I say it to both of them, but I'm looking at Leo, and even as I speak I feel like I'm talking down to him.

'What,' says Leo, 'if I don't want to fucking forgive her?' He stands up and storms out, but halfway to the door turns back to me. 'You just push and push . . . This is on you.'

Matilda cries and Sian starts to shake.

Elena picks up Matilda while I rest a hand on Sian's shoulder, to show her she isn't alone. But I don't have anything to offer her beyond platitudes: 'Give it time.' I can't say to her: *I'm sorry – I fucked up. I'll fix it.*

'Oh my god, I'm so sorry,' I say to Elena when we're clear.

'What for?'

'For what I said that made Leo leave.'

'You didn't make anyone do anything. We didn't have a plan, and we ended up reinforcing each other, which he'll have read as everyone being against him.' Elena must sense my devastation. 'Reflect on that, for sure, but don't let it get in the way of thinking about the case as a whole.'

—

Andrew is someone I picture – in normal life – wielding barbecue tongs and wearing a *World's Best Dad* apron. He intended to end his life outside his ex-girlfriend's house, where she lives with her new partner. She recognised the car pulling up in the early hours of the morning. He was unconscious when the police pulled the hose from the exhaust pipe.

I know I've avoided seeing him. There's something about his manner, a nerdiness or deference, that reminds me of Fifty-Three – *Aaron* – though physically there's no resemblance.

Andrew's had ten days on an antidepressant started by his GP a few days before the suicide attempt. He's been changed from an involuntary to a voluntary patient, and he'll have day leave this weekend for Easter before being discharged after Prof Round on Tuesday. He's agreed to be interviewed during the round because he wants people to understand that major depression is not the same as grief or sadness. And because he's the sort of guy who doesn't push back.

I see him in one of the interview rooms adjoining the Low Dependency area.

'I'm wondering if we can go back to how you were feeling when you tried to suicide,' I say.

'Do we have to?'

'Only if you're up to it . . .'

He takes a few breaths. 'When I lost my mum, I was sad and felt bad that I hadn't seen her and missed her birthday, but I was still functioning. I still went to work; I could watch the footy and put it aside for a bit. But this? I mean, it isn't like I haven't been depressed before, so I should have seen it coming, but . . . bang.'

Andrew's a plumber but hasn't worked for a while: a sign, if someone had been looking. He's survived two previous suicide attempts. The first was six years ago, when his wife left him and took their two kids. He overdosed, but not on anything that was genuinely likely to kill him, and there's a sense from the notes that his treating team thought it was a cry for help. The second attempt, three years ago, had no obvious precipitant, except that he'd stopped his meds. Both times he ended up in hospital with suicidal ideas and a plan.

Andrew pauses for a long time before continuing. 'I remember reading about those Thai boys – the ones that got stuck in the cave and couldn't get out.'

Not a bad analogy to choose: the story culminated in a successful rescue.

'And that's what depression felt like?'

'It was like I was in that cave. Alone. No way out. Wasn't seeing or hearing anything. Didn't eat, had to drink myself to sleep. I'm not talking about *sad* misery. It was black nothingness. I think part of me believed I was in hell.'

'You managed to find a hose, though, and get yourself over to Mandy's.'

'I'm a plumber and I can drive. I guess I was able to focus enough on one thing – ending it. I had this idea that Mandy needed to know I loved her right up to the end. I didn't want her to find me or anything. I wasn't thinking past the moment of oblivion.'

'Did you blame her? Or her new partner?'

'He's a loser – but who'd want to be with me?'

'Do you ever get angry?'

'Sure. I was pissed off at her when I found she had a new boyfriend, and who it was, but to be honest I was more sorry for myself.'

After my conversation with Andrew, I run my presentation past Nash, and he makes some useful suggestions – as well as checking that I really am comfortable about doing it.

'You don't have to stick your neck out,' he says, but of course I do. He smiles. 'Should be a good turnout tomorrow.'

'How do you mean?'

'Nicole heard we were presenting a case of depression and wanted the admin staff to come. There's a lot of ignorance around about the difference between sadness and clinical depression. But she's going to fix it by teaching medicine to people who deliver meals and analyse data.'

'Like Carey?'

'Carey's different.' Nash laughs. 'Educating the public is important, but it's not your job. Speak to Prof and the clinicians.'

'It's only a small room.'

Nash smiles. We've been moved to a larger venue, he tells me. It seems Andrew is going to get his audience. I'm just relieved I confronted my demons with my peer group before I had to do a public performance.

—

My second parkrun is on Easter Saturday. The weather is cool and I'm feeling fit, rested and ready to nail it.

'Powerful stuff at Jon's,' says Ndidi, as we take off at much the same pace as last time. 'What you shared opened the door for the rest of us. Are you okay?'

'I'm fine. And you guys were great. I think I just needed to say it out loud. How's Sian?'

'Taking no shit. So, better. But she'll stay a bit longer. Still having difficulties with attachment to the baby.'

'She's been in a long time.'

'Better that than going home to no support.'

Rowers on the river wave to us and I wave back. We do the loop. I push it a little. All according to plan – the twelve dollars I paid for the personalised training program was worth it.

I'm keeping pace with Ndidi as we cross the bridge, follow the river to the turnaround point, then head back. And a few minutes later, there's Xavier again, with kids and loping dog, running toward us. This time, I can see he's placed me; he might have worked it out between the two runs. For a second, the mask falls away, and life goes into slow motion. Which is not helpful when you're running. By the time I hit the bridge, Ndidi is gone.

My time's better than for the first parkrun, but not what I was shooting for.

'Good therapy,' says Xavier, coming over to where Ndidi and I are having coffee afterward, partner and kids in tow. The mask is firmly back in place.

He introduces his wife Sarah, who is carrying a thermos, and his kids. 'This is Dr Wright, who was on the ward with Dr Ashwood when I had depression. She didn't see me at my best. No-one's at their best in hospital.'

He's singing the right tune. *It's a disease like any other.* If he actually had depression.

The kids seem fine with it, but his wife, holding his arm, looks a little uncomfortable.

'How are you finding the mental health system?' he asks, as the kids move off.

I can see Ndidi doesn't want to let the opportunity pass. And she never had any contact with him in hospital. I let her start, then walk off to dump my coffee cup. I'm waiting for Ndidi, looking at Xavier's kids staging an informal sprint competition, when he comes up behind me, alone now.

'I understand you're being discreet,' he says, 'but I'd like to thank you – not just for what your team did for me, but for choosing this profession of service. I speak from experience when I say you won't always be appreciated. But your family should be very proud of you.'

I guess I could interpret his words as a reassurance for himself as well: *Do good, don't worry what people say about you, family's your rock.*

Without waiting for a response, he heads off toward someone who's spotted him. Doing his VIP thing.

'He asked if he could have a quick word with you,' says Ndidi, joining me. 'If you'd treated him for a broken leg, it wouldn't have been an issue.'

'Just erring on the side of caution. What did you think?'

'He's my local member. More a grassroots kind of guy than a mover and shaker. I've met a few politicians, and until I made the connection that he was Alex's patient, I'd have said he was okay.'

'Did he say anything about . . .'

'Being a sexual predator? No. He said suicide prevention is high on his list. I guess you could read that two ways.'

'Alex would, for sure. But I'm not planning to tell him about running into his patient.'

—

On Monday, Alex walks with me to the lecture theatre for my Prof Round presentation. I've dressed a bit more formally than usual in a black pencil skirt. Alex notices but I can see he's in two minds about commenting.

'So, am I looking good or not?' I say.

'You're asking *me*?'

So he had noticed Jon shooing him out after our last study group.

'Yes. You're the only person I'm asking.'

He smiles. 'I can't answer that without a definite breach of boundaries.'

'Any tips for dealing with Prof?'

'You're asking *me*?' he says again.

I laugh. 'Experience. But I was thinking more about my history with . . .' I raise my eyebrows.

'With humiliating him? I've thought about it. What I'd say is, watch for him giving you an opportunity to take him down. It won't be over something life or death, just who's right. He'll be wrong – but it'll be a test to see whether you call him out.'

'What's that got to do with clinical judgement?'

'I guess it's some sort of judgement – reading a situation, deciding what's important.'

'And you're saying I should agree with him.'

'I'm saying that on the one hand there's your dream, your career, your whole mission in life; on the other, you show a bit of respect for one of your elders. Hmmm, which to choose?'

—

There must be a hundred people. We're in a modern lecture theatre with tiered seating and swing-up desktops, lots of technology and a plaque to say it was named for a former health minister.

Oliver, the senior registrar, takes me aside before I start. I realise now he's quite visually impaired – very heavy glasses and a huge font on the tablet he's holding with his notes.

'I should tell you that if Prof makes a criticism, it's nothing personal – but of course it always is. But he does it to everyone. And let him talk. Like you would a patient.'

He introduces me and my presentation: 'I Thought I Was in Hell'. It's a reminder to myself that, no matter what Prof throws at me, I'm in a better place than Andrew's been.

I outline Andrew's family history: the harsh father, the mother who was in and out of hospital from the time he was born. I mention that his mother's absences might have caused an attachment trauma. I discuss suicide without my voice quavering. I finish with a diagnosis of recurrent major depression, precipitated by the break-up of his relationship.

Prof steps up.

Do not publicly correct him even if he says black is white.

'Is Andrew currently expressing suicidal thoughts?'

'He has them fleetingly. He went on weekend leave, but it was structured – he stayed with his brother and sister-in-law. I believe there is an ongoing risk if he were to experience another trauma.'

'And how will you manage the risk that an event of this kind could lead to another episode?'

'I will ensure my consultant agrees with my assessment that he is safe to be discharged.' I risk a look at Nash, who nods. I'm nearly there. 'Andrew will have the CATT team number to phone and will be referred to a psychiatrist to see on an ongoing basis. He'll have his life back and, with it, the responsibility to manage his illness.' I've almost forgotten something obvious. 'And, of course, he'll be on medication for the rest of his life.'

Prof nods. 'You'd better bring him in.'

'Doing well,' Jon whispers to me as I walk past.

I open the door, invite Andrew in and introduce him.

'Lot of shrinks,' he says as he sits down opposite Prof and me.

'You've seen a few over the years,' Prof says. 'What's helped the most?'

'The meds.'

'Why do you stop them?'

'Hate the side effects. You know what I'm talking about.'

Antidepressants often affect sexual function.

'So, are you going to take them this time?'

'I guess so.'

'Because it will come back otherwise. The depression.'

Andrew nods.

'And you know that, and you know how bad it is, but still you stop them.'

'Not a good patient, am I?'

Prof nods thoughtfully. 'I think you try hard to be a good patient and partner and person. But I'd imagine that sometimes you get angry at the unfairness of it all.'

'Not really. Life's not fair. We St Kilda supporters know that.' He smiles at the audience.

'When you think of your father, back when you were a child, tell me the first five things you recall.'

'Ah. Always took us to the footy – we were footy mad. Hard-working. Good provider. Tough as nails.' Andrew pauses before adding: 'A pisspot.'

'What was he like when he was on the drink?'

He hadn't told me about his father drinking; had I asked? He'd said his father could be 'harsh', but he'd qualified it with 'not that often' and I hadn't followed up. It's the first crack in my presentation.

'A monster,' says Andrew.

'Abusive?'

'Beat the shit out of us all, until my brother got big enough to give him one back – only needed to do it once.'

'Bet you didn't want to be like him.'

'Too right. Swore I would never, ever touch my wife or kids – and I never have, nor any woman.'

Prof thanks Andrew, tells him he can leave, and then turns to the audience. 'I'm conscious that we have some non-clinical staff here, and I want to emphasise that all depressions are not the same. Your friend or partner or you yourself may not exhibit the same symptoms or behaviour as today's patient but still have a severe and dangerous illness.

'Dr Wright gave us a sound description of Andrew's disease – what we diagnose – and the illness – the patient's experience of it. Enough for the examiners. But we also need to consider the patient's *predicament*: his life as it incorporates the illness and the treatment.'

I'm relieved. Prof's doing what Prof does and I'm sidelined for the moment.

'Now, for the clinicians: will he stop his meds this time?'

No-one thinks he'll stop them immediately. But what about if he finds a new partner and wants a sexual relationship? There is discussion about managing this risk.

Prof asks: 'If he does stop taking his medication then, Hannah, what will be the underlying reason?'

And there it is. It's not the trap I was watching for; just a straight clinical question. But I freeze. I want to say: *My brain has seized up because you're holding my future in your hands, not because of any issue with suicide that I can't handle.*

I manage, 'Because he hates meds controlling his life? Thinks that taking them is admitting to a weakness?'

'That's what he'll tell you. But what hasn't he dealt with in his life?'

My mind is blank; I can't make sense of the question.

Prof waits, shifting his gaze from me to the audience.

I'm looking out at them too and see Alex miming a word, but I can't make it out. And beside him is Omar, making a stupid face: eyes narrowed, teeth bared and . . . I've got it.

'Anger,' I say.

'Exactly,' says Prof. 'Because to be angry in his household was to be terrifying. Rather than identifying with the aggressor, which is the defence many men from abusive backgrounds find themselves employing, this man's genetic heritage has offered an alternative – the depressive position, which is a repression of the unacceptable anger at his father for terrifying him and at his mother for not protecting him. And until he deals with his anger, he will be destined to relapse, and choose to die rather than face the anger he can't express.'

Yep. That's exactly what I was trying to say.

Prof looks in Nash's direction. 'Antidepressants notwithstanding.'

'But he wouldn't know he was making a choice,' I say, before I can stop myself. 'Because he doesn't recognise his anger. And if *we* know that, and don't offer him an opportunity to deal with it . . .'

Prof smiles condescendingly. 'We can do that. But he's the one who has to choose to take it. Choices, always choices, *most* of them not ours to make.'

It's not a disaster. People clap and ask good questions, and Nicole says a bit about the importance of all staff knowing what we're here to do and the problems we face.

'You owe me a drink,' says Omar when we're done. In case I've forgotten, he demonstrates his angry face again. 'I guess you want to know my secret.'

'Of screwing up your face?'

'Of diagnosing underlying psychopathology.'

'Go on.'

'We nurses spend far more time with the patients than you do. We actually have training, and eyes and ears.'

'Okay . . .'

'Plus two techniques from the Omar bag of tricks. Number one: when in doubt about the underlying emotion, go for anger. That's actually a lesson from our friend Elena.'

'And number two?'

'I was sitting next to Alex and I heard what he said. Teamwork.' He puts an arm around me. 'You did good.'

But the message from Prof, communicated without words in those endless seconds while I cast around for an answer, was clear: *I saw you. I told you this would bring up unresolved issues. And I've known all along that Jùnjié stirred up more than you realised.*

For once, he's right.

—

I go and sit in the registrars' room, and Alex finds me there.

He starts: 'You didn't miss a trick question. I was probably wrong about that.' Then he looks at me properly, draws up a chair and waits. There's some of the magic that Prof showed with Veronica: the capacity to make you feel nurtured and cared for without touch or words. This time, I accept it.

'Aaron,' I manage to say finally. 'The kid who suicided. I thought I felt guilty . . . but it's much more.' I don't want to say it out loud. My voice catches. 'It's anger. At the foster kids, for fucking up my childhood, making my parents even more unavailable. So I ended up doing shitty things to fucked-up kids.'

Alex is silent. I can see he's tempted to put his hand on mine, but he reads me right. Yes, just not now. What I need now is his take on what's going on for me.

'How can I be angry?' I say. 'I mean . . . it's not just anger I'm feeling. I'm *furious*. I want to scream. I want to fucking bring Aaron back to life so I can kill him with my bare hands.'

Alex just waits.

'What sort of horrible person am I for being angry at someone who suicided? For being so self-centred that all I can think of is how *I* feel? What about his poor mother, and my parents, and –'

'Breathe,' says Alex. 'Should you be angry at Aaron? I wouldn't believe you if you told me you hadn't been, okay?'

He waits until I look at him, until he's sure it has sunk in.

'But,' says Alex softly, 'it's better directed at his parents or whatever it was that left him so desperate – which was not of his making. Once you make sense of that, you can reclaim the narrative.'

It's the same message that Elena wants to convey to Chloe's family. It's okay to be angry at someone who's suffering – or who suffered. Or was acting with good intentions. But try to put it in perspective.

I nod. 'I think I can work through that.'

'With someone?'

'I guess that'd solve the problem with Prof at the same time.'

'Too easy.' He's smiling.

'What?'

'If you go into therapy, your anger at Aaron's parents is going to be just the beginning.'

—

I've already done a discharge interview with Andrew. The paperwork is done, the appointments made, the boxes of medication dispensed. But he's still here, waiting for a visitor. I'm going to have to miss watching Chloe's second family therapy session, but this is more important. I want to at least give Andrew a chance to deal with his buried anger.

When I get to the unit, his visitor has arrived. I sit outside his room, waiting, and it dawns on me that I've come here for myself – because of my own issues. If he stops medication down the track and suicides, I don't want to be left thinking there was something else I could have tried. But he's not going to sign up for therapy. Takes one to know one.

As I'm getting up to go, his visitor emerges. He looks to be in his early twenties, a tradie of some kind, closed in on himself. We don't speak as he passes, but I can feel the rage coming off him: at the father who didn't take him into account when he decided to suicide. I think of Xavier and his kids: how hard it must have been for him to be so open about what he did, how he risked being seen by them as weak – but how it gives them a better chance of getting through it together.

I go into Andrew's room. 'Your son?' I say.

'One of them. The other's still pretty pissed off. Frankly, I don't know why. It's not like I've been much use to them.'

'Probably pretty hard to be, given what you've been dealing with. Which is what I wanted to talk about.'

'Being a better father?'

'Being well, so you can be. Staying on your meds would be a good start. Ask your psychiatrist to try a different med if you feel you might stop this one because of the sexual problems. Sound okay?'

'Sure.'

'But I'm wondering . . . You haven't dealt what triggers these episodes. I don't know if doing that will stop the episodes and if you'll still need medication, but –'

'So why do I need to deal with whatever it is?'

'Because . . . When you drove your car to Mandy's house, what were you thinking?'

'I told you. I wanted to her to know I still loved her.'

'And how angry you were at her.'

'What if I was?' Andrew says after a moment, sounding defeated. 'Can't say I blame her for leaving me, though. I put a downer on everything. First wife took the kids – same reason.'

'And you were angry about Mandy's new partner?'

He shrugs. 'She could have had better taste.'

He's been repressing anger all his life. With the drugs on board, I figure, it stays buried.

'If you want to understand that it's okay to be angry and that it won't turn you into your father,' I say, 'then here's the name of a good guy. A therapist.' I hold out a card. 'It wouldn't hurt to try.'

'Sure.'

'Maybe so you don't pass on to your sons what your father passed on to you. Or at least show them another way of dealing with it.'

We sit looking at each other for a long time, and then I see something: a tiny nod that tells me he's connected the dots.

He holds up the card I've given him. 'This guy you mentioned, do I call him or go through my shrink? She's not going to get upset that I want to see someone else?'

It shouldn't be an issue, but of course it is. Biological versus psychological approaches. 'Your GP will give you a referral. Maybe let your psychiatrist know after it's set up.'

'And we can talk about my boys?'

'Definitely. But, I need to tell you, it's not going to be cheap . . .'

Andrew gives me a strange look. 'Have you paid for a plumber lately? It'll give me some motivation to get back to work.'

Then he does something I haven't seen him do before. Out of nowhere, he laughs.

NINE

BREAKTHROUGHS

A solid, unremarkable house in a leafy suburb. Tidy lawn, Subaru in the driveway. Two cops are knocking at the door, gently at first, then more insistently.

'Jacq. Jacq! Are you okay?'

One points to a double-hung window. They force it open and the first cop climbs through. Shouts, 'Jacq?' again. Then: 'Shit.'

The second cop follows. A woman in a red negligee is sitting in an armchair. Frozen, unresponsive. But alive.

'You'll love this one,' says Alex. 'I saw her in ED and she was wearing a red nightie. A fairly . . . small one.'

Here I am, thinking it's time I took some initiative and texted him about a drink or dinner or possibly more, when he appears in person and starts telling me about a scantily clad woman.

'Cops forced an entry, and that was what she had on,' he says. 'Not in bed – in the living room.'

I wince at the thought of being hauled into ED in my birthday gift from Marcus. 'Who called the cops?'

'No-one – she's one of theirs. Detective Sergeant Livermore, in charge of media liaison. There was an incident she was meant to deal with, and she didn't answer their calls.'

Detective Sergeant Livermore is in the interview room, in a wheelchair, staring straight ahead. She's maybe forty, with shoulder-length hair that sees a good stylist, in a hospital gown, but I can't help imagining her in the red nightie. Something about her tells me she could carry it off.

Through the glass, I can see Omar and another nurse speaking to her. She's not responding. The nurses help her up and place her on a normal chair. Her upper body remains oddly rigid.

'I take it there was no foul play?' I say.

'At this point in time, our investigations are ongoing,' Alex says in a cop-speaking-to-the-media tone. Then, in his regular voice, 'No. She was sitting in an armchair, completely frozen – way worse than she is now. I'm thinking personality disorder . . . for a start, anyway.'

Alex has his own admission to do: 'Guy you saw a few weeks ago.'

Ahmed, the truck driver who nearly killed Alex's Mr X – or was nearly pulled into his suicide plan – has been undertaking group therapy for his post-traumatic stress disorder. It's triggered flashbacks and nightmares.

'We'll get him settled, give him something for the nightmares, then move him over to the PTSD ward,' says Alex.

'Not exactly a win for psychotherapy,' I say.

'Not a win for anyone,' says Alex. 'It's not like antidepressants are miracles – the studies say if the patient doesn't get better after the first two you try, then they're basically screwed.'

'Good to know the technical term.'

I look up Jacq on the system. No psych history. The neurologists have given her the works, including an MRI scan, presumably after they'd got her out of the chair shape, and decided she's not their problem. I guess there's always the chance she has some seriously weird neurological illness. But for now, she's ours.

They've contacted her husband, a detective inspector who left the marriage a week ago. The intern recorded his statement verbatim: '*I last saw her when I collected my stuff on Saturday. She screamed at me and started throwing glassware. I left and won't be going back.*' The neighbours called the cops. Awkward.

There's nothing in the section on past and family history or her premorbid personality. It's hard to take a history from someone who isn't speaking. She doesn't respond to questions or to me touching her arm. I'm tempted to prod her harder, but the notes say she didn't react to blood being taken.

Nash wanders in. 'Ah, this is Constable Livermore? I think we'll have the nurses put her in her room for her own protection. If she hasn't eaten or had anything to drink in a couple of days, we'll put a nasogastric tube down. Hate to do it, it's pretty unpleasant, but there's not much else we can do.'

'Urgh,' says Omar. 'Wouldn't wish it on my worst enemy.'

All this in front of the patient. Nash, at least, is normally respectful, but that 'Constable' was a pretty obvious provocation. When Omar has wheeled her out, Nash smiles. 'She'll likely come around by tomorrow at the latest.'

'But . . . what's wrong with her?'

'Born in the wrong city in the wrong era.'

'Thanks. I'll put that in the notes.' I follow Nash back to the glass house.

'If you believe Freud,' he says, 'Vienna was full of women like this in the 1920s. Physical manifestation of psychological issues.'

'You're saying this is psychosomatic? Triggered by her husband leaving her?'

'In contemporary terms, we'd say she has a histrionic personality disorder, which makes her vulnerable to this type of presentation under stress.'

'So, what do we do?'

'We'll wait her out. She won't like being left in a room.'

A Freudian diagnosis and no medication. A first in the time I've known Nash.

—

Sian is going to be discharged later in the week. She deteriorated after Leo walked out of our last therapy session, but has picked up since. No delusions. The fight that went out of her has returned, but she's still struggling to connect with Matilda.

Elena and I head to the Mother Baby Unit, where the art and music therapy room, with its stacks of coloured paper and walls covered in artwork, has been freed up for us. The patients have been working in clay and there's a table with half-finished sculptures in the Madonna and Child genre. One is breathtaking in its depiction of maternal pain. Another is missing both heads.

Sian comes in alone and sits down. Matilda is sleeping and Leo hasn't shown up.

'Can we get started?' says Sian. 'If he doesn't want to be part of it, that's his problem.'

Elena nods. 'Maybe that's where we should start. Tell us how things have been between you and Leo.'

'He's asked his mother to stay on when I go home. I always said I'd be the one to look after the baby. I've got plenty of leave. His job pays more, but he's away a lot. That was working okay for us. It's the way it's still going to work.'

'But things have changed.'

'Not because of anything I did.'

Her look challenges Elena to disagree with this, but she just smiles.

'How do you get on with his mother? It's Deirdre, isn't it?'

Sian looks at me. 'You've met her. How would you like to have your partner's mother living with you? As long as it's short-term, I'll cope. I'm not going to say no to a bit of help at the moment. Hopefully we can get her an Airbnb.'

'Would you have preferred your own mother to help?'

'I'd have preferred to be able to manage on my own. I'd have preferred not to have got ill. But those choices aren't open to me. My parents are overseas and everyone's telling me to take it slowly. I thought you were here to help me bond with Matilda' – she takes a breath, steadies herself – 'emotionally. So we can both go home.'

ECT has delivered its miracle. Sian is no longer psychotic or even depressed. But she is having to deal with the aftermath of a serious mental illness, and the impact on herself and her relationship. There's no medication for reality. At least nothing that I'm allowed to write a prescription for. But my bet is that they'll be buying Deirdre a return ticket sooner rather than later.

Elena talks Sian through some mindfulness techniques: being in the space, focusing on the here and now. 'You have to look after yourself,' says Elena, 'because no-one else will.'

'You've noticed?'

'If Matilda is screaming and hungry, yes, give her breakfast before you get your own. But when she's asleep or your mother-in-law is caring for her, do you do the ironing . . . or do you light an aromatherapy candle, play some music and have a bath?'

Sian manages a smile. 'Fit your own mask first . . . I'm so fucking tense, Matilda probably picks up on it.'

'Which upsets her and makes you feel things aren't working . . .'

Sian hasn't mentioned what I'd say are the big two issues; she waits until Elena suggests we might wind up.

'Sandra says the medication will stop a relapse.'

Elena looks to me.

'It should,' I say. 'But you need to keep the stress down. Right down. For a while, at least.'

'I've got that message. I hate meds and I thrive on stress, but . . . you do what you have to do.' She takes a deep breath. 'For Matilda. That's why I'm doing it. If you want to help me out, make sure Leo knows that, and that I'm going to be okay with her. And that this isn't going to happen again.'

'You feel Leo needs that reassurance?' Elena asks.

'You heard him last time. He's going back to work in WA next week. For a month. He's expecting everything to be back to normal when he comes home. But maybe things can't go back to the way they were. I've changed. We have a baby. *We* need to work differently. If you're worried about stress, keep Child Protection off my back. Maybe tell them that if they speak to me again, I may not be as sweet as I was when I was bombed out on meds.'

When she called them fucking Nazis.

'I look at the photos of Matilda and me when she was born and I look so happy. But I can't remember any of it.' For a few seconds, the mask drops and she chokes up.

As Elena leaves, a nurse who only needs a red hat to be Mrs Santa comes in with Matilda in her arms. 'Here she is, love. I've changed her nappy and she'll be right for a wee play before it's time for a feed.'

Matilda is in a matching pink-and-white bunny outfit, including a headband with ears and, of all things, a daisy poking out from under it.

'Where did the daisy come from?' I ask.

'Special delivery.' The nurse winks at me. I'm still looking at Matilda, perched awkwardly in Sian's arms, when the nurse returns. She's holding an ice-cream container of daisies, the kind that you see growing wild. Someone's picked these for Sian.

'Why don't we put Matilda on the rug and sit down with her?' I say.

Matilda looks pretty cute there; after checking me out, she focuses on Sian.

I grab a few daisies and scatter them around her, like an Anne Geddes scene. It's not exactly Sian's style, I suspect, but I'm doing the best with what I've got.

Sian sits on the rug. She's frowning. I suspect her lack of delight is being registered by Matilda as *I'm not delightful.*

Then it happens. Sian idly picks up a daisy and Matilda sees it. Her eyes light up and she smiles.

'She likes the daisy,' I say.

Sian splits the flower's stem and threads another daisy through the hole, before splitting the second stem and repeating the process. As she does, she starts humming. I vaguely recognise the tune. It's upbeat, and though Sian has only a faint smile, it's enough for Matilda, who kicks her legs and arms as if trying to dance. I ask Sian if she'd like a photo. She's noncommittal. I frame them up, then change my mind and switch to video.

We're there for fifteen minutes. When Matilda finally decides it's time to eat, she and Sian are both wearing daisy-chain necklaces and Matilda's head is on a pillow of flowers.

While Sian sits with Matilda guzzling on a bottle of milk, I replay the video.

Sian watches it, stunned.

'Matilda was really connecting with you,' I say. The evidence is right there in front of her.

'I guess. I was humming the song my mother used to sing. I didn't even realise I was doing it.'

'What's it called?' I ask.

'"It's Only the Beginning".' Sian turns to her baby, smiles. Behind her eyes, the light has switched on.

—

The next day the light hasn't exactly switched on in Jacq's eyes but there's a shift.

'She's moaning a lot,' her nurse says. 'And out of the chair, moving around, bumping into things.'

Psychogenic blindness? No, it's clear that Jacq can see me when I introduce myself.

She's still in a hospital gown; they haven't been able to find someone to bring her clothes in.

'Why am I here?' she mumbles, rocking in her chair. 'Who did you say you were?'

She repeats this several times and doesn't really seem to be listening when I respond. I hit her with a mini mental-state examination – a set of questions designed more for dementia than hysteria – and she mostly doesn't answer. I try some general knowledge, but if I extrapolate from the questions she does reply to, she'd qualify for end-stage dementia. Prime minister: George Washington?

She comes across as a really bad actor. I'm going to have to trust Nash when he says she's not that. I need to work on seeing her in my mind when she's well.

If she's a detective sergeant, she's probably been pretty tough. Dealt with a sexist culture, the hard people in the criminal world, probably corruption inside and out. Climbed the ladder. Yet a relationship break-up has shattered some part of her psyche.

'Is she eating?' I ask the nurses.

'Yeah. As long as we deliver her food on a spoon. I keep wanting to pretend it's an aeroplane. She asked the night staff to brush her teeth for her, for pity's sake.'

'Let's hope she isn't here at that time of the month,' says another.

Schizophrenia, with its delusions and hallucinations, is, surprisingly, easier to find sympathy for.

'Projection,' says Alex when we cross paths in the glass house. 'If someone competent and capable can snap so easily, it could happen to us, and we don't want to admit to our own vulnerability.'

Yeah, yeah. Jon is in the registrars' room, and I let my frustration out.

'She just literally crawled down the corridor begging people for help. *Whispering.* It's not like her larynx has been affected. She's a cop. How can she bear to be so pathetic?'

Even as I say it, I'm aware of the sexism: because Jacq's a senior professional woman, I expect her to not let the side down. But I'm expecting only a wry smile from Jon.

Instead, he gives me an un-Jon-like serve. 'She's sick,' he says bluntly. 'She may be a cop – which isn't exactly a positive to some of us – but she's still a patient. I know you do this thing where you try to imagine your Acute patients without their disease. In Extended Care, the patients are never going to be well, so we've got to accept them as they are. I'm not saying it's easy, but it's what we should be aspiring to, even when a condition isn't permanent. It's what you and I would want if we were sick.'

Jon sees my expression and gives me a goofy smile.

'Sorry. Lecture over. I'm just having a shitty day. My boss thinks I should be an expert on child abuse.'

—

I take Jon's words to heart and spend some time on the phone with the police HR department, trying to persuade them to give me the details of her next of kin, but I run into a wall. Finally, a neighbour calls to check on her and is happy to talk without being 'authorised to comment'.

'She and Ed were the total power couple,' says Lucy. 'I mean, they rocked. Literally. Loud parties. They both got promoted faster than anyone else in their year; we heard that more than once. Ed'll be chief commissioner one day. Maybe Jacq will. But they broke up.'

'Recently, I gather.'

'We heard it. Couldn't not hear it.'

'There was violence?'

'Maybe. I was more worried *she'd* kill *him*.' There's an embarrassed silence before Lucy says, 'Ed left her for a younger woman. Another police officer. Who's pregnant.'

'So, what was Jacq like before this?'

'Like I said, fun. I wouldn't want to get on the wrong side of her, but she was the life of the party. Give her a drink and – well, let's say I wouldn't let my husband go over there alone. I thought she and Ed were perfect for each other.'

No past or family psych history that Lucy knows of, but she finds a phone number for Jacq's sister.

I can check some of the boxes for histrionic personality. I've known a few who fit the definition: friends who dress a bit wildly, are the first to come over with a bottle of wine if you've had bad news and are always happy to chat if you ring at 3 am. That's the good side of the personality type, and I'm doing my best to focus on it.

The sister gives me a similar picture to that of the neighbour, at first.

'Jacq is the most self-centred person I know. She never phones unless she wants something, never asks about me or my kids.' There's a pause. 'But that's only since she got together with Ed. He's a charmer, but he can be a jerk, too, and she couldn't see that. Suddenly she was into clothes and parties. But there was a caring side, and she wanted to be good cop. I mean, decent. There was this veteran who'd been in trouble, and she made a bit of a personal project out of him.'

I try to replace my image of Jacq in her red nightie with something more suitable for interacting with the vet. She's still got a button undone on her shirt.

'I blame our dad,' her sister says. 'He was such a shit. Jacq adored him and he adored her – when it suited him. But he was also a cold fish if she ever stepped out of line. I remember once when she was maybe eight? She was sick and Mum had to take her to the bathroom in the middle of some big ceremony where Dad was getting an award. He didn't talk to Jacq for a month. Not a single word. My mother finally made him speak to her again because Jacq had lost a ton of weight.'

You didn't have to be in Vienna to be shaped by things that happened in your childhood.

'Is she going to be okay?' asks her sister.

'The consultant's optimistic.'

'You know, while you're getting her back to normal, if you could take her back a few more years to what she used to be . . .'

Easy. At least, no more difficult than a lot of what we're expected to do in this job.

—

'Ed is probably narcissistic, like her father,' says Nash when I share the results of my detective work. 'When PDs' – personality disorders: *people with personality disorders* – 'pair off, they can neutralise each other. Keys and locks. Keeps them functional and out of our system.'

Until the key gets lost.

Nash doesn't seem to have much in the way of treatment in mind other than trying to paint her a picture of an acceptable life without Ed. Rebuild her sense of self, even if it's on shaky foundations. When she's ready to talk and listen, that is.

—

The next day she's a bit more lucid. 'I fell,' she says when she sees me looking at a bruise on her head. 'I'm just too weak to walk. Why am I here? Someone needs to work out what's wrong with me.'

'Someone' meaning a real doctor rather than a psychiatrist.

'What do *you* think is wrong?' I ask.

Her eyes open wide. 'You're the doctor.'

'How did you feel . . . how are you feeling about your husband leaving?'

'Ed? Oh, he'll be back.' Heavy sigh. 'When he gets tired of his slut.'

'Let's just say that doesn't happen. What would life look like for you?'

Jacq laughs. 'After I get out of lock-up because I've hacked his balls off?'

I'm not going to report that as a risk to another person; it's a sign of life.

'Break-ups are hard,' I say. I was there not too long ago, though it's Marcus's experience that's more likely to have resembled Jacq's. I felt empty and lonely – but not rejected. I think of their power-couple image and of the neighbours being told over and over of her and Ed's successes. It's more than rejection: it's humiliation.

A word pops into my head – the tongue-in-cheek term that some doctors and nurses would have used in the past to describe Jacq's response to her separation: *acopia*, failure to cope. Pejorative – the successor to *nervous breakdown*. It's probably my own inability to manage Jacq – to cope with her – that's brought it to mind.

I ask about her career, but she tells me she's feeling faint and zones out.

I suggest to Omar that he wheel her into the common area. Surely she won't want to be on display in a psych ward. I'm hoping to shock her into some sort of action.

Omar seems to have the same idea. As he wheels her in, he points to the TV: 'Holy shit – look what that cop's doing!'

Jacq doesn't move.

Omar grins at me. 'Worth a try.'

—

There's nothing helpless about Alex's patient, Ahmed the truck driver.

'If I was looking for a flatmate, he'd be perfect,' says Alex. 'Makes his bed, tidies his room and wants to give the cleaner a hand in the kitchen. I think his helping others is a way of avoiding looking after – looking *at* – himself.'

'So, increased meds or intense psychotherapy?' I'm half-kidding: the second, other than in group format, isn't really an option, given our resources.

'He isn't exactly reflective at the moment; nothing beyond: *Other people have it so much worse than me.*'

When I walk past Ahmed in the ward, he stands up as if I'm royalty. Omar grins and says, 'Don't go thinking he's got a thing for you. He got his friends to bring in a plate of Afghan desserts for us. All gone.'

—

I'm looking forward to hearing my study group's take on Jacq and my management of her – or lack of it. It's not something we're likely to get in an exam, but maybe I'll pick up some principles for dealing with the stranger cases.

Tonight we're at Ndidi's two-storey in the upper-middle-class suburb of Kew. The front garden has one substantial tree, but the remainder has been taken over by ivy. If anything else was ever alive there, it isn't now.

'Nice place,' says Alex, and Ndidi answers the implicit question.

'Not ours. House sitting for a friend of my father's who's got an overseas posting.'

Her husband – 'I'm Torben, the handbag' – has led us to the open-plan living area at the back of the house, under a glass roof and backing on to a garden with another large tree and grass almost as tall as the barbecue. A banquet of snacks is laid out on the coffee table.

'Don't look at me,' says Ndidi.

'Mr Handbag?' I ask.

She laughs, but it's a little forced. 'In my dreams. We live on takeaway. My mother made all this. She's filling in time feeding us until someone gives her a grandchild.'

I catch her eye and the message back fits with the one she sent me on the parkrun: that someone is supposed to be her.

Jon and Alex are already seated. Alex asks about Torben. He's a film director, Ndidi tells us – not famous yet. It comes across as 'not earning money right now'.

We run through a bunch of cases over a stew – chicken, of course – with peppers and tomatoes. It's getting late by the time we get to Jacq. I give them a pretty detailed summary, thinking I might get some insight from talking about it. Nup.

'Oedipus complex,' says Alex.

'I thought only boys had that,' says Ndidi.

'Boys for mum, girls for dad,' says Alex. 'Bet her dad was either a top cop or a top criminal. Regardless, she had to marry someone bigger and better. The treatment plan is challenging because the problem is her underlying personality structure. You can't re-parent someone in two or three weeks.'

'So, you're doing nothing?' says Jon.

'Containment isn't nothing,' says Alex and laughs. 'We don't have a clue.'

Then he pulls a book from his backpack and gives it to me. 'This might help.' It's *Love's Executioner and Other Tales of Psychotherapy* by Irvin Yalom.

'Not just Freud. This is current, insightful, covers a whole range of presentations . . .'

I realise he's bought it for me as a gift and is talking to cover his embarrassment.

'Where's mine?' says Ndidi, taking the book from me. Alex is already beating a retreat, with Jon right behind.

Ndidi flips through the book then passes it back to me.

'You're both being pretty discreet,' she says.

I laugh. 'Not much to be discreet about.'

'Early days. But don't worry about Jon and me. Pairing up with other doctors has its downsides, but so does the alternative.'

At the gate, I open the book. There's an inscription, which Ndidi probably saw. *Love's executioner seems to be our work. A love we have in common. Love, Alex.*

Torben comes out, pushing the wheelie bin, and sees me standing there, rereading to make sure I've understood what Alex meant. *Work has brought us together but gets in the way. But I want to keep trying.*

'Hannah, right? Don't tell Ndidi I told you this, but she really needs these meetings. You guys help a lot – especially you.' He puts the bin in place, then adds, 'You've probably gathered she's struggling a bit.'

—

I pass through the Low Dependency common area on my way to see a patient and find Ahmed doing what Ahmed does: helping out. A guy's come to replace the big fridge, and it seems his hand truck is broken. He and Ahmed are discussing the problem. Despite Alex's concern that Ahmed is keeping busy to escape his own issues, engagement of this kind is probably contributing to his short-term recovery.

I return in time to see Ahmed, Sonny the martial arts instructor, Zac – who had the near-fatal response to clozapine – and the actual repair guy lifting the fridge together.

'Put it down!' I yell.

Ahmed shakes his head. 'We have it up now. Safer to take it to the truck.' He may be right: putting it down could need more coordination than these guys are capable of, especially given their illnesses and medication.

The sole nurse in the area, Aurora, dashes off, presumably to find help. Then Zac loses concentration and wanders away, leaving one corner unsupported.

'Dr Wright,' calls Ahmed. 'Take the corner.' No option, really.

Now there are four of us holding the fridge, like pallbearers. And I'm the only person with a door key. I'm figuring Ahmed's plan is probably the least-worst option: just get it to the truck. These guys aren't likely to abscond and wouldn't be much of a risk if they did. And if I start thinking about anything other than holding up my corner – well, I'm the famously clumsy one.

But I need someone to open the door. Maybe I can kill two birds with one stone. 'Detective Livermore!' I shout. 'We have a situation here.'

'You can't ask her,' says Ahmed. 'She's too sick.' Then: 'Chloe, please, we need your help.'

Chloe is, like Jacq, in a wheelchair, though she can walk a bit. And that is what she does: rises from the chair like she's the object of some sort of miracle, walks slowly over, lifts the cord on my key card over my head and releases the door. Fridge guy, who's in front, kicks it open.

'How far?' I say.

'Fifty metres or so. Be easy with the hand truck.'

'Concentrate on the work,' says Ahmed. 'Don't think about getting into trouble. And don't worry about Dr Wright. She is a practical person. Knows about tyres.'

We get the fridge to the truck. Fridge Guy opens the back with one hand, and we slide it in. We're high-fiving as Omar and Aurora arrive to escort Ahmed and Sonny back into the unit.

'Now we bring in the new refrigerator,' says Ahmed. I'm not sure if he's kidding, but he doesn't pursue it. 'If there is trouble,' he says, 'you can blame me. But these people have lost their self-respect in this place. This was a good thing.'

'These people' amount to Sonny. Unless he's counting himself and me. The way I'm going with Jacq, I'm thinking this may be the only useful thing I've done this week.

—

I know the fridge story has got around when Carey sends me a recommendation to do the module on safe work practices and includes a link to a tutorial on lifting. I send them back a link to a Durham University study which suggests that wearers of red clothing can be perceived as aggressive and angry.

I need the laugh because I've barely hit *send* when my mother phones. 'You need to get your brother to come home.'

Lennon has been taken to the Mount Isa hospital with food poisoning. He's going to be okay, but I should talk to him. Sure, but what my mother wants is for me to pressure him to come home and finish his apprenticeship. Get him to make an important life decision while he's feeling sick and sorry for himself.

I text him and he calls right back: he's already been discharged.

'What'd you eat?' I ask. Can't stop myself taking a history.

He's silent. Then, 'What do you reckon?'

'Shit. Are you drinking again?'

'I stopped for a while. Then . . .'

'Is that what happened with your apprenticeship? Mum and Dad know about this?'

'We haven't talked about it.'

'What does it mean for the jackarooing?'

'They're okay if it doesn't happen again.'

'Mum thinks you should come home.'

'I know. One of the reasons I came up here was to make a fresh start. Coming home would only make it worse.'

'You getting some help?'

'There's a guy I talk to on the phone. A social worker. He's good. And I know you're a psychiatrist, but I'd rather you didn't . . .'

'I won't. But I'm glad you told me. And that you've got him.'

Except his social worker is probably working on the behaviour and not on what I guess is the cause. Lennon's been drinking since he was thirteen. Peer pressure from a horde of foster kids. I have to ask.

'When I saw you at home, you mentioned what happened . . .'

'I didn't. You did.'

'Do you want to talk about it sometime?'

'Not really.'

I shouldn't feel so relieved.

—

I'm walking with the other registrars, sandwiches in hand, when we hear a mother and baby in the garden. It sounds like laughter. Through the plants that provide some privacy – less since one of the patients incinerated a patch – we can see Sian and Matilda. Sian is making faces and Matilda, sitting in her pram, is giggling.

'She's like a mother hen on steroids, trying to make up,' says Ndidi. 'Which is not who she actually is.'

'Maybe she's changed,' says Jon.

Ndidi nods thoughtfully. I sense that she's considering – maybe identifying with – Sian's transformation. Not just the clinical recovery, but motherhood. I'm guessing she's trying to get pregnant, and it isn't happening. Maybe her weight's a part of the problem. If so, she drew a lousy hand with Eating Disorders *and* Mother Baby.

'At least Child Protection won't need to be involved,' says Jon.

'They're waiting in the wings,' says Ndidi. 'But if they try to separate mother and baby . . . Sandra's huge on the importance of attachment for the baby's long-term mental health. We'll make sure it doesn't get messed with any further.' Ndidi looks at me. 'The daisy chains were what did it.'

'So not the drugs or the ECT,' says Alex.

'I hope you're kidding,' says Ndidi. 'You saw her when she came in. Good luck giving her flowers back then.'

Alex smiles. 'Where did they find the daisies?'

'Hannah mentioned it when we were at Jon's,' says Ndidi. She looks at me again. 'I'm guessing you brought them in.'

'I thought it was you,' I say.

That only leaves Jon and his big smile.

—

There's no miracle for Jacq – at least not yet. No antidepressants either. And still no management plan. Elena is too busy to see her till next week. In the meantime, I hit her up for suggestions.

'The histrionic who's been rejected? You're right about the humiliation: there's a core of shame about not being good enough. Narcissists are similar but with different coping styles.'

'She's pretty hard work.' I think of Taylah, and even her mother, with their likely borderline personality disorders: pains in the neck, but they had an energy that was almost fun. Jacq just takes the air out of the room. But that's my problem to deal with.

Elena seems to be thinking along the same lines. 'The *well* version of DS Livermore would hate this type of person, I'd imagine – she'd have no time for them.'

'So how is she going to deal with it?'

'Denial and repression. I imagine she's pretty good at that.'

'But she can't think forever that Ed is going to return.'

'So she needs a different narrative,' says Elena. 'Such as: she is better off without him, and she left him because she found out about the other woman.'

We're not talking about Jacq gaining any sort of insight. 'Then the next time someone leaves her, the same thing happens again?'

'It's what keeps us in business.'

No shortage of problem analysis – just nothing that looks like a real solution, except time and good luck.

—

Ahmed's recovery is short-lived. I'm in the ward when the television shows a news report from Afghanistan that triggers his PTSD. I recognise it from the day he showed up in ED and, thanks to Prof, I know what to do.

I pull out a pen, hold it in front of his eyes – and drop it. So much for *nothing to break* in psychiatry. It seems to have rolled under one of the armchairs, and when I look up from trying to fish it out, I see a repeat of Chloe's rise from her wheelchair – but this one is closer to being a miracle.

Jacq walks over to Ahmed, squats beside him and begins a calming monologue: 'Take some deep breaths. You're safe and secure here, if you're feeling anxious, let it pass . . .'

She's done this before. And Ahmed seems to be responding. It takes him only a minute or so to settle.

Now, Jacq pulls up a regular chair and begins chatting with him. I watch for a bit, then Omar beckons me over. He's writing up the incident report for the fridge-moving episode and wants me to look it over. It occurs to me that if Prof sees it, it'll be nice, documented evidence of the poor judgement he's got pinned on me.

It's a wordy mess. I'm mentioned, but I'm called 'the registrar' in one place, 'the doctor' in another and misspelled as 'Dr White' in a third. It would be hard to work out that I carried a quarter of a fridge or even that there was a fridge involved. Just some sort of patient activity conducted under 'professional supervision'.

'That'd be Ahmed,' says Omar.

'And the safety officer?'

'Sonny. He's worked as a security guard. They have to be licensed. Anyway, it says "in the *role* of safety officer".'

'No offence, Omar, but this is pretty hard to make sense of.'

'Yep,' says Omar.

—

On Tuesday morning, a week after I first saw her, Jacq is scheduled for an interview with Nash and me. She walks in wearing jeans and a shirt. She looks . . . normal.

'I need to be back at work,' she says crisply. 'So, I'll be leaving.'

Nash gives her his blessing. She isn't exactly complimentary about any of us, and thinks we've failed to establish the real diagnosis. I hate to think what she's going to put on the feedback form and what that will propel Nicole to do.

On my way home, I pass the PTSD ward, where Ahmed has been transferred. I get the usual catcalls from the vets, which I ignore, but in the garden, sitting together on a bench, are Ahmed and Jacq.

Apparently Nash was right about the lock-and-key therapy. But I'd never have picked Ahmed as the key.

TEN

IDENTIFICATION

'Why didn't you share this with me earlier?' asks Professor Liron Gordon, psychotherapist, struggling to hide his shock.

The patient opposite, in the professor's man-cave of a therapy room, considers his question for some time. She reaches out and takes a tissue from a box on the coffee table. After a few moments, she blows her nose, then speaks through tears.

'You didn't ask.'

It's so surreal that I genuinely wonder if I'm hallucinating: if someone has spiked my coffee; if I've accidentally taken a patient's meds; if working in a psych ward has sent me over the edge.

Carey is walking into the ivory tower cafe. Except they're now presenting as a woman. And beside them is . . . Carey, in low-key brown chinos and jacket, rather than their signature red. What the hell?

Stop, Hannah. Process.

The woman is physically quite similar to Carey – tall and slim, short brown hair – and is wearing Carey's red suit. They must have given it to her. Possibly because they read the paper I sent them about red indicating aggression. If you think things through instead of just reacting, there's a logical answer. Most of the time.

I'm sitting at a table alone, waiting for Alex, who's sent me a text message: *Need a coffee. 5 minutes?* An hour earlier I'd seen him going to his supervision session with Prof. Now there's another message: *Sorry, back at the ward. Def need a drink, talk, your stimulating company.* And another: *Three of my favourite things ;-)*

I text him back. *Looking forward to that drink. With Ndidi and Jon.* Study group tonight, which he seems to have forgotten.

He's straight back to me: *Be good to talk before that. Some news.*

As I'm getting up, the two Careys come over.

'Amy, this is my friend, Hannah,' the original Carey says to their companion.

Up close, the similarity is not so disconcerting, though they could easily be brother and sister. They're about the same age: I'd guess early thirties. And there's something they have in common that I can't put my finger on. 'My friend Hannah' is a stretch, but maybe it's a sign that they've forgiven us for not inviting them to join our study group.

'Hi, Amy,' I say.

'Can we join you?' says Carey.

I am sort of curious. 'Sure. I've already had lunch, though.'

'We also just had lunch, but Amy wanted to get a coffee before she drove home. Metaphorically. Amy only drinks tap water. No ice. But I'll have a coffee.'

Amy smiles. Carey's on their way to the counter when they turn back. 'Do you want one, Hannah? Sorry, I assumed that you had coffee in the cup in front of you, but in fact you appeared to be leaving, so . . .'

'I'm good.'

Carey joins the coffee queue and Amy wastes no time getting to the point. 'Are they in a relationship?'

'You don't know?'

'I just met them, and if I ask them, and they *are* in a relationship, they'll think I'm offering sex. Which, if I was, I'd just say straight out. Most men wouldn't be offended – don't know about non-binary. So, better to ask a friend, right?'

'Right . . . um, how do you know Carey?'

'I was coming out of Professor Gordon's rooms, and they saw the suit I'm wearing. I bought it at a charity shop. Turns out they'd just donated it. I could have had it for free if we'd met earlier. But of course the suit was the reason we met.'

'You were meeting with Prof?'

'He's my therapist.'

All the Menzies' psychiatrists – the consultants, not the trainees – have a half day off each week to see private patients. Prof is the only one I'm aware of who sees them in his office at the hospital. I doubt Nicole approves.

I don't know if Carey's violating any regulations in socialising with Amy: they're not a doctor and she's not their patient, nor is she a patient of the hospital, strictly speaking. Not that it matters: Prof would still totally lose his shit.

'What do you do?' I ask.

This could take us anywhere, but she gives a conventional answer.

'I'm a researcher. I used to be an academic – early music – but I got retrenched. Not fired, retrenched. There was a staff cut. I was really good at what I did. Now I'm in government. Politics, actually, but I say "government" so people don't ask what party. So, please don't. Still research, but not early music, obviously. And I teach piano. Just a bit. I've got an anxiety disorder, which gets in the way.' She spots Carey returning. 'I answered your questions. And shared information about my mental health. So what about . . .'

'I don't know if they have a partner,' I say. 'They've never mentioned one.'

Carey puts their coffee and Amy's water on the table, and any hope that we'd move on from Amy's psychopathology is immediately dashed.

'I was telling your friend that I have an anxiety disorder,' she says.

'Who diagnosed it?' asks Carey.

'I saw three psychiatrists and one psychologist before Professor Gordon. The psychologist was the best, but obviously it's not a big enough sample to make generalisations. I'd sort of given up, but then I changed jobs, and everyone there said Prof Gordon was the top psychiatrist in the state, and I thought: new start. Someone at work got me an appointment with him. He's expensive, but what price do you put on your mental health?'

'What else did the therapists say about you besides anxiety?' Carey asks.

They've definitely crossed the line. Even as a research assistant, they're still staff and she's their boss's patient. 'Hey,' I say, 'I think that's Prof's job.'

'Hannah's trying to tell me I'm asking an inappropriate question,' says Carey. 'She's a psychiatry registrar.'

'No, you're not,' says Amy.

I start to protest, but Carey explains, 'I think Amy was responding to the implication that I was asking an inappropriate question, not the follow-up statement.'

'Of course,' says Amy. 'I have no reason to believe you'd lie about your job. I'm happy to tell you what everyone's said, including Professor Gordon. It might help with your training.'

I'm thinking *borderline personality disorder* and *time to leave* when Carey says, 'Let me have a try. No charge. Tell me when I'm wrong. Depression.' As they say it, they tap their thumb. Checking off a list. 'Query bipolar, query schizo-affective disorder, obsessive-compulsive disorder . . .'

I'm mesmerised. I know Carey has picked up some medical theory, and enjoys showing it off, but this is next level. They keep going, counting off the diagnoses, and Amy nods at each one. Is this a routine the two of them worked up over lunch?

'Borderline or narcissistic personality disorder – they wouldn't mention that to you.'

'Wrong. I mean, Professor Gordon did mention them, but as things he'd considered and eliminated.'

'Rightly so. Possibly gut problems?'

It's a shift from diagnosis to symptoms. Carey has made a diagnosis and is testing it. Impressively.

'Wow. Since I was a kid.'

Carey laughs. 'That was a bit of a guess. Which is why I said "possibly". Didn't want to risk my perfect record. But now I know, I'd be saying inflammatory bowel disease or possibly just problems digesting carbs. And you hated certain foods. All kids do, but you were worse. You got stuck on certain special interests and you had a lot of tantrums. Maybe you do now when it all gets too much.'

'Meltdowns.'

'That's the correct word. So you know you're autistic?'

'Sorry?' says Amy. 'People have said I might have Asperger's . . . but it's pretty uncommon in women, right?'

'Wrong. On four counts. First: it's recognised less often in women, but almost certainly that's only because they're better at masking. Second: the term Asperger's is rarely used these days, partly because the man the condition was named for did some terrible things, but also because the term's been absorbed by autism, including in *DSM-5* – that's the diagnostic manual, which I don't recommend you read, because it's about disorders. It focuses on deficits rather than strengths.'

I've figured out what's going on. I've always assumed Carey was on the autism spectrum and it's in character that they'd have read up on the subject – swallowed the manual. But if you're an expert on only one thing, you're going to see it everywhere. That said, I think they've guessed right. And they haven't finished.

'Third, you don't *have* Asperger's or autism. It's not a disease, or an add-on. It's the way you are, the way you're born and, if you're authentic, the way you live. You *are* autistic.'

'What's the fourth thing?' says Amy.

'Actually, that was it, thanks to the vagaries of English grammar. *You* are autistic. You can go and get an adult diagnosis if you want, but I know what I'm talking about. You're a researcher: I'd put the *p* value at point zero five. Conservatively.'

'So you think that's what's wrong with me?'

'I think that's what's wrong with you and what's right with you. What four professionals in their *absolute fucking ignorance* about a condition with a prevalence of at least two per cent failed to identify.'

Carey takes two slow breaths, genuinely angry, having to rein it in before continuing. Like the time they got upset with Nash for suggesting they didn't have experience delivering bad news.

'Get a book. Not a medical book. Read an autism memoir, preferably by a woman. I'd recommend *Late Bloomer* by Clem Bastow. A lot of things are going to fall into place. And don't go back to Prof until you've processed it all. That's your starting point, not a bunch of unrelated symptoms.'

I think I need to say something here. So I say, 'I think I need to say something here.'

And Carey says, 'Yep, that your training isn't covering this, but you'll fix that deficit.'

I have my issues with Prof, but I don't envy him dealing with this all day.

They turn back to Amy. 'Take it on board, realise that it all makes sense, and that a lot, maybe all, of what's wrong with you is just stuff that happens to a certain kind of person. And acknowledge the good things. As Max, my pub-trivia teammate, might say: *Amy, you're a star.* Today might be the best day of your life. It was the best of mine.'

I'm not sure if Carey's referring to the day they were diagnosed as autistic, or today, when they met Amy.

Amy has started crying, an outpouring of emotion that seems to affirm what Carey has said.

'You should speak to Professor Gordon about it before you make any decisions,' I say to Amy as I leave. Right thing for her – maybe not for Carey.

—

Everyone seems to be in the glass house except Alex. Whatever he wants to talk about, it can't be as outrageous as a research assistant critiquing *DSM-5* while they re-diagnose, treat and terminate therapy for one of Prof's private patients.

Nash and Sandra are dissing the other boss: Nicole. She's requiring everyone to do yet another module: hand hygiene. In case our medical training didn't cover bacteria. Maybe we should be doing an autism module.

Omar spots me and raps a spoon on the table.

'Now that we have a quorum . . .' He's holding a rolled-up piece of paper. I know what it is: his tongue-in-cheek award for Acute Unit Employee of the Month.

'Easy call this time. On the shortlist were Joanne, for her contribution to police dental care, and me, as always, for the example of professionalism I provide to you all – but saving a life is in a different league. We do it every day, of course, but we're subtle about it. The guys with their crash carts and defibrillators in the middle of the night are always going to get the glory. But this time, it was one of us. So, from all of us, and Zac, who's alive to say it, thank you to Dr Hannah Wright.'

Omar's speech is met with a big round of applause. Naturally I'm chuffed, but . . . for emergency medicine? Is one straightforward physical intervention – that happened only because I was on call – worth more than all the complex psychiatry I've been doing?

Omar hands me the printed-out award. And then ('But wait, there's more') a small package. I open it to find a miniature tool set.

'Fridge repair kit,' he says.

Alex has joined us and adds to the applause. It's a little strange that we're so close to each other's successes and screw-ups. On the one hand, we're getting to know parts of each other's lives that we might try to keep to ourselves, at least in the early stages of dating; on the other, well, same thing: there's no hiding, no space of our own if we do start seeing each other seriously. My head and heart are sending me different messages on this one.

'You go first,' I say. 'You're still coming to study group tonight?'

'I'm never going to say no to an invitation to your place. But I may not have a psychotherapy case to talk about.'

'Xavier . . . Mr X . . . has pulled out?'

'*Prof's* pulled out. He said he can't supervise me anymore. Not *won't* but *can't*. Wouldn't elaborate, except to say I'd done nothing wrong, which is a big statement from him.'

'Nothing to do with the Prof Round thing?'

'Ancient history. I made him look good, so it was never a problem. But I can't continue with Xavier unless I find a new supervisor. Sandra's too busy and, in case you hadn't noticed, we're light on here for psychotherapists.'

I think of Elena, but I doubt Alex would accept a psychologist. Not that she has any spare time either.

'I'm wondering if something serious has happened,' says Alex. 'Some family or health problem. Or . . . Xavier's a politician, so maybe Prof's got some connection with the advisory board he's been appointed to.'

'Makes sense.'

Before we can speculate further, Omar calls Alex over. My Carey story will have to wait till this evening.

—

Carey has never phoned me; it's always text messages. But today, they phone. While I'm seeing Chloe. Someone's got her a hot chocolate from the cafe and she's holding it when we sit down.

'Looks delicious,' I say. 'Therapy helping?'

As soon as the words are out, I know I've made a mistake. Chloe's lips tighten and there's a tremor in the hand that isn't holding the cup as her finger carefully moves around the edge of the froth, collecting it and a sprinkling of chocolate powder. There's been no eye contact. Maybe I'm wrong. She slowly raises her eyes and in the steely greyness that has been so hard to access I see a tiny flash of anger. It's so fleeting I wonder if I imagined it.

And then my phone goes.

'Hannah, I need you *right now*.'

'I'm with a patient.'

'Is it a life-threatening situation? For the patient?'

'No, but . . .'

'Prof's office. Now. If you can't come, send Ndidi. Or Alex. Or the nice guy.'

'Jon?'

'Yep. In that order of preference.'

Chloe is still playing with her hot chocolate. I don't wait to see if she drinks it, or if I can save the situation – I'm scared anything I say will make it worse. 'Sorry, emergency,' I say, and run.

Carey is standing outside Prof's office, but Prof's secretary, Goldie the Goth, is between me and them and isn't going to let me through.

She points to a container of hand sanitiser. 'Nothing's so urgent that you need to take the germs with you.'

'You've just done the hand-hygiene module, right?'

'Times two,' she says and winks. She's done it for Prof as well.

She opens Prof's door before I have a chance to speak to Carey. Prof waves us both in but doesn't offer us chairs.

I check out my enemy's den. There's no moose head on the wall, but it wouldn't be out of place. Deep leather chairs, a wave-shaped analyst's couch, a coffee table. Big polished-wood desk littered with paper and pens, files and a silver box. A photo of him getting his Order of Australia.

He looks calm, but stern. I'm assuming that word of Carey's intervention with Amy has reached him and am mentally constructing a defence of my part in it.

'Has Carey explained why you're here, Dr Wright?'

'No. No, they haven't.'

'Well, Hannah, this is a meeting that I very much wanted to have in private with Carey, and while he tells me –'

'*They*,' says Carey. They're trying to look impassive, but there's a twitch. That was hard even for them. I don't know if I could correct my boss in a disciplinary interview, with my job on the line, if they got my name wrong. That's *Hannah*, not *Helen*.

'My apologies,' says Prof.

I suspect he's gritting his teeth but determined to take zero risks. If he's intent on firing Carey, he wants to be bulletproof as he does it.

Prof turns to me. 'While *they* tell me that *they're* entitled to have another employee present, they can't compel you to be here.'

He smiles. He knows the position he's put me in.

Carey saves me from the dilemma. Or digs a deeper hole for me. 'If Hannah leaves, I'll call someone else. Ad infinitum, until I find a witness who isn't intimidated.'

'I'm not sure that's in your best interests,' says Prof.

'Is this about my conversation with . . . your patient?' says Carey.

'That's what it's about.'

'And you're unhappy about it?'

'I'm very unhappy about it.'

'Then I want a witness.'

Prof looks at me. Smiles. 'If you insist, then I think Hannah's an appropriate choice.'

Meaning, if I do whatever he wants, he'll credit me with good judgement. While I'm throwing Carey under the bus. Except . . . Carey probably does deserve to be fired, and it's not like they won't be able to find another research assistant or admin job.

Prof rises and leads us toward some armchairs grouped around a coffee table. He indicates where he wants us to sit, then takes a third chair for himself. I realise he's set it up so he and I are facing Carey.

'So,' says Prof, eyeballing Carey, cutting me out, 'you took it upon yourself not only to socialise with one of my patients, but to offer your own diagnosis.'

'Not a diagnosis,' says Carey. 'Diagnosis refers to diseases. I offered her some insight, and then I offered her fellowship. And community. She may well have a psychiatric disorder, but without understanding the common basis . . .'

I have to say, Carey isn't shying away from the fight.

'You're suggesting you've helped me out? Well . . .' I can hear the sarcasm in Prof's tone, and I'm guessing that's not going to land well – or effectively – with Carey.

Carey interrupts. 'Prof,' they say, 'we're both doctors . . .'

What the *fuck*? Carey may have a PhD, but PhDs don't call themselves doctors – especially to professors of medicine.

'Excuse me, Professor Gordon,' I say. 'Could I have a few moments with Carey?'

Prof nods – readily, I think – and I take Carey's arm and drag them into their own small office opposite.

'What sort of doctor are you?' I ask.

'Same sort as you. A medical doctor. I *want* to be a psychiatrist. I did my medical training in Tasmania, two years general medicine and then a year as a psych registrar. But I got rejected from the training program. You can guess why. If I'd had a physical disability or . . .' And suddenly they're shaking, their whole body trembling.

'Are you okay?' I ask.

'I just need a minute. Less.'

They do some steady breathing, and after less than a minute, as promised, nod that they're ready to continue.

'Why didn't you tell anybody?' I say.

'Prof specifically said he didn't want me saying I was a doctor while I was doing the research job. Patients want to talk to someone they see as unaligned, I suppose.'

'But why are you doing this job at all?'

'Prof promised me a place in the training program next year if I did the research work. For basically no pay.'

No wonder Prof didn't want a witness in the room. And I'll be competing with Carey for a place in the training program. If they survive today. Which is at least partly in my hands. As Prof is aware: *I think Hannah's an excellent choice.*

'If he fires me,' says Carey, 'I'll tell Nicole about the deal. It's almost certainly unethical.'

'You're going to confront him with that? Threaten him?'

'If necessary. I imagine it would be awkward for Prof but for me as well if I carried it out. Lose-lose. I'm hoping he'll see that and we'll find a win-win solution.'

'When I pulled you out of the room, I thought you were going to try to convince Prof that you did him a favour with Amy.'

'Exactly. I spotted something he'd overlooked.'

'Oh, he'll have loved that.'

'Apparently not.'

'Carey, doctor or not, you're way junior to him.'

'It's not about seniority . . .'

'For god's sake, Carey. Listen to me. If you're humble about it' – what chance of that? – 'maybe, *maybe* that could work . . . but *you do not want me in the room*.'

'Because?'

'I just know.'

'How?'

'He's a fucking narcissist, Carey. If he has to back down a centimetre, he doesn't want to do it – he won't do it – in front of a registrar. Especially this one.'

Carey nods. The clinical formulation has got through.

I have a flash of inspiration – courtesy of Ndidi. 'Turn on the voice recorder on your phone. You don't need his permission; you're an employee and you have a justifiable fear that you could be bullied. Don't use the recording unless you have no other option. And don't ever tell anyone it was me who suggested it.'

I'm thinking that they have a chance. As long as I'm right about Prof's reason for not wanting me in the room.

Carey nods and gets out their phone.

'*Hide* it.'

'Thanks, Hannah. I called the right person.'

—

Late in the day, Elena calls me to say that Chloe's parents have cancelled the third family therapy session – and terminated therapy altogether. Chloe didn't want to do it anymore. *Nice work, Hannah.* And she didn't write the letter to her sister that was her homework from the first session.

I've heard nothing from Carey, so I figure I'll walk past their office. Goldie the Goth is packing up, but I get a squirt of hand sanitiser. By the time I've verified that Carey has locked up and gone, she's alerted Prof to my presence and he's stepped out of his office. Just when I thought my day couldn't get any worse.

'Hannah. Come in.'

I enter his office and take a seat. I feel like I've been summoned to see the principal. I'm reminded of Nicole's observation about infantilisation of junior doctors. *Get over it.* He isn't going to let me into the program, and I'll work out what I'm going to do about that later.

Rather than sit behind his desk, Prof stands and paces, which eases the formality a bit. There's a sandwich on his desk; he must be planning to work late, or else it was lunch and his day has been disrupted by the situation with Carey and Amy. And whatever's happened with Mr X and Alex.

'I haven't told Dr Grant yet, but since you're here . . . I gather you were witness to their intervention today. They likely know more about autism than everyone else here combined. Their diagnosis is almost certainly correct. But it was made without context. Without an understanding of the patient's *predicament*.

'Imagine, hypothetically, that there were other factors, beyond the simplistic answer to everything. Imagine – I'm saying *imagine* – it had taken months of work with me for my patient to disclose that she was a victim of sexual assault. And then, having been handed the simple key to happiness, she terminated therapy.'

I'm putting the jigsaw together. Amy works in politics. All her colleagues know Professor Gordon, the psychiatrist of choice. And Prof suddenly ceased his supervision of Alex, who was seeing an MP who's admitted to sexual harassment of a colleague. Harassment, not assault, but Xavier might be talking it down. Or Prof might be talking it up. No great coincidence, just a small world.

'You'll be pleased to know that she has been persuaded to continue therapy, and that Dr Grant has used their standing with her to support that decision. Things will continue as they were, as much as they ever do when we've survived traumas, major and minor. I'm sure you'll treat everything that's been discussed today as if it involved patients, as it does.'

I nod. 'Of course.'

'And regardless of what you may or may not have been told, I shall assist Dr Grant in gaining the skills – and judgement – needed for the psychiatry training program, but I shall recuse myself from any say in their selection.'

I want to say, 'Sounds good, can I have that too?' Maybe, if they were in my situation, Carey would.

Prof spots a crumpled tissue on the floor and tosses it in the bin, then resumes eating his sandwich.

'Which brings me to you. Good work today. I don't want you to confuse political astuteness with the clinical judgement I'm looking for. That's a different attribute and, as I've said before, a different journey. But, the modern expression is *reading the room*, and that's important too.'

I'm about to get up – actually getting up – when Prof adds, 'Please don't discuss this with Dr Grant until I've spoken to him.'

Totally reasonable. Except for the pronoun. Prof's used the right one at least twice in this conversation. I look at him and, whether the mistake was deliberate or accidental, he knows he's made it and, yes, he's waiting for me to correct him. And now he knows I've noticed.

I say nothing.

Prof smiles and nods. I'm dismissed. Carey's not in the room – there's nobody I need to defend. No public point I need to make. No reason for me to call him out except . . . it's a tiny, micro, exercise of power. As Alex predicted, a test. Failing it would be a third strike. Is this the pronoun I want my career to die on?

'*Them*,' I say.

'Quite right, Hannah,' says Prof.

—

As I walk back to the ward, I feel an odd sense of relief, of a burden lifted. If Prof doesn't want me in the program . . . screw it. And even if he does? I'm ready to walk away.

Stop. Reality check. I'm casually considering giving up on my dream. Something's been brewing without me realising it.

I try a bit of CBT: What is the negative feeling I'm having about psychiatry? And the word that comes into my mind, after about ten seconds of reflection, is . . . uselessness.

And the unproductive thought that led to this feeling? The answer, if I were to write it in a four-column book, is that the interaction with Prof reminded me of him beating up on Alex when he missed Veronica's tumour. All that psychotherapeutic formulation when the answer wasn't even in our wheelhouse: a simple physical cause with a complete recovery. Presented, diagnosed, fixed. Thanks to surgical procedures and medication, which just keep getting better.

It's not just that.

There was Jacq getting better independent of anything we did. And Elena pulling out all stops on top of Chloe's sixteen admissions and the best efforts of people like Nash, with years of experience – for what? A hope that one member of the family will make a decent life for herself, which she might do anyway, without our help? And we'll never be able to measure our miserable contribution.

Psychiatry is heading down the biological path: brain rather than mind, medication rather than talking. If a pill could fix writer's block, Sabriya the journalist would have taken it. If medication could get Chloe eating again, wouldn't that fix most of the family's problems? No medication is going to fix my family's issues, but nor is anything I've got to offer.

Maybe I just need a drink.

—

'I can buy you a drink, if that's not inappropriate,' says Carey. I'm back in the glass house, and they're working at a bench with their laptop, presumably having decided to put some space between themselves and Prof. 'To say thank you for today. You may have saved my career.'

Possibly at the cost of my own, I think. But I'm being a drama queen. We both have other options.

'I'd love to have a drink with you,' I say, 'but not tonight. I have to get home.' For study group. Sore point with Carey. But I can't leave them hanging. 'I've seen Prof and I think you're going to be okay. But you'll have to convince the selection panel for the psych training program that you can read a patient, and a room, and that you've got judgement . . .'

They smile. 'And of course they'll be equally cognisant of my positive autistic qualities. Memory, focus . . . ability to be objective in an emotionally charged situation. And my non-aggressive clothing.'

I'm not sure if they're being sarcastic or not. When in doubt, opt for sincere, certainly with Carey.

'The aftershave may be a bit of a distraction,' I say. 'It's pretty strong.'

'I think that's the idea. Wouldn't be much point if you couldn't smell it. It was a gift from my great-aunt. Probably an unsubtle reminder that I shave and should identify as male.'

We both laugh.

'So,' I say, 'you're a doctor?'

'As I told you. I'm a specialist in telling people they're going to die. Or that their kids are.'

'You want to explain?'

'I'd be happy to. As I said, I did medicine at the University of Tasmania. Planned to be a physician. Two years out I did a medical rotation, and one day a colleague of mine couldn't face telling a couple their child's prognosis. So I did it for them. I read what I could in a couple of hours, then did it as well as anyone can do these things without training. My colleague was appreciative, but indicated that he thought that it wasn't as hard for me as it would be for him. Because . . . autism.'

'Shit. I mean, sorry to ask, and tell me if I'm being ignorant about autism, but . . . *was* it hard for you? Emotionally?'

'You're being ignorant about autism, and yes. Very hard. But it's something we have to do, so I read up and learned about it. Which people noticed. And I became the go-to person for delivering bad news. You know: *I'd do it, but Carey does it better.* Which is what happens with practice. A vicious or virtuous circle, depending on your perspective. We had a paediatric cancer ward. I got a lot of practice.'

Carey stands and starts walking around the glass house; it's not a big space and there are people coming and going. I walk with them to keep the conversation private.

'I realised that, despite what I'd been told all my life, I was actually adept at understanding interpersonal dynamics. Not intuitively, as you do, but analytically.' They laugh. 'Today wasn't a great example. That's what stress does to your functioning.'

'But you decided you could be – wanted to be – a psychiatrist. You don't think you'll find it frustrating?' Asking for myself.

'Challenging. The profession's made huge progress. Easy to forget when you encounter a difficult case. But there are numerous problems that won't ever be solved with medication alone and that's what makes the job so interesting.'

They could have left it at that. But they add, 'We've got one-way mirrors, electroconvulsive therapy, psychedelic drug trials. We're the weird guys and that's a familiar place for me.'

—

I make it home half an hour before the others are due to arrive for study group. Despite Carey's words of encouragement, my doubts about psychiatry haven't receded.

It's a spectacular autumn evening and the lawn is carpeted in elm leaves. I text the guys to rug up, then drag a couple of the kitchen chairs to the shared garden, opposite the bench seat. I've got a takeaway roast chicken and salad.

Jon is the first to arrive, carrying an esky with beer and dips.

Ndidi is next, with mineral water and more dips, then Alex, who pulls a bottle of wine – pinot gris – from his bag.

While I'm cutting the chicken, Alex brings the others up to speed on Prof terminating his supervision. He's connected the dots between Mr X and Prof's patient, though he doesn't know about the Carey connection.

'But,' says Alex, 'X is still worried about . . . let's call her A.'

'No,' I say, 'let's call her Y.'

Alex looks at me, eyebrows raised in query, before telling us that Xavier is showing no clinical signs of depression, but has been afraid Y will go to the media, possibly encouraged by the party fixer, who has been undermining him.

Alex wants to challenge Xavier about his motivation for the suicide attempt. Was he just trying to scare Y into silence?

'If so,' says Ndidi, 'and if that's all there is to it, he doesn't have a mental illness. Try to set him straight if you want, but I don't see how that's something you do forty sessions of for credit towards being a medical specialist. Sorry, but there have to be limits around the talking-cure thing.'

I don't say anything. Last time Alex started dismissing Xavier's risk, I had flashbacks to Aaron. *Leave it alone.*

'What did Prof think?' says Jon.

'We didn't really discuss it. To be honest, Prof wanted me to go pretty slowly.'

'Seems like good advice.' Jon opens another beer.

'That was before X was under pressure from the fixer. He could try again and miscalculate.'

'Hopefully you'll have a new supervisor when you get back,' says Jon. Alex is about to take a week off for a friend's wedding in Fiji.

'I'm with Jon,' says Ndidi. 'If you need advice, ask someone who's into doing what psychologists – or friends – are supposed to do. Anyone else got a case?'

I talk about Chloe pulling out on Elena after I commented on her eating and linked it to the family therapy.

'Why did she agree to remain in hospital in the first place?' asks Alex. 'Did the therapy session address what she was staying for?'

I don't have the answer and I guess it will keep me awake tonight.

'By the way,' says Ndidi, looking at me, 'Sian and Matilda have gone home. Luckily Sian's mother-in-law's around; her own family's missing in action.'

'Lucky? You think? Did you meet Deirdre?'

'Briefly.'

'They don't exactly get on. I think Sian will have her on the plane back west even if she's got to pay for child care.'

'Not so easy. Child Protection got a temporary court order. Abundance of caution, blah blah blah. Mother-in-law has to be there. She's technically the baby's carer.'

'Shit.'

Jon is shaking his head.

Ndidi shrugs. 'Goes to court properly in three weeks. If she can't last that long . . .'

I have my doubts Sian and Deirdre will be able to function together more than a few hours at a time, particularly if Deirdre plays the legal-responsibility card. Sian is still regaining confidence after a big blow to her sense of herself. The right mother or mother-in-law could be a huge help – but my guess is that isn't Deirdre.

Ndidi is getting up to leave when I remember that there was something else I needed to bring up.

'Carey.'

'What've they done now?' says Ndidi. She's laughing.

I haven't thought through how to do this. 'You realise they're autistic, right?' I say.

'Have autism,' says Alex. 'Careful or you'll have Nicole sending you on a sensitivity course.'

'Actually,' I say, 'you could have a good argument with Carey on that one. Disorder versus identity. But we haven't exactly been sensitive to them as a person.'

'Fair comment,' says Jon. 'If they were a patient . . .'

'Or,' I say, 'if they were one of us. If they were a doctor trying to get into the psych program, we'd have them in the group, right?'

'We accepted you,' says Alex. 'Despite . . .'

'It's not hypothetical,' I say. 'Carey *is* a doctor.' I fill them in.

There are a few moments of shared incredulity. In our world, there are doctors and non-doctors, and Carey has crossed the divide – or has been on our side of it all along.

'Not telling us gave them a certain power,' says Alex. 'If they weren't autistic –'

Ndidi doesn't let him finish. 'Running errands for Prof for a year! Maybe they were good enough to get in, but Prof held them back so they could be his lackey.'

'Regardless, maybe we can help them get into the program,' I say.

'Are you sure they're ready?' says Alex.

'Plenty of people get in when they're not,' says Ndidi. 'And Carey's been fucked around. Could have been any of us.'

Could be me.

'They wanted to join the study group,' I say.

'If they'd told us . . .' Ndidi starts, then shakes her head. 'Doesn't matter. They're in as far as I'm concerned. Hope they like chicken.'

'In,' says Jon.

'Can't argue,' says Alex. 'Can I tell them it was the bottle of wine?'

Ndidi and Jon take off, and Alex and I exchange looks.

'Bit of pinot gris left,' he says.

'Back in a minute,' I say and dash inside for a bathroom break and quick tidy-up.

When I return, he's cleared the table and, from somewhere, produced another bottle and a mini cheese and fruit platter on a plastic plate. Very cute. And his timing is good: after the day I've had and with my doubts about where my career is going, I'm ready to de-stress.

I sit down, sip my wine, and suddenly Jess, who'd been inside while we had our meeting, bursts into the garden in a panic.

Alex and I jump up.

'Something's happened,' says Jess. 'I need to talk to you right now, Hannah.'

'Can I do something?' asks Alex.

'No. You need to go. Please.'

Jess has me by the hand and Alex picks up his bag and heads to the gate. And then he's gone.

I break free of Jess's grip and put my hands on her shoulders. 'Calm. You'll never be an ambo if you can't keep calm. What's happened?'

'I *was* calm. I was just getting rid of him for you.'

Jesus Christ. Omar at work and now Jess at home.

I speak very slowly. 'What made you think I wanted him to go?'

'I was watching. You didn't see. While you were inside, he was getting all this stuff out, he was just about licking his lips. *Lying in wait*. You'd been drinking, so . . . What sort of guy does that to someone in his study group?'

'You were the one who told me to date doctors.'

'I meant Alex. Him doing it to Alex. Who's basically dating you. As soon as Alex left, he –'

And the penny drops. For me, at least.

'Alex is the guy you just sent away,' I say.

It takes a little longer to drop for her.

'Oh shit. I thought you were seeing the hot guy. I thought Alex was the hot guy and that Jon was the funny guy. Not that the real Alex isn't hot, but . . . oh shit.'

I text Alex. *So sorry – crisis under control. Another time. Safe travels. xxx*

He texts back straight away. *See you in a week. Shame the two registrars can't take leave at the same time ;-)*

Then Jess and I head inside with the wine and cheese.

ELEVEN

BOUNDARIES

'Buddy, I hear you, but I need to see it run without trouble for three months. You told me it was the Rolls-Royce solution, and I'm happy to pay for that – when I see it working without having to call you back. Am I being fair?'

Jarryd wants to argue but he's feeling too stressed. He and his client are walking toward his van: *Baker Solar*. The client breaks off, heads back into his garden and gives his attention to a wayward rose.

Jarryd shakes his head, but the pressure is physical, a tightening in his chest. He stows his toolbox, wipes his brow, not feeling good at all.

In the driver's seat, he puts the keys in the ignition, then changes his mind and pulls out his phone, but realises he won't be able to talk. He pushes the door open and staggers out.

'You okay, buddy?' the client shouts from the garden.

Jarryd shakes his head; he can't breathe. Is it the pain or the stress or the rising panic? He thrusts his phone toward the client.

I guess a normal person in a normal job would lie awake thinking about the screw-up with Alex. Or his text message suggesting he'd like to take me to Fiji. Instead, I lie awake thinking about my screw-up with Chloe, which is bound to be the reason her family has cancelled therapy. I don't get anywhere, but then the dream sleep does its thing and I wake with a plan. I get in early and see her before handover. She hasn't even had her shower.

'I'm going home today,' she tells me. There's a solid core of defiance there, and my heart sinks.

'I heard. It's always been your choice. But I wanted to say thanks for helping out with the fridge.'

Chloe gives me a blank look.

'When Ahmed and Sonny and I were carrying the fridge and you opened the door,' I explain.

'Oh.' She manages a smile. 'No big deal.'

Except by Nash's standards, it is: *The end-stage anorexic is totally focused on themselves – and even then only food and weight.* Uncharacteristically brutal for him. And untrue in Chloe's case, even if only in the form of that walk from her chair to take the card from around my neck and hold it against the door sensor. How much can I push into this chink?

'Can I ask you to do something else? Nothing to do with eating, I promise.'

'Then what?'

'Brianna asked for your help.'

'She doesn't need my help.'

'She asked for it. In the first therapy session.'

'How do you know?'

Shit. But good pick-up. I give her a straight answer. 'I was one of the team observing. Maybe keep that one between us?'

'I have no idea how to help. She got a nose ring. I'd never have done that.'

'Elena asked you to write a letter to your younger self and then give it to Brianna. Maybe it'll help her understand where you're coming from.'

'What am I supposed to write?'

'I think Elena said to write what you'd have done differently. Wisdom from her big sister.' Bad choice of adjective.

There's a long pause. I feel for her. When I first saw her, it was like looking at a photo of a concentration camp survivor – too far from my own experience for me to be able to empathise in an instinctive way. Now I see the twelve-year-old and all she aspired to be, still there in this woman whose development has been tragically arrested. Inside, I think she still is mostly that child.

Chloe looks at me – *really* looks – and says, 'I wouldn't have gone to camp.' A long pause. 'Church camp. It was the first time I lost weight.'

I stay silent until it becomes clear she won't be offering any more.

'Maybe share that with Brianna. The therapy with Elena isn't about your weight, you know.'

Her eyes flash. My suggesting it *was* about her weight caused her to sabotage the session. Then she lets it go.

'You think if I write the letter, Brianna will stay off my case?'

'Maybe it'll help her work better with you and your family. She'll appreciate that you cared enough to do it.'

Later in the day, Chloe's mother, Sue, and Brianna visit. Chloe doesn't go home with them, and I see her pass an envelope to her sister. As I'm walking home that evening, Elena calls to tell me that the family has rescheduled the third therapy session.

—

The following Wednesday, Alex is back, but I'm on call again and we don't cross paths. He's sent me daily text messages: mostly what's-happening-on-the-ward? stuff, but more than he needs to unless he's *really* unable to let go of work.

The Acute Unit is full, so the CATT team will have to find a bed elsewhere if someone needs an admission. I get dinner at the hospital cafe: protein, carbs and water, as the running program specifies. Plus a load of fat.

The psych nurse in ED calls.

'There's a guy here who's been medically cleared but he's refusing to go home. Might be one for you.'

I wander into ED – it's my third time on call and I know my way around. The cubicles are full, but the place feels calm.

Kate Rigby, the senior registrar, is on tonight. Lucky me.

'Panic attack, cubicle five,' she tells me. 'Jarryd Baker. First time, so I guess it's no meds, send him home, wait and see.' And in case her usurping of my role isn't sufficiently clear, she adds, 'Unless you're here to fix the fridge.'

The story of that little incident has apparently been widely shared and no doubt embellished – the fridge will have been full of restricted drugs, the patients carrying it dangerous sociopaths.

The nurse is waiting for me outside the cubicle. 'He refuses to believe the intern. She's told him there's nothing wrong.' She catches my look. 'I mean, physically.'

I can see Jarryd through the half-open curtain. A thirty-two-year-old electrician, shirt open from where the ECG was attached. It came up normal apart from a racing heart, which is consistent with anxiety, under which 'panic attack' is classified.

Nice body. (Where did *that* thought come from?) And, when he smiles in greeting, dimples.

I introduce myself – just Dr Wright, no mention of psychiatry yet – and ask him what happened.

'Haven't felt great all day.' His voice is deep and a little husky. Probably a smoker – which is *not* sexy, I remind myself. 'Did some lifting yesterday and got a bit of a stiff back from that, but then I get into the car to go home and I can't breathe. Thought I was going to die.'

'Have you experienced anything like it before?'

'Never.'

'How long did it last?'

'Five minutes? They're trying to tell me it's all in my head.' The smile again, but there's fear behind the bravado.

'The tests look normal.' They've done a chest X-ray and blood tests for the tracers that appear when you're having or have had a heart attack. Doesn't happen often at his age, and it hasn't on this occasion. 'Any stress lately?'

'A bit. Couple of difficult clients and I've just gone out on my own.'

'Are you an anxious type? A worrier?'

'I worry about screwing up a job. Not getting paid.' He laughs. 'Getting sick. Stuff everybody worries about.'

'Does it keep you awake at night?'

'Sometimes. You think it's in my head, too, don't you?'

'I have to check. You could be anxious and still have something physically wrong. But one thing at a time, okay, Jarryd?'

He likes the *Jarryd*. 'I'm all yours.'

'Any family history of anxiety?'

'Nope. I mean, not that you'd see a doctor for. My mother . . . let's say I haven't told her I'm here.'

'Family history of heart problems?'

'My dad. Died at forty-nine.'

'Heart attack?'

'Uh-huh. He wasn't with my mum.'

'How old were you?'

'Thirteen. I was pretty knocked around by it . . . Can't help thinking that I might go young like that. Like I might have inherited something.'

Can't help thinking. He gets short of breath and subconsciously worries he'll die like his dad – is that what's behind his panic attack?

'Can I speak to your mum about your dad's heart?'

'If you really need to, but don't freak her out. Like I said, she's a mum. Aren't you going to examine me first?'

Cute. I leave the cubicle to call his mother and, as Jarryd warned me would happen, she instantly panics and I have to spend a couple of minutes calming her down. Eventually I'm able to ask after her late ex-partner.

'It was a shock,' she says. 'We'd split up but, you know, on good terms. He just dropped dead with no warning.'

'Were you told the cause?'

'Yes, it was his heart.'

'As in heart attack?'

'Definitely his heart. He wasn't overweight, didn't smoke. They said it can just happen like that sometimes.'

If Jarryd has grown up with that message . . . He's got a family history of anxiety, acknowledges at least some on his own part, there's current stress and a reasonably comprehensive physical work-up has come back clear.

I reassure him that everything looks fine and, reluctantly, he agrees to go home.

Inevitably, I pass Kate on the way out, and inevitably she smiles and says, 'Panic attack.'

The best comeback I can manage is 'provisionally'. I'm too pissed off. Not with Kate personally, but . . . *What thoughts have led to your feelings of utter fucking uselessness?* Answer: *The emergency medicine registrar has flippantly diagnosed something in my space, when she'd be outraged if I ventured into hers.*

I once aspired to have her job. I'm not sure if that's what starts the train of thought. I also have my instincts telling me that 'panic attack' doesn't quite fit with the guy who's been gently hitting on me. And Prof taking down Alex for missing a physical symptom – after Alex's *if you're looking for something, you'll find it.* I was primed to look for a panic attack. What would I be looking for if I'd gone through the other sliding door and been the emergency-medicine registrar?

I run through the symptoms again, including those that *didn't* contribute to my diagnosis of a panic attack. The husky voice, the family history of heart attacks . . . No, that wasn't what she said.

I hit redial on Jarryd's mum and have to repeat the calming-down process.

'You said Jarryd's father had a heart attack.'

'That's not exactly what they called it,' she says. Now.

'Does aortic aneurysm sound familiar?'

'Yes! Aortic, definitely.'

'But not aneurysm?'

'I thought that was a brain thing.'

'Aortic dissection?'

'That's it. Definitely. Oh my god. Are you saying –'

'No. I just needed to be clear on the history.'

I put down the phone and walk back to ED. Jarryd's still there finalising the paperwork. I ask him if I can repeat the physical that the intern has already done. Jarryd's happy to comply and we return to the cubicle.

His abdomen suggests he works out. Nothing abnormal there.

'Where's the back pain?' I ask.

Jarryd points to the region around the second or third thoracic vertebra.

'Is your voice always husky?'

'Nah, just some virus I've picked up over the last few days.'

'Okay, we're going to do another test. I'd like you to lie down until then.'

I go to find Kate. There's every chance I'm going to give her another reason to take me down, and I expect an eye roll. Instead, she pauses, nods, and heads off to organise a CT scan with contrast.

I decide to hang around for it. I'm tingling all over in anticipation of what they might find. If I'm honest, I *love* this feeling. And I'm anxious about Jarryd too.

I chat with him for the next forty minutes. About his work, not mine. About whether we should add batteries to the solar-power system at the family home.

I take him to radiology, watch them inject the dye, sit with the radiographer as the images are taken. We both look and our eyes widen.

'I'll be back with you in a minute, Jarryd,' I tell him. 'Just got to talk to someone.'

I find Kate, drag her over to a workstation and bring up the scan.

'Chest X-ray missed it,' she says. 'The heart got in the way.' As it does. 'You talk to him. I'll get a cardiac surgeon.'

'Jarryd,' I tell him, while Dr Rigby is making it all happen, 'you were absolutely right: there is something wrong.'

His smile fades.

'Your aorta, the big artery from your heart, has a weak spot, and it's started to blow out.'

'Like a tyre?'

'Like a tyre.'

'You're saying it could burst?'

'That's the risk. Aneurysms run in families, and you are the luckiest and smartest man alive, because we usually don't get to diagnose them in time.'

It takes him a moment to work out what I'm saying. 'It's what killed my dad, isn't it?'

'Because he probably ignored the sore back and the hoarse voice, which is the aneurysm pushing on a nerve. You're going to need an operation.'

'Um, you mean . . . right now?'

'Yes. You'll have to sign some forms first. Trust me – just sign them.'

'You're saying: don't fuck around?'

'I'm saying there are risks, but the alternative is . . .'

'I hear you. I'll sign the forms.'

'You want me to call your mum?'

'After you find out what's taking them so long.'

I make a point of walking past Kate on the way out.

'Good work,' she says.

I smile. 'Did you want me to check the fridge before I go?'

—

Alex has asked Elena if he can join me in observing her third session with Chloe – a response to my enthusiasm about the first one. I had to skip the second to catch Andrew before he was discharged.

It's the first time I've seen Alex in over a week, and I'm conscious that I've missed him. I've *been* conscious of missing him. And not just because I've had to do all the Acute admissions and discharges by myself.

I lead him to the storeroom with the one-way glass. An observation *team* – team Hannah and Alex. Family therapy done properly, except for our total lack of experience and expertise.

Elena joins us, carrying a white cardboard box that she puts on the table. She's wired. It's harder to sense in her than it is in most people, but fiddling with her beads is the giveaway. Today's are green, matching her earrings and shoes, against an off-white dress that's on the floaty side. On Elena, it looks stylish.

She props against the table; tells us that the second session – the one I couldn't make – didn't go well.

'Therapy takes time. Including time for them to reflect, rather than just bolster their defences. But Nash wants her discharged.'

Chloe is steady at thirty-one kilograms. An increase, but hardly anything to get excited about. Mentally, which is supposed to be what we're about, I've seen no change. Unless you count the letter she wrote to her sister – her homework from session one, delivered late. I've briefed Elena on that, and she seemed pleased.

'The mother – Sue – made a bit of an effort: only ringing Chloe once a day,' says Elena.

'Was David able to say what he'd lose if she got better? The father's homework,' I add for Alex's benefit.

'Not directly. But he wouldn't have a purpose. Keeping Chloe alive is his mission, part of his identity as protector of the family. When I asked about the trip to Greece they supposedly dreamed about, I may as well have asked about visiting the moon.'

'So Chloe's illness is the glue that holds the parents together?' says Alex.

'Yes,' says Elena. 'The question is whether it will hold Brianna, and what will happen when Chloe dies.'

I'm conscious of the time; the Youngs will be here any minute. 'What's the plan?'

'I've got this session and maybe one more.' Elena's fingers are still on those beads. 'I'm going to throw everything at them – if it doesn't work, it can't be any worse than where they are now.'

What about Brianna? I wonder. But I don't want to put Elena any more on edge.

'I will definitely be taking a break, so feel free to think of any messages you might want to give them. And I'll warn you: I may be taking an unconventional line.' Her tone says: *Don't try this at home*. She points to the cardboard box. 'I'll leave this with you for the moment.'

The box is about thirty centimetres square and five or six deep, sticky-taped shut. There's nothing to suggest what's in it.

'Is this really a thing?' says Alex when Elena has left. 'Suggestions from the gallery?'

'Makes sense. We have time to watch and think.'

'Can't imagine Prof doing it.'

In the darkened storeroom, Alex and I watch through the glass as Elena enters the therapy room. Sue follows, then David pushing Chloe in her wheelchair and, finally, Brianna. They take up the same seats in the circle as in the first session: Chloe between Sue and David; Brianna between David and Elena.

'They're looking at a mirror,' says Alex. 'I wonder what impact that has on the process?'

'It's a pretty crappy mirror,' I say, and Alex's response is cut off by Elena's voice coming through the speaker.

'We talked last week about how hard it is to change. And how *not* changing can be as risky as doing things differently. I'm wondering if this has brought up anything for any of you.'

Chloe looks uptight. So does Sue. David looks angry – I wonder if he'll be able to admit this. Brianna looks like she's given up. No-one's going to respond. Almost immediately I realise that the ache I feel for Brianna has some of my own childhood pain tied up in it.

'In the first session, Brianna,' says Elena, 'you said you wanted a life and hoped Chloe would help you.'

Sue jumps in. 'Chloe can't help herself; she can't be expected to help Brianna.'

'Really?' Elena's tone is mild. 'Able to fool nursing staff with weights under her wig, able to smuggle them into the hospital, but can't help herself.' She's nodding as though ruminating on a curious phenomenon. 'Brianna, what do you think about what your mother said?'

'Chloe wrote me a letter.' She looks at her sister and smiles – earns a half smile back.

'Would you like to talk about it?' says Elena.

The sisters exchange glances again. 'We thought it was private,' says Brianna. 'So, no.'

'Have there been any other changes?' says Elena.

'We went to see *Swan Lake*.'

'If Chloe had been home, would you still have gone?'

'No. We'd already changed tickets twice.'

Sue interjects: 'When Chloe's home, she can't get around easily, and I don't like to leave her alone.'

Elena nods. 'So, Chloe coming in here gives your family a break. Brianna, you got to do something you wouldn't have done otherwise. Chloe chose to stay here: perhaps it was her way of letting you have time with your parents.'

Brianna looks confused.

'Elena's trying to shift their perspective,' says Alex, whispering, though they can't hear us.

'Really?' I whisper back, and he smiles an apology.

Elena turns to Sue and David. 'What do you do in the evenings when Chloe's in hospital?'

David replies. 'We aren't . . . we aren't all that social.' More confidently, 'We get a great deal of support from our church community. Our pastor is actually a qualified therapist.'

Alex rolls his eyes. There are no rules about who can call themselves a therapist.

'So, when you're at home, do you watch TV? Do you walk the dog? Talk?'

'We're still worrying about Chloe,' says Sue.

'Brianna, when Chloe's in hospital, is there anything you do that is different? Or anything you would like to?'

'I have to study. I want to be a vet, so I need really high marks. To be honest? It's better when she's in hospital, because Mum and Dad aren't hovering around her, and running to her favourite cake shop because just maybe this time she'll eat it and we won't find it in a box at the bottom of her cupboard covered in mould. Which, by the way, I saw her eat once, mould and all, though of course she threw it up again afterward.'

'Brianna . . .' says David.

'Oh, no, she doesn't throw up, does she?' says Brianna. 'She just has a *sensitive stomach*.' Brianna starts crying. David puts a hand on her arm and she pushes it off angrily.

'Chloe,' Sue murmurs softly and puts her hand on her older daughter's arm.

'Wow,' says Alex.

'Sue, can I ask why you thought Chloe needed comfort?' Elena says. 'It's Brianna who's crying.'

'But this is hard on Chloe, too,' says Sue.

'I'd say it's pretty hard on Brianna, from where I'm sitting. But, Brianna, you pushed your dad's hand away. Are you ready to be comforted yet?'

Brianna's still fighting back tears.

Elena moves to sit next to Sue, vacating the seat next to Brianna. 'Chloe's with us at the moment – so, Sue, can I get you to sit next to

Brianna and see if she'll let you comfort her? David, you're welcome to try again too.'

Alex and I – and probably Elena – hold our breaths.

Sue doesn't want to move, and I'm sure the only reason David doesn't storm out is that he'd have to admit he's angry. In the end, Sue does move chairs, and she gives Brianna's shoulder a perfunctory pat. It's awkward. Cringeworthy, if not for the pain that must be sitting behind it.

'I don't need you to pretend,' says Brianna, crossing her arms.

'I think maybe it's hard for your mum to comfort you when you're angry,' says Elena mildly. 'Even your dad doesn't show his anger. They're relying on you for that.'

'Fuck,' says Alex.

'Me? They hate me being angry,' says Brianna.

'Yes, I imagine it's pretty scary for your mum and dad,' says Elena. 'Because this is a family that deals with problems by showing how much they care.'

Elena looks at her watch. 'I need to meet with the team. While I'm gone, I wonder if you can think of all the ways you care for each other.'

When she joins us, Elena sits on the arm of my chair and watches them.

'It looks like they're digging their heels in,' I say. 'Except Brianna, who's desperate.'

'They're enmeshed,' says Elena. 'They're all trapped in this toxic interplay. Chloe being the focus makes Brianna feel unloved – but it gives her the chance to leave and find what she needs elsewhere.'

'Where she'll recreate the same dynamic with a partner,' Alex says.

'Not necessarily,' says Elena. 'She might do a few years of psychotherapy or – who knows? – work it out for herself.' She looks hard at us, then takes a breath. 'Wish me luck, and call Security if . . . if you think you need to.' She smiles – not really serious – and heads off, taking the box with her.

Alex and I turn to the window.

'The team is very clear,' says Elena. 'That first week, they told you that you really do care about each other – Sue and David not going on holiday, David not taking the promotion, and Brianna trying to get help despite the risk that means in your family. I'm sure while I've been out, you've thought up lots more ways you care.'

The Youngs are listening, watchfully. Ready to counterattack.

'Can you maybe give me some examples?' Elena asks.

Sue and David rattle them off: buying cakes for her, making her favourite dinners, cooking with her, sitting with her during meals. *Her* being Chloe, of course.

Elena nods. 'All to help Chloe gain weight.'

Brianna is slouched in her chair, arms folded and looking at the ceiling.

Elena picks up a folder she must have placed on the floor when she first arrived. She opens it and then unfolds a graph covering several pages of A4 stuck together.

'This,' Elena says, pointing, 'is Chloe's weight when she was fifteen.' She guides a finger along the horizontal axis. 'And this shows how her weight has changed over time.'

Even from where we are sitting, we can see a monumental drop at around fifteen, and a further drop in the past two years.

'Dr Sharma did not want to admit Chloe,' says Elena, 'because he knows that Chloe will get what she wants and no-one can stop her.'

Chloe looks a little vacant. David's mouth is a grim line, and Sue has started to tear up.

'Chloe,' says Elena, 'I think you've made it pretty clear that only Brianna has got it right.' She gives a theatrical sigh. 'David, Sue, I was on your side, but the team sees the big picture. And they asked me what you *actually* do when you care for someone.'

Alex and I look at each other. 'Where's she going with this?' he says.

I have a sense, but don't want to say it out loud.

'So I said to them,' Elena continues, 'well, *I* do whatever that person asks of me. What *they* want. I cared for my sick mother and she wanted to watch James Bond movies, which I loathe, but of course I watched them with her.'

'We buy Chloe her favourite cakes,' says Sue.

Elena looks pained. 'But that isn't what Chloe wants, is it?' She turns to Chloe. 'Do you want to put on weight, Chloe?'

Chloe doesn't respond. She looks spaced out, dissociated.

'Your mum thinks you want cakes – vanilla slices are the favourite, I believe? She drives a long way to your favourite cake shop to get them.'

Elena picks up the cardboard box and puts it in front of her. 'Imagine this is full of vanilla slices.'

Alex and I both stiffen and we're pretty much mirroring what happens in the room. Chloe doesn't move, but she blinks faster. Brianna has sat up and is watching her parents as much as her sister. Sue looks anxious. I'm feeling for Chloe. She's my patient and this feels like abuse.

David's anger brims over. 'Obviously she wouldn't eat them in here in front of everyone.'

'Really? If you want to gain weight, why wouldn't you, Chloe?'

This time she answers. 'I like vanilla slices.'

Alex and I look at each other, surely thinking the same thing. The lie is ludicrous, or at least the implication that Chloe wants to gain weight is. Yet it's what holds her family together. Elena's voice is measured, conversational, as she dismantles it.

'But even if you did, you'd throw up afterward, as Brianna told us. As the nurses have observed. Because, of course, what you want more is to lose weight, and we just keep ignoring you, don't we, Chloe?'

Elena sighs again. 'You obviously care, Sue and David. You're well-intentioned, but you're not giving Chloe what she's been showing you for years that she wants, which is to lose weight regardless of the consequences. That's what the team said, and they pointed out that what Chloe wants is not unexpected for someone with this illness.'

'So you're suggesting we don't try to help her?' David looks aghast.

'Of course not. But you need to help her with what she wants, not work against her.' Elena turns to Chloe. 'When you go home, I imagine that would be not calling you to meals? Not asking you about what food they should buy? Letting you go running?'

'Um . . .' Chloe is lost.

I've been holding my breath as I watch David and Sue.

'Chloe can't articulate it for you,' Elena tells them gently, 'because she's been relying on Brianna to do that. She knows what she wants hurts you, and she doesn't want to do that.'

Elena turns to Brianna now. 'You were her last hope, because you're the strong one who's allowed to be angry – she isn't strong enough.'

Brianna has tears rolling down her face. She pulls her chair over to sit opposite Chloe. 'You know I'm not really angry at you? I get mad at you, but I'm mad at myself for not being able to . . . change your mind. But I know you're not going to, and I accept that.'

Chloe smiles – all teeth and jaw and so little flesh. She leans forward and hugs Brianna.

'Chloe wants you to do the same, Sue,' says Elena. 'If you really love her and want her to have what she wants, this is what you need to do. And David, you have to support Sue to let Chloe do what she wants.'

Sue lets out a piercing wail. 'I can't – I won't – you can't make me.'

'No, Chloe can't,' says Elena. 'Even though she's tried every way she could think of for more than twelve years. If she dies – and all the doctors say it's only a matter of time – you'll never have said goodbye and never have shown her that you love her. You'll have made her struggle all this time because of what *you* wanted.'

I'm not sure if I grab Alex's hand or he grabs mine. I'm shaking. I think he is too.

'If Chloe dies,' yells David, 'it's on your head! We'll sue!'

'Oh shit,' Alex and I say together.

'If Chloe dies,' says Elena calmly, 'it will be because anorexia nervosa killed her, and because Chloe chose to let it do so.'

'What sort of damn quack are you?' David shouts.

'Do we call Security?' Alex asks.

David is still in his chair.

'No,' I say. 'Let's knock on the window – the team's allowed to do that.'

I knock.

It pulls David up as he looks toward us. Elena doesn't miss a beat.

I just love this woman.

She lowers her voice, but we can still hear her.

'That will be the team reminding us that we all agreed to show each other respect. And I respect that I have made you angry, and I understand this. It was pretty shattering to me to realise that Dr Sharma was right and that we needed to respect Chloe. And her wishes.'

Sue looks at Elena likes she wants to murder her. I have never seen a look like it before. It's not Jack Nicholson in *The Shining* or Anthony Hopkins in *The Silence of the Lambs*. It's unadulterated murderous rage, like you'd feel toward someone who'd killed your whole family. Which is close to what Sue must feel Elena is doing. Then the rage is gone – and in its place is a crumpled woman who looks like she's aged twenty years.

There was a moment during the first session with the Youngs when I fantasised about being in therapy with my family; helping my parents come to terms with the pain they've been carrying, and helping Lennon, Mel and me, I guess. Maybe give that one a miss.

Sue stands up and walks toward the door, but is hardly able to stay upright. David rushes to her side and whispers something. Whatever it is, they keep going, out of the room.

'How are you feeling, Brianna?' asks Elena. She leans forward and rests her hand on the girl's shoulder. Brianna still has both hands on Chloe's knees.

Brianna takes a minute to pull herself together. 'Will I lose them too?' she asks.

'Let's hope not,' says Elena. 'It's hard, very hard for them. Be patient. And kind. I think . . . Would you like to wheel Chloe back to the ward?'

When Elena joins us, we're still frozen in our seats, and still holding hands.

Elena slips to the floor, rests against the wall. We sit in silence until Alex breaks the spell with, 'We'll write up our observations.'

The unspoken reason: *In case David follows up on his promise to sue.*

'Are there any stats on whether this is likely to work?' I ask.

Elena shakes her head. 'I doubt it. Research, yes, and shared experience. It's the equivalent of an experimental drug. But getting the parents to relinquish control is a widely accepted goal in anorexia nervosa.'

'Have the Youngs done that?' asks Alex.

'You saw Sue. What do you think?'

'You broke through.'

'I think so, too. But I don't know if it's going to hold up when David pushes back.' Elena is shaking her head. It's all been so intense, and now, looking at the aftermath, that seems to be the flaw in the plan. David will have the power, and Sue will have the comfort of returning to the status quo.

'Was there ever any chance of persuading David to let go?'

'As I think you observed, David's need is to be needed by Sue. That's what I'd have tried to work with if they were coming back.'

'And Chloe?' I ask.

'I've kept in mind that she's an inpatient, and we'll have a chance to follow up with her.'

'We?'

'Let's talk tomorrow.' She stands up and opens the box. 'Do you want a vanilla slice?'

—

I'm still buzzing when I get back to the ward.

'You're late,' says Nash.

'I was observing Chloe's family therapy session with Elena.'

'Went to plan?' His tone tells me he isn't interested in an answer, but I give him one.

'Amazing. Scary. Yelling, tears. Change? I don't know.'

'Spectacular.' Nash smacks his hand hard against the side of the filing cabinet and the drawers shudder. 'There's a certain personality that's attracted to psychotherapy because of the power to do that sort of thing, and the intellectual gratification of connections and insights. But where are the trials that show it can be reproduced? It's not medicine.'

'What else have we got for Chloe?'

'You should be asking what else *they've* got. Aromatherapy and reiki. Beat the devil out of them. When you don't require evidence, you never run out of options.'

'But –'

'Can it make things any worse? That's what you're about to say, isn't it? Yes, it can. The family's found a way of surviving. What if therapy undermines that? What if the marriage breaks up? What if the sister develops an eating disorder?'

'Elena didn't –'

'I'm not saying she did. I'm not criticising Elena: she's an experienced psychologist doing what she does in a case she knows well. I'm warning people like you and Alex – Alex in particular – not to be seduced by it.'

—

It's been a huge day, beginning with a phone call at 3 am to say that Jarryd the electrician had made it through his operation with a synthetic tube replacing a section of aorta, and then watching one of the most dramatic and emotional interventions I've seen in psychiatry – in medicine. And sharing that second experience with someone who, as much as you can ever tell, felt the same way.

Seems I'm right, because that evening there's a text from him: *Dinner Saturday next week at my place? No work talk.*

There's a connection with Alex that isn't going to happen with some guy I swipe right on. If I do stay in psychiatry, we won't run out of things to talk about. But Saturday *next week*? What's wrong with now?

He's working back. I walk home quickly, pick out a pair of jeans, a tight black top and heeled boots, and spend a bit of time on my hair and make-up. It's pretty much my best look. I text Jess, telling her it might be a good evening to keep a low profile, preferably not in our apartment. She sends me a smirking emoji.

'Tonight's the night,' says Omar, who's walking out as I walk in. 'He's just packing up. Not looking as hot as you.' He laughs and points back at the door. 'I'm allowed to say that out here.'

Alex can't have read the rule book about what can be said inside and out. He's very happy to be taken to drinks and dinner. And to talk work.

'I've just seen Xavier again,' Alex tells me as we walk.

'You've got a new supervisor?'

'Not yet. But I don't want to suspend the therapy. I figured being appointed to the mental health advisory board position had given him a certain amount of security – that was the message he was sending – so I pushed a bit harder on the suicide thing. Whether it was, consciously or otherwise, manipulation.'

Challenge was the word he'd used with the group. I guess he took our silence as an okay to go ahead. I feel uneasy and Aaron's face pops into my head. It takes effort to focus on Alex.

'You took a risk,' I say. 'I guess I'm always going to want to play it extra safe whenever there's a hint . . .'

'Which is why you need to have your own therapy.'

'You been talking to Prof?'

'I don't need to. I'm sure he'd say the same. But I guess I was a little inspired by what I saw Elena do today.'

'Not by your patient's arrogance?'

He stops walking. 'Fair question. If Prof were still my supervisor, I guarantee he'd have asked that.'

'You mean you'd have checked with him before you took the risk?' We're standing in the middle of the footpath, pedestrians flowing around us. On a big date, consumed by work. 'How did he react – Xavier?'

Because I saw him in ED when he arrived, then in Acute and again at the parkrun, he's not an anonymous Mr X to me. I remember how scared he looked in ED. He'd a brush with death and was shaken. And, whatever his motivation, he engaged voluntarily in psychotherapy and is continuing it.

'I broke through the . . . arrogance,' says Alex. 'But he held the line on why he jumped in front of the truck. He insisted that it was genuine. Frankly, he convinced me, but the value is in what it opened up. I think there's a lot of shame there. So, huge progress.'

—

We share a bottle of wine, and dinner, at the Italian place I've chosen. The conversation doesn't run out, even when we finally move on to personal stuff. His renovations: under control but he needs a tile cutter, which I can borrow from my dad. Travel: we're earning the money for it, but having trouble finding the time. Art: surrealism versus expressionism, but neither of us know shit and we laugh when we both realise this at the same time.

It doesn't matter that much what we're talking about: the chemistry is there and it's the most fun I've had in a long time. I want to ask him about the piano and whether he plays, but we shift back to career plans – dreams. I'm sharing some of my reservations about psychiatry with Alex, at the same time as trying to deal with a semifreddo which is completely *freddo* and resisting my efforts to get a spoon into it.

Alex points to my dessert. 'Metaphor for the fact you're struggling. You know I think you should do psychiatry, and that you'll be great at it, but you're not sure, are you?'

He looks at me intently, just as I apply some serious force to my spoon. My ball of semifreddo flies into the air, and Alex catches it in one hand. We both burst out laughing, and then he stops, puts it soberly on his plate and heads to the bathroom.

When he comes back, he's paid the bill – that wasn't the plan – and, without discussing it, we walk back to my place. He's quiet. But we hold hands.

'Sorry about the semifreddo,' I say. 'Actually, I thought it was pretty funny.'

'I know you did,' says Alex. 'That's how you and Marcus bonded, right? Over the broken beakers. And let me guess: he told that story forever.'

He's right. So I tell him the full story of the dropped resus kit. 'Marcus thought it was a joke. Clumsy Hannah. And that was the beginning of the end for us as well as for emergency medicine.'

Even as I say the words, I'm thinking, *And maybe it doesn't have to be that way*. Emergency medicine, not Marcus. Clumsy Hannah is walking around with Omar's employee of the month award for wrangling a resus kit to save a life, and just diagnosed an aneurysm that the ED guys missed. There's a simple solution to my disillusionment with psychiatry.

We arrive outside my place. I've had a good evening. Alex gets me like no-one else ever has. I find him sexy. Especially the eyes but even the messy hair. Particularly the messy hair. I'm picturing ripping his shirt off, but wondering about what will happen to the buttons. Is he the sort of guy who likes to fold his clothes? I'm actually nervous.

'Want to come in?' I say.

Then comes the pause. Alex looks awkward and my stomach drops.

'Thanks, but . . .' He doesn't put his hands in his pockets but that's the look. 'I wasn't expecting . . .'

'No, my bad,' I say doing my best to smile. 'Let's never speak of it again.'

I'm trying to open the door and get through it so I can put a slab of wood between us as fast as possible. So much for intuition being my strong point.

But Alex grabs my arm before I can escape. 'I don't want the night you launched the semifreddo to be some big moment. Like it was with you and Marcus. Which became pathological.'

'Sure.' *Just let me go.*

And then, to add to my complete confusion, he kisses me. Not a button-ripping kiss. But it's not nothing. And then he's gone and I'm inside, turning on the lights.

Jess, who's apparently been waiting in the garden, takes this as her cue to come in.

'You were going to invite Alex in, right? But I just saw him walking away. I'll get the ice cream.'

I'm about to say that I've already had dessert – but I never ate the semifreddo.

She gets the rocky road, I sit on the sofa, and she pulls up my desk chair to perch opposite me. The only light is a beam from the streetlamp that hits the floor between us.

I tell her everything.

'Wait,' she says, 'he invited you to his place?'

'Saturday after next. Not going to happen now.'

'Maybe – I might be wrong, but I'm usually not – he wanted that to be the special night.'

'Maybe I wanted tonight to be that night.'

'Maybe he just panicked because you tried to jump him and he wasn't ready. If it was the other way around . . . I mean, if you weren't ready, you'd expect him to understand. Or maybe he's got some, like, medical issue.'

Maybe all sorts of things.

'Leave it,' I say. 'There's something else I want to tell you – and it's more important in the long term.'

'So Alex is, like, just for fun? Because the way you've been talking –'

'I'm thinking of changing specialisations,' I say. 'Applying for emergency med.'

'No!' She shouts the word and I'm totally thrown. Does she have an issue with me being in her space?

She gets out of the chair and paces around. 'For someone so smart, you can be incredibly dumb. It's not like I haven't told you, like, fifty times.'

'Better tell me again,' I say. I've got no idea.

'A lot of people were fucked up by what happened with Aaron, okay?'

'I know. I was there. But sorry . . . talk to me.'

She does, for half an hour – about how it impacted her class, my parents, my brother and sister. She saw things I didn't, or things I just accepted because I was too close. Then she turns it back on me.

'You've done something about it. Someone had to and it's you. You're the one who has the gifts. Do you get that? The teachers who gave you extra help –'

'Hey, if you want to help me, you have to listen. That's how therapy works.'

'*You're* the therapist.'

I asked for that. But I'm carrying enough guilt without having to atone for the whole town.

'Sorry, Jess. I'm done.'

Jess sits down and looks at me for a bit. 'I'm sorry,' she says. 'This is my stuff. I shouldn't be putting it on you. You do whatever's right for you. Emergency medicine is good; I just had it in my head that you were going to do therapy.'

'I get it. It's okay. But understand that there are other ways to make up for what happened . . . like doing what you're doing.'

'You think I don't know that?'

—

The next morning, there's a delivery of flowers waiting for me in the registrars' room. And a card.

Thank you for saving my life. They tell me you're a shrink. For the sake of everyone with a thoracic aneurysm, go and be a real doctor. Jarryd the Sparky (and his mum).

TWELVE

JUDGEMENT

Two cars speed across the drawbridge as it opens, racing against time and the widening break between the two halves. The first jumps the gap, recovers, presses on. The second, in pursuit, is flung into the air by the upward slope. Its momentum carries it toward the other side: it touches, then falls back, tumbling into the void.

The movie stops abruptly.

'Dad!' Three kids in unison, in the suddenly silent home theatre, as the lights come on.

It's their mother, Sarah, who speaks. 'Your father and I need to talk to you.'

'Does Dad need to go back to hospital?' It's the oldest, trying to show he's on top of it, but there's anxiety in his voice.

'It's not that,' says their father, Xavier Farrell MP. 'There's going to be an article in the paper. A very unpleasant one.'

'Politics,' Sarah says. Her expression says something else.

Xavier's kids are looking at him.

Tomorrow they'll be looking at him differently.

It's raining on Saturday morning – winter is coming – and numbers are a bit down for the parkrun. I look around for Xavier Farrell and his family. In my uncertainty about psychiatry, the smiling kids and the bouncing dog are a reminder of the upside.

'What's happening with Sian?' I ask Ndidi as we set off at the usual pace. I haven't had an update since she was discharged with baby Matilda, with a court order requiring that she be supervised by Leo's mother, who is not exactly her BFF.

'Child Protection is asking for the order to be extended,' says Ndidi. 'Twelve months.'

'They don't give up, do they? I presume Sandra will shoot them down.'

'Sandra doesn't want to take any risks, and Sian's mother isn't available as an alternative.'

'What about the attachment? The baby's long-term mental health? I thought Sandra was big on that.'

'Who'll ever know? But if Sandra gets the physical risk wrong and Child Protection were shown to have been right . . .' She grimaces. 'I've told Sandra what I think. But it's me in court next week, and I can't go against her.'

I've picked up the pace, and Ndidi is now working hard. I think of all those foster kids, of what happens when families fracture or carers die. And Sian, who became ill through no fault of her own, put aside her objections to medication and ECT, and is now having to submit to her mother-in-law or potentially lose her baby.

I try one more time. 'If you're asked – I mean, if they actually bring up Matilda's future and ask what you'd recommend – what are you going to say?'

'You know me. I'll tell them what I think and deal with Sandra later.'

The words are right, the conviction not so much. Glad it's her, not me.

I realise she's dropped back. Or I've pushed on. I'm feeling a little peeved, more at the system than Ndidi.

There's no sign of Xavier and his family as I cruise back over the bridge.

I run a personal best and get the coffees.

—

The following Thursday, I'm in the glass house early, when my phone buzzes with a text message from Sandra, sent to me and Nash.

> *Nash: Ndidi is due in Children's Court 9.30 today but is unwell. It's my private practice day and senior reg is on training course. Hannah is familiar with the case – see discharge notes.*
> *Hannah: stick to them!*

I misread the last line as *stick it to them*, but no . . . Fuck, fuck, fuck.

There's no message from Ndidi. She wouldn't have expected Sandra to ask me to appear in her place.

Before I can respond, Nicole walks into the glass house. I hear her before I see her: the click of her stilettos is unmistakable.

'Just the person I was looking for,' she says. 'Actually, I was looking for Dr Edozie, but apparently she's off sick, and the nurse in the Mother Baby Unit suggested I speak to you.'

'I've been asked to attend court in her stead,' I say. 'I'm due there . . .' I look at my watch to make the point as politely as I can.

Though, if she stops me from going, maybe that would be a good outcome – she can take the blame.

Nicole ignores my hint. 'This is about the placement of Sian Tierney's child?'

I'd like to say, 'None of your business,' as Sandra or Nash surely would. They're getting increasingly angry about Nicole using her position to butt into clinical matters, and she's already interfered in this one. If she hadn't given Child Protection an early heads-up, they might never have intervened and we wouldn't be dealing with this mess.

'Sandra asked Nash if I could cover,' I say. 'I saw Sian when she was in Acute.'

'What are you going to say?'

'I'll have to read the discharge summary.'

'Is she safe with the baby?'

'There's always a risk.'

'That's not an answer. I worked for Child Protection. They're not trying to manage risk, they're trying to eliminate it. If it was your sister . . . Do you have a sister?'

None of your business. I nod.

'Does she have children?'

Damn. I nod again.

'What would you say?'

I'm worrying about the court appearance and about my own appearance: the white t-shirt I threw on only because I hadn't done my laundry. *My Brain Has Too Many Tabs Open* isn't the ideal message to display.

And I resent a non-clinician using her power to put words in my mouth. Except that they're the words I'd say, if I was allowed: 'I'd let her have her daughter. Without the mother-in-law.'

'Fine. Don't perjure yourself today.'

Jesus Christ.

Nicole spots Alex. He and I have been dancing around each other all week, which is not quite what I intended when I said we should never speak of our screwed-up date again. And exactly what I was concerned about, way back, when I had a rule about dating colleagues.

'And it looks like you'll have work to do,' Nicole says to him.

'Sorry?' says Alex.

'Your psychotherapy case,' says Nicole. 'The MP who jumped in front of a truck. You've seen the news?'

I wonder if she realises that Xavier Farrell is Alex's psychotherapy case only because she basically dared Nash to assign him to a trainee.

Alex shakes his head, looks uncomfortable.

'He's come crashing to earth. Usual reason. Shame, actually – he was at our review of the Mental Health Commission findings last week and seemed pretty engaged.'

And, having thrown two hand grenades into the ward, she's gone.

—

The Department of Families and Housing versus Tierney is listed for Court Three. It's a modern building off one of the smaller city laneways, down from the Magistrates Court and a block from the County Court, and the streets are full of robed lawyers carrying briefcases and pulling wheeled bags.

I'm held up at the scanner by a family with a pusher and backpacks that spill across and off the conveyor belt, and a child that runs back and forth setting off the alarm.

When I get through, the clerk at the window says the case won't start till ten. They haven't gone in yet.

I skim the discharge summary. There's nothing about the risk to Matilda of separation from her mother. To be fair, Child Protection isn't proposing that. There's probably no research on the impact of compulsory oversight by your mother-in-law.

In the upstairs foyer there are people everywhere in huddles, babies in arms, children in prams and on seats next to harassed parents, instructions being issued over a loudspeaker. I look around and see Sian, Leo and Leo's mother, Deirdre, who is holding Matilda.

Leo glares as he sees me approach. He's in a suit, tie loose at his neck. Sian's in jeans and sneakers. Deirdre is neat in black and white. I button my oversize blazer over my t-shirt.

'Dr Edozie is off sick,' I say.

'Any advice for me today?' says Leo. His tone suggests it wouldn't be well received.

His mother gives him a dirty look. Pulling him up for being disrespectful, or just reminding him who's supposed to be doing the talking?

Ndidi had described Sian as pissed off. That seems accurate.

'Matilda looks like she's doing well,' I say to her.

'Except for the runny nose. Nothing serious, according to the doctor.'

'Which is what I told her,' says Deirdre. 'I've raised five children. You'd expect me to know what I was talking about.'

Can Sian handle a year of this? Unless her lawyer is across the deal, she may think she only has to hold it in for a few more hours.

A tall middle-aged woman who looks like the kind of lawyer I'd want on my side in a child custody battle comes over, accompanied by a short guy with a serious gut: Homer Simpson to her Marge. 'Has anyone seen Dr Edozie?'

I explain who I am and they pull me into a small room next to the court. Homer's the lawyer for Child Protection. I don't catch his real name. Marge Simpson is in fact Cynthia, the senior child protection worker whose voice I heard on Ndidi's tape.

'You'll be on first,' Homer says, and – seeing my reaction – adds, 'This is the second day. We only need you to confirm Sian was psychotic when she came in.'

They're in luck. I saw more of Sian when she was really unwell than Ndidi did. That's not going to help her.

'She'd be hard work,' says Cynthia, obviously fishing.

'Having psychosis is pretty hard,' I say, then, before she can press me, 'I'm new to this, just standing in, but I'm curious: what would happen if Leo and Sian were to break up?'

'Deirdre is the primary carer,' Cynthia says, not answering the question.

A crackly voice over the loudspeaker calls us in. The courtroom is small, and we seem to have three lawyers: Homer for Child Protection; a baby-faced man for Sian; and a serious-looking young woman with heavy glasses for Deirdre. Why does the mother-in-law need a lawyer?

There's a lot of talking among them before the magistrate comes in. He's middle-aged, with the look of someone who's been doing a tedious job for a long time. He reminds me a little of Max the barrister, who we treated in the manic phase of bipolar disorder.

It's after eleven before I'm called up and sworn in. I sit in a chair with the magistrate to my left and the line of lawyers in front of me to my right. Leo and Sian are sitting behind her lawyer, not touching, and Deirdre is with hers. Matilda is in a pram in the aisle, beside Sian.

Homer asks about my role and qualifications, and what contact I've had with Sian, given I'm not the doctor who was subpoenaed.

The magistrate seems happy enough with my response.

Then Homer asks me to explain Sian's diagnosis.

'Sian was diagnosed with postpartum psychosis,' I say. 'It occurs in one in six hundred deliveries and is an affective psychosis – a bit like bipolar disorder.' Textbook.

'And she left her baby alone in a cupboard: is that correct?'

'Yes.' I know what Sandra would say – *just answer the question* – but add, 'While Sian was unwell, and untreated.'

'And she didn't tell anyone when she was admitted that she had even had a baby?'

'That's correct.'

'Do women with postpartum psychosis often do dangerous things and put their baby at risk?'

'Untreated . . . sometimes. Often there's a partner with them who spots the warning signs and gets them into care before anything happens.'

Dirty look from Leo.

'So, you would agree that she needs someone with her?'

'If she has another baby, certainly she will need monitoring.'

'But now? You'd agree she needs someone supporting her?'

'All first-time mothers need support.'

'But we aren't talking about that, are we, Dr Wright? Sian isn't just a first-time mother; she's a first-time mother who has psychosis. Who abandoned her baby.'

'Who hid her baby. And is now taking medication for the psychosis she *had*. She does need support – it's a matter of how much and for how long.'

'Can you tell us about her treatment?'

I outline the medication and ECT, then the support to help her reconnect with Matilda.

'So, she wasn't bonded to Matilda?'

'For a while, she thought her baby was gone – that was part of the illness. Then ECT impacted her memory. Then she felt guilty.' I remember the daisy chains and throw it in for balance. 'My colleague told me that when Sian was discharged, she was like a mother hen on steroids. So, I'd say she has since bonded.'

Homer's mouth twists but he doesn't pursue the bonding line. He takes me through her follow-up. Then, predictably: 'And there's a risk of relapse. So this could happen again, and not necessarily with such a fortunate outcome.'

'If she stops medication or has another baby. But stress could also have an impact.' Before he can stop me, I add: 'She's currently not psychotic, and is insightful and compliant with treatment.'

'Has she cared for Matilda, without assistance, for any length of time since her breakdown?'

'Not to my knowledge.'

Homer hands over to Sian's lawyer, Babyface.

'When my client was psychotic,' he asks, 'did she ever actively try to harm Matilda?'

'No – from her perspective, she was doing everything she could to protect her. Hiding her from what she perceived as danger.'

'Do you think my client loves her daughter?'

'I have no doubt about that. This child was planned and wanted, and in my recent interactions with them, I've seen clear evidence of that.'

Deirdre's lawyer now: 'Are you aware of any *strong psychiatric reason* why Mrs Walker, Matilda's grandmother, should not care for her? And, for clarity, as the primary carer, for an initial period of twelve months?'

'I haven't assessed Matilda's grandmother.' I immediately regret not going further, but Deirdre's lawyer has stepped away.

The magistrate asks if the lawyers have finished with me.

Homer notes, in light of the previous question to me, that Child Protection has assessed Mrs Walker and approved her as a carer.

'And the maternal grandparents?' says the magistrate.

'They've also been approved but, as they're currently overseas, the parties have agreed to the paternal grandmother.'

Babyface, Sian's lawyer, hasn't finished, apparently. *Please ask me about attachment or toxic supports.*

'Can I ask what you meant when you said that it's a matter of how much and for how long Sian might need support?'

Clumsy, but it'll do. 'Sian needs support to help increase her confidence in caring for Matilda. That can be hard for grandparents, who may find it easier to just step in and do it themselves.'

I cop a withering look from Deirdre.

'With the right support,' I continue, 'Sian is likely to be able to take full responsibility for Matilda within a month or two.'

I've heard Sandra say this. *Full responsibility* doesn't preclude calling in some help when she needs it.

'So you'd say that a twelve-month order, as the department is suggesting, is excessive?'

I force myself to take a breath. 'Yes.'

The magistrate addresses Babyface: 'I'm still not clear what the issue is here. Is your client happy to accept help?'

'Yes, Your Honour.'

The magistrate turns to Child Protection: 'Can you explain why we need the order?'

Homer leans over to Cynthia, then straightens up. 'Ms Tierney is not yet recovered from a serious mental illness where she put her child at grave risk. Matilda is not safe with her alone and, because of his job, her partner is away for weeks at a time.'

'But why can't . . . er' – the magistrate checks his notes – 'Mrs Walker just stay with Ms Tierney until the doctors give the all clear?'

'There is a vulnerable baby involved and we've heard there's at least some risk of relapse.' Homer must see that the magistrate isn't sold, because he adds, 'I'm advised that Ms Tierney has been less than cooperative with Child Protection. We see that as a risk factor for compliance.'

Compliance with what? I look at Cynthia and see what's gone down: they like Deirdre and they don't like Sian, who'd have a strong idea of her rights and not hesitate to exercise them.

Sian's in her lawyer's ear, demonstrating exactly that.

While they're conferring, Deirdre's lawyer raises her hand. 'A small matter: my client's home is in Port Hedland. And the baby's father also spends time in WA. Over a twelve-month period, Mrs Walker will need to make trips home, and we would like the court order to acknowledge her freedom to do that – with the baby, of course.'

So *that's* why Deirdre has her own lawyer.

I look at Leo, the partner who spends half his time in Western Australia. There's no frantic whispering in his mother's ear: this was the plan they came in with. It buys him a year before he has to make up his mind about whether to leave the relationship. If that happens, I guess there's a good chance that, in the turmoil that would result, his mother would keep Matilda.

Sian gets it. She leans in to Babyface, but he's already rising to his feet. He gets it. Everybody gets it, including the magistrate, who's probably seen it all before.

'It seems to me that the parties' intentions have not been fully shared, and that you' – the magistrate points to Cynthia – 'need to review the plan, taking into account Mrs Walker's intentions.'

All that conniving and all those legal fees down the drain in about fifteen seconds. I like this magistrate.

'Apologies, Your Honour,' says Deirdre's lawyer. 'If we could have a short recess?'

'Can we excuse the witness?'

The lawyers decide they can. I feel the weight of the world rolling off my shoulders, though I'm not sure where all this leaves Sian. Matilda starts to cry and I look over to see Deirdre about to pick her up. A venomous glance from Sian stops her dead.

But before he lets me go, the magistrate asks me a question. 'Do you see any psychological impact on the baby if she were to go to Western Australia with Mrs Walker?'

It's a straightforward question, and surely Sandra would answer it in the same way I do – just more articulately. I'm struck by the obvious, though it probably hasn't been obvious to Ndidi either: the magistrate decides this; I just need to give him the right information.

'In this first year, it would be very destabilising, particularly if Sian wasn't able to relocate with Matilda. Having two primary carers is confusing enough, but if she lost touch with her mother for an extended period? Matilda would divert all her attachment needs to Deirdre – Mrs Walker – and on return . . . I don't know. But she would be at risk of an attachment disorder.'

'What would that mean?' asks the magistrate. He actually seems interested.

I outline how the attachment between mother and baby gives them a basis for dealing with later problems in relationships, and how it plays into the risk of anxiety and depression. I sound like I'm reciting a textbook. There's a reason for that.

'So,' he says, 'it's a matter of balancing risk. And that includes the risk of Ms Tierney relapsing and causing harm to the baby. How great do you think that risk is?'

I can see Homer's about to get up. I give a safe answer.

'All of us are at risk of mental illness. It can happen to any of us, out of the blue, as it did to Sian.'

I see nods in the courtroom. I've summarised the reason for acute psychiatry in two sentences. The magistrate nods too. It's the perfect moment for me to step down, but he slips in one more question.

'Though realistically,' he says, 'she's at greater risk than you or me.'

'I don't know your history.'

Shit.

There are enough people in the courtroom whose future is not hanging on these proceedings that I earn a round of laughter, and time to reflect on my faux pas – which has surely come from a deep belief that we *are* all at risk and shouldn't divide ourselves into them and us. Maybe that recognition is why the laughter goes on so long.

Eventually the magistrate cracks just the slightest smile. 'Thank you, Dr Wright.'

And that's it. The Carey-style response aside, I feel I've done okay, but I sense that the magistrate's last point is going to stand. The fear of mental illness, and the association with physical harm to others, will trump everything else. I wonder how Sian's parents will feel in retrospect about the three-month sabbatical that deprived their daughter and grandchild of the option to stay in Melbourne.

—

When I leave the courtroom, Leo comes after me. He's not aggressive, just guarded. 'What you said about . . . bonding.'

'Attachment?'

'Matilda could just . . . attach to my mother, right? She's brought up five kids. No psychosis.'

If he's so sure, why is he asking? But he's confirmed their strategy.

'Your mother is a lot older than when she brought you up,' I say. I've been careful with my testimony, but now, one on one with the person who has it in his power to change the outcome, I decide to use a little of my own power. 'If Matilda does have problems later in life, she may point the finger at your mother. And if she's missed out on growing up with her mother, she may blame you.'

He takes it in. Then, 'Tell me the truth. Is Sian ever going to be right again?'

'Nobody's ever the same after something as big as this. I guess you're not. But will she recover totally from the psychosis? She has already. She could relapse, but we'll be watching for it. And it's treatable.'

He nods. 'Like you said, we can all get sick. Could've been cancer. But . . . you saw what she was like. That wasn't her. It scared the shit out of me.'

'She seems to be finding her mojo again,' I say.

To my surprise, Leo laughs. 'She's not easy. Has to be the boss of everything.'

'That was then. Maybe you can negotiate something a bit different now.'

'Easy to say.'

'If this scared you, what about her? And you've got a baby now. I guess the question you've got to ask yourself is whether you can build a new life that keeps the good things and adapts to what's changed.'

I've budged him: I can feel it. What else have I got? What would Elena say?

'So, it looks like your mother's in for a tough time. You've got two strong women in your life.'

'You don't like me, do you?'

Deep breath. 'It's more disappointment. After you put Sian first when you brought Matilda into the Mother Baby Unit, and took on the hospital staff – including me – when you thought we weren't doing the best for your family . . . I was hoping you might have been able to step up.'

—

First thing next morning, I see Alex outside the registrars' room. I follow him in: it's been awkward between us since the date that went wrong, and maybe I've overreacted. Or maybe he'd like to explain himself a bit better. But before we can get started, Ndidi bursts in – looking pretty energetic for someone who was too sick to go to court twenty-four hours earlier.

'What happened?' she asks. 'You must have been awesome!' I guess she does sound a little husky.

'What do you mean?' I say.

'I just spoke with Sian. They dropped the case. No order.'

I open my mouth and just shake my head.

'Leo's mother is on her way back to Port Hedland,' Ndidi adds.

'Wow. Is Sandra okay with that?'

'Can't complain: all parties agreed. Support's in place. Leo has quit his job, too; he's going to look for something local when she doesn't need him around as much.'

I'm gobsmacked. I don't know which of the things I said to him did the trick, or if it was something else entirely.

'And sorry,' says Ndidi. 'I had laryngitis. You know the rules about coming in sick. My voice was shot; I couldn't even have done a video link. But you did better than I'd have done anyway.'

Laryngitis. Unable to speak. Wow. I sneak a look at Alex, the Freudian, who's struggling to keep a straight face. He heads out the door, and I feel a wave of sadness about what's happened with us. Two aspiring psychiatrists who can't get their own shit straight.

—

Chloe's mother, Sue, asks to see me and she comes in – without David.

'This is very, very hard for me,' she says. 'I hated those sessions with Elena, but that last one? I don't know why, but it suddenly struck me. I really have done everything I could to get Chloe to eat, and I've failed. But I don't want her dying without being able to say goodbye properly, and having to spend whatever time she does have left fighting and worrying.'

She wipes away a tear. 'I know she's going to die, Dr Wright. I hate that I can't do anything about it, but it's time to let her go . . . and try to make it up to Brianna, as well as decide what it is I want to do with my life.'

My life. Alex may have been right about what David feared.

There's a knock on the door of the interview room, and Omar comes in and pulls me aside.

'Chloe's father is here. Do you want me to get him to do the bullying module?'

I shake my head – not in the mood for jokes – and ask Sue if she wants him to join us.

'Will you stay?' she asks.

David comes in, a dark cloud, and Sue answers the question that's emanating from him.

'I'm here to see Chloe, David.'

'You didn't tell me you were –'

I interrupt. 'I guess this is a discussion you can have at home. Sue, I wonder if you'd mind me speaking to David for a few minutes, as I've been doing with you?'

Sue's already getting up. This is my moment to pick up the pieces that Elena didn't have a chance to. *Keep it simple.*

'How did the therapy session with Elena go?' I ask David when his wife has left the room.

'I'm sure Sue's told you. We've been told to give up on our daughter. Let me tell you, as long as I'm here, that's not going to happen.'

I remind myself that I'm not Elena. I've looked after Chloe, been sympathetic in our dealings. I'm the good cop. And I've just had some success in getting a partner to step up. David's not Leo, but I have a limited repertoire.

'Can I be direct with you? More direct than I've been with Sue?'

'If you're going to tell me that Chloe's very ill . . .'

'I'm sure you know that. Maybe it's best that Sue prepares herself for the worst-case scenario, but I'm going to tell you that backing off may actually be your best hope. You've tried everything else, and I don't think she actually wants to die. I'm sure you know that with children, there's a time to let them make their own decisions and sometimes you're surprised by how well they do.'

I actually doubt he does know it.

'But that's going to be very hard for you and your wife. I've been talking to Sue, and she wants to try it, wants to give Chloe the best chance we think she has, but for a mother to just let go . . . She'd need a huge amount of support.'

He sits back. Not angry, thinking. 'And she's told you she doesn't expect to get it. Is that right?'

'No, she hasn't said that. But she's being asked to act against all of her instincts – and I'm sure yours too. It's a very hard thing to do.'

'We've had to do a lot of hard things. We've always done what we believe was best for Chloe and we have a source of strength that you might not understand.' He pauses. 'First Peter, chapter three, verse seven.'

Afterward I look it up. Weak women and strong men, with an instruction to treat your wife with understanding. At least the second part's right.

Now for Chloe, my actual patient. I call Elena, and she's happy – thank god – with my intervention. She communicates the strategy to the Eating Disorders team, who'll now give Chloe the space that I promised her when she was admitted. She'll stay in for a few more days before we see whether the family can hold the line – and whether it'll do any good.

After a couple of days, I ask Omar how he thinks she's doing. Increasingly, I'm trusting his take, and those of the other experienced nurses, on my patients. They spend more time with them than I do; I seem always to be on the phone to relatives, pathology or other hospitals and doctors. Not to mention doing paperwork. 'Time spent on accountability,' Nash says, 'is time spent away from patients. Someone should be accountable for that.'

Omar thinks there's been some change. 'Did someone take her mother's phone away?'

He's right. When I see Chloe, there is something different about her. She's not as bright – the brightness always felt false, anyway – but maybe more settled? Calmer.

I ask about the therapy session. She remembers that I was on the observation team for the first session, and I confirm that I watched the third.

'My mum and dad came in the day before yesterday. Did the big-talk thing. It's a little weird.'

'In what way?'

'They basically said they're not going to be involved in my . . . eating.'

'How do you feel about that?'

'Like I said, weird. It's been like this for so long. You said if we went to therapy, they'd get Brianna to back off, and now . . . everybody has. Even the nurses, right?'

'I think they're saying that it's your life. Any thoughts on what you might do with it?'

'Not really.'

'You mentioned social work.'

'What happened to backing off?'

—

Elena's in the glass house when I return from talking to Chloe. I try out my attempt at a formulation. 'So now the parents aren't controlling her, Chloe doesn't need to control food?'

'More or less. It'll be a lot more complicated than that, and she's really messed up her body. And the parents . . . we'll see. Brianna, incidentally, has asked to see me privately. In therapy.'

Brianna probably hero-worships Elena. She's not the only one. Nicole and the Butterfly Foundation appear to have been right: family therapy should have been tried a long time ago. Or maybe it had to be the right intervention at the right time.

Not everyone agrees. 'Chloe has gained five hundred grams,' Carey tells Nash in the glass house. 'Some evidence for the experimental treatment.'

'Who told you to tell me that?' Nash slams the door on his way out.

I want to ask Alex if there's any more news on Xavier, but he hasn't been around all day. Probably still avoiding me.

—

That night, Jon, Alex, Ndidi and I have scheduled what was supposed to be a purely social outing, though, inevitably, we've managed to tack on a work agenda. No-one's suggested we include Carey; we'll invite them to a regular group meeting first. We've given up on dropping hints that they lose the aftershave: subtle doesn't cut it, and we don't want to be less polite than we'd be with a neurotypical person.

Jon has a long-term patient ('schizophrenia, a bit thought-disordered, a lot in her own head'), who was a successful musician before she became unwell, and she still plays on weekend leave. Her stage name is DJ Voices, and that's what she prefers to be called on the ward. She's picked up every Friday by a couple of friends and returned to care on Sunday.

Jon's boss thinks the electronic music scene is weird and dangerous, but doesn't actually do anything to ensure that the DJ is not exposed to whatever risks he thinks it poses. Jon wants to take a look by showing up, hopefully unnoticed, at one of her public performances. His concern is that she may be being exploited, financially or sexually, or not taking her meds. 'If she's like she is on the ward, she's going to fall asleep.'

We've discussed the ethical issue. Alex's response was instant: you don't insert yourself into your patients' lives. And anyway, what was Jon going to learn from seeing her perform?

Jon had a raft of counterarguments: it's a public event; she won't see us; one of her visitors gives flyers out to staff; nobody else is looking out for her. And it's only an issue for him, as the rest of us have no relationship with her. As for the diagnostic value: 'I'll be looking for affect, signs of coercion . . . I know this person from the five days a week she spends locked up against her will; I'd like to be a little more holistic in my understanding.'

Like seeing Xavier at the parkrun. I'm glad I didn't mention that to Alex.

DJ Voices is performing on Friday night in a basement bar beneath a Greek coffee shop in Thornbury. We're going to eat beforehand, as the doors don't open until nine.

I've splurged and bought a dress – kind of figure-hugging, with a low-cut neckline – which I try to keep casual with my usual Docs. Not a dress I'd ever usually wear. It may be an unconscious response to the awkward evening with Alex, which I still haven't really processed. If he wants to interpret it that way, he can.

As I jump on the tram, I get a text from him saying he can't make it. Fuck him.

Then one from Ndidi: still not feeling 100 per cent.

And now Jon, responding to the cancellations. *Meet at the venue?*

I get a burger. And as I'm sitting in this crappy takeaway, all dressed up, the phone screen lights up with my brother's name.

'Lennon?'

'Sorry, you doing something?'

'You've been drinking?'

'Doesn't matter. Lost the job. Moving on.'

'Are you coming ho—'

'No!' There's a pause while he gets his anger under control. 'Sorry. I lost it with Mum a couple of hours ago. I said sorry to her too, but I'm still . . . like this. Better you talk to her. I need you to tell her not to call me again. Same for Dad.'

'Shit, Lennon. For how long?'

'Maybe forever. If something happens, I'll call you. But – I'm sorry – can you tell them? Maybe tell Dad first.'

'I'll call you tomorrow, okay? Try to chill.' That's all I've got right now.

If I was in another place, emotionally, maybe Lennon's call would have pushed me back toward psychiatry – where I'd have the chance to learn how to deal with what he's thrown at me. Instead, it's reinforced my desire to escape from it. To run.

—

Jon is outside the venue when I arrive, and I'm instantly comfortable with him. When I've been out with Alex, I've felt challenged, wondered what the agenda was. But Jon's easygoing; I've never had a sense of him wanting to be anything more than a reliable support.

We head downstairs and get beers. It's dark and noisy, with about fifty people in the room, and fifteen minutes later Jon's patient, DJ Voices, is introduced. She steps onto the stage, says something I can't make sense of and dives straight into making music. I recognise her from a night when I was on call. Can't miss the green hair. The people around me are dancing, and there's a definite energy. More punters straggle in.

Jon suggests we move closer to get a better look. It's not easy, but we find a wall to prop against.

DJ Voices looks scrappy and maybe spaced, large headphones over her ears. But she's really into it. Her hands fly over the turntables while the rest of her dances. Occasionally she calls out to the crowd, punches the air and whoops.

'This is pretty amazing,' shouts Jon over the music. 'I've never seen her engaged in anything.'

And then, mid-performance, she stops, shakes her head and walks offstage. Even from here, I can tell she's in some distress.

Nobody ever asks, *Is there a psychiatrist in the house?* but here we are. Automatically I start moving forward, expecting Jon to follow, but he grabs my arm.

A nerdy-looking guy comes to the microphone. 'DJ Voices has to take a little break. She has some major mental health issues and she has to go through a lot to do this for us. Let her know we appreciate it.'

Everybody claps. There's an overwhelming feeling of support – love, even.

Jon nods to me. 'I'd guess this isn't the first time. They seem to be on top of it.'

After a few minutes, DJ Voices comes back and resumes her set. We weren't needed; her community supports were enough. That's obviously a good thing, but if it had been a physical accident and I'd been an emergency medicine registrar, I would have stepped up without hesitation. And everyone would have recognised I had skills that they didn't.

'Definitely not falling asleep,' I say when she's done. 'You think she skipped her meds?'

'Hope not – she's on a depot as well as oral, but she'd be risking some ugly side effects from withdrawal of her clozapine, on top of the psychosis. My guess is she's taking them.'

'Maybe whether this is exploitative isn't the point,' I say. 'They're giving her something we can't give her.'

'I'd still like to know where the money goes. Do you feel like dancing?'

Not really, but I allow Jon to drag me into the midst of the crowd. I've had enough to drink that I can relax into moving freely, not something that comes naturally.

I feel his breath on my neck, his chest next to mine and it would be easy to think we were on a date. I remind myself we aren't – and that recently I was thinking Jarryd the electrician looked hot. It wouldn't take an analyst to figure out where all this is coming from. It wasn't Jon I dressed up for tonight.

We leave after a couple of hours, tired out from the dancing, and as we walk to my place from the train, I have my first real chance to talk with him one on one.

His life has been very different from mine, but there's common ground in our chaotic extended families. When I get him on to photography he describes the Country where he grew up in such a way I can almost see it. We talk about his Bilinarra heritage, and how that's influenced his medical career. His mum ran a clinic in Darwin, so health care has been front and centre all his life. He considers himself privileged to have got a good education and to have the chance to give something back to the community.

It strikes me that Jon is like my family and Alex is like . . . what I left them for. Or Jon is like the familiarity and fit of emergency medicine, and Alex is like psychiatry and what it asks of you at a deeper level.

'Why psychiatry?' I'm asking him because it's what I'm asking myself.

He takes a while to answer, and I spend the time just enjoying the walk. We're off the main street, it's a clear night, and quiet after the noise of the club.

'There's a lot of pressure to treat what's seen as urgent, and tangible. Obstetrics, blindness, drug abuse, plain life expectancy . . . plenty of work to do. Psychiatry's seen as a luxury, as the medicine you do after everything else.' He laughs. 'Maybe not breast implants.' I look at him and can see he's regretting the example.

'Yet depression is one of the leading killers,' I say. 'Suicide . . .'

'Preaching to the choir. But do we do what we love, or do we do the most useful thing?'

'Tough question.'

'Not really. We can't all be epidemiologists or prime minister or full-time peace activists. You know the story about the kid throwing a stranded starfish back into the sea. *Maybe I can't make much of a difference, but I made a difference to that one.*'

We get to my door. No lights on, so Jess is asleep or has gone out.

'So,' I ask, 'was it worth doing? Seeing your patient?'

'Definitely. And thanks for coming.'

'I enjoyed it. And good to talk about psychiatry.'

He laughs. 'You don't get enough of that?'

'I could talk all night . . .' I'm more relaxed than I've been for a long time and the words just pop out.

'Really?' He's smiling.

He leans toward me, but I get out my keys and open the door. The two of us step inside.

Then my phone rings. I automatically pull it out: three years as a doctor is going to do that. I see who it is and silence the call.

'Alex,' I say, in answer to Jon's expression.

'Call him back. He's not going to ring you at eleven thirty just to chat . . . Is he?'

Before I have a chance to reply, Alex calls again.

'I'm sorry,' he says, 'but this is work and I really need your help. Xavier's sexual harassment stuff is turning into a big story.

He's being asked to step aside. I wanted your advice on whether I should call him.'

He's asking me? My instincts, the instincts I had before I had any education in medicine or psychiatry, say yes, reach out, make the human connection. *Be his friend.* My dad wouldn't hesitate a moment.

But Xavier isn't our friend. Alex is Xavier's therapist. He knows that and he knows the answer. But he wants me to give him moral support. And, though he's probably not thinking it consciously, to share the blame if anything goes wrong. Asking me to do what I least want to do: participate in a decision about a patient who's threatened suicide. Maybe he's doing me a favour.

'Call Prof,' I say.

'I'm not going to do that.'

'Then you know what to do.'

Jon nods his approval.

'I was just thinking it wouldn't hurt for the guy to be reminded that there's someone he can talk to, someone who isn't judgemental.'

'He may not see you that way. You said you've been challenging him.'

'So you're saying I shouldn't call.'

'First, do no harm. If you can't call Prof, wait till you've spoken to your new supervisor.'

Alex hangs up and I fill in the detail for Jon. We're both back in work mode, and the moment between us has gone.

When I'm finished, Jon looks at me for a few moments. 'You're going to lie awake half the night worrying about whether you gave him the right advice.'

He's so right.

'Look at me,' he says. 'If you and I want to survive in this profession, we have to learn to let go. Do our best, which we've just done, and then go to bed knowing that our patients will do what they will, that we're only a small factor in it.'

Easy to say.

He hugs me, just briefly. 'Try meditation. Find something that works. But learn to let go.'

That's exactly what I plan to do.

—

Mercifully, Jess seems to have gone out. I sit down, put on some familiar music, and instead of churning over what I said to Alex, I find myself just feeling for him, and for us. Thinking about how *sorry, but this is work* trumped everything this evening; how our work is so consuming, even driving the way we try to help each other, that it's screwing up any chance we have of a proper relationship. Love's executioner. I want to go over to his place, but I know that we'd spend all night thinking about a troubled politician. Is this the life I want?

Intuition is my superpower. And it's telling me to get out. I've got some good things from psychiatry. I've faced my issues with suicide, not to the degree I'd need to be a psychotherapist or, according to Prof, any kind of psychiatrist, but enough to make me a better doctor – and a more resilient person.

I'm on the way to discarding the Clumsy Hannah narrative. I can thank Alex for that. And there have been some good moments with patients. Sian and her baby. Chloe. I was never going to save my family. And maybe if I wasn't doing psychiatry, there would be some hope for Alex and me. I should take the good stuff and run.

THIRTEEN

SEQUELAE

It's late evening when two police officers pull up outside an anonymous but well-kept house in a quiet suburban street and emerge from their car, faces set.

The woman who opens the door to them is Sarah Farrell, wife of Xavier, the disgraced politician. She knows, instantly. Her hand goes to her face, and her legs give way. The female cop catches her as the three kids come running.

—

Seb – solid, suited, fifties – is dining with four other men of similar age and dress in a white-tablecloth Italian restaurant, big glasses of red wine in front of them, everyone showing signs that they've been drinking them, when his phone buzzes. 'Sorry, have to take this one.'

He steps into the city street, ducks around the corner into a laneway. 'What the fuck? When?'

There's a long pause as he gets the details. Not much fazes Seb, and he can deal with this. And any awkward questions.

'You know I'm not going to answer that. I talk to journalists all the time; everybody's first guess has to be the woman . . . Maybe some feminist got in her ear, her shrink . . . she's seeing Ron Gordon. Look, it's sad for the family but, I mean, he had a choice. You know my brother had cancer – pancreas, it's a bastard, he fought it right to the end – and . . . he only had to step aside.'

He paces, impatient, as the briefing continues. Finally, he's had enough. 'Mate, that's all well and good, but we can't change the past. We move on. Travis is ready to step up, and of course this isn't the way he'd have wanted it, yada yada. But he'll get over it.'

He wanders back into the restaurant. His steak has been waiting and he checks the temperature with the back of his fingers. He summons a waiter and it's whisked away.

'All okay?' says one of his dining companions.

He laughs. 'They'll probably just bung it in the microwave. Sorry, guys, I need to make another call. Just a quick one.'

—

Amy takes the phone from her ear, stunned. It's a little after 10 pm and she's sitting at McDonald's, sharing nuggets and chips with Carey. They've been to a movie, but they both like to eat late and have discovered a shared passion for junk food.

'All done?' says Carey. Then, 'Is something wrong?'

'That was a guy from work . . . not officially from work, just a supporter of the party who knows everyone. If you're in trouble and you need the best lawyer or just need a problem to go away, he's the one you go to. I talked to him after what happened at the function with the MP.'

'They're blaming you for the leak? I think that was inevitable.'

'He said they probably will. But the MP . . .'

'We can use his name now. Everyone knows who he is.'

'Was.'

'What do you mean?'

'He died. Hung himself.'

'Hanged.' Carey mentally upbraids themselves for the reflexive response. *Hung* is also acceptable, in a grammatical sense. Not in any other. And it distracted them for a moment from seeing Amy's distress, even though Amy is autistic like them. They should be able to recognise distress in anyone if they want to be a psychiatrist.

'How are you feeling?'

'Guilty. I mean, like I told you, I wasn't traumatised by what he did. More annoyed. It was noisy where we were and I suggested we go somewhere quieter and I think he thought it was an invitation to have sex. It wasn't the first time I'd sent the wrong signal. And he wasn't pushy or anything when I told him he'd got it wrong. More embarrassed. I only asked for help so I could learn how to avoid those kinds of mistakes, and now . . .'

'You're not responsible for anything he did. Including this.'

'I could have told him I wasn't going to make a complaint.'

'It came out anyway. Neither of us know what was going on in his head. I get that you're feeling guilty. It's a reaction, part of the grief.'

'I'm not crying, because I tend not to when I hear that someone's died.'

'I understand. I don't either.'

'Also, I hardly knew him. But I do feel guilty . . .'

'That's totally normal. Because you're a human being and you care about others. Not because you've done anything wrong. Hold on to that thought, okay? Would you like a hug?'

'Not really. I'm not much of a hugger. But thank you. What you said helps.' She hesitates, but Carey, like a good analyst, waits, and Amy continues. 'I've been trying really hard not to send *you* the wrong messages. I told your friend whose name I always forget –'

'Hannah.'

'– that if I wanted sex, I'd just ask. Pretty cool, huh?'

'I wish all women were as cool as you.'

'Seriously? All right: here I go. If I get it wrong, don't hold it against me. First, I think you need to know that I've never met anyone who wears aftershave before. Not so I can tell, anyway. There's probably a reason. It smells bad.'

Carey nods.

'And,' says Amy, 'I'd really like to have sex with you. Maybe not immediately, but some time.'

Carey smiles. 'I think you did an excellent job of communicating that. That's a big step forward in our relationship. Worth ditching the aftershave for.'

—

Early morning: a police officer races into a public-housing complex, presses the lift button, then decides to take the stairs, two at a time. There's a newspaper under her arm.

On the third floor, she knocks hard at the door of a flat. And again. The door opens, revealing a bleary-eyed truck driver in a robe. The police officer, incongruously, throws her arms around him.

'I was so worried,' Jacq says.

'Why?' Ahmed is still waking up.

Jacq waves the newspaper. 'The guy who stepped in front of your truck. Xavier Farrell. He died. It doesn't say suicide, but there's the phone number for Lifeline at the end of the article.'

Ahmed takes it in. Slowly. 'He was a good man. He paid for my tyres.' Then he begins to shake.

Jacq is ready for this. 'Take some deep breaths. You're safe and secure here . . .'

Ahmed calms a little.

'Do you want me to take you to hospital?'

Ahmed shakes his head. 'I don't know.'

'I'll stay here till you do.'

—

Sian is feeding her baby as Leo, bored, scrolls the news on his phone.

'Hey,' he says. 'There's a guy in the paper – topped himself. I'd swear he was in the ward at the same time as you. I think I talked to him in the lounge. He's a pollie. Was.' He shows Sian the photo.

She shakes her head. 'Maybe. It must have been when I was in Acute.' She laughs. 'Not likely to have been in the Mother Baby Unit.'

'He was up for sexual harassment. Most of these guys just tough it out, right?'

'Most of them,' says Sian.

'He could've resigned, would've still had a life. I mean, shit, things change, you rethink, you find a way of getting on with it.'

'Easy to say,' says Sian.

Leo smiles wryly. 'You know, I told you I was talking to the guy – I'm sure it's him now – and he seemed totally sane to me, and at that time you were . . . I didn't even know you.'

'*I* didn't know me.'

'Turned out he was in more trouble than you.'

'Did I ever tell you I had this aunt who was pretty bizarre – bag-lady clothes, hair a total mess. We kids thought she was a witch. Obviously she had some sort of mental illness, because she had ECT. She told us all about it. What she said was nothing like what I remember of my experience, which is basically nothing, so it was probably bullshit. But we thought the ECT had caused the illness.'

'You never told me.'

A long pause. 'You were right to let them give it to me.'

'Wasn't an easy call.'

'I fucking hope not. If you'd grown up with my aunt, you'd definitely have said no.'

Leo is imagining his partner as a child, frightened by the witch. He rubs her head, musses her hair. It's not something he would have done three months ago, and Sian might not have smiled back as she does now.

Matilda chooses the moment to throw up her dinner.

'Shit,' Sian says. 'Get me the wipes.'

'Get 'em yourself.'

But he's already up and they're both laughing as he puts his phone down.

—

'You see that politician killed himself,' says David Young, by way of making dinner conversation. Or, as he does, setting up a sermon. Chloe, Sue and Brianna are seated at the table, though Chloe doesn't have a plate in front of her.

'Terrible waste,' says Sue.

'And a sin,' adds David. 'I bring it up because I've been following the story. Some young woman led him on, and then threatened to have him charged with sexual harassment. Now he's dead. Brianna, I hope –'

'Bullshit. Total bullshit.' Brianna isn't having any of it.

Nor is David. 'Young lady, you're in our home, not in a place where you're . . . indulged.'

Brianna gets up to leave the table.

'Sit down,' says David. 'You stay here until you've eaten every scrap on your plate.'

Sue shakes her head. 'Go and do your homework.'

—

'I blame myself.' Elena is having coffee with Omar in the hospital cafeteria.

'I didn't know you'd seen him,' says Omar.

'I didn't. I'm so angry. Prof asked me if I was willing to take over the supervision. I could have, but Nash wouldn't sign off on it.'

'Because you're not a psychiatrist?'

'You know how much training psychiatrists get in psychotherapy?'

'Not much.'

'Forty sessions under supervision and they can do whatever they like. Do you know how much training a clinical psychologist gets? Do you know how much I've done?'

'A lot more.'

'A *lot* more. And it's ongoing. Alex has none. He sees me taking an extraordinarily confrontational line with a family, because one of their daughters is in a life-threatening situation . . .'

'Chloe?'

Elena nods. 'The risks I took were proportionate to that situation, the absolute opposite of what you'd do with a patient with one suicide attempt and no history.'

'But you think Alex picked up on it.'

'If a psychologist, a female psychologist, a Greek female psychologist can do it . . . I'm sorry: I'm venting. He – Xavier – was an inpatient in your unit?'

Omar nods.

Elena takes his hand briefly. 'I'm sorry.'

'Goes with the territory. In theory. In the time I've been here, we've never lost one on the ward. But once they're discharged . . .'

'What was he like?' says Elena.

'Like every patient. Trying to deal with something scary about himself that he maybe didn't know before . . .' Omar trails off. 'But Alex: I work with him. I've seen way, way worse. And after today, he won't be the same.'

Elena nods.

'Nash too,' says Omar.

'To lose anyone who's been a patient . . .'

'I was thinking about the fact that Nash didn't let you supervise.'

Elena shakes her head. 'I never asked.'

—

Nash Sharma looks across the table at his wife and children, the youngest strapped into a highchair, having breakfast together with a level of formality that is one of the vestiges of their cultural heritage. On the wall in front of him is a family photo taken at Chennai airport: Nash, his parents and his sister, Sarita. She was fifteen and he was eighteen. It was the last time he saw her; she died from anorexia nervosa while he was doing his medical training in America.

Nash has three children. Same as Xavier Farrell. How are *his* children now? How will they be in a year, in ten years, in fifty?

Professionally, Nash does not deal with the effect of parenting and loss on the psyche, but this is through choice, not ignorance. He knows that Xavier Farrell's death will haunt his children for the rest of their lives. And though he, Nash, will never be brought to any meaningful account, he is – at least in part – responsible.

A conversation plays over in his head. Not the one he could have had with Elena, asking her to supervise; that was Prof's responsibility. No, it's the one with Nicole Ogilvy. She couldn't have been in the director's position more than a week when she took it upon herself to warn him that Alex shouldn't see Farrell as his psychotherapy case.

Nicole's concern was all about the politician's public profile and influence: she didn't want the hospital assigning a junior to a VIP. That had rankled with Nash, but more so the arguments about Alex's inexperience. 'Farrell's a player. He'll run rings around a first-year trainee.' At some level, at *every* level, Nash agreed with her. But his pride, his loyalty to another doctor ahead of a social worker reborn as an administrator, and his hubris – yes, his hubris – had affected his decision. He wasn't going to take Nicole's direction on a clinical issue.

Nash doesn't know to what extent Alex failed to spot the signs or intervened inappropriately. Only Alex is alive to know what was said with the door closed. But circumstances put a green trainee with a patient at risk of suicide and then removed his supervision.

Circumstances? It's a mealy-mouthed word. It began with Nash. And finished with Alex's supervisor, Professor Gordon. Together, they'd had a chance to prevent this.

—

'I'm afraid I have a rather distressing story for you.'

Professor Liron Gordon has the attention of his peer-review group, lunching in a private room at the University Club. Wine open, cheese course served. Two men, three women, including Sandra Byrd, and himself. All well past fifty, all serious.

'The gentleman in this morning's paper – the member of parliament and representative on the mental health advisory board who suicided . . .' He lets it sit for a moment, before releasing the tension. 'Not one of mine. It's been a very long time since I've lost one, and never one who was actively in therapy.' Another pause. 'But the woman in question, the victim of the assault: we've discussed her, without me sharing the connection with the MP, on a couple of occasions. I imagine you can guess who she is: the woman with a blunted affect – a complex array of symptoms.'

One of the women speaks up: Margaret McDonald, the psychiatrist who occasionally sits on the ECT tribunal. 'This is the one who self-diagnosed as having Asperger's.'

Prof nods. 'Autism, she'd say, and I suppose we should let *DSM* be the arbiter there.'

'This year,' says Margaret, and there's a ripple of amusement.

'I had no idea of the connection,' says Prof. 'In fact, we were working on other issues and the harassment hadn't come up.'

They've stopped eating. Prof's tone says there's something even more interesting to be revealed.

'But I was supervising the trainee who had the MP as his psychotherapy case.'

There it is.

He waits, letting them know that questions are welcome.

'How experienced?'

'He's a first-year. Unusual, I know, but permitted. It'd make sense if he'd come to psychiatry with some background – in clinical psychology, for example – but this young man had nothing but a few volumes of Freud. And his consultant is about as psychologically minded as an orthopaedic surgeon. So he asked me to supervise.'

'How did our trainee encounter this patient?'

'He was admitted to the Acute Unit, where our trainee works. After a suicide attempt. Apparently . . .' This is a weak point in Prof's story and Margaret interrupts his attempt to move on.

'I'm sorry? This trainee's consultant assigned him a suicidal –'

'I was about to explain. There was strong evidence, both clinical and circumstantial, that the behaviour was . . . calculated.'

'This was the opinion of your orthopaedic surgeon?'

One of the men intervenes. 'Margaret, let Ron tell the story. I presume he was employing a bit of hyperbole. Nash Sharma is pretty sound.'

'Well,' says Margaret, 'history suggests the assessment was wrong, and an inexperienced trainee was assigned a risky patient who has now –'

'Sorry,' says the man to Margaret. 'We've been remiss. This is your first time with the group – and, as we said earlier, welcome, and an honour to have you with us. But we have a few informal rules, and I guess the most important is that we're first and foremost supportive. Some of us have to hold a line in court, with patients, with their families. Here we can admit to our failings and mistakes, seek counsel if we want it . . . Questions for clarification, not as challenges.'

'I understand, Isaac,' says Margaret. 'I'm just a little shocked. I think suicide puts us all off balance.'

'Thank you both,' says Prof. 'I think we can all see that mistakes were made – and, as Isaac says, we can still learn. I imagine Dr Sharma, since we all know to whom I was referring, is having a difficult morning, and our young trainee more so. Nobody need tell me that it would be no surprise if he was lost to the program.

'But, as I said, I was asked to supervise, and our trainee had seen the patient for a dozen or so sessions, and I was, obviously, counselling a very conservative approach. The patient had previously disclosed to our trainee details of the alleged assault, and that level of trust did bear on the original decision to allow him to proceed. And then I discovered the conflict of interest.' He looks around the group. 'I don't feel I had any choice but to terminate the supervision.'

General nodding.

'And, of course, advise Nash that he would need to find another supervisor for the trainee.' He pauses. 'Perhaps I should have taken a more active role, given that the trainee was not making arrangements to suspend the therapy.'

He pauses, expecting not approval, but a silence that gives him some sort of absolution.

'You're asking us a question,' says Margaret, 'and I'm going to answer it. The failure of you and the consultant jointly either to find an alternative supervisor or instruct the trainee to suspend therapy was the last, and I would contend the most serious, in a series of consequential mistakes. Including those surely made by the poor trainee.'

—

'I'm just so fucking angry.'

Ndidi and Jon have moved from the registrars' room to a pair of benches outside, so as not to be interrupted. And to have some clear air around them, because Ndidi's barely keeping a lid on it.

She's had a tough year. Her job's very different from her husband's, and trying to get pregnant has only highlighted their different priorities. She's less and less confident that they'll be fixed by bringing a child into the world.

'You know, I've had patients die, I've probably made mistakes that contributed to it, but this is different. If Alex had done nothing – never offered him psychotherapy – this might not have happened. Worst case, *worst case*, he might have suicided anyway, but that's what happened after all the self-examination and therapeutic insights: the worst case. First, do no fucking harm.'

'You're being harsh,' says Jon. 'I know how you feel about psychotherapy, but if you think of it as a legitimate treatment, well . . . treatments don't always work.'

Jon's coming from a different place, where a therapist or health worker is the last person you'd blame for a suicide, but he's arrived at the same point as Seb the fixer: wondering, in his gut, why a privileged guy like Xavier would choose to end his life.

He lets Ndidi go on, waiting for the right moment to say something.

'Right from the start, you heard what I said. If he wanted to be a psychotherapist, he could have studied psychology, where he'd have been taught to do it properly: stuff that works, instead of a fucking religion.

'And then . . . you know a whole lot of people are going to be blamed for this, but at the end of the day, it's Alex who wanted to do it, who pushed to take it on, who kept going. He's an adult, a doctor. And you know what really pisses me off?'

'Besides everything you've just said?'

'It's that he won't change. He won't learn from it. Remember when Prof took him down over that woman with a brain tumour? Prof was doing his best to shame him into taking a hard look at himself, but you saw what Alex was like after. *We'll be selling tickets next time.*'

'You're pretty angry,' says Jon.

'Good pick-up. But what really, *really* pisses me off is not that he isn't going to leave the program with his tail between his legs. No, he's already constructing his story. I can see him in the exam: *This experience taught me so much* . . . What pisses me off is that *he's* not going to leave the program, but Hannah probably will.'

'You think so?'

'I've just spoken to her. Right now, she's feeling more responsibility than you and me. Maybe more than Alex.'

Jon nods. 'I'm feeling some. I should have pulled him up when he talked about challenging Mr X – Mr Farrell. Do you feel that yourself?'

Ndidi sits back, spends a few moments looking up at the sky full of dark clouds.

'Why do you think I'm so angry?'

—

Alex has come into work. The show must go on, and he has to go on. Might as well be now: he has a chance to do some good every day, a sustaining thought. A thought to pull him out of the devastation he felt when he heard the news, out of sitting at home with a glass of whisky that felt theatrical rather than comforting.

It hasn't escaped him that his way of dealing with his trauma has little to do with the long-term reflection he wants to encourage in his patients and more in common with the cognitive behavioural therapies he dismisses.

Suicide is how psychiatrists – even the most experienced – lose patients; the scenario that triggered Xavier was there before he started therapy; there are lessons to be learned, lessons he can share with others. He hasn't begun to reflect on what those lessons might be.

Instead, he's found himself involuntarily constructing some sort of explanation, narrative, defence.

He's in the registrars' room when Hannah comes in. He'd texted her when it happened, told her he'd already made the decision when he phoned her that night. It's not true, of course. She, more than anyone, could have changed his mind. He'd added: *Please don't call.*

'I didn't think you were coming in,' she says. 'I did your admission for you.' As she would. Hannah has always been not just the organiser, but the energy and heart of the group. There's no facade with her: not Ndidi's pre-emptive aggression, Jon's studied detachment or his own hubris, flippancy, analytical posturing. Hannah has an intuitive sense of what's going on that he doesn't think he'll ever achieve.

And he's in love with her. He stuffed up the big date, trying too hard, overthinking it, wanting to create the perfect moment over the dinner he'd planned. A dinner he'd have cooked, where they didn't talk about patients, where afterward he played the piano and Hannah sang. Jess told him she sang. None of that will happen now – and he feels guilty even thinking about his personal life after what's happened.

'You probably don't want to talk about it,' says Hannah, 'and I'll respect that. But if our roles were reversed, you'd be offering me a space to be heard without judgement.'

He hasn't talked to anyone yet about Xavier and he realises now that's because he's been wanting to get it straight in his own head. The narrative.

'You want to know the truth?' Alex says. 'He's gone. I never met his kids. I'm going to live with this for the rest of my life. Glad you asked?'

Hannah nods. 'You know when you stuffed up the presentation of the woman with the frontal-lobe tumour –'

'Could've been another casualty of my incompetence.'

'Could have. We've all got "could haves". We related to you that day, because it could have been us. And . . . again. We're all feeling sorry for you, so your own feelings are pretty appropriate.'

It's okay to feel sorry for yourself, she's saying. She's better at this than she thinks she is.

'I guess,' Hannah says, 'you'll look a lot deeper when you do your own psychotherapy.'

'If that's a message, I've heard it. Before I take on another psychotherapy case.'

'And . . .' Hannah stops.

'Go on. You were going to say something insightful, weren't you?'

'You've given me some good advice, and I've taken it on board. I want to give you something back, if you want to listen.'

Alex squashes his urge to say something flippant.

'When you do see a therapist, maybe tell them the real story, and not the one you're going to tell your dad.'

—

Jess knows. Jess knows everything that's happening in Hannah's life. The other way around: not so much right now. Jess got the news that she'd been accepted for the paramedic program and put a bottle of sparkling wine in the fridge, but when Hannah came home after the mess-up with Alex and talked about Aaron and not doing psychiatry, it wasn't the time to tell her. And now this.

If Hannah doesn't become a therapist, Jess will do it herself. Someone has to. The thought of what she'd need to do to get there terrifies her.

—

Ndidi turns up at my home. I've taken a day off – a non-mental-health day. The chat with Alex, which turned into a two-hour reflection on family and image and shame, took more out of me than I'd expected. A trained therapist would have done better, just as an anaesthetist would have done a better job of intubating Zac on the floor of the Acute ward, but the timing was more important.

Alex and me, always talking about work or playing therapist to each other. I never asked him about the piano.

There's an envelope with my name on it on the table – in it, a card from Jess with a picture of a cartoon puppy looking up at its owner adoringly. The caption says: *You're my hero.* She's added: *Whatever you do. Just so you know.*

I had intended to avoid the group debrief, but Ndidi is insistent. I get that there are lessons to learn, a chance for collective bonding and healing. Except I'm in the process of separating from this group.

I'd made the decision already, but the suicide cemented it. I spent a while beating myself up, talked myself past the guilt. I should have told Alex to call Xavier. Listened to my instincts and had the courage and judgement to balance them against a textbook reading of the situation. I had the chance to save a life. I didn't, and I'll have to live with that.

Ndidi's parked outside. A white BMW: 'Doctor's car. Parents bought it for me, so no choice.' It's less than a kilometre to the hospital, and she doesn't waste any time getting to the point.

'Two years ago, they had a consultant walk away from medicine altogether after a suicide. He'd debriefed everyone except himself. Registrars, less experienced . . .'

'I think Alex will get through. He's –'

'You know who I'm talking about.'

I might as well tell her. I'm going to have to explain it to Nash in the next day or two.

'It's pushed some buttons.'

'That suicide when you were fifteen.'

It's not a question. A trauma that I thought I could overcome by seeing a couple of at-risk patients under close supervision and sending home Taylah Keane from ED, someone whose number I had. Maybe if Xavier hadn't *hanged* himself.

And if I hadn't seen him at the parkruns. That's the picture I can't get out of my head now: him and the kids and that loping dog, running toward me over the bridge. Gone forever.

'I've had a few flashbacks. But that's not why. I decided before I knew about Xavier.'

Ndidi doesn't look convinced.

'I left emergency medicine for the wrong reasons. Doing psychiatry has helped me realise that. It's all short-term fixes, or years of work for no result that anyone can measure.' I dump it on Ndidi – all the stuff that's been brewing this whole term. 'The Nicoles and their KPIs that have got fuck-all to do with outcomes for patient; the Nashes and their refusal to accept anything that hasn't had a randomised control trial, which means pharmaceutical; the Profs and their power games.'

'Every medical specialty comes with a narcissist professor. And adminstrators.'

'True. But Alex talks about the battle for the soul of psychiatry, and I think we . . . they . . . are going to lose it. Have lost it already. Whatever he did wrong with Xavier, antidepressants weren't the answer either.'

'Uh-huh,' Ndidi says. 'You've written your resignation?'

'No,' I say. Instead, in my pocket, is the card from Jarryd. *Be a real doctor.*

—

I walk with Ndidi along the familiar path to the ivory tower. The meeting room is about half-full and Nicole is looking around, checking off a list. Pretty much everyone from Acute is here, except Nash. I guess he's holding the fort.

After taking the roll, Nicole walks out. I'm a little surprised she's not sticking around.

I sit between Jon and Alex; Jon sees Carey coming in and beckons them to join us.

Sandra is running the debrief. She stands in front of us, in pale pink, including her hair, which seems right in some strange way. A calming colour.

Nash walks in. With Nicole. Sandra takes that as the cue to begin.

'When one of our patients suicides, it affects us all,' she says. 'Maybe now, maybe later. Maybe only in a distant way, maybe viscerally.

'This is a space to talk, but only if you want to. First, though, I know that some of you are sitting here feeling a sense of personal responsibility. You feel there was something you could have done, or not done, that might have made a difference. If that applies to you, and only if you want to, I'm going to ask you just to stand up.'

Absolute silence. And without words, Sandra, who was too busy to take on Alex's supervision, sends us a message: *I am standing.*

On either side of me, Alex and Jon stand, and I follow. Ndidi hesitates for a moment, but she's one of us. The group that didn't push back hard enough. The registrar whose resignation it's triggered. Admitting our culpability in front of our bosses and our colleagues.

Carey is sitting, looking horribly conflicted and pressured. Like they need a time-out to get advice. They weren't involved in advising Alex but, of course, there's the connection with Amy. If they're still seeing her, they may have been involved in her decision to go to the press, if that's what she did. Or been in a position to stop her. Or had the opportunity to counsel her on resolving the issue. All actions or inactions are revisited when they might have contributed to someone's death. But I guess they're worried about signalling that there's a connection. Nobody's going to work that out. I nod to them, and they're up like a shot.

Nash stands. I turn to see that Nicole has followed suit, as if she'd been waiting for his cue. While Nash is facing forward, looking only at Sandra, Nicole is surveying the room.

Elena is already up – Elena, whose confrontational approach to therapy inspired Alex to try it himself. I can feel her pain: *We didn't debrief properly.* I can tell that Alex is near tears: I hope he's sensing solidarity and not feeling that he's dragged all these people down with him. Omar stands, and a couple more nurses follow.

Sandra is looking into space: not at anyone, but somehow it's directed. I realise what she's waiting for, and I guess everyone does. The longer she waits, the more awful it gets.

Finally, a chair leg scrapes at the back of the room. Prof rises, is still for a moment, head bowed, as if paying respect to the dead, then leaves the room.

'This is what happens,' says Sandra. 'We don't like uncertainty and try to come up with a narrative. People feel responsible when they are not. This was Xavier Farrell's decision and we will never know what exactly went into the complex mix that took him to that moment at that time. But it wasn't any one thing or one person.'

Sandra gives us time to sit down, for the tension to dissipate. 'So, would anyone like to say anything?'

She doesn't have to wait long. Nicole speaks and, despite her show of solidarity with Nash, I feel offended. *She isn't one of us.* But of course she is, at least in this. The problem's mine.

'Traditionally,' she says, 'these sessions have been large, like this, but I have also organised a separate debrief with the senior staff, including Sandra, Nash, Professor Gordon and myself.'

Sandra nods, but why should the senior people get their own session? I look at Nash and his folded arms give me the answer. At these group meetings, they're busy being strong for – or afraid to show weakness to – the rest of us. I guess that was what held Prof back. Maybe Nicole has got it right, though I wouldn't want to be running that debrief.

Omar raises his hand. 'He wasn't in the ward long. He was a bit full of himself. But we never really know, do we? What's going on underneath. I feel sorry for his kids.'

I think, inevitably, of Aaron, and of shame, and the difference between how we view ourselves and the places to which we sometimes fall. And, thanks to the parkrun and Alex's presentations to the group, I know about Xavier's wife and kids. The fifteen- and ten-year-old boys whose male role model has sent them a message: button it up and, if it really gets hard, bail. The twelve-year-old daughter who may spend her life with a succession of older male partners, none of them able to fill the gap her father has left. Xavier's death will have left a whisper in their minds that he did not love them enough to stick around. Harsh, not in his control, probably not what he was thinking, but once you're dead you don't have control of the narrative.

'Maybe we need to offer them support,' Sandra suggests.

'I'll speak to Prof,' Nash says.

Someone mentions suicide running in families, another legacy Xavier has inadvertently left.

I can't and won't talk in front of this group. Not because I'd be ashamed to, but because I want to be able to offer something and I can't. Depleted, numb or just incompetent: I'm not sure. But in seeing my more experienced colleagues – even Elena – standing with me in acknowledgment of their fallibility, and opening up about their feelings of powerlessness, I am feeling less . . . self-critical. Not just that: less critical of what we're all trying to do. Our patients' problems are so complex, our treatments so crude, ourselves so human. We're not unscientific: we're at the leading edge, still working out the science.

I realise, too, that I've been dishonest with myself, with Jess and with Ndidi. My issue isn't with psychiatry, the system or my colleagues. The flashbacks to when I was fifteen aren't just part of it. They're all of it. And my real anger isn't with *Aaron's* parents.

The things that led me to psychiatry – Aaron's suicide, my parents' struggles then and now and, surely, the impact they've had on my own psyche – are the same things that will make it impossible for me to do it safely and sanely. Unless I deal with them, which means uncovering trauma I'd rather stayed buried.

I love my parents and, intellectually, I know they did their best. I want to be able to visit and sing with them and give advice on eczema ointments and paleo diets without thinking about how much they've fucked me up – and why. But that's the price I'll have to pay if I want to be a psychiatrist.

—

I walk out alone and stand outside, taking deep breaths.

Elena comes over. I'm expecting her to ask if I'm okay, but no: it's business.

'I told you Chloe's sister wanted to see me in therapy?'

I nod.

'I wondered if you'd like to work with me, as a co-therapist. It'd count toward your accreditation, but I was hoping that wouldn't be the only reason.'

Elena waits for me to respond and, when I don't, she continues.

'You know, Brianna's only fifteen. I look at my patients, even David and Sue, and I'm in awe of their courage just in living their lives, as well as facing up to the things that frighten them most. It'll be a challenge, but I think we can make a difference.'

I stand for a while, just taking it in slowly. It's the work I've wanted to do boiled down to its essence: the patients and their courage, the knowledge that the person I've learned the most from, admired the most this year, wants me to work with her. To get one starfish to safety.

'I was thinking of dropping out of psychiatry,' I say. 'I guess I'd have used not getting into the training program as an excuse. Lay some guilt on Prof. I may have sabotaged myself just a little there.'

Elena nods. 'I'd forgotten you weren't in the program. Take that as a compliment. But you've changed your mind?'

As of a few minutes ago.

I nod.

'You'll apply interstate if Prof blocks you here?'

'I haven't really thought it through. I'll do whatever I have to.'

—

I'm left thinking about Sue and David, almost the last people I'd have expected to be inspired by. I tried to put myself in Chloe's shoes;

I related to Brianna instinctively, but I never felt much empathy for the parents, who, faced with a terrible crisis, have had to come to terms not only with what it means, but with not being able to fix it themselves, from within their hopelessly enmeshed family.

Maybe it was like that for my parents. Maybe if I . . . I stop myself. Realise what I was about to do – what I've been doing for a long time. Putting myself outside my family, setting myself up as the problem solver for Mum and Dad and Mel and Lennon without acknowledging that I'm part of the problem.

Standing outside the ivory tower, I call Lennon.

'Hi, Doc.' Well, that pretty much sums it up.

'Hey, Bro.'

'Bro? You sound like a Kiwi. Since when do you call me Bro?'

'Since now. Since I realised it might be a while till you came back, and I don't want to lose touch. I've been doing a lot of thinking about what happened with Aaron. It messed me up, too, and I'm going to try to do something about it.'

'I guess you're in the right place to do that. But if you're saying I should . . .'

'I'm not. It's just that you and Mel and I went through the same stuff, and I'd like to talk about it sometime.'

'As part of your therapy?'

'More just getting my memories straight. And figuring out what it means to us now.'

There's a long pause before he answers.

'You think I should come home?'

'Not for me to say. I don't come home all that often. And not just because I'm busy.'

Another long pause.

'You think it'd help with kicking the drinking if I . . . did what you're doing?'

I manage to stop myself. And say what I need to say rather than what I want to say. 'Probably one to ask your social worker.'

'Okay. I might do that. Keep in touch. Sis.'

—

I walk back toward the unit and there, sitting alone on a bench near the path, is Prof. There's no easy way to avoid him, and he's already seen me. He beckons me over.

'I understand Alex sought your advice.'

'He phoned me the night before. If I'd given him permission, I think he'd have –'

'Sit down. Please.'

I sit beside him. And stop talking. Look up at the fluffy white clouds in a blue sky. I sense that he's also looking up, rather than at me.

'If you'd advised Alex to call the patient,' says Prof, 'it might have turned out differently. It's a burden, of a kind that's intrinsic to our job. To medicine. I can only say that I would have given Alex the same advice that you gave him. And similarly be examining myself.'

If he tells me I've shown good judgement, and that he'll recommend me for the training program on that basis, I think I'll punch him.

Instead, he says, 'What have you learned this year?'

I say, through gritted teeth, 'That I've got some stuff to work through before . . .'

'Before you become a psychiatrist. Most people do. And you'll get help to do that work.'

It's a statement, not a question, but I nod anyway.

'I'll look forward to having you in the program. Never know when we're going to need to move a fridge.'

ACKNOWLEDGEMENTS

The Glass House is a novel, its characters and cases fictional. But we wanted it to be as accurate as possible a portrayal of mental illness and its treatment, and of the mental health system – not as we might wish them to be, but as they are.

Our first-reader group, always important to us, was expanded to include clinical experts in each of the areas we touch on. Our aim was to check that the cases and their treatment were realistic, which is not the same as being typical – or stereotypical. We also included a number of readers with personal histories of mental illness and its treatment – *consumers* – but again emphasise that everyone's experience is different.

So, all errors are ultimately our responsibility, but there are far fewer than there would have been without the help of Dr Catherine Acton, Prof Sophie Adams, Prof Michael Berk, Prof Philip Boyce, Lahna Bradley, Prof Ernie Butler, Tania Chandler, Dr Hannah Cross, Robert Eames, the late Dr Edwin Harari, Prof Mal Hopwood, Prof Richard Kanaan, Dr Charles Landau, Prof Shari Lusskin, Dr Michael Mazzolini, Dr Jess McConnell, Prof Pat McGorry,

Rod Miller, Georgina Penny, Jan Phillips, Yenn Purkis, Dr Joy Quek, Dr Suzy Redston, Dominique Simsion, Dr Daniel Simsion, Donna Stolzenberg, Prof Anne Sved Williams, Geri Walsh, Dr Chamali Wanigasekera, Janifer Willis and a number who have chosen to remain anonymous.

We would also like to thank Rebecca Saunders' team at Hachette Australia for their faith in and enthusiasm for the book, and editors Rebecca Allen, Alison Arnold and Ali Lavau, who demonstrated just how much good editors can contribute to a book you thought was finished. Prior to its acquisition by Hachette, the manuscript benefited from the input of David Winter and Michael Heyward of Text Publishing, and Sarah Lutyens of Lutyens & Rubinstein.

The Glass House was inspired by the courage of patients and the dedication of mental health workers who deal with issues which are often poorly understood, inadequately resourced, and for which there are few complete solutions. We hope this book will contribute to a better recognition of the challenges they face.

The starfish story is from Loren Eiseley's *The Star Thrower* (1969).

BOOK CLUB QUESTIONS

1. Which of the patient stories in *The Glass House* did you like or relate to most and why?
2. Sian undergoes electroconvulsive therapy (ECT). Have you read or seen other stories in which ECT is used? How do those depictions compare with how it's portrayed in *The Glass House*?
3. Hannah advised Alex not to phone Xavier at a time of crisis. Do you think Xavier received appropriate treatment?
4. On page 62, Hannah comments about Chloe's multiple admissions for anorexia nervosa: 'Would we say the same if it was sixteen admissions for asthma? . . . We do think differently about mental illness.' Do you agree?
5. There is an argument that mental health stories should be told from the point of view of the patient(s) rather than 'those in power'. Do you agree?
6. The episodic structure of *The Glass House* is unusual for a book but common in television series. Why do you think the authors chose it? Did it work for you?

7. *The Glass House* is set in an acute mental health ward. Did you have any previous knowledge or experience of this aspect of health care?
8. There are a number of controversial issues dealt with in *The Glass House*: medication vs 'talking' therapies; admission and treatment against the patient's will; use of physical and pharmacological restraints. Did the book change your opinions on any of these?
9. Have you read any novels or memoirs written about mental health journeys? How did their portrayals of health workers compare with those in *The Glass House*?
10. On page 40, Carey says, 'It's called empathy . . . Too many psychiatrists never really try to understand the patient. They're always on the outside looking in. Not in – *at*.' Do you think the clinicians in *The Glass House* showed empathy for their patients?
11. If you had a mental health problem, who would you want to treat you: Hannah, Nash, Prof, Alex, Ndidi, Jon, Elena or Carey?
12. Hannah tells us that work got in the way of her relationship with Alex. Do you think that's the real reason it foundered?
13. As the first book in a series, the conclusion of *The Glass House* is quite open-ended. What do you think is next for Hannah?

Professor Anne Buist is chair of Women's Mental Health at the University of Melbourne, with thirty years of clinical and research experience in perinatal psychiatry. With a multimillion-dollar grant from Beyond Blue, she established an Australia-wide screening program for perinatal depression. Anne began writing at eight, but medicine intervened until 2012, when she wrote an erotic fiction series (under a pseudonym). This was followed by four crime novels and a standalone thriller.

You can find Anne at annebuist.com, on Facebook @annebuistauthor and on Instagram @anneebuist

Dr Graeme Simsion's debut novel, *The Rosie Project*, has sold over five million copies in forty languages, spending sixty-five weeks on the *New York Times* bestseller list. A film is in development with Sony Pictures. The two Rosie sequels were also international bestsellers, as were *The Best of Adam Sharp*, in development with New Sparta Productions, and *Two Steps Forward*, which was written with Anne and optioned by Fox Searchlight/Disney. Graeme and Anne are married and live in Melbourne.

You can find Graeme at graemesimsion.com, on Facebook @graemesimsionauthor and on X @graemesimsion